RANDOM HOUSE

LARGE PRINT

THOSE WHO
ARE SAVED

THOSE WHO
ARE SAVED

ALEXIS LANDAU

R A N D O M   H O U S E
L A R G E   P R I N T

Published in the United States of America by Random House Large Print in association with G. P. Putnam's Sons, an imprint of Penguin Random House LLC.

Cover design by Vi-An Nguyen
Cover images: (mother and daughter) Jelena Simic Petrovic / Arcangel; (background) Alexandre Rotenberg / Arcangel; (planes) Berliner Verlag / Archive / dpa picture alliance / Alamy Stock Photo

The Library of Congress has established a Cataloging-in-Publication record for this title.

ISBN: 978-0-593-39581-3

www.penguinrandomhouse.com/large-print-format-books

FIRST LARGE PRINT EDITION

Printed in the United States of America

10 9 8 7 6 5 4 3 2 1

This Large Print edition published in accord with the standards of the N.A.V.H.

For Lucia and Levi

For Laura and Levi

Motherhood is a bright torture.
I was not worthy of it.

—ANNA AKHMATOVA

All the goodness and the heroisms
will rise up again, then be cut down
again and rise up. It isn't that the evil
thing wins—it never will—but that
it doesn't die.

—JOHN STEINBECK

CHAPTER I

VERA

FEBRUARY 1945, MALIBU, CALIFORNIA

She cupped the lukewarm water and splashed it over her face again and again. The obsessive remembering ceased. A boon, if even for one breath, not to think. She reached for a nearby towel, but sensed someone standing behind her. Her eyes fluttered open. Eyelashes wet, chin dripping, she adjusted to the white sunlit bathroom. In the mirror above the sink, a young woman calmly watched her from the doorway. Helix of dark hair curled over one shoulder, brown liquid eyes, yellow silk blouse, gold chain around her neck with the heart dangling from it. Her daughter, but her daughter at eighteen, all grown.

Not the four-year-old daughter Vera had left behind in France.

When she spun around, the girl was gone.

Vera stared into the vacant doorway and steadied herself against the sink basin, the cool ceramic pressing into the small of her back.

"Lucie?" she whispered into the still air. "Lucie?"

She never stopped thinking of the day they left Lucie, as if reliving it would crystallize or explain something that she had overlooked. But no matter how many times Vera circled back, that day remained implacable; it cared nothing for how swiftly a life could darken.

They had gone on holiday early, leaving Paris in the beginning of May 1940, in anticipation of the occupation, decamping to the southern seaside town Sanary-sur-Mer, where they kept a summerhouse. The Werfels, the Freudenbergers, and Hugo Lafont and his wife, Ines, were already there, and Max and Vera felt safe in the south, among friends, discussing the war in lowered tones as they sipped chilled champagne in Elsa Freudenberger's garden among the lemon trees, the scent of lime blossom infiltrating their fear, lessening it.

And the heady scent of fig trees, azure waters lapping against a long sandy coastline, a forest full of pines Vera loved to stroll through, notebook in hand, preparing for an image or a phrase that might present itself, made it seem as though their circumstances had not been greatly altered. She had just finished her third novel, about an old French farming family from Vosges. The family's attachment to the land and its customs stretches back generations, until the Great War upends their lives, taking away their sons. The novel is from the mother's point of view, and the loss of her sons causes delirious grief. After the war, one son returns, only to relay that the other one died on the Eastern Front. The son who survived has changed, no longer caring for the farm, the family, or the land he's inherited. He only cares for freedom. His own personal freedom. And so the mother learns another kind of grief.

Some afternoons, Vera spread a cardigan over the coniferous earth and lay down, contemplating the thrushes rustling overhead, replaying bits and pieces of dialogue the mother has said, or might say, to her estranged son, and, cupping a fuzzy peach in the palm of her hand, she felt lucky.

But one early evening in the beginning of June, the setting sun filtering through the linen curtains, Vera listened to the news in the little room on the ground floor where she kept the radio. The terse male voice on the wireless reported that the situation did not look positive, neither in Belgium nor in the Netherlands.

Lying on the small worn sofa, she closed her eyes, palms resting on her abdomen, calmed by how naturally, without any effort, her breath rose and fell, wondering what Sabine, the cook, had prepared for dinner, deciphering various smells emanating from the kitchen on the far side of the house: Salmon with fennel and raisins? Then she heard: "All foreign nationals residing in the precincts of Paris, and all persons between the ages of seventeen and fifty-five who do not possess French citizenship, must report for internment." She sat up, light-headed, a metallic secretion flooding her mouth.

Blinking into the falling dark, she switched on the lamp.

"Max," she called, standing up.

Walking out of the room, trying not to break into a run, she yelled, "Max," with a startling roughness.

She burst into the dining room, finding the table set, the silver gleaming, the wineglasses waiting to be filled with their preferred dry white, from the Marsanne grape.

Max smoked his pipe in front of the open French doors, surveying the olive trees, their delicate branches cut out against the silvery night. Lucie was sprawled across the sheepskin rug, colored pencils strewn around her. She had drawn a picture of their cat, Mourka, with his dangling pink tongue and elongated whiskers.

"What's all the racket?" Max asked, resting his pipe on the windowsill.

Lucie glanced up from her drawing.

Vera stared around the room, as if some irrevocable change should be evident.

"I heard on the wireless, about the internment."

"Oh, that," Max said in his usual nonchalant

manner. "The precincts of Paris. Remember now, that's all they said."

He strode over to her, pushing up the sleeves of his crisp white shirt.

Lucie watched them closely.

He cupped Vera's shoulder, his warm hand lingering there. "From a military point of view, there's no conceivable reason for interning us here in the south."

"What about Paul?" Vera asked, searching Max's face at the mention of his younger brother, who had stayed in Paris. Max had urged Paul to join them, but he brushed off the occupation as if it were a trifle—he couldn't be bothered to worry. She missed him, thinking about how he always arrived late to dinner parties, but was charming, regardless. Lucie adored him, treasuring the miniature green alligator purse he had given her for her last birthday, an extravagant and unnecessary gift, but that was Paul.

Worry bloomed across Max's face. "He said we're all overreacting, like a bunch of lemmings jumping off a cliff."

But she could see that he feared for Paul and his parents, as well as for the rest of his extended family, whereas Vera had so few relatives, comparatively. Her father had died of heart failure just before Lucie was born. And she'd fallen out with her mother, who, after her father's death, took up with a South American polo player. The last time they spoke, her mother flaunted having paid for forged papers and suggested that Vera not call on her again, as such contact would compromise her new identity.

Agnes came through the double doors that led into the opposite hallway. "Is everything all right?"

Normally, she would have knocked, waiting timidly for permission to enter. She had the night off, and Vera had expected that she would take one of her beloved long walks and return after dinner with bits and pieces of gossip she had picked up in town.

Vera said that of course everything was all right, casting a look at Lucie, but there was a sharp knock at the front door just as Agnes started explaining something she'd heard from the neighbors.

A gust of wind caused the open windows to swing shut. For a moment everyone froze, and Vera thought: **Now they have come for us. They are going to throw us into a camp. I'll be separated from Lucie.**

She began to sweat, and tried to walk, as naturally as possible, to Lucie. Kneeling down next to her on the rug, Vera felt her breath shorten, her pulse accelerating.

Sabine appeared from the kitchen. "Shall I get the door?"

It was only the Freudenbergers, thank God. Just seeing Elsa in her silk kimono decorated with golden koi, her hair pulled back into a severe bun, and Leon in his pin-striped suit and straw fedora washed Vera with relief when she ushered them inside.

They looked the same.

Perhaps things weren't so bad.

But then Leon asked, somewhat shakily, clutching his hat in his hands, "Have you heard?"

Max sauntered out of the living room and retorted, "Oh, yes. We've heard. Come on, let's have a drink."

Over a bottle of whiskey, they obsessively discussed the situation. The later it grew, the blurrier all the reasons appeared for why the internment had been put into effect, and whether it would apply to Vera and Max. Both were from St. Petersburg; their families had immigrated to Paris during the revolution, over twenty years ago. "Since then, we've lived happily and quietly in France. It's our home," Max reflected, stroking his silvery beard.

Vera paced the length of the Oriental rug, rubbing her palms against her pleated skirt. "But we're foreign nationals. We don't have French citizenship, and the radio said all foreign nationals must report—"

"Yes, but you see," Elsa interrupted, perched on the edge of the cushioned settee, "the French government has more reason to intern us because we're German, and this is a time of war, whereas you are merely Russians, having resided in France for much longer than we have."

"We're Jewish arrivistes," Leon remarked sardonically from the corner.

Max said, "The Germans have persecuted you,

not just for being Jewish, but Leon, you publicly de-
nounced Hitler in your many articles and books.
You're the 'enemy of the state number one.' Where
was that printed again?" He poured more whiskey
into Leon's glass. "Well, the point is, the French government will directly realize that you are an enemy
of Germany and a lover of France. They won't intern you."

"Or," Leon offered, shifting in the deep leather
chair, "the French government will proceed against
us only to give the public the impression that France
is actually doing something to repel the Germans."

Vera noticed the sweat sprinkling the back of
Leon's pale blue dress shirt, despite his cool de-
meanor.

"Even if that were the case," Max interjected,
pouring himself another thimble of whiskey, "there's
one thing we can be sure of." He paused for dramatic
effect, relishing how they waited for him to inject
some reason into this tangled night. "As we have all
experienced countless times, the utterly ineffective
workings of the French bureaucracy will ensure that
it will take ages for the paperwork to arrive here in
Sanary to intern us. By then, we'll be gone."

Elsa and Leon heartily agreed, placated by Max's
logic; they could remain in this summery cocoon a
little longer. And Max, smoothing down the front of
his shirt with panther-like calm, was satisfied with
himself for saving the evening, as he would later say

in bed, expecting praise from Vera when all she felt was cold dread.

After the initial shock of the news that night, the tone turned less manic, and during the momentary lulls when the conversation drifted elsewhere, the evening nearly recaptured the languor they had enjoyed on other summer nights. But even as they entertained the possibilities, and examined the various angles of their predicament, Vera felt her fixed place in the world beginning to unhinge and loosen. Every noise grated; every gesture appeared imbued with portentous meaning. The occasional birdcall trilling in the night made her jump, and the clatter of dishes cleared from the table in the next room sounded hostile. Lucie's barreling run down the hallway, attempting to escape the bath, sent a sharp pang through Vera, as though all had turned irretrievably dark, even as Elsa's heady perfume, with its hints of benzoin, reminded her of other times when they would sit idly after dinner, smoking and drinking and lamenting some insignificant, comical aspect of their lives.

The following morning, while Vera sat at the breakfast table, nursing a coffee, her head pounding from too much whiskey, the cook, Sabine, appeared before her with a stricken face. She announced, with an air of self-importance, that she had read a notice posted in the town hall: all persons of foreign birth living in the Var department in the Provence–Alpes–Côte d'Azur region who had not yet reached

the age of fifty-six must report to the Gurs internment camp in southwestern France, effective immediately.

Max, listening from the doorway, barefoot in
silk pajamas, asked casually, as if to reassure Sabine
that this was all an overreaction, "Surely there's been
some mistake? Two days ago, the wireless specified
that only those living in Paris must report for internment."

Lucie barged into the living room, demanding
something. Vera wished now that she could recall
what: A glass of milk, a jam sandwich? Vera sharply
replied that she must request it politely. Lucie pouted
and then bolted into the sunlit garden. Watching
her daughter's birdlike shoulder blades protrude
from beneath the cotton straps of her sundress, her
smooth skin browned from the sun, Vera understood, in a chilling flash, that she and Max were not
French. It didn't matter that they were here now, in
the South of France. As a foreigner, she could not
shield Lucie, and pictured them at Gurs camp, lying
on the filthy hay-covered ground where animals had
been corralled, lice roving through the hay. Taking
a sip of coffee, she could already taste the camp's
metallic water, and the watery broth they would
call soup.

Lucie yanked off a few lemons from the tree and
lobbed them over the low stone wall.

Agnes's voice twitched with irritation: "Lucie,
please stop. You're ruining the lemon trees."

Vera blinked into the white sunlight, watching Lucie disobey. Pressing the heel of her palm into her forehead, she was thinking: **How are we going to get out of this?**

Sabine muttered in the background, wondering if they would leave Sanary, and then who would look after the house?

Max rejoined, "But Lucie is French! Born in Paris. She has citizenship. Let's not panic."

This should have temporarily relieved Vera, but the words "stateless" and "foreigner" looped through her mind. Words people had often used to describe her family when they had immigrated to Paris in 1917, when all she wanted was to be the daughter of a baker or a shopkeeper, living near Javel station with a name like Charlotte Moreau or Cecile Laurent . . . a common, ordinary name, a name that would never disturb or give pause, instead of Vera Dunayevskaya. When she married Max, she took his name, Volosenkova, equally unpronounceable, inducing the same silent derision to pass over people's faces, as clouds can momentarily block the sun.

When Vera enrolled Lucie in the lycée, the same questioning looks crossed the teachers' faces, and she knew that Lucie would also be marked as not quite French enough for the French.

And yet, despite always being described as "exotic" and "foreign," in a tone coated with false admiration, France ran through her blood: columnar cypresses lining dusty roads, cool stone churches offering shade and respite, the language she knew before any other. Soft and bending, sharp and brooding, it captured all she'd ever felt, harkening back to Agnes, who was once her own governess, singing her to sleep: **"You may have taken Alsace and Lorraine, but in spite of you, we will always be French!"** The language of dreams, streaming through her fingertips, into the pen, onto the page. A phrase, a certain word, provided the incendiary for all else. Without this language, this soil, what was she but a nebulous entity drifting through time and space?

Light, shade, stone. This was her home, her self.

But, Vera thought, forcing a smile at Sabine, who eyed her warily while pouring more coffee into the china-blue cup, a few drops spilling onto the saucer, the last time she and Max had applied for citizenship, two months ago, it was denied for the third time.

After breakfast, Agnes took Lucie to the beach to allow Max and Vera time to think and plan. Max stood on the bedroom balcony, his back to her, smoking furiously. "We'll wire Paris immediately. Figure out some way."

"Flames," Vera called out from the bed.

He turned to face her, the sunlit sea behind him. "What?"

"That's what Dr. Adler said. We should have listened to him then. We should have left Europe. We should have gone to America. It's too late now."

Dr. Adler, a cousin of Max's mother, was a famous psychiatrist practicing in Manhattan. With painful clarity, Vera remembered the dinner party he had attended at their newly renovated top-floor apartment. It was 1938, just after Hitler had disposed of his war minister, and rumors of another war swirled. After the other guests had left, Max and Vera bid Dr. Adler goodbye in the oval entryway, all of them bathed in the chandelier's amber glow. "You must leave France. Immediately," he said. Vera glanced into the adjoining living room, where she had installed Lucie on the velvet chaise, dreaming beneath a cashmere blanket the color of snow. "Come to New York," he pressed. "I'll write you an affidavit. Still now, you can get exit visas." Max nodded, as if he were seriously considering such an offer, but Vera knew he wasn't. He had just secured a new contract with the Paris Opera. She was deep at work on her novel.

Perched on the edge of the bed, Vera still felt the scratchy sensation of Dr. Adler's beard against her cheek when they hugged goodbye, and the letters he sent from New York in the following months that remained on top of the high glass table in the foyer, imploring them to leave Europe, because the Europe they knew and loved would soon erupt into flames.

Max stubbed out his cigarette on the balcony railing and came inside.

"We have to decide about Lucie," Vera said.

"Take her with us, of course."

She gathered up her linen skirt, fisting the fabric, her knuckles whitening. "I've heard in the camps children are separated from their parents. We might lose her. Or something worse could happen. And **she's** not a foreign national . . . She shouldn't have to go . . ."

Max knelt down before her. "What do you want to do?" His gray-green eyes watered. His tan skin suddenly appeared wrinkly and old, hanging from his face in heavy folds.

It was a plan that had been constructing itself in Vera's mind since last night, the architecture of it forming, stone by stone, until it now blazed before her, crystallized and finished. "Agnes will stay with her here, until we're released. Hopefully only for a few weeks. Nothing much needs to change. If things worsen for any reason, she can always bring Lucie home with her to Oradour-sur-Glane. You know she has a large family with many sisters. They all have children. Lucie will blend in. She might even enjoy it. And then, when we're released, we'll get Lucie back."

"Okay," Max said simply.

The pit in Vera's stomach tightened. Was this right? Was there any idea in taking Lucie with them? But once at the camp, no one knew what to expect, and the conditions . . . She had heard they made the bread with sand and the drinking water was contaminated. People suffered from dysentery, with barely enough water for cleaning themselves.

Shuddering, she stood up and walked into the hallway, opening the closet door to bring her empty suitcase down from the top shelf.

Two days later, they were to appear at the town hall to obtain a special pass to travel from their home to the camp. Once this was issued, Vera and Max, along with the Freudenbergers, would report to Gurs camp. Max had telephoned Paul last night, urging him to at least flee to the free zone, pleading with him to take their parents, but Paul insisted that Paris was safe for Jews, lightly reminding Max that many of their friends had even returned to Paris in the last few weeks, given the recently signed armistice with Germany. Vera had also spoken to Katja, her old friend from the Sorbonne, who insisted that Paris was still Paris, the only difference being the swastika flag flying over the Eiffel Tower. But while Vera listened to Katja, her palms started to sweat, thinking that Katja's French Catholic roots afforded her the luxury of staying in her apartment near Place Saint-Michel, commenting on the situation as if it didn't affect her, and maybe it didn't.

Leon's driver was due to collect them at noon. The sun glared on the whitewashed walls of the house.

Vera's eyes watered in the harsh morning light, watching Lucie standing in the garden in her black pinafore, listlessly watering the lemon trees with a dusty hose.

Last night Lucie had practiced a song at the dinner table, her high sweet voice lucid and piercing: **"France, mother of the arts, of arms and of laws, long have you nourished me with the milk of your breast. Now, like a lamb who calls out to her nurse, I fill caverns and forests with your name."**

She sang it so seriously. In better times, Vera would have suppressed a smile, but now she asked, the question catching in her throat, "Where did you learn that?"

Lucie shrugged, dipped a crust of bread into her milk, and then took a savage bite out of it. "Madame Agnes. We sing it on the way to the beach."

Lucie dropped the hose at her bare feet, watching the thin stretch of water filter into the dry soil. Then she strode off, in search of Camille, her doll. Vera watched her dart through the trees. The cat, Mourka, trotted after Lucie, his tail a black arrow, pointing into the cloudless sky.

Vera didn't hear Agnes come up behind her and was startled by her low, hoarse whisper. "I promise she will be safe with me."

Vera stared into Agnes's pewter red-rimmed eyes. Agnes smiled hesitantly and offered Vera a handkerchief. "I only worry about the war, and what will happen to France. But Lucie, I protect as my own daughter. She is mine too, in a way."

"I know," Vera said softly.

Agnes had no children, and seldom spoke of her youth. Once, Vera was aware, she had been in love, but it had ended badly and she'd slipped into spinsterhood, as if the role had awaited her all along, although she radiated a youthful efficiency at the age of fifty-two, always tidy and lean, shunning waste of any kind, reminding Vera to be thriftier and more careful. Vera's mother had hired Agnes when they still lived in St. Petersburg, nearly thirty years ago. All the wealthy Russian families sought French nannies to care for their children and, in the process, perfect their French, as French, not Russian, was the preferred language of the elite. Agnes stayed with the family during the revolution and fled with them to France, continuing to care for Vera once they began their new lives in Paris, not wanting to return to her rural village in southwestern France, where her younger sisters shared a farm with a constellation of uncles and brothers-in-law, a family brimming over with frequent clashes and disagreements, all of which Agnes was happy to escape. When Vera moved out of her parents' apartment and married Max, it was only natural that Agnes come with her.

Vera held Agnes's hands. She had thin papery skin, spidery blue veins running beneath it. With renewed urgency, Vera repeated the instructions again.

They'd gone over the details of the departure yesterday, but she needed to repeat it all, like a chant or a prayer: "If you must, first sell the furniture in the Paris apartment, then the furs, the silver, and, as a last resort, the jewelry. You also have the sixty thousand francs for living expenses. I've made arrangements with Jacques for the garden to be looked after here. There is the request for back taxes from Paris, but do not pay them. Dr. Delafontaine, you have his address. Lucie has been vaccinated for diphtheria. She has a slight case of enteritis, so no unpasteurized milk or unpasteurized cheese." Vera paused, catching her breath. "Of course you know all of this."

She tugged her wedding ring over her knuckle and back down again. "I also left a letter with Maître Vernet giving you power of attorney to make all decisions for Lucie as you see fit—" Her voice broke off, and Agnes embraced her.

She pressed her cheek against Agnes's starched collar and instantly felt small again, crying about her mother, who had flown into another rage and slapped Vera across the face, the emerald-encrusted ring leaving a stinging scratch under her eye. Agnes's thin arms held her in place, her insistent whisper tunneling into Vera's ear: "Don't worry. It will be all right in the end."

Max ambled down the stairs, dapper in his linen trousers and white shirt, his graying hair slicked back, still wet from the bath. He gave her an apologetic look. Last night they'd fought because Vera's weeping had distressed him. He told her that she must remain calm about the events that were about to occur, avoiding the words "camp" and "internment."

"Calm!" she had screamed into the windless night, backing up against the balcony's wrought iron railing, imagining how she might hurl herself over it, landing with a thud on the dry, dark earth. "How can I be calm in a situation like this? And you, drinking glass after glass of wine at Café des Voyageurs with Leon yesterday. I found you lying facedown on the couch, and Lucie asking why you were asleep at four in the afternoon. What was I supposed to say? That you were drunk and sunburnt? And you think I'm not acting properly!"

Max now placed down his valise. "Where's Lucie?" he asked, holding out the pocketbook edition of Balzac, seven novels in one, that Vera had been frantically searching for this morning.

"She's in the garden," Vera said, taking the book and pressing it to her chest.

Max strode over to the open French doors to find their daughter racing through the mazelike hedges, chasing Mourka, whose tinkling collar with its little brass bell always betrayed their location.

Vera hovered a few inches behind Max. She fought off the pressure mounting in her throat when she said, "The car will be here any minute."

Lucie disappeared behind a copse of olive trees,

dragging her doll by one leg, the straw-colored synthetic hair flecked with dirt.

"Lucie!" Vera called.

The morning grew hotter.

Already Vera had sweat through her white crepe blouse. She fidgeted with the front button. Her clothes would turn to shreds in the camp. What was the use?

Lucie's thin silvery voice rang through the trees: "Come find me!"

Vera and Max had told her about their "little vacation" and that she would stay with Madame Agnes for a bit. Lucie made them promise that she could eat ice cream every day after lunch, and that Mourka would sleep at the foot of her bed, and that they would return with presents. A blue dress and blue shoes.

Yes, yes, they said, of course.

After these negotiations, Lucie was content, having, in her eyes, won. It pained Vera to see how such small things mattered to her, belittling all else to abstraction. And yet this was the grace of childhood, the wondrous emphasis placed on cats and ice cream, on blue dresses and dusty coins buried in the garden, unearthed the next day and proclaimed a treasure—coins Max routinely buried the night before in preparation for Lucie's exultant discovery.

She reappeared between the trees, triumphantly squeezing a small silver coin between her forefinger and thumb, her dark hair a tangled halo, her cheeks flushed, tiny beads of sweat percolating along her upper lip. "Mama! I found more coins!"

Vera knelt down, opening her arms.

Lucie barreled into Vera's chest, knocking the breath out of her.

She held her tightly and whispered into Lucie's curls, "Enough to buy ice cream."

Just then she heard the dreaded honk of Leon's cabriolet, a sound that in other times had signaled motoring in the moonlight after dinner, or a trip down the coast to a neighboring town.

Lucie touched Vera's necklace, a heart hanging from a thin gold chain. It was an unconscious habit, something Lucie did all the time. "Are you leaving now? Can I first show Papa the coins I found? And will you tell Agnes about the ice cream after lunch? Every day?"

"Yes," Vera said, pressing the back of her wrist into her eyes, but insipid hot tears leaked out. She scanned the garden, the lemon trees blurring, the bougainvillea flowering over the stone wall a menacing blend of violet and apricot. And Lucie's doll, Camille, abandoned under the green bench on the far side of the garden. The doll lay facedown, and she had heard Lucie instruct the doll, in a strict tone, that it was time for bed and that was that.

"Let's go show Papa the coins," Vera whispered, noticing traces of butter smeared across Lucie's cheek from a recent snack, and that each fingernail housed a thin line of dirt beneath it. She worried

Agnes might overlook such details in their absence, while also knowing that Agnes would never neglect Lucie, as she often noticed the stray hair escaping from Lucie's braid or a miniscule stain on Lucie's pinafore long before Vera did.

Together, they walked up to the circular driveway.

Vera clutched Lucie's hand, changing her mind.

Lucie would come with them.

She already felt Lucie's weight on her lap in the crowded back seat.

Lucie trilled, "Leon and Elsa are here!"

The forsaken doll, Lucie's unfiled nails, the sun and heat lightened her head, made it spin.

Leon and Elsa sat grimly in the back seat, staring straight ahead.

Max waited on the other side of the car, glancing down at his watch. Their suitcases were already strapped onto the car roof.

"Oh," Vera said, throwing up her hands. "Where's Camille? We can't forget her."

Lucie frowned. "She was naughty. I put her under the bench."

"Vera," Max said, walking around the side of the car. "It's time." His left eye twitched. A sky blue handkerchief spilled out of his breast pocket.

Vera whispered to Lucie, "Don't forget about Camille under the bench. She'll get so very cold at night."

Kneeling down one last time, she pulled Lucie into her and whispered that she loved her and that she must always be good with Madame Agnes, and they would return soon, with a blue dress and blue shoes. She kept whispering—she couldn't remember now what else she said, only that it had allowed her to hold Lucie a few seconds longer, the warmth of her small body flooding into hers, Lucie's shallow breath on her neck, her tangled curls between Vera's fingers. She took one last inhalation of Lucie's natural milky scent, overlaid with the rosemary bushes she had trampled through earlier.

Agnes stood in front of the house, columnar in a navy shift, long sleeves even in this heat. She gestured for Lucie to come.

"Oh, wait," Vera said breathlessly. She undid the clasp of her necklace, her fingers working quickly, and then watched the delight unfold on Lucie's face when she lifted up Lucie's hair and fastened the chain around her neck.

"Keep it safe?"

Lucie nodded, squinting up at her before she ran to Agnes, as casually as any other day.

Vera slid into the back seat and gently closed the door.

Elsa gave her a pinched smile, meant to encourage, but it only made Vera's heart beat faster. She jerked around to look through the dusty rear window and saw, to her relief, Agnes rubbing off the butter from Lucie's cheek with a fresh white handkerchief.

Then Agnes glanced up and locked eyes with

Vera. She nodded as the car started down the road. A nod that reminded Vera of childhood evenings when Agnes administered medicine for Vera's asthma before bed, a nod that communicated empathy but also a resolute firmness, a firmness that Vera had never dared cross. That same nod presented itself now, indicating that certain decisions were irreversible, and certain moments in time could never come undone.

Vera looked down at the little black and white diamond tiles patterning the bathroom floor. **Of course**, she thought, **I'm seeing things. Things I shouldn't see.**

Spinning around, she examined her reflection in the mirror, willing Lucie to reappear, but Vera only caught her own dull face: sunken cheeks, blue shadows, like half-moons, under her eyes, her lower lip chapped and puffy. She tilted her head toward the doorway, listening for him, but she only heard the crashing surf and seagulls cawing at the rising sun, as if rejecting it.

It was strange, finding herself in a clean little motel room, this box on the sand, with a man she barely knew, who now slept deeply.

She stared at Sasha from the bathroom doorway: his arm hung off the bed, knuckles grazing the carpet, his palm loosely open, as if entreating her to come back. His face was turned away from the morning sun splintering through the blinds, and she tracked the slant of his cheekbones, the tendons in his neck, his body barely containing all the life running through it.

Last night, when he had delved into her, she felt tightly warm and dark with bursts of jagged light, that dislodged each piece of her, as though the carefully placed glass squares in a mosaic were coming undone: her marriage to Max, the war, fleeing France and losing Lucie, her stilted existence in Los Angeles, and the heavy history of before: leaving Russia on the eve of the revolution, the china-blue walls of her childhood bedroom, Agnes's hands caressing her into sleep, the same hands that had held and comforted Lucie.

The sheets were twisted at the foot of the bed. She studied the scene, perplexed by how easily she had gone with Sasha in his convertible, speeding down the highway, and then she had suggested they spend the night together, taken aback and intrigued by her own boldness.

She smiled faintly, remembering the English term for it: **a one-night stand**.

Sighing, Vera lit a cigarette and leaned into the door frame. She wondered when Sasha would wake up and realize the error in assuming she was the type of woman who took pleasure easily and lightly, unburdened and spilling over with desire, as she had seemed last night. It almost caused her to laugh, struck by this sardonic illusion, as if the farce of herself was finally coming to light.

What a mess, she thought, inhaling deeply. **I'm going mad, just as Max said I would.**

She watched Sasha sleep, unable to ignore the pulse between her legs, as if he were still inside her, his fingers tracing the curve of her ribs, his stubble against the side of her neck, which she touched now, her skin slightly razed and red.

She thought to yesterday, blue-black hair falling in his eyes, his jaw tensing when he saw her at Villa Aurora, as if he'd always been waiting for her. With his Russian name, there was something sweet and familiar about him, and the hum of energy between them contained a lilting melody that maybe only she heard. When he sped down the highway, he glanced over at her, and with his hand resting on her thigh, his bemused smile suggested that he could easily take her away from all this.

She looked at herself in the cloudy mirror of the armoire, shrugging off the towel, letting it fall to the carpet. She noted her smooth stomach and upright frame, her wavy hair skimming her bony shoulders. It had been a long time since she'd looked at herself like this. She touched her abdomen, her hips, the swell of her thighs, and, for an instant, she returned to a younger self, before she was a mother, before they fled Europe, before grief had made her invisible.

CHAPTER 2

SASHA

OCTOBER 1940,
NEW ROCHELLE, NEW YORK

Sasha sat in the back seat of Dubrow's Cadillac, fidgeting with his cuff links, his jacket too tight in the shoulders, and stared out at the manicured lawns and white mansions on the way to the Hampshire Country Club. He felt out of place in this sedate affluence, with its circular driveways and spiral-shaped topiaries. The suit didn't fit right, having gone unworn for over a year. In California, no one wore suits. But he was home for the High Holidays, which dictated dark suits and ties, and that you sit in shul for hours on end while intermittently a congregant blew the shofar, the whole room quaking with centuries of expectation for that long, sob-like blast.

During the ride up to New Rochelle from the

Lower East Side, he thought about how different "home" was, since his mother, Leah, had moved into Dubrow's New Rochelle house five years ago, after they got married. But Sasha was still a kid from Rivington Street: broken storefront windows and toy guns, games of cops and robbers under the shadowy arcade of the rumbling El, and pushcarts rattling down the uneven streets selling everything from dead chickens with the feathers still on to plump watermelons in the summer, Mr. Ferrucci bellowing out, "Red like fire, sweet like sugar."

Leah and Dubrow now rated the merit of the sho-far blower, joking that because Schiller's teenage son had performed the task, the sound was a weak imi-tation of the blast meant to rouse the dead and re-joice in the new year. Sasha half listened to their griping, in a mixture of English and Yiddish, while trying to hear the radio on low, reporting that Vichy France had enforced new legislation in regard to its Jewish population. Leah and Dubrow brushed the news aside, casually, as if swatting a pesky fly, but this was more or less their general attitude, as if the trouble in Europe didn't apply to them, believing America was exempt, an unquestionably safe haven, whereas Sasha wasn't so sure.

Leah turned around in her seat, her dark eyes flashing with mischief. "What did you think, **bubbala**?"

"Schiller did all right." Sasha tried to smile, see-ing how much she loved that he was home, even for a few days. She was forever betrayed that he'd moved away, and forever hoping he'd move back. The High Holidays, the "Days of Awe," as they were called, pe-rennially filled his mother with heaviness and light, with sweetness and angst, her gaze retreating inward to a distant place when she recited the evening kid-dush before dinner. He always wondered why this time of year affected her so much, guessing that she remembered the Jewish holidays in the shtetl attract-ing violence, pogroms, though here in America they were safe. Sasha used to remind her of this when he was young, when they lived in the tenement apart-ment, just the two of them. And yet, when leaves began falling and the light turned golden, her emo-tions heightened, her eyes glistening with the past.

Waiting for him to say more about the Schil-ler boy, about the service, about the new rabbi, too young in her opinion, so that they could return to their joking and gossip, to the way it used to be, she added, "Are you sure you can't stay until Yom Kippur? It would be so nice if—"

"Ma," he began, but then she interrupted, "Fine," and turned away from him, refocusing on the road.

When Rosh Hashanah ended in a few days, he would return to Los Angeles, where he'd been work-ing as a screenwriter for the last two years, writing one-offs for the studios. And Leah knew, as much as she didn't want to, that she couldn't keep him

here. Ever since he was young, she'd called him a
dreamer, a **luftmensch**, head in the clouds, uninterested in life's practicalities. That's how she saw his
choice to live in California, where he knew no one,
had no one, when in New York, she used to say, opportunity presented itself like a rich salty oyster. She
thought he was crazy not to take advantage, when
for most of Sasha's childhood, they had been so dis-
advantaged. Things had changed after Leah met
Dubrow. Dubrow owned a string of cafeterias, and
with no children of his own, he'd groomed Sasha
for the business, starting him out as a busboy at fifteen, and then a waiter, and finally a manager of
the Lower East Side location under Leah's watchful,
hopeful eye.

But Sasha couldn't force himself into wanting
that life. He'd grown up on the streets, intrigued
by the heated arguments unfolding on every corner,
the women yelling from one window to another over
laundry lines crisscrossing alleys and tiny gardens,
betrayals and sacrifices pulsating behind every door,
while lovers, leaning against a chain-link fence on
the schoolyard's edge, made promises they couldn't
keep. On their rooftop, he and his friends kept
pigeons, giving them names and distinct personalities, with innate desires and dislikes, much like the
people they knew.

The neighborhood was rich with gossip, but poor
in every other respect, and his mother taught him to

love the stories that circulated from tenement to tenement like wildfire. Together they found a special joy in reporting that Mrs. Markowitz had left her nice husband for a Polish painter, a lout who drank, or that Tedora Binaggi, who lived upstairs, had lost her parents at the age of three on the voyage over to America from Italy. She had waited at Ellis Island with a white placard hanging from her neck, until a nice Italian woman took her hand, and whispered, **"Vieni con noi."**

These stories, they grew inside him, gaining momentum and energy, as though he carried blueprints of great cities in his mind, urging him to construct plots with gut-wrenching twists, characters with secrets, hidden pasts, and unexpected futures, awaiting them all. It wasn't really a choice, to write, as he was propelled by the unconscious need to rescue the truth from vagueness and omission, from the distortion of memory, from the desire to alter the story so that it reflected better upon the storyteller. And maybe this urge to know more, to understand what had really happened, grew out of the silence that blanketed his own past, with its many gaps.

Sasha was born a year into the Great War, in a shtetl twenty kilometers from Riga, and his earliest memories were blurry, as everyone's were, but more so given the unsteady times: all the men left to fight, and then other men arrived, German soldiers. The war bled into the revolution, the czar's

White Army against the Reds. Certain images persisted: his mother stoking blue embers in the fireplace, willing the smoldering sparks to warm them, dipping small pieces of bread in salt; a forest full of pine trees; the sound of a bullhorn roaring from the town square, barking orders he couldn't understand, Germanic, harsh, unbending. The fear in his mother's eyes when they ventured outside, her hand clenching his. A fear that persisted long after the war because, he later realized, she was husbandless, with a little boy to fend for, which left her subject to hostility and judgment, but only later did he guess the full extent of it.

During the worst of their arguments, Leah often said that if he didn't like the cafeteria business, then he should at least consider college, where he could learn a respectable profession like law or medicine, and Dubrow would pay for it. But again, living under someone else's thumb, no matter how generous and gentle that thumb might be, Sasha couldn't do it. So he started thinking about how he could make a living from telling stories, and got a job writing copy at the **New York Daily Mirror** his last year of high school, and then, because he wrote fast, he became a crime reporter at seventeen. He smoked cigars to look older, and what began as an affectation grew into a natural part of his personality. Soon, he started handing out cigars to cops for leads, which worked better than passing out sticks of chewing gum. Most nights, he came home late, or not until breakfast, and after a shower and a peck on his mother's cheek, he dashed off to high school, barely waiting for the bell to ring, when he could return to his disorderly office desk, a few steps from the men's room, waiting for a hot tip that would launch him back onto the streets.

Leah shook her head, muttering that he was a "vulture for bad news," chasing leads of bank robberies, tenement fires, murderesses, gambling rings, and "leapers," as they called those who threatened suicide from the rooftops of skyscrapers as Sasha and the other reporters barked out questions from below. With crime scenes and the city morgue his regular haunts, he knew this work disappointed his mother, despite his increasingly numerous bylines, to the point where she stopped reading his articles; they were too disturbing, too bloody, too human. But when he went out on assignments, adrenaline coursed through his veins. He often arrived at the scene before the police, prowling for anything incongruous, pressing down harder on a detail that didn't quite fit, something closer to the truth but not close enough, and often then, the truth came tumbling out.

He did this for five years, juggling crime reporting and managing Dubrow's to keep his mother happy, and he felt as wet and malleable as concrete when it's first laid, unmarred by footsteps, pleased by the thought that he could easily shift paths.

Just after his twenty-third birthday, his mother set him up with Margaret Altman, of the Altman department stores. "She's home for summer break from Vassar," his mother explained, adding proudly that Margaret studied anthropology and music. Sasha took her to a dance at the Hampshire Country Club, where many matches of the Westchester Jewish elite were made, her chaperone watching from the corner. "My aunt," Margaret said with a touch of embarrassment. Generous diamonds twinkled in her ears, a corsage of baby white roses gracing her delicate wrist. She asked, trying to make small talk, if he enjoyed the cafeteria business, quickly adding when she saw his confusion, "I mean, aren't you taking over Dubrow's . . . eventually?"

Eventually.

The word hung in the air, accumulating weight, his chest constricting with the notion that the concrete was beginning to set, hardening under his wingtips, even within the time it took for the song to end, the band playing "April in Paris." The longer he stayed here, dancing with Margaret, the sooner the grand vista of his future would narrow down to a fine point, with little chance for something else, something more.

Shortly after this, a query on gold-embossed letterhead showed up from an executive at Warner Bros., offering Sasha five hundred dollars to write a script based on the Waldorf Astoria double-suicide case. The week prior, Sasha had written an article about these newlyweds who had supposedly taken their own lives, found naked in the bathtub with a bullet shot through the man's head, but the woman, save for light bruising around her neck, was left untouched. Convinced the fancy letter was a prank, cooked up by one of his fellow reporters, Sasha telephoned the studio in Los Angeles and asked to speak to the man from Warner's.

"Is this real?" Sasha asked, the phone receiver balanced between his neck and hiked-up shoulder as he buttoned up the white pressed shirt he had to wear for his shift at the cafeteria, along with the silly black bow tie.

The man explained that they thought the case would make a good picture, and when Sasha retorted that he knew everything they did, it was right there in print, the man said, slightly exasperated, that because of legal constraints, they couldn't just pluck the story from the pages of the **Mirror**.

"So, how's this gonna make a good picture, with the case still unsolved?"

"You don't get it." The man sighed. "This is the movies. Make up the ending."

"Just make it up?" Sasha repeated, feeling slightly dumb as the words tumbled from his mouth. At the same time, he wasn't sure if he could just make things up for a living . . . it had been hammered into him to hunt down the truth, untangle fact from fiction, not create more fiction.

Even though Sasha turned down the offer, the seed had been planted. As he greeted customers and handed out menus, he imagined his stories illuminated on the wide screen, viewed by thousands in the anonymous dark. As a kid in the summer, he and his friends would watch three shows a week, stealing into air-conditioned theaters, sinking into plush velour seats, the cowboys swaggering and towering before them, guns drawn, jaws clenched. He never thought he could actually make movies like those, until this seductive fantasy began to throb through him while he loitered around the cold morgue in the early dawn, waiting for a scoop, his clothes stinking of formaldehyde. Images of the stories he'd reported demanded more life: A matronly ambulance attendant tagging a corpse with such gentleness and care, as though bidding goodbye to her own son, or a young woman's body found in the middle of Park Avenue, her alligator purse flung a few feet away, after she had jumped from a moving car. A police chief smiling down at a pair of newborn kittens he cupped in his palms, having just rescued them from a dumpster when searching for the murder weapon. He started jotting down these observations in a notebook, and soon, he was experimenting with "making things up" and writing a few story outlines.

And so, a year later, another telephone call came from RKO, this time about an article he'd written, "Close to the Edge," about a psychiatrist specializing in talking leapers out of jumping, who, as it turns out, was battling his own demons. They offered him seven grand for the film rights and to adapt the article into a script.

Sasha said yes.

And what he couldn't fully articulate but had started to feel in every particle was that California promised space, as if time could be stretched and elongated out there, and in its velvety emptiness he could re-create himself. No one would know he didn't have a father. No one would know his mother had worked in a sweatshop sewing buttons onto jackets, lace onto collars. No one would know he was an immigrant kid who had struggled to lose his Russian accent in grade school, or that the other boys threw gravel at him on the playground, and when he came home with a black eye, his mother demanded in Yiddish, "Who did that to you? Tell me who."

The night before he left, he sat with his mother at the kitchen table. Her face, wan beneath the shaded lamp hanging from the ceiling, echoed with more than just his leaving for California. It was the same unsettled, absent expression that he recognized from childhood, as if a ghost were hovering between them. He felt the urge to ask about his father, about the war he was born into, about the details of their life in the old country that she intentionally blurred. He hunched forward, sitting on his hands, readying himself to broach the subject, when she pushed the plate toward him. "Here, eat." It was a herring sandwich on rye bread that she had just prepared.

Sasha stood up and folded his arms around her, and for a moment a thick, strained silence settled over them until he broke the tension by joking that she could always come with him to California.

Leah sighed, her body softening. "What would an old woman do in California?"

"What do old women do in New York?"

Their eyes met and they both laughed.

He arrived in Los Angeles on a hot July evening in 1938, his chest loosening when he first glimpsed the Pacific, a shimmering blue that bled into the horizon. He walked along the beach, breathing in the salty air, his loafers stuffed under his arm, his bare feet sinking into the still warm sand, and the eucalyptus trees on the bluffs up above emitting that sharp, clean scent. When he'd walked far enough, he sank, fully clothed, into the sand, his mind flattening into a blank canvas, a blankness waiting to be filled.

. . .

Glancing out at the lush suburban greenery of New Rochelle now, he saw they were almost at the country club, and it was too late to take off the pinching suit jacket, as his mother would only make him put it on again. He hadn't been listening to Dubrow and his mother chitchat, but Dubrow was now saying something about how Europe wasn't our fight to fight, parroting a speech that Joseph Kennedy had given over the radio. Maybe, Sasha thought, Dubrow didn't understand, given that he was born deaf in one ear and couldn't fight in the Great War.

Leah turned around in her seat again and announced that she sided with those Philadelphia mothers who had stormed the White House in protest against the war. "They don't want their boys sent off to fight. And quite frankly, neither do I."

"Joel Binaggi and Harvey Feldman already enlisted," Sasha countered, naming his childhood friends from Rivington Street.

Making a wide turn onto the tree-lined lane leading up to the club, Dubrow remarked that those kids didn't have the opportunities Sasha had. They were only using the war to fill a void.

"Feldman's in law school, and Binaggi is taking over his dad's grocery business," Sasha shot back.

The air inside the car stiffened as Dubrow pulled up to the club: a white colonial mansion with a wraparound porch, a circular gravel driveway leading both in and out, the smooth rolling golf course

behind it. White-gloved valets stood at the entrance.

Dubrow sighed heavily and turned off the igni-
tion. "Come on, let's have a nice time."

The valets approached to open the car doors.
Leah rearranged her gold-and-burgundy brocade
skirt and gave Sasha a tense look, her face a shade
paler, and he felt a stab of guilt, realizing that she
feared he would enlist, and for once, her worry was
justified. He almost couldn't bring himself to get
out and walk over the pretentious gravel driveway in
his hard leather oxfords into that ridiculous and imposing place where he could be sure they'd be playing Glenn Miller with a vengeance, as if such forced
gaiety could help people forget the dark storm gathering over Europe. But he did it for his mother,
who shot him another anxious look when the valet
opened her car door.

Together, they walked up to the club. She clung
to his arm, and he felt her pressuring insistence that
he at least pretend to enjoy himself, but then she
added, as if it were an afterthought, "Oh, I forgot to
tell you. Margaret Altman is here tonight. I told her
you were home from California, and she was hoping to—"

Sasha stopped short. "Ma. Come, on. Seriously?"

She looked at him with injured eyes. Dubrow
paused, his arm extended toward the open double
doors, waiting to escort Leah inside.

Couples in evening attire passed, furtively glancing at Sasha, and a wave of embarrassment washed over him, knowing that he was making a scene, but it couldn't be helped.

"Sasha, please, it's only dinner?"

"I can't, Ma. I just can't."

He turned away, unable to take her disappointment any longer, and overheard Dubrow whisper hoarsely, "If he wants to go, let him go! The tighter you hold him, the farther he'll run." Leah muttered something back, and Dubrow added, "My **sheifale**, don't make a storm in a teacup."

Sasha walked toward the sunset, streaked with pink and gold, and the spidery elms, silhouetted against the inflamed colors, and thought of California: the mountains and the sea, the dry desert winds, the lucky sunshine, and the sky, endless and blue.

CHAPTER 3

LUCIE

AUGUST 1940,
ORADOUR-SUR-GLANE, FRANCE

She played outside with the other children, who had hair the color of clarified butter and lips stained from eating wild blackberries. Stripping the bushes of the ripe fruit, they called her "Agnes's girl," because they knew Agnes had worked for a wealthy family with only one child, a girl, and Lucie was that girl, and they had been instructed to now call her "Agnes's girl" instead of "Lucie from Paris." At first, she felt ugly compared to them, with her dark hair and white skin, but after a while it mattered less.

Pointed cypresses lining gravel paths that led to nowhere, the brush of lavender and sage against her fingertips, the soft purr of the cat on her lap. She felt his breathing through the calico fur. And now there was a new puppy, the runt of the litter, and they'd

allowed her to keep him, a small act of generosity—
Agnes's sisters were going to drown him otherwise. Lucie named him Giles. She loved to stroke
his velvety ears and smell his puppyish breath, full
of newly chewed grass and dirt, and feel his little
pointy teeth gnawing at her knuckles. Sometimes he
left regurgitated honeysuckles on the doorstep, but
Lucie cleaned it up before anyone noticed.

She fed bruised apples and old carrots to the
horses and stroked the bridges of their downy pink
noses. They flicked their tails in appreciation, their
large liquid eyes asking for more.

Inside, the oak floors creaked under her feet. The
walls were made of stone, some light and rough,
some dark and smooth, a varied landscape running
beneath her palm. Chinks of light bullied their way
through the recessed windows. In the drafty front
room stood a piano, older than the one her parents
had in Paris but still functioning. It had been in this
farmhouse for over one hundred years, Agnes whispered, adding that Lucie was never to touch it.

But sometimes, when the sisters weren't around,
Lucie played a few chords that her father had taught
her. The mournful notes pierced her with homesickness, and she would gently place the heavy wooden
lid back over the keys, swallowing down a hard
knot. The only other time she neared the piano was
when Monsieur Durand came to tune it. He gave
her a conspiratorial wink and motioned for her to
come over, showing her his tools, various levers and

wrenches that he kept in a special black case. After he finished, he lingered in the kitchen, where Agnes served him coffee at the table and they spoke for a while, their animated talk echoing through the house, and Lucie wondered what was so interesting. Before he left, he palmed her some pastilles that she hid deep inside her pinafore pockets, waiting until she was in bed to savor them.

At night: a blanket of stars. Orange candies dissolving under her tongue.

The sisters' faces were rough and red from windburn, their hands blistered and full of miniscule cuts. Lucie thought perhaps the sisters were rough with her because their lives were rough, their work often requiring their backs to bend and curve for many hours. Plucking chickens, darning socks, scrubbing floors, pulling root vegetables from the soil. Lucie thought that because they had to bend so much, they couldn't bend any more with her, or with anyone. Whenever she came near, their faces looked like the stones that surrounded them, hard and impenetrable, but then she would creep up on them in gentler moments: feeding a baby, smoothly brushing out their daughters' hair, the flaxen strands gleaming in the firelight as they murmured little stories about lost treasures and cats that could talk. While she listened, a desolate sadness permeated her, knowing that she must carry something within herself that they found repellent.

. . .

A long time had passed since her parents went on vacation, the longest time ever, but it had only been one month, Agnes explained.

"Mama said they were only going away for two weeks," Lucie retorted, monitoring the small muscles twitching along Agnes's neck when she replied, "You misunderstood. Not two weeks. Two months."

Lucie also wondered why they had left Sanary. They were supposed to stay there until her parents returned. But a few days after her parents left, Agnes suddenly decided that they should leave too when a French officer visited and spoke the entire time in a reassuring tone, suggesting that they should vacate, given that other officers would visit them tomorrow morning, quite early. The cook and the gardener looked pale and frightened, but Lucie did not understand why because the officer had kind eyes and a large mouth, and spoke with his hands, and ate all of the biscuits that Sabine had set out on the porcelain plate.

Before he left, he knelt down and stroked her cheek. "You look just like my little girl."

Immediately after this, Agnes made preparations for them to catch the afternoon train to Limoges. From there, they would stay with her sisters on a farm in Oradour-sur-Glane. "Just for a bit," Agnes kept repeating as she tore through drawers and shelves, stuffing clothes and shoes into suitcases. She did not pack in the orderly fashion she always did before big trips, folding the clothes first on the bed and then eliminating what they didn't need. She was sweating, wisps of hair sticking to her temples, and her hands shook when she snapped the suitcases closed. Lucie watched, frozen in the doorway, touching the golden heart pendant that hung from her neck. She knew not to speak, as one more question might cause Agnes to start sobbing or screaming—she couldn't tell which—but she kept wondering why they were leaving, and how her mother and father would find her. They were supposed to remain here, she kept wanting to remind Agnes, but Agnes's flustered, quick movements and exaggerated sighs, the way she seemed to see and not see Lucie, gave her pause. It was the same expression Agnes wore when Lucie asked her a question while she was reading the newspaper and she mumbled an answer, her eyes glazed-over with distraction.

It was the same, but with more fear in it.

CHAPTER 4

VERA

AUGUST 1940, GURS INTERNMENT CAMP,
SOUTHWESTERN FRANCE

Her hands trembled as she tore open the thick cream envelope. Agnes's familiar handwriting slanted across the page, and Vera devoured the words that would have to sustain her until the next letter arrived. Vera and Elsa had been here for a month, and this was the second letter from Agnes. Vera knew she was lucky to get it. People complained that letters weren't coming through, or if a letter arrived, it often took months, especially if a letter was traveling from the occupied zone to the free zone. At least Oradour was in the free zone, but tucked just below the Maginot Line. Gurs camp, also in the free zone, was much farther south, the blue Pyrenees rising up in the distance.

Agnes wrote: **The weather is clement. L. loves**

sleeping with the older girls in the big bed. She got a new puppy today, we tied a blue ribbon around its neck. Camille was left outside in the downpour overnight, now we are drying her by the fire—she is safe and warm. Sincerely, A.

The stone farmhouse, the new puppy with its soft dark pelt, the sky blue ribbon Lucie had tied around its neck swam before Vera's eyes. She walked around in a daze, not registering the camp's ugly bareness, the letter a salve, a palimpsest obscuring the surroundings: barbed-wire fence up against purple mountains, rows of unheated barracks with corrugated roofs, piles of stones they had assembled yesterday, only to be commanded to disassemble them today for no other purpose than to instill a sense of deprivation and meaninglessness within them.

Vera wondered if Max and Leon were suffering the same conditions, as the men had been detained in a nearby camp. Crude pipes ran alongside the barracks that they used to wash themselves. The toilet a slab of concrete with a hole in it, separated by low partitions. The unbearable stench as she squatted over the concrete hole, staring up at the changeable sky, thankful at least that Lucie had fresh air and plenty of milk, unlike the children here, who roamed the camp in packs, lawless, scavenging for food or for some cheap trinket: a filched marble, a toy soldier, a broken yoyo. These child gangs hoarded black bread, ersatz coffee, scraps of meat, lost coins, their lice-ridden heads peering into the huge pot where the daily watery soup simmered. Over the last two weeks, the children had transformed into cunning thieves, adapting to the camp, as opposed to their bourgeois mothers, who shuffled around, frightened and indignant, demanding to know when they would be released, demanding to send letters and make phone calls, requests the guards casually dismissed while chewing tobacco, waiting for the right moment to hurl the wad, glistening with saliva and spit, at anyone who asked for too much.

The women grew depressed and lethargic in the face of these daily injustices, while their children grew more daring, their elbows sharpening, their once plump faces angular.

Vera listened to the mothers lamenting their children's former selves. Jean Paul, who had always sat obediently at his school desk, his beautiful cursive streaming across the page, and now look at him. A bare-chested savage leading a pack of savages, face smeared with dirt, blond hair matted, depositing at the end of each day a bruised apple or a few split-open figs onto his mother's pillow, the same way their family cat used to drag in dead birds and expect a reward for it.

"Well," another mother interjected, "you must have seen my Claudette scratching her legs like a flea-ridden dog, scratching until she bled, and then running after the boys in her stained pinafore, all those years of piano and ballet lessons discarded in an instant."

Some of the women envied Vera for having managed to stow Lucie away somewhere safe and clean. When they noticed Vera staring at their children, they would say in their light chattering way, "Oh, but it's really better. This place is a disgrace. Just look at this soup, nothing but diluted broth," holding the half-filled spoon under Vera's nose. For a few moments, Vera felt consoled, even flattered, that perhaps they thought she was a better mother, a more cautious mother, for having sent her daughter to the country, but doubt always returned.

What had she done?

It was a huge mistake. She should have kept Lucie with her no matter what.

Once, in the early dawn, while the women dressed and she lay still on her pallet, feigning sleep, she overhead them.

"Poor Vera. Can you imagine?" one of them whispered.

"Absolutely not," another mother hissed. "I would never leave my child, not under any circumstances. I must see him, touch him. How else can you know if your child is truly well?"

The question hung in the air long after the women finished dressing and left. It hung there every night as Vera tossed and turned. After many wakeful hours, she often fell into a deep sleep just before dawn broke. This morning, Elsa was shaking her, repeating that they were here in the camp, it was time to wake up and wash, but Vera kept staring into Elsa's browned face, both seeing Elsa and not seeing her, both knowing that they now lived in this cement room full of strange women and also that she held Lucie close in the garden at Sanary, sun filtering through the treetops, Lucie prattling on, her voice soft and lilting, reciting a story Vera had now forgotten.

A dull gray light shone through the one dirty window. Vera stumbled around the little makeshift bed, searching for her shoes, not wholly believing she was here. If Lucie had felt so real in her arms, only to melt into a mirage, then perhaps these old clothes she wore day after day, the dirt between her toes, the metallic taste in her mouth, this camp with its surly French soldiers, wasn't real either. Perhaps **this** was a dream, and she would soon find herself next to Max in their four-poster bed, while he munched on a croissant, reading the paper, spectacles having slid down the bridge of his nose, buttery flakes of breakfast decorating his furry chest. She imagined telling him about this dream. No, a nightmare, she would correct herself, describing how they'd been separated and interned at different camps. Agnes had taken Lucie to Oradour-sur-Glane because it was no longer safe in Sanary. She would include that Elsa was as industrious and clever as ever, even in dreams.

She thought about this with a half smile, watching Elsa magically produce a bottle of cold milk for a pregnant woman who slept a few beds away. Then Elsa helped with the woman's bedding, expertly tucking the sheet under the loose hay. Following this, in one continuous motion, Elsa slipped a stolen apple into a nearby woman's apron. Later, Vera saw the woman cutting the apple into quarters for her children, and Vera considered how Elsa did so much and she so little. Within their first days here, Elsa had instructed the women to arrange their beds in rows, and told them where to store their shoes, and explained how to keep the ever-present dust at bay by shaking out their belongings every day, to stave off disease, lassitude, filth. She seemed to know when a woman's labor was coming and arranged for her admission into the infirmary. After a child was born, she could tell, even before the mother could, if the child had fever or jaundice, just by the touch of her palm.

Waiting for the toilet, the line coiling and infinite under the punishing sun, Vera and Elsa glanced around, increasingly aware of the German soldiers, elegant in their gray-green field uniforms, who, over the last week, had multiplied and replaced the French ones.

Fresh rumors circulated that, due to the recent armistice, all prisoners could be surrendered on demand to German officials. Over the last few days, the German prisoners had been released, except for the German Jews, leaving behind Elsa and

Vera and other foreign nationals, such as a young Dutch mother, an Algerian grandmother, a slew of Englishwomen, the supercilious Russians (whom Vera avoided), and the Spanish Loyalists who had escaped the civil war in Spain and were now interned here, as well as many Frenchwomen who for one reason or another were under suspicion. Perhaps they had communist husbands, or had married foreigners.

Elsa's hand encircled Vera's wrist, and in one quick motion, she pulled her behind a crumbling brick wall.

"Now our places in line are lost for the day," Vera whispered.

Elsa shook her head. "Listen. We can't stay here any longer. It isn't safe. Ingrid, you remember Ingrid? She was released after the armistice."

Vera nodded, recalling the young German girl who had clung to Elsa, seeking instruction on how to care for herself in these primitive conditions, untrained in the ways of women. When Ingrid needed help making a sanitary pad, Elsa didn't flinch, and after this, Ingrid fashioned herself as Elsa's little secretary, the others joked, but all of them admired Elsa's ingenuity and wit, which lightened the gathering darkness, making the sordid surroundings appear a little less so.

Elsa continued, "She risked coming back here a few days ago to tell me very soon we will all be transported to a camp in Poland. The foreigners, political enemies of the Reich, Jews, all the undesirables will go." Elsa paused.

"If we can make it to the Spanish border, it's less heavily guarded. Varian Fry, a young Quaker and American journalist and a great admirer of Leon's, has promised to get us across. We'll take the night train to Cerbère. Then we'll have to climb the Pyrenees." Elsa stopped, noticing Vera's distraction.

"You're not listening."

Vera stared down at her worn shoes, the T-straps fraying. Her head felt light, empty.

Elsa smoothed back her already smooth hair, coiled into a severe bun at the nape of her neck. **Economy**, Vera thought. **Elsa is all economy, and I have nothing to offer but prevarications and doubt. But of course she can afford to act so briskly when she has nothing to lose.**

By "nothing," Vera meant a child.

Elsa said, "There's the question of Lucie."

Vera started at the sound of her daughter's name.

"It's not safe, or even possible, to send for her."

"I know," Vera said, her throat closing up. She tried to swallow, but a mounting thickness prevented her. They'd heard from recent refugees entering the camp about the horror of the roads: thousands had fled Paris and the northern provinces with mattresses strapped on top of cars; farmers had abandoned their fields; once cherished family dogs now roamed the streets. People pawned the family silver for a few liters of petrol. Train stations resembled refugee camps, overrun with families huddled on benches, people sleeping on the floor for days, hoping to make it onto a train that would carry them south.

Vera leaned against the cool brick wall, shaded by the overhanging plane trees, and closed her eyes, the sting of tears pulsing behind her lids.

Elsa ran the back of her hand against Vera's cheek, and Vera recalled Agnes's last letter alluding to the plentitude of bread and milk, how Lucie slept peacefully, the new puppy curled into the crook of her arm. She knew what Agnes meant beneath those images of hearth and home: **We are much safer staying put, even with the German advance, than leaving and becoming subject to the roads, to the lack of food and petrol, to the chaos of a country in flight.** Vera knew Agnes was right, and yet she still thought there would be time to collect Lucie somehow, or that this internment would only last a few weeks and they would reunite. This was what she had believed in the back seat of Leon's car, staring through the rear window watching Lucie, in her black pinafore, growing smaller and smaller.

"She will be all right," Elsa whispered, the words as warm and soft as her hand, which had now slid down to Vera's shoulder. "But Oradour is just below the demarcation line. It's too far. Too dangerous. On the way here, Lucie could be apprehended and taken into custody." Elsa's hand dropped.

"I know," Vera repeated, opening her eyes, tears blurring Elsa's severe cheekbones, turning her hawkish nose less distinct.

Elsa glanced around, taking stock of who might be watching. The only face that smiled back belonged to Madame, as she was called in the camp, based upon her former profession in Paris. An elderly woman whose rippling obese body appeared to move in various directions at once, supported on either side by one of her girls. Her black wig wobbled on top of her head, and her crimson velvet dress trailed behind her in the dust. Her face, white and heavily powdered, a slash of red across her lips, reminded Vera of a Kabuki mask, eyebrows arched into manufactured surprise, and Vera, unthinkingly, smiled back.

CHAPTER 5

VERA

On her last night at Gurs, the children debated if they could see their fathers in the moon. Vera lay on her pallet, knowing that tomorrow morning when they filed out with the others, she and Elsa would walk in the other direction.

After Elsa had told her that soon German soldiers would replace the last French ones, they had taken turns digging a hole under the barbed wire fence between soldiers' rounds and covering it with leaves and brambles. On their final morning, when the soldiers changed, they dove to the ground and wiggled through the space between the fence and the dirt. Sliding on their bellies for hours, they weaved, like water snakes, through the tall grass until they reached the road.

Once on the road, they blended in with all the other filthy refugees escaping the north for the south. Planes flew overhead, and everyone looked up, gasping. Abandoned rusted cars festered in the hot dust. Women and children jumped on the back of German military convoys, leaving their husbands behind. "Meet you in Marseilles," they yelled into the wind, the men shielding their eyes with the palms of their hands.

In the throng, Elsa clutched her arm, explaining that they had to first locate Leon and Max, get them out of the camp in Nîmes, and from there leave France. "America. America is the only place we can go," she said.

Franz Werfel's complaints rang in Vera's ears, echoing from another time, when they still had a choice: **Don't go to America. Here in Europe we are established, we have renown. Nobody knows us in America.**

French officers still ran the military office in Nîmes. Somehow Elsa had found this out in advance. The officers said that Leon and Max were not in Nîmes, but at a camp called Saint-Nicolas. The only way to get there was by taxi. No other way. No bus, no train, nothing. "The roads are also very bad," they added. "You cannot walk. It will take all day, at least."

Elsa begged the officers for help, saying all the

right things about having lived in France for many years, and that Vera—she nudged Vera forward—was a celebrated French novelist. "And of course, you must be familiar with my husband's work, Leon Freudenberger." She sighed. "He has a stomach ailment and is unwell."

The French officers listened, nodding at the appropriate times. After Elsa had finished her speech and the silence in the room grew uncomfortable, one of the officers strolled over to Elsa and sat on the edge of the desk. He held a cigarette between his fingers, contemplating whether or not to light it.

When he finally spoke, his voice sounded like tires crunching over gravel. "I must explain something to you. If the Nazis asked us to sell our mothers, we would do it. That's how afraid we are of the Nazis. Do you understand?"

That afternoon, Vera found herself perched on the lap of a black marketeer in the back seat of an old Peugeot. Next to her, another man smoked a strong cigar while periodically scratching his balls. Elsa sat on the other side of him, pressed against the taxicab door. The roads were bumpy, filled with potholes, and with each bump, the black marketeer's knee wedged deeper into her groin. She felt oddly aroused. He was attractive. Gray stubble, muscular forearms, reptilian eyes a slate color she couldn't trust. When the driver swerved and Vera tilted to the side, he gripped the curve of her waist, stopping her from colliding with the car window. The taxi driver locked eyes with Vera in the mirror, but she nodded and his gaze returned to the road. She had felt dirty and ugly for weeks, and the realization that this man actually enjoyed the feeling of her body gave her brief pleasure, recalling days not so far gone.

Vera ground down on his knee, sharp pleasure rippling through her limbs. She wondered if this is what war did, stripping people down to an elemental state, revealing their true nature. All along, when she was studying Russian literature at the Sorbonne and marrying early and having a child, keeping regular hours hunched over her desk, ensconced in a roomy moth-eaten sweater and searching for the perfect metaphor, underneath such pursuits, certain inherited proclivities that she had believed she was immune to were stirring within her, waiting to burst forth. **Yes, it's happening**, she thought, burning with shame. The shame of finding her mother's torn negligee in the bathroom, the shame of the man with pomaded hair and cedar aftershave who spent the night whenever Vera's father was away on business.

Getting out of the car, Vera wondered if Elsa noticed the blood flooding her cheeks, but Elsa was too busy haggling with the driver over the price of the fare, trying to hold on to their last few francs that she had hidden up until now, sewn into the hem of her skirt.

The driver stood with the car door open, shaking his head, his bald scalp pinking in the sun.

Even from here, the camp's stench was unbearable because the inmates defecated along its barbed wire boundary. Vera hooked her fingers through the rusted metal fence, calling out Leon's and Max's names to the men milling around on the other side of the fence. The attractive man from the cab was unloading cases of whiskey from the trunk, his eyes flat.

Vera called out Leon's name again because he was better known than Max. A murmuring overtook the prisoners, and they repeated Leon's name, one man calling out to another in an uninterrupted echo until finally Leon and Max waded through the crowd. Even after six weeks, Max appeared as robust as ever, his olive skin darkened, his cheeks tinged red from a sunburn. Vera's chest swelled at the sight of him. He was alive and healthy, smiling even. She glanced down at her torn hem, her unshaven legs and dirty fingernails. She touched her face, feeling the layer of dirt and grime that had amassed there, and forced herself to smile back at him.

Leon clutched Max's arm, visibly weak, no longer the well-dressed charming figure he had been in Sanary. Amidst the sun and dust, he appeared drained of his vigorous wit. A young Austrian doctor held Leon's other arm, and explained that Leon had suffered from dysentery, but luckily his high fever had subsided a few days ago.

"But he needs unripe apples and bitter chocolate. The best remedy."

Elsa stifled a cry and then announced that she had chocolate from Paris and some unripe apples stolen from Gurs. The men cheered, Elsa's prescience a sign of grace to them all.

Through the barbed wire, Elsa passed the apples and chocolate to Leon. Their fingers touched.

Elsa whispered, "Not to worry. We have a plan."

Max motioned for Vera to come closer, his breath stale and bitter. "What is it?"

He didn't even ask about Lucie, so consumed was he with his own survival. Just like those greedy wives jumping onto German military trucks, speeding away, leaving their husbands to fend for themselves.

"Elsa and I are going to Marseilles. The American consul general is there, and we'll get our papers in order. We must leave France." She paused, wanting the effect of this to settle. "America is our only chance."

She willed him to ask after Lucie. Instead his eyes glazed over, and Vera thought he was imagining his escape, if the berth on the steamer would be comfortable enough, and when he could eat a good meal.

He inhaled sharply. "How will I get out of here?"

"I don't know."

She did know, but she wanted to torture him with vagueness, leading him to believe that they might have to leave him behind, in this wretched camp. Of course Vera would relay the details of their plan to get them out, but in these tense moments she wanted him to feel something other than relief.

His face fell. It gave her a strange tingling pleasure.

"And Lucie," she began, her voice catching. She clenched the metal fence between them. "We can't take her with us. There's no way she'll make it to Marseilles from Oradour, with the roads the way they are, the stalled trains and the checkpoints. I have to write Agnes that we're leaving, somehow, without saying too much."

She stopped talking, hoping he would interject, that he would refuse to leave Lucie behind, that he would offer alternatives, no matter how farfetched, or even suggest that they stay in France and remain with Lucie throughout the war, even if it meant going into hiding.

He only looked down at his shoes, the sole separating from the upper tip.

Vera now noticed that Max had sweat through his shirt, and fresh red blood bloomed in the corner of his eye, a burst capillary from lifting heavy stones in the heat.

He looked away and then spat a ball of tobacco into the dry earth. "She's safe there, with Agnes."

"You don't know that," Vera snapped.

His gaze turned inward and darkened, and that boyish naïveté she had always cherished, now she stomped on it, wanting to smite it.

"You're right," he finally rejoined. "I don't know anything anymore."

Vera pulled on the fence, willing it to rattle, but it barely moved.

They left Leon and Max in the camp and boarded the first train they could find to Marseilles, where the American consul general was located. It was a military train full of drunk French soldiers, laughing and swearing and elbowing one another, delivering dirty joke after dirty joke. A lieutenant stoically smoked a cigarette, staring out at the French countryside. "How devastating. We've already lost the war." He flicked his cigarette out the window.

Stretching at least a mile, a line of people curved around the American consul general for exit visas from France and immigration visas to America. Elsa and Vera were instructed to stand at the rear. People murmured that they had already been sent back three, four, five times.

In an imperious flash, Elsa marched to the front of the line and thrust a note at the doorman, who nodded and disappeared into the building.

"What did you write?" Vera asked.

"I wrote 'Leon Freudenberger.' The American government, notably Eleanor Roosevelt, knows he's interned, and they've promised to get him out.

Varian Fry, you remember, the American journalist I told you about in Gurs? He's heading the Emergency Rescue Committee in France. He'll get us the right papers. He'll get us out."

A few seconds later, the door opened and they were ushered inside.

Varian Fry stood before them in a cream linen suit holding a glass of seltzer in one hand, his thick tortoiseshell glasses in the other. Vera passed Elsa a look, acknowledging the shift in the air, a sudden fluidity permeating their surroundings. Guiltily, she thought of all the others still outside, locked in an eternal wait. The other refugees might not get out, and yet, if they were able, they would have done the same, grasping after survival as she grasped after it now. If nothing else, she must survive for Lucie.

Elsa repeated her name, and he instantly asked them both to sit down on the plush sofa, motioning to the tea service nearby and offering Vera and Elsa cigarettes, coffee, and plum cake all in the same breath.

Vera took in the slender brass lamps, restive and serene, the oil paintings of landscapes along the paneled walls, the rose-colored carpet, the trilling of telephones and banging of typewriter keys echoing down marbled corridors, the click-clack of high heels and the rustle of thick creamy paper, paper she had once used in abundance, her penciled notes filling pages and pages.

Her eyes stung with tears as she settled into the sofa, and in the same moment, Elsa stifled a sob that was both strategic and authentic. The possible outpouring of emotion, of female distress, caused Fry to lean forward, push his glasses onto his face, and in a stern, conspiratorial tone explain that he would personally get Leon and Max out of Saint-Nicolas, as well as arrange for their escape to America. "It will be done," he concluded, looking them both in the eye.

In a flurry, in a daze, the plan was assembled. Vera watched the paneled walls change from cream to violet, late-afternoon light seeping through the arched windows. She half listened, drinking cup after cup of tea, her body loosening, her mind accelerating, planning the moment when she would ask Varian about her daughter, if there was any way to get her now. In the baroque padded comfort, all seemed possible, the Germans ineffectual, the bureaucracy of escape an afterthought.

She smiled and smoked a cigarette, crossing her legs. And yet she knew the silk sofa was a dream, and the ease with which Varian now explained the plan a fantasy that hinged on the impossible intersection of luck and strategy. Why else were those poor people still squatting outside the consul, in front of the locked iron gates?

"Tomorrow, I'll travel by car to Nîmes, to

Saint-Nicolas camp. Only the American consul has petrol. As you said, Elsa, around five o'clock in the afternoon the prisoners are taken to the river to wash themselves. The men are lightly guarded because who would try to escape half naked and wet? Yes?" He paused, his light eyes expectant. "This is when I approach Max and Leon with Elsa's note, written in her hand, that Leon will recognize, convincing them to come with me."

He produced a note from the inside pocket of his blazer and read it out in perfect German. "'**Komm jetzt mit mir, es ist sicher, geh mit.**'" (Come with me now. It is safe. Don't ask any questions.)

Vera caught her reflection in one of the large windows, and all she saw was sleeplessness and dirt. She shook her head, tossing her greasy hair back from her face, watching Varian closely. He excused himself to retrieve his coat and hat from his office. Elsa had gone to the powder room. Varian would soon escort them to an empty attic above a bakery that had recently been vacated by other refugees who were now on their way to Ecuador.

He returned from his office, hat in hand, a light cashmere coat folded over one arm. His loafers clacked over the parquet floor as he walked toward her. "Are you all right?"

"Yes, thank you so much for your help," Vera said, pursing her lips. "I can't imagine what we'd do otherwise."

"You don't want to."

A heavy silence followed.

She touched his coat. "I have something to ask you."

He gestured for her to continue.

"My daughter is in Oradour-sur-Glane with her governess."

"Was she born in France?"

"Yes."

"Does she possess French citizenship?"

"Yes." Vera paused. "But she's Jewish."

He ran a hand through his silvery hair. "Oradour is quite far north. Just below the demarcation line."

"She was baptized a few years ago. We all were."

"I see." He scanned her face. She couldn't determine if he felt sorry for her or if he thought this was a genuine advantage.

"It might provide some security," she added.

"You're asking me if this is so?"

Vera glanced away, fighting off the sinking feeling that he couldn't do anything, or wouldn't do anything. **My hands are tied, there's nothing to be done, we can't work miracles, it's too late now.** The phrases of denial throbbed through her, as if he had already uttered them.

He switched on one of the brass lamps, and a gentle glow filled the room.

Elsa closed the bathroom door behind her, clicking it shut.

He stepped into the amber pool of light. "Listen. There isn't much that—"

"I know how difficult it would be," Vera said, touching his coat again.

Varian threw an uncertain glance to Elsa, who watched them from the hallway.

He sighed. "This could very well endanger the entire escape plan."

"What is happening?" Elsa asked, her voice turning harsh, more Germanic.

Vera's cheeks burned. Elsa would call her selfish and she would be right. But she couldn't stop herself. "But is there any way to arrange it? She's only four years old."

Varian perched on the arm of the sofa. Looking down, he frowned at a coffee stain marking the white cuff of his shirt. "I'm afraid not."

Elsa walked over to them. "Vera, I'm sorry. But you know that the German authorities are searching for Leon. His photograph is everywhere. He's a hunted man. We barely have enough time as it is. God knows how long it will take Lucie to travel from there to here . . ." She softened and drew a breath.

Varian stared at the rose carpet. Their silence communicated what no one dared to say: it was only because of Leon's international literary fame and political connections that Varian was helping them. Otherwise Vera and Max would be left to perish with the horde, at the mercy of the lackadaisical French government, which would eventually turn them over to the Germans.

"Perhaps," Elsa began, "Vera could send a cryptic

message, a signal of some sort to Agnes, through you, of course, and without endangering us, that we are leaving for America. At least this way, Agnes will know what has happened. It won't just be as if, poof, she is gone!"

Vera winced at how cutting yet true the re-mark was.

Once on that ship, they would vanish from Europe.

Poof.

All Vera wrote: **Little golden America.** She thought of the phrase straightaway. It was what her father had often said about Russian Jews fleeing to the New World for a better life. Vera and her father had mocked those panicked White Russians who chose barbaric Manhattan or gritty Chicago over sanguine Paris. Naturally Agnes, from old French stock, agreed, and she often joined in on their mock-ery. Whenever news circulated of another relation immigrating to that strange and bloated country filled with roaming cowboys and hucksters, Mafia bosses and harlots, Agnes would shake her head and mutter, "Little golden America," like a bell sounding off in the dark.

Vera clenched the note before giving it to Varian.

He took it, slipping it into his blazer pocket, and smoothed it down with his thin, reedy hand.

CHAPTER 6

VERA

OCTOBER 1940, SOUTHWESTERN FRANCE

For five days, Vera and Elsa hid in a pension attic outside of Marseilles, awaiting Varian Fry, who promised to take them to the small village of Cerbère, in the foothills of the Pyrenees, over which they would cross into Spain. They couldn't go yet, as Fry first had to smuggle Leon and Max out of the internment camp. Vera secretly felt relieved. She was still in the same country as Lucie; they slept under the same night sky, and felt the same crisp October air. In unexpected moments, a wild hope stirred within her, suggesting that maybe, somehow, she could go get Lucie, or Agnes could bring her to this little pension, and together they would escape. When she imagined it, she almost felt happy, as if by believing this were true, even for a few moments, it somehow reversed the mistake she had made. But then Varian's insistent voice from their conversations at the consulate, with his emphasis on how difficult, nearly impossible, it was to escape at all, cut into her thoughts, and she realized none of them might get out.

A few days later, they took the train from Marseilles to Cerbère. Varian had managed to get Leon and Max out of the camp, but to safeguard against the exacting French police, the men traveled in first class, Vera and Elsa in third with the scant supplies Varian had been able to procure. Because there were no seats left, Vera and Elsa stood next to each other, their feet swelling in their uncomfortable shoes. As sweat trickled down the sides of her torso, a pervasive hum filled her ears, and her head lightened. She crouched down, putting her head between her legs, gripping her valise. The increasing distance from Lucie, intensifying with each jolt of the train, made her feel faint, knowing she couldn't stop what had already been set into motion.

At first light, Vera and Elsa went through the village of Cerbère, which led into the foothills of the Pyrenees. They passed early-morning workers bent over vines, snipping off bunches of grapes and tossing them into panniers fastened to their backs. The workers did not even look up when Elsa and

Vera stumbled past. Sweat peppered Vera's thin blouse. She anticipated a whipping wind drying the sweat, chilling her.

Steep slopes rose up before them, filled with rubble and rock, covered in gnarled Grenache vines, whose knotty roots webbed over the uneven terrain. Varian had outlined their route, explaining that it would take eight hours in total, pointing out a halfway summit point where they would rest before continuing. He advised them that it was safer for the women to lead over the mountains, with Max and Leon following two hours behind, warning them that maps were forbidden. His grave voice pounded through Vera's head: **Only spies and smugglers carry maps in the mountains, and if you are caught with one, they will send you back to France, immediately.**

She swallowed hard, remembering Varian's long straight back moving confidently through the narrow cobblestoned streets of Marseilles. He was immune to the threat of closing borders, and how quickly valid visas could turn invalid on the whim of the police, and the precariousness of getting Leon and Max out of the men's camp. It was all because he was American and tall, Vera thought.

Clutching an overhanging cedar branch, Elsa whispered, "We have to climb up to Col de Cerbère. The border is just beyond that," making it seem as if the crossing were nothing to fear, even though Vera detected a tightening in her voice.

The wind picked up and the sun blazed.

They paused, taking in the barrenness of the landscape, listening to the workers' voices carried up by the wind.

"Leon and Max are probably starting now," Elsa added, reassuring herself. "We'll meet them in Portbou, at the restaurant with the yellow awning, as Varian instructed." From there, they would take a train to Barcelona, and then from Barcelona to Lisbon.

The steep incline of the mountain trail gave way to a blanket of pinewoods and scrub, peppered by small conical huts where the vineyard workers could rest. Without speaking, they started moving toward this plateau, chests bursting for air, Vera hoping this would be the worst part and knowing it probably wasn't.

After two hours, the sharp incline finally relented, and they stumbled over fallen pines into the shaded scrub.

They sat for a while in silence, feasting on the meager food Elsa had packed: butter smeared over heels of bread, a few hard pears.

Dense clouds passed over the sun.

Elsa sipped some water from the canteen. "I was angry with you at the American consul. When you asked Varian to get Lucie and bring her with us."

"I know," Vera said, examining the pine needles, luminescent, glinting green.

"I'm proud that you've carried on since then."

Vera bent a pine needle into an arc and laughed bitterly. "What choice do I have?"

Elsa shook her head and started to pack up the remaining pears, the dirty napkins. "Agnes will get the note. Varian promised. And you will return to France when this madness ends, and you will go to Oradour and get Lucie back. I know it in my bones." Seeing the doubt on Vera's face, Elsa added, "You are not abandoning her. You are saving her."

Wading through the broom and scrub, trekking up uneven paths that dead-ended only to jut off in another direction, Vera took in the silvery gray sea flecked with whitecaps, restless and wild in the distance. Tremors of hope radiated through her, a pulsing force that carried her up the mountain, hastening her pace. Ignorant hope, maybe, but hope nonetheless that her daughter was safe.

The Pyrenees breathed, hazed in blue.

Vera squinted through her sweat. Up ahead, Elsa traversed the rubble slopes, zigzagging up the incline, moving as steadily as a goat. She paused a moment, shielding her eyes from the sun.

Vera waved, indicating all was well.

Elsa made a sharp signal with her hand, drawing Vera's gaze over the cresting slopes of the dirt paths to a red-tiled roof held up by decrepit ocher walls.

The customs house.

A lanky Catalan soldier smoked in the arched doorway, his eyes narrowing when Elsa and Vera approached. Tossing the smoldering cigarette butt into the debris, he ground it down with his boot while adjusting his holster. He was young, barely twenty, dark hair falling into his eyes, a thin disappointed mouth.

"Good afternoon, Officer," Elsa said in broken Catalan.

His eyes lingered on Vera's long smooth neck sheened with sweat.

"Good afternoon," Vera managed, forcing her dry lips into a cracked smile.

He nodded and ushered them inside.

Another officer sat with his feet propped up on the desk, swatting flies with a folded-over leather belt.

Afternoon heat thickened the air, made it stand still.

Elsa watched her with catlike intensity, her black eyes narrowed into points.

"Oh!" Vera gasped on cue, letting the backpack slide off her shoulder, the front of her blouse slicing open to reveal her breasts encased in a brocaded brassiere. "This pack is too heavy." She sighed, unzipping it halfway.

The zipper stuck. Her hands shook when she tugged at it.

The younger soldier crossed his arms over his chest.

Vera felt Elsa tensing, and she swallowed hard, trying to maintain her focus.

With one last violent jerk, the zipper gave way and the Camel cigarette packs cascaded onto the stone floor.

Vera stepped back from the pile and lifted her hair off of her sweaty neck. "It's much too burdensome to take along." She paused, scanning the soldier's impassive face, but then his eyes flickered over her skin and her breasts.

She smiled again, this time more naturally. "It would help us so much if you kept all of this. Would you mind . . . ?"

The tail end of her question was swallowed up by the jerk of the officer's chair as he lunged to collect the cigarettes.

The younger officer glanced over their papers, which Elsa had laid out on the desk. He took a moment to look at Vera again, his face stirring with approval, before stamping the papers.

And then, with one limp hand, he waved them out the door, mumbling, **"Déu sigui amb tu."**

If there is a God, Vera thought as they stumbled toward Spain, **He is in these blue mountains, and in the sea that glints before us**. Too frightened that their luck could still be snatched away, they silently ran down the lower foothills, Vera's hand clutching

Elsa's, both of them half crying with relief, but Vera also cried for Lucie, for the pain of separation that pierced her, more real and throbbing than when she was within France's borders, when she could still turn back, even if turning back meant death. Her eyes swam with tears, blurring the sun's golden orb as it dipped into the solid gray ocean.

CHAPTER 7

SASHA

OCTOBER 1940,
BEVERLY HILLS, CALIFORNIA

Sasha perched on the edge of a chaise longue in Charlie's cool dark living room, the patio doors open to a long rectangular pool and overhanging oak trees. Charlie, his agent, sat in a low leather chair next to him, finishing off a cocktail. It was a warm Sunday afternoon, and Charlie had suggested Sasha come around for a drink while they talked over **Cyclone**, a script he'd recently written about a young German woman who falls in love with her literature professor who opposes the Reich, despite being engaged to a top Nazi official. She tries to save the professor—he is about to get arrested for his political beliefs—and together they make a run for it, almost reaching the Swiss border, but they are pursued by her fiancé and his gang of thugs.

Accidentally, one of the thugs shoots her instead of the professor, and she dies in the professor's arms, leaving the fiancé racked with guilt.

Unlike most in Hollywood, Sasha couldn't ignore the war, sensing it was only a matter of time before the European conflict would hit US soil. A dark foreboding crept over him every time he opened the paper to read a headline about another devastating air raid on London. Or when he went to the movies and the newsreels of those poor Polish Jews, with their belongings bundled onto their backs as they waded into the streets during a roundup, cut through him, as he knew it was merely luck and circumstance that separated his mother and him from those Jews. Staring plaintively into the camera, their ghostly expressions carried the knowledge that there would be no return.

Charlie had submitted **Cyclone** to studios before Sasha left for the High Holidays, and now Sasha felt jittery, wondering if Charlie had heard anything yet.

Adding to his jitters, he wanted to talk to Charlie about directing. He'd been thinking about it ever since he saw how that hack director had taken **Close to the Edge** and transformed the story into something entirely unrecognizable. The script Sasha had written brimmed with tension and excitement. But the picture he'd seen two months ago was so poorly made that he felt nothing. And neither had anyone else, given how the movie had bombed at the box office.

Sitting in the dark theater watching the credits roll, Sasha had sunk farther into his seat, overcome with defeat, knowing that once any script of his was handed over to someone else, he lost all control. He'd felt betrayed by what he'd seen on screen, worst of all by himself. Directing was a craft like any other. He would learn it.

Nerves jangling, wondering how Charlie would react to such a thought, Sasha remembered making his first telephone call to Charlie two years ago, sweating through his shirt, staring down at the scrap of paper his mother had given him with Charlie's number scrawled across it. When the secretary put him through, Charlie sounded rushed and unimpressed, telling Sasha to send him a few sample scripts and then they would talk. Two weeks later, Charlie agreed to meet him at the Polo Lounge in Beverly Hills.

Charlie was tall and svelte, with little pineapple cuff links that caught the late-afternoon light. Pulling his eyes away from a Betty Grable look-alike in a low-cut dress, he said, "Imagine my surprise when I get a call out of the blue from my aunt Ida in New York. She says that her good friends the Dubrows from the Hampshire Country Club have a son coming out to California, he's new in town, even sold a script, can I help? She mentions **Close to the Edge**, yada yada yada, and then I say, sure, it's good, but what else has he got? Opportunities don't just materialize out of thin air, like I'm some kind of goddamn fairy godmother."

"Sure," Sasha said, taking a stinging gulp of his gin and tonic.

"Even if you'd single-handedly murdered Hitler and stopped this whole damn mess in its tracks, it wouldn't matter if your writing was shit."

"Let the work speak for itself."

"That's right." Charlie's gaze drifted back to the blonde, who now mouthed something to him over the rim of her frosted cocktail glass. "But then I read the first half of **Double Suicide**, and I thought to myself, hey, this kid's got balls. The characters are realistic, sometimes even unlikable, but still, I found myself rooting for them."

"Yeah," Sasha said, taking another long sip of his drink. Charlie shifted positions on the green velvet banquette and explained that his director clients were always keen to find a gem in the rough, casually rattling off some of his clients, as if Sasha didn't already know that he represented Lauren Bacall, Charles Boyer, and Tyrone Power, and directors such as George Stevens and Howard Hawks. Charlie raised his glass. "Welcome to town, kid."

Their glasses clinked just as the blonde glided by their table. She deftly slipped her number into the front pocket of Charlie's blazer and kept on walking.

He grinned. "Happens all the time."

. . .

Charlie wore that same irresistible grin now as he turned his gaze toward his wife, Jean, in a strapless white dress, her honey-colored shoulders shrugging when she gestured to the coffee table overlaid with grapes, Swiss cheese, rye bread, and deviled eggs. "Sasha, have something to eat. I bought too much."

Charlie took a puff of his cigar. "Enjoy it . . . Pretty soon we'll be on rations like the Brits."

"Do you think we should get involved?" Jean asked Sasha.

"Someone's got to stop those dictators from destroying Europe, don't you think?"

Jean shrugged her perfect shoulders. "Oh, I don't know. Why should the burden always fall on us?"

Charlie yawned, staring up at the coffered ceiling. "I did read something troubling in the paper, about Hitler decreeing a law for a 'New Europe' or some such wild thing."

Maybe, Sasha thought, the inveterate beauty of this place could lull someone into believing that the war wasn't actually happening, or that it wouldn't dare touch this paradise. A framed photograph of Jean serving coffee to actors backstage stood on the mantelpiece, next to another photograph of Charlie slinging an arm around Bing Crosby, both men laughing.

Jean's melodious voice rang out, "Sasha, you're miles away."

He shook his head and smiled apologetically.

"Well, here's a better question," Jean said, drumming her elegant fingers on her knee. "How about a blind date with my cousin? She's new in town."

Sasha laughed and leaned back into the chaise. "Oh, I don't know about that." He was a disappointment to women. His large-featured face—the Roman nose and full mouth, the heavy dark eyebrows—lent him an air of seriousness, of intent, but really, half the time he found himself listening for a hint of a story idea, something he might use later for a script.

"She's a bearcat, that cousin, believe you me," Charlie said.

Sasha waved Charlie's comment away; he never quite connected with anyone. On his last date, with a secretary from RKO, they'd gone to the Santa Anita Race Track in Pasadena. It was a long drive there and back, and he asked her question after question, about what Colorado was like, if she grew up with horses there, why she'd broken off her engagement to her high school sweetheart, and so on and so on. She answered blithely, barely stopping to catch her breath, until she turned to him before getting out of the car at the end of the date, her hand gently on his shoulder, and said, "I had a nice time, Sasha. But I know absolutely nothing about you."

Momentarily jarred by her comment, he made some joke to dodge what she'd said, but the words stung. All his questions served as a kind of armor, a trained way of negotiating the world, ingrained in him since childhood. When people asked too many questions about why they'd left the old country, or who his father was, or how come they barely had any family to speak of, his mother would sidestep such probing with a witty remark, pointed enough to quiet them, or she'd deftly change the subject. But most of all, she deflected the questions that hit too close to home with questions for them, asking after their relatives, or if they liked the new yeshiva teacher, later telling Sasha that people loved to talk about themselves—they couldn't help it. Always better, she said, to ask and listen, especially in a neighborhood such as this, bustling with nosy housewives. Even a whiff of gossip will get them salivating, she added scornfully. While Sasha watched his mother pepper the neighbors with questions, her tone breezy and unbothered, her eyes met his, and in them he read: **Keep things close to the vest. That way they can't hurt you. That way you are safe.**

Jean nibbled on a grape and smiled gamely at Sasha. "So, my cousin, what do you think?"

Sasha smiled back, calmed by the late-afternoon light spilling into the room, and the sound of water continuously trickling from the stone fountain outside. He shook his head. "She sounds nice. But maybe another time."

Jean stood up and lightly touched Sasha's shoulder, and he inhaled her sharp gardenia perfume. "All right, but she won't be free long. Please excuse me. I have a tennis match in half an hour."

They watched her lithe frame cut through the room before she disappeared down the hallway.

Charlie sat up and swirled around his drink. "It's tough." He gave the empty hallway a hooded glance. Then they heard a door close. "She wants a child, and I don't. We had a big blowout last night. She threw a crystal ashtray into my temple." He turned his head to the side, and Sasha saw a long thin scrape nestled in a bruise.

Charlie emitted a dry laugh. "She thought I was dead when I fell back against the bed, blood on the carpet and all over her dress. By the time the ambulance came, I was having a drink and smoking a cigar, and it was a big hassle to convince everyone to go home."

Sasha shook his head. "All that because you don't want kids?"

"I'm at the point in my career where I can do whatever the hell I want. Travel, buy new cars, go to Vegas every weekend, you name it. But with a baby, that all goes out the window. You know what I mean?"

Sasha snapped off a few grapes. "I don't know, Charlie. Wouldn't it be easier to just do what she wants?"

He balanced his forearms on his muscular thighs. "She wants a lot of things. Like a darkroom in the back of the house so she can become a lenswoman, even though she knows I don't want her to work. I don't even want her to cook."

Sasha didn't see a problem with any of this, but in truth, he had no knowledge of marriage, so it was best just to keep quiet. And best, he thought, to not bring up his directing ambitions at the moment, when it was hard enough just to sell a script, let alone attach himself as a director with no experience.

Charlie shifted in his chair. "So. **Cyclone.** Columbia and Paramount passed." He hesitated, seeing the disappointment on Sasha's face, and then continued, "They don't want to provoke Germany. A picture like that will be banned in most of Europe, and God knows how it will do here."

"I think America is ready for a movie like this."

"I don't know if Hollywood is." Charlie swirled the ice cubes around in his drink, staring into the amber liquid. "You know what Schaefer's people said about it, over at RKO?"

"What?" Sasha asked, trying to stave off the sinking feeling that he wasn't getting anywhere in this town.

"They said such an anti-German picture could be seen as advancing the Jewish agenda to intervene in the war. That it's clannish."

"Clannish?" Sasha rose up from his seat, but Charlie gestured for him to sit. "What's happening over there isn't just about the Jews. It's about that sonofabitch toppling Western democracy, crushing all that we stand for. They're bombing the hell out of England, and now in France . . ." Sasha trailed off.

"I know," Charlie agreed. "I know. But listen, it's not all bad. Warner's liked **Cyclone**. I set a meeting for next week."

"Okay. That's something."

The sound of Jean starting the car in the driveway distracted them for a moment. She tooted the horn three times before speeding away.

Charlie's gaze drifted off for a moment. "She always does that." Then he took off his glasses and gave Sasha a hard look. "And in the pitch meeting, don't be a **groyser tsuleyger.** Got it?"

Sasha grinned at the phrase his mother used to say when he got too cocky. "Sure."

Charlie shook his head and let out a disbelieving laugh.

CHAPTER 8

VERA

OCTOBER 1940, EN ROUTE TO
MANHATTAN, NEW YORK

The golden light of early October fell over Lisbon, bathing the red-tiled roofs and white-washed colonial buildings in a nostalgic tint. Or perhaps, Vera thought as the hulking steamer pulled away from the Portuguese coast, it was just the light of sadness.

When they arrived in Lisbon, German police teemed in the streets, while refugees flooded the cafés, the scent of panic pouring off of them like a fine vapor. Nazis motored down the wide boulevards that ran parallel to the sea, swastika flags rippling in the wind. "Lisbon is death," Varian had warned them. "You must not stay even one day there."

. . .

The SS **Excalibur** buffeted the open sea, and the rough pounding waves drove everyone into their cabins during those first few days. The constant motion and the incessant ocean air, that mix of saltiness with pungent fish, made Vera's stomach churn and clench. She clamored for the tiny bathroom, vomiting into the toilet. Afterward, doused in sweat, she lay there, the cool tiles calming against her cheek. At first, when Max came into the cabin and only saw her legs stretched out on the floor, he gasped, thinking she had collapsed, or worse, only to find her peacefully resting, forehead pressed into her folded-over hands, the dry dark as quiet as a crypt.

Vera wondered if he feared she had killed herself. Various friends and acquaintances had done it, suspecting that a terror much worse than death awaited them. Last month, Walter Benjamin had overdosed on morphine tablets when he found out he would be sent back over the Spanish border into France. Walter had taken their exact route over the Pyrenees, but on that day, the Spanish police proved less forgiving. The poet Walter Hasenclever killed himself in the des Milles internment camp when the Germans overtook it. Apparently, he'd used barbiturates. And the playwright Ernst Toller had hung himself in his New York hotel room by the silk cord of his robe after learning that his brother and sister had been sent to a concentration camp.

When Vera sat up, blood rushed to her head, and she gave Max a weak smile.

No, she could never do it.

Not as long as Lucie was alive.

Vera often smoked with Elsa after breakfast along the balustrade of the ship. On the upper deck, their fellow travelers, the fabulously boring bourgeoisie of continental Europe, as Elsa called them, reclined in chaises, bundled and wrapped in fur-trimmed blankets, gazing up at the slow-moving clouds, as if the ship were a floating hospital where they took the cure for exile. Everyone discussed the weather and what types of foods to expect in America. They muttered "peanut butter" and "Jell-O" in devastated tones. Many of them, including Vera, read **1001 Words in English**, which they found comical and puzzling. She was still on the **A**'s, repeating certain words under her breath as she walked laps around the deck: "able," "accelerate," "accentuate," "accommodate."

Elsa found the passengers' languorous comfort distasteful, insinuating that other refugees, who were less wealthy and famous but objectively stronger, should have been saved from burning Europe.

Then she would cock her head and listen to the squabbling Eastern European Jews traveling down below, in third class. Elsa leaned over the railing, straining to see their exaggerated gestures. The caftan-clad Jews relentlessly cajoled, accused, and chastised one another, a never-ending cycle of human interaction that excited Elsa. Her eyes lit up, watching them, but Vera looked away, stung with shame for having believed she was different from them. She used to cling to the idea that she and Max, and all the other Jews they knew and associated with, were nothing like these newly arrived Jews from the east whom everyone mocked—undesirables, **Juifs**. Vera even used to avoid the overly Jewish sections of Paris, the Marais and Belleville, averting her eyes from the pious men with their **payos**, sputtering Yiddish. She had actually felt embarrassed for those poor Jews, in clothing from the last century, as if they still waded through the decrepit streets of Vilna, refusing to assimilate.

And yet here she was with them, on the same ship, all hurtling toward an uncertain future, and it struck Vera with painful clarity that it didn't matter if she could travel first class, or that her daughter had been accepted into the most prestigious lycée in Paris, or that she had won the Prix Goncourt for her first novel, or that her husband wrote symphonies for the Paris Opera.

In the eyes of the enemy, they were all **Juifs**.

There were no exceptions.

Sometimes, before dinner, Max accompanied her on the upper deck. He lit her cigarette, and if she seemed especially lost in thought, he recited her favorite Akhmatova poem to cheer her, the one about

Tsarskoye Selo, the gardens in St. Petersburg, where Vera had lived as a little girl.

She rested her head on Max's tweed shoulder. The poem brought her back to Morskaya Street, where she and her father always used to walk, stopping to admire the window of Fabergé featuring a row of golden enamel eggs patterned with emerald leaves and ruby petals, blood red, and tiny yellow diamonds dotting the egg's circumference. Her father whispered into her ear that the emperor gave the empress one of these eggs each anniversary of their betrothal. Now, as she watched the white-capped waves carry her away from France, the overlapping pain of two exiles pierced her.

Turning to Max, Vera caught the tail end of a conversation about the merits of South America. "Why would you live in icy New York when you could easily immigrate to Buenos Aires?" an older woman exclaimed.

At first, Vera and Max decided that they would wait out the war in New York. After all, it was closer to France than California, and they knew many others who had settled there, nestling into an established community of exiles. But Michel Toch, Max's professor at the Mannheim conservatory, whom he had looked up to ever since his student days, bitterly complained in a letter to Max that there was no money in New York for composers. When Hitler came to power in '33, Michel immediately fled, first to Paris and then to London. In the late thirties, he immigrated to New York and taught at the New School before finally going to Hollywood, which he now claimed was the only place to go. Michel promised to help Max get a job scoring for one of the studios, or at least, he wrote, secure a foothold. He had recently composed the score for **Heidi**, and Max often said that Michel was flush with opportunities, the money steadily pouring in from various channels. But everyone knew of other composers who fared less well, and the shadowy figure of Nikolai Petrovitch, a fellow émigré, hovered on the outskirts of these blazing success stories. Once, Petrovitch had composed symphonies for the Vienna State Opera; he now tuned pianos for a living, traveling door-to-door with his black leather box full of tools. At least, Vera thought, Max had been able to transfer a quarter of their savings into an account in Canada before leaving Paris, at the recommendation of a banker friend who warned assets might be frozen.

Leon stated that all that mattered to him was his library, no matter where he ended up. "I lost my first one in Berlin, the second one in Sanary, and now I'm adrift, with no books to speak of."

Vera considered her own mazelike library, divided between Sanary and Paris. She couldn't think without her books. The collection reflected the inner workings of her mind, past obsessions, future ones, all accessible with one tour among the spines, her fingertips tracing the titles as if gliding along piano keys, each book, each writer emitting a certain note that, when pressed, revealed a close, breathing universe.

But even without a library, she should still be able to write. And yet she wasn't sure she could do it. She had left her typewriter along with her manuscript in Sanary, and now debated whether to rewrite it from memory. But the story, about an older woman mourning her sons, set in the French countryside during World War I, felt trite and pointless. Even the various details swirling around her that she might have taken note of and formed into a narrative refused to congeal. For example, an Italian countess who insisted on feeding her Pomeranians caviar for breakfast, and the young waiter who didn't know what to do with her endless demands, glancing desperately around for someone to intervene. Or the man and woman who clearly were carrying on an affair, only ever meeting when the deck was deserted, after everyone had gone in to dinner; after the soup was served, Vera watched the woman enter the dining room first, her eyes radiant, her neck inflamed from the man's stubble, and settle down next to her husband with practiced nonchalance. Vera observed their respective husband and wife eating lunch or reading the paper, and a dull pang of disenchantment overcame her, wondering if they knew, or didn't know, and what did it matter anyway, given the state of things? But she couldn't bring herself to construct a narrative from these observations. In the past, she could have conveyed, in a biting short story, the main idea: the man and woman only wanted to hold each other, freely and openly, but if given such freedom, their desire would evaporate, as swiftly as when the emergent noonday sun dissipated the morning mist.

During the weeklong sea voyage, Leon worked feverishly on his Josephus trilogy, and she wrote nothing, did nothing, except anticipate that stab of self-loathing every time Elsa mentioned Leon's progress. And her seasickness hadn't subsided, which wasn't helped by the fact that all night, when everyone else slept, she obsessively thought of Lucie, wondering if Agnes had received the note and knew they had immigrated to America, or if she still thought they were interned at Gurs. Even though they had made it over the Pyrenees and onto one of the very last ships, bombs and roiling storms could still undo them. And once they got to America, then what? Max reassured her that a network of European contacts and friends would help them find a place to live in Los Angeles, suitable for Lucie, near a good school, in a nice neighborhood. And he already had meetings set up at the studios, which were apparently willing to hire European composers for their music departments.

But Vera secretly feared that something would go

wrong, and they would die on the open sea from an errant German torpedo. She had done this to her characters many times. Killed them off just when the long-awaited moment of hope lurched into view, but she refused such a fate, pushing away the idea that she might die before seeing Lucie again.

Perhaps now all those blighted characters would have their revenge, she thought, listening to Max and Leon make fun of various English expressions. "He's hairy at the heels!" Leon bellowed, after which Max barked out his favorite one: "Come on, Leon, let's keep chomping fat!"

"Let's **chew** the fat," Elsa corrected.

Max winked at Vera, his clever eyes mischievous, recapturing the boyishness he'd had when they first met and he took her to all the jazz clubs and racy cabarets in the Latin Quarter, squeezing her thigh under the table while the saxophone crested over them in dark rich waves.

"It was just announced on the wireless. Greece has entered the war," a man called out from the other side of the deck.

The wind picked up, cutting through her.

During the last few days of the voyage, Max drank less in the evenings, his eyes gleaming, as if he could already see the New York skyscrapers towering above him, touching heaven. The expectancy in the rippling sea air, and the knowledge that soon they would greet the Atlantic coast, with Manhattan shining before them, made everyone, including Vera, slightly manic.

Vera spent the last night on board lying awake in her monastic twin bed while Max slept soundly in his. She sat up and opened the nightstand drawer, pulling out the photograph: Lucie running toward the camera in a white dress, holding Mourka out in front of her. Her unfocused smile, eyes bright and laughing, her dark hair, the morning sun streaming into the Parisian living room; in the background, coffee cups and breakfast rolls on the table.

Vera studied Lucie's face, remembering the perfect bow of her upper lip, the cleft in her chin, how warm she felt when Vera lifted her from a long nap, her skin smelling of lavender from the scented sheets. She closed her eyes, willing sleep to come. And it did, with images that bent time, crushing it and then straightening it out again, as only dreams do. Her father sank into a velvet armchair before the fire, his face dewy from the bathhouse, and yet he still perspired while reading the newspaper. Vera watched him read, vaguely wondering about all the families fleeing to Shanghai, Odessa, or Tehran. The kitchen maid, a plump Ukrainian peasant, crossed herself and prayed for God in heaven to protect the czar.

Her body jerked in sleep as time hurtled forward to Lucie's birth. Max walked over to her and stroked her cheek with the back of his hand. Those days were long and listless. Her only preoccupation was Lucie, with her translucent skin and milky blue eyes, ensconced in a bundle of muslin, lulling Vera into the predictable routine of changing and feeding and washing her tiny perfect body. And then, at the end of the day, the hum of the elevator rising up to the top floor was a welcome sound, signaling that Max would unlock the front door, remove his hat and gloves, and come toward her with open arms, asking after Lucie in a playful tone.

She had temporarily stopped writing to care for the baby, and so now she found herself asking him questions about what he had seen out there, in the world, while she was cloistered and padded by the baby's soft blankets and toys, the tiny cashmere socks and satin coverlets, almost as if she herself were an infant in need of protection. When the baby fell asleep on her chest, she would rest her hand on Lucie's downy back and time her breath to match Lucie's breath; in the suspended calm, her eyes closed, and her mind flattened into serene blankness.

Vera woke with a start. She sat up and curved her body forward, as if to catch Lucie from falling from her chest, sensing the weight of a baby no longer there. She turned her head to the side and something jagged and unkind jangled inside of it. Cabin doors slammed shut with the particular fierceness of departure. Voices echoed in the ship's corridors. Loud talk vibrated through the thin walls. Max's suitcase sat open, expertly packed, on the bed opposite hers, as if reproaching her for her lateness, announcing that many important things were underway, and here she was, stunned, still in her nightgown, sleep crusting her eyes while she hugged her knees into her chest, blinking into the small bright room.

The cabin door burst open. "We're nearly there. You can already see the Statue of Liberty. The skyscrapers. Everything!" Max beamed.

She reached for some unknown object. A hairbrush, a cigarette. She didn't know what.

"Come quickly!" he added before closing the door.

Vera spotted Max in the crowd, pressed up against the ship's railing, waving a little American flag along with Leon, Elsa, and some others.

Where did those magical little flags come from? She squinted up at the statue that everyone was gazing at in awe, taking off their hats to it, waving handkerchiefs in the air, as if the torch carried real fire. Of course, Vera thought, most of them probably didn't know that the statue was a gift from France, and yet here they stood, panting and trembling before it. And the women, glossy fur coats thrown over their shoulders, hats tipped at exaggerated angles, their painted faces veiled by dotted net—ready to greet the New World, they had utterly transformed themselves to appear richer and more beautiful, and they had succeeded.

She stood next to a staircase that led to the upper deck, and she steadied herself against the banister, looking down for a moment at the wooden planks. Embarrassed by her plain woolen dress and her one hat, the peacock feathers bent, she attempted to smooth them down now, to at least look presentable. The morning sun shattered her vision. Too bright, too sharp, too many colors, languages, and perfumes. Her heart drummed as people cheered, and she focused on a little boy in a sailor suit wobbling in the middle of the deck as his mother yelled for him to stay close. He decided not to hear her. A group of older children hung over the railing for a better look at the skyline, and Vera tried to imagine people living in those impenetrable concrete structures.

Her eyes watered in the brightness. She squeezed them shut for a moment.

Was this what it meant to be American: to stare into the sun and challenge its strength?

CHAPTER 9

VERA

NOVEMBER 1940, NEW YORK, NEW YORK

She knew she should feel lucky that Agnes was watching over Lucie, hidden away in a stone farmhouse in the middle of France, but she didn't. A piercing anxiety woke her in the middle of the night, harshly insisting that she had failed to protect her daughter and now her daughter would perish. A couple fought in the next hotel room, a radio program switched on and then off again, fireworks or maybe gunshots popped in the distance, the subway rumbled—it all coursed through her, lived in her, the city's sharp malice jangling in her mind like pieces of mismatched cutlery.

She shook Max's arm to wake him. "Max! Do you think Agnes knows we're in America now?"

Max yawned. In the shadowy predawn, he

appeared wholly unbothered. "If Varian managed to get her the note—"

"Even if he didn't," Vera hissed, "I sent her a letter the day we arrived in Manhattan, so she should know by now that we're here."

He sat up, rubbing his eyes. "You only sent the letter a week ago."

She sighed, sinking back into the soft mattress. "It seems like ages ago."

He patted her bare thigh, and then let his hand rest there. "She probably hasn't gotten it yet, with how impossible the post has been."

She wanted to add that the post would be even more impossible once they reached California, the distance between them and Lucie widening beyond comprehension.

They would be so far away.

So very far.

They'd argued about it last night, before going to bed, and now she felt the pull of the argument again. She had tried to persuade him they should stay in New York, at least for a little longer, but Max said that she was being irrational; there was no reason to stay here. He couldn't get work as easily in New York, if at all, and they had already decided on Los Angeles.

An ocean separated them, whether they were in New York or California.

The groan of the early-morning garbage trucks

filtered through the window, which they had left open a crack. Max turned over onto his side, his back to her before she could say something nasty, implying that her need to stay close to Lucie was greater than his.

She felt for the gold heart pendant that always hung from her neck, but of course it wasn't there. Max snored steadily.

She had to get out of here.

Vera pulled her coat tighter against the chilled wind and dug her chin into its collar. The city was less abrasive in the early morning, before its incessant activity unfurled. A few cabs lumbered by, off-duty lights dimly glowing in the fog, and an elderly man walked a small shaggy dog, tugging the leash whenever the dog paused to sniff the damp concrete. White-hot steam billowed out from the windows of one of the many towering brick buildings, as if a trapped dragon exhaled through the wrought iron bars, something she might have made up for Lucie, if Lucie were beside her now, but it was only a hat-steaming factory.

She stopped in front of a cafeteria window, enticed by the idea of food, but men in fedoras and overcoats crowded the place, all reading the **Jewish Daily Forward**, in Yiddish from what she could tell. She moved on, in search of another place, as she'd heard cafeteria food ruined the stomach.

A few blocks down, wide plate glass windows and a spacious interior bathed in amber light drew her inside. It was still a cafeteria, Dubrow's, but less crowded. The waitress called her "honey" and directed her toward the metal trays and coffee. She hesitated in front of the pastry case, confounded by the gleaming rows of unidentifiable foods. The waitress saw her looking and said loudly, "The cherry pie is a favorite. I personally like the apple cheese strudel, but it's up to you." A few men glanced over their newspapers at Vera.

She ordered the cherry pie, keeping the sentence as short as possible. She didn't like the sound of herself in English. Tentative and halting, with too many breaths and pauses between each word. And the look on the waitress's face confirmed this.

The coffee was hot and strong. The plump syrup-coated cherries combined with the buttery thick crust tasted surprisingly good, though it sat heavily in her stomach. She began to relax into the leather booth, and the sprawling mural along the far wall comforted her. She stared at the peaceful afternoon scene: couples strolled by cypress trees, and shallow steps led up to a civic building lodged in the middle of a perfectly planned park. The scene made her feel civically inclined, as if such afternoons were possible in a country like this, allowing everyone the freedom of leisure.

She pressed the back of the fork against the roof of her mouth, savoring the last bits of pie. Of course, she knew it wasn't true, the "liberty and justice for all," but the promise was seductive, making her feel as if she were on the inside looking out for one fragile moment.

Men in trench coats and heavy black shoes passed by the cafeteria window, eyes trained on the sidewalk. Vera sensed the building momentum of more cars, more people, more noise as the city gained speed and tension to challenge the day, crushing those not strong enough to face it.

Every few minutes the door clanged open as the place filled up with morning commuters. The din of utensils scraping against plates and lowered voices discussing Roosevelt's reelection and how Germany was bombing the hell out of London.

She wondered if Max was up yet. They were staying at the Wyndham Hotel, on Eighth Avenue in the Garment District. Despite its vastness, with the many ballrooms, bars, and even a barbershop, all the European refugees had been relegated to the eleventh and twelfth floors; anytime Vera and Max went anywhere, they encountered people they already knew, or vaguely knew, and others who looked strikingly familiar. Thomas Mann and Stefan Zweig held court in their rooms, nonchalantly tossing around accounts of a doomed Europe. Given that none of the world dictators had any formal academic education, they concluded that the barbarity would only worsen. In the same breath, they bemoaned the absence of coffeehouses in Manhattan. "Where does one converse, scribble down notes, play chess, and observe the people while lingering over a cup of black fire? Nowhere!" Zweig lamented.

To combat the pressing throng of refugees they encountered on every floor, in every elevator, Leon had shut himself away in his hotel room to write, while Max started drinking as soon as the sun went down. Elsa wrote endless letters, using Leon's name, to try to secure affidavits for family still in Europe.

Vera avoided the lobby and all other places of congregation, which only left the overheated hotel room as a safe haven. As she waited for the elevator, all it took was one sympathetic smile to another refugee, and out it poured: abandoned children, demolished houses, disloyal staff, no money at all.

Vera cringed, knowing that if she were to tell her story, she would sound exactly the same.

It was better to write. Even if all these letters were lost or delayed or never delivered. Pushing aside her plate, she took out some hotel stationery, careful to tear off the embossed address at the top, and her fountain pen.

November 5, 1940

Dear L.,
    We miss you terribly and think of you every day. Cold wind sweeps through the city, which is full of canary yellow

taxicabs and garbage trucks and loads of glamorous lonely people, and barely any trees. There's an ice rink that you would like, and they also serve hot chocolate there.

Vera paused, imagining Agnes reading the letter aloud, her soft voice massaging every word, trying to get the most out of it for Lucie's sake. But she didn't want to give too much away, about where they were, because of the censors. America would sound so distant and far away, and this might frighten Lucie, and California sounded even more foreign and unimaginable. And even now, Agnes might maintain the idea that Vera and Max were still on vacation, but because of the war, they had been delayed. Yes, it was important that Lucie not know they had gone to America. She might boast to someone about her parents in America, the way children do, and this would raise questions about why she wasn't with them. Questions that would put her at risk.

> **Send my regards to Agnes and her family. And remember to listen to her. Soon we will be together again.**
> **Love,**
> **Mama**

She drew a heart with an arrow through it on the back of the envelope.

. . .

That night, at a cocktail party at Jules Romains's penthouse apartment on Riverside Drive, rain streaked the wide glass windows, and sinewy figures flashed before Vera as if outlined in a silvery light. Gardenias stood, freshly cut, in crystal vases. Bookcases curved around the room, undulating and wavelike. The hostess wore one of the gardenias tucked behind her ear as she welcomed them, her slender arms encased in long silk gloves that reached up to her elbows.

Men with famous names introduced themselves to Leon and Max. Vera vaguely recalled reading their work and wondered if they had read any of her essays or novels, but they didn't seem to recognize her in the slightest, not even Paul Brasillach, with whom she had given a joint lecture five years ago, when her first novel came out. He looked the same now, with his carefully combed blond hair and imposing stance. She remembered that he was very dogmatic about rejecting realism in literature because, he had argued, surrealism was the only way to upend the oppression of bourgeois values, which were stifling society. He purposefully targeted her work, and not only her work but also her personally, knowing that she led a comfortable domestic existence, and perhaps also knowing that she was not a communist. But he didn't know what her family had witnessed on the eve of the Russian revolution:

students rioting and attacking bystanders on the street for no good reason other than that they could get away with it. The revolutionaries proved just as violent as the White Army when they caught a whiff of power. It was human nature.

Of course, afterward, on the steps of the Bibliothèque de l'Arsenal, he smiled innocently and complimented her novel, while in the same breath admitting he hadn't read it. He now coiled his arm around a woman in a pale lavender gown with fur-trimmed armholes. So much for upending the bourgeoisie. His wife delicately ate an olive off a toothpick.

A waiter handed Vera a glass of chilled champagne, and she felt a stab of nostalgic pleasure. She used to drink chilled champagne before the war.

Leon was explaining to someone that the severe anti-communist sentiment was difficult here, and that some people even inferred he was a communist just because he'd taken such a public stance against fascism.

"He's depressed about it," Elsa interjected.

Paul pompously added, "In America, everyone thinks in such literal terms. There is absolutely no opportunity for nuance. For instance, if I say I oppose Mussolini, then they all immediately assume I love Stalin!"

"If you find it so intolerable here, perhaps you should return to Europe," Vera said, leveling her gaze at him.

"I can't," he snapped.

"I'm sure **Gringoire** and **Candide** would welcome you back with open arms." These were right-wing magazines for which he had written many editorials and reviews.

Paul gestured to his wife, who was trying to light a cigarette with a faltering lighter. "She's a Jew."

He thrust out his chin, expecting Vera to challenge him or concede it was true, they couldn't go back, but she only felt a hot shame flood through her because of the way he had said "she's a Jew," as though it were a category outside of human, hated and stateless, a fate he now shared.

Paul's wife finally lit the cigarette, and Max, as he often did, rescued the moment. "Well, I greatly admire Roosevelt, I'll tell you that much."

They all raised their glasses.

After their little crowd dispersed, Leon lumbered toward Kurt Weill and his wife, Lotte, who had been a brunette in Germany but, Elsa whispered to Vera, looked much better as a blonde. Renee, a French dermatologist from Paris, was smoking on the couch with Lotte. Renee's son had attended the same nursery school as Lucie, Ecole Jean Dolent. Vera wondered if he had escaped with his mother.

Max clasped both of Kurt's hands in his, his body lurching forward, unable to contain his enthusiasm at encountering a fellow musician. Among his colleagues, he appeared to expand and inflate, feeding off their shared energy.

Kurt said they felt safe and happy now that they were finally here in America.

Vera looked at the women in silken gowns, willowy figures in peach and pearl gray and silvery white, jealous of how languidly they moved around the room, as though they hadn't just arrived here, bedraggled and exhausted by the long sea crossing. Perhaps these women had come over months ago, with many dresses to choose from, given their air of relaxed luxury, whereas Vera wore her single formal dress. Max had bought it for her yesterday at Bergdorf Goodman, but it was an extravagant purchase and they both felt guilty about it. Running her palm along the velvet, she felt strange and at odds with herself, thrown off by Paul's comment about his wife. He now rested his forearm on the fireplace mantel, talking with the hostess as though he didn't have a care in the world.

Through the large windows, a yellow moon hung over the dark Hudson.

Elsa instantly became enamored with Renee, discovering that they had fled south on the same road that Vera and Elsa had traveled when they escaped Gurs. Renee began to recount the terrible ordeal of fleeing Paris, and Vera recalled a garden party Renee had last spring, the grass wet from a recent rain, dabs of black caviar on sour cream couched in endive, and then Max accidentally tipped a glass of red wine onto her paneled dress, the light beige silk instantly ruined and then the comic attempts to fix it by pouring massive amounts of salt onto her lap, all of them laughing about it. Elsa sat close to Renee now on the settee as Renee described, with birdlike intensity, that she had left her mother-in-law behind, on the side of the road, because she had to carry her son to the nearest hospital. He'd been injured by a bomb blast. Her husband had apparently gone missing at that point, but they later found each other. Parts of her story were swallowed up by the big band music streaming from the phonograph, but from what Vera could infer, Renee had no idea what had happened to her mother-in-law.

Wishing she could disappear into the wallpaper, Vera drained the last drops of champagne from her glass.

"Lost in the tropics?"

Vera immediately detected a German accent, tidy and curt, beneath the English.

"Sorry?" she asked, for though she'd heard him, she didn't know what to say. It seemed easier to smile and appear confused.

The German, dressed meticulously in navy trousers and an ironed shirt with a silk bow tie the same port-wine shade as her dress, looked at her expectantly, and she realized he was one of the men Elsa and Leon had embraced when they all first walked into the apartment, making exclamations in German about the happy coincidence of finding him here, followed by his sarcastic retort that every intellectual between Budapest and Paris eventually ended up in this apartment.

He now gestured to the palm-treed wallpaper with his cigar, enveloping them in a cloud of blue smoke. "Dreadful." He deftly spirited away her empty glass and replaced it with a new one, ice cold to the touch. Her dress, backless and all velvet folds, fell in a low-slung loop that rested in a heap at the base of her spine, and she noticed him noticing this.

He introduced himself as Otto Beckmann. When she said her name, he added, "Of course. You recently arrived from France with Leon and Elsa. They often spoke of you. And Max."

"We were all in Sanary-sur-Mer, but then we had to leave, like everyone else. It happened very quickly."

He nodded. "I was thinking of going there too, but in the end, I thought it better to come here." He paused. "Are you and Max joining Leon and Elsa in Los Angeles?"

"Yes," she said regretfully.

"You could get work out there, as an actress," he teased. "You're certainly beautiful enough."

Vera blushed. "Honestly, I don't know what I'll do out there." Then she took a sip, the ebullient bubbles dissolving in her mouth.

He asked what she did before the war, and she said she was a writer, but as she explained this, she felt embarrassment wash over her, because now those historical novels about ill-fated love affairs seemed insignificant. Trifles not worth mentioning. And the writing itself often fell into a lyrical haze, which came easily to her, too easily, coating over the raw emotions of the characters with a shiny patina, making it all so smooth and digestible. Yes, maybe Paul had been right. She shouldn't write like that anymore. How could she, after what had happened to her, to Europe, to everyone? The problem was, she didn't know how to write without the crutch of beauty. And hadn't beauty lulled everyone into the kind of passivity that made possible what was happening in Europe right now?

Vera stared into Otto's arctic blue eyes. "It all seems like a long time ago, writing those books."

He stubbed out his cigar in a nearby ashtray. "It's true, we're living in a different world now. But you can always write."

From across the room, Max chatted with Heinrich Mann and his wife, Nelly, on the couch, her plump breasts cascading out of a low-cut dress. The music picked up, drowning out conversations.

Vera touched her pearl earring, the weight of it heavy on her earlobe, having already noted the dark line of paint beneath Otto's fingernails, which explained his arrogant way of looking, as if he could already envision how this scene should appear on canvas: heavy black lines outlining female forms, distorted faces grimacing, mordantly laughing at nothing but their own inanity. He might even paint himself into the foreground, a lone figure glowering at the viewer. Then she realized that this painting she imagined had hung in the living room of Elsa's house in Sanary. Yes, it was by the famous German expressionist painter Otto Beckmann, entitled **Paris Society**. She had always loved it and now she knew this man had painted it.

"I know your work. Elsa owned one of your paintings."

He smiled, his ironic edge softening for a moment, and he explained that he had been in New York for three years already. "First, I lost my teaching post in Berlin, and then, the day after that, they featured my work in the **Entartete Kunst**, the Degenerate Art Exhibit. A week later, I left Germany forever. According to the Nazis, the Jewish racial spirit of filth and depravity infused my work. And I'm not even Jewish." Seeing the expression on her face, he added, "I have nothing against the Jews. I'm a target, same as they are. One of my closest friends was a Jew. We fought in the Great War together."

"What happened to him?" Vera asked.

Otto paused, his gaze reflective. "He went to Argentina. Or maybe it was Venezuela."

She felt a chill even though the room was warm, static catching on her gown, the fire crackling behind the grate.

Otto joked, "And here **I** am too, swept up in this exodus." He gestured with the tip of his newly lit cigar at Leon and Max, who spoke to a man in an ill-fitting suit.

Vera smiled at him. "We're stuck with each other." Then she sat down next to him on the couch. He sipped a glass of cognac, asking where she was staying, and when she said the Wyndham, he groaned. "Oh, God, no. I'm at the St. Moritz. Same crowd. Can't stand it."

"Why don't you leave then?"

Otto placed his drink on the marble coffee table. "I am leaving."

"Where are you going?"

"The same place as you."

"California?"

"Yes."

CHAPTER 10

VERA

DECEMBER 1940,
LOS ANGELES, CALIFORNIA

A gypsy woman once foretold that she would escape the sting of sorrow if she lived near the sea. She'd read Vera's fortune at one of those Parisian parties with masked people laughing on balconies, the beaded curtain demarcating the little room where the gypsy sat on a heap of pillows, the garnet lampshade's glow bathing them in premonition. Of course, it was all for show, the gypsy a prop, an attraction to enliven the evening.

Vera thought of her now, staring out at the purple-smudged dawn through the bedroom window, the thick white and brown limbs of the eucalyptus trees, the blue jays clustering on a bush before dispersing.

When the sun came up, it singed the brown mountains gold.

But her heart, tight and fragile, wobbled in her chest like a glass orb. With still no word from Agnes, Vera willed a letter to come. Michel Toch had suggested that Vera and Max use his address as a forwarding one, until they were settled in Los Angeles, but even now, after a month had passed, no letter arrived. Every morning, they read the newspaper in Michel's breakfast nook, the ticking of an ornate grandfather clock the only discernible sound, hoping that reading the paper cover to cover would somehow bring them closer to understanding what was really happening over there, to Lucie, but the headlines only made Vera more fretful: "New Warsaw Ghetto Completed" and "United States Ambassador to Great Britain, Joseph Kennedy, Stands against American Entry into War." And those unbelievable pictures of the Coventry Cathedral reduced to rubble. Right next to this, an article detailed Hitler's decree for a "New Europe," heralding that soon, Europe would be "**Judenfrei**."

Elsa and Leon found a Spanish villa nestled in the hills of the Pacific Palisades overlooking the sea, and they tried to convince Vera and Max to live up there too. But with no schools, hospitals, or grocery stores nearby, such a place would be unsuitable for Lucie, once they brought her here. Vera explained this in Michel's kitchen, where they were temporarily staying while looking for a house to rent. It was Sunday. Max prepared miniature mustard cheese sandwiches, even though, he muttered, the cheese tasted like wax paper, before skewering each one with a toothpick, the ends of which were wrapped in blue-green cellophane reminding Vera of a children's party.

"And with the petrol rations, how will you get anywhere?" Vera wondered. "The house is so far away from everything."

"Oh, I won't have to drive much," Elsa said with a wry smile. "I walk down to the water, there's a little grocery there, and I hike my way back up."

Leon threw up his hands in mock surrender. "All the windows are broken, the backyard is entirely overgrown, and the basement is knee deep in mice and lizards, but we bought it for nine thousand dollars."

Elsa turned to Vera and whispered, "He just sold his latest book to Martin Secker in London, so he's feeling flush."

"The last one in the Josephus trilogy?"

"No, **The Lautensack Brothers**."

Of course, Vera thought, he's working on two manuscripts simultaneously, managing to sell one that she didn't even know he was writing, causing her to feel oddly betrayed, as if they had purposefully kept it secret until they could flash around news of the sale with artificial nonchalance.

"There's not a scrap of furniture. We'll have to sleep in the backyard until the house is habitable,"

Leon added, swiping one of the cheese sandwiches off the platter and popping it into his mouth. "In sleeping bags."

"A Persian prince lives in one of the neighboring villas," Elsa said. "At least that's what the agent said. It can't be entirely wild up there."

"The landscape reminds me of Tuscany," Leon rejoined, chewing pensively on the sandwich. "That's why we took it so quickly." And then he reminisced about their sojourn throughout Italy when they were young and first married; they backpacked, and he wrote his manuscripts while she prepared the food and tent, arranging all the details so he could focus on his work.

"Clearly, nothing has changed," Elsa said, giving him a peck on the cheek before pouring coffee into each porcelain cup.

After another week of searching, Max and Vera found a house to rent on Adelaide Drive in Santa Monica Canyon, a quaint English-style cottage with avocado trees and azaleas in the garden and rooms with slanted ceilings and views of the sea, for eighty dollars a month.

But there were still so many practicalities to arrange. Everyone said they would need a car, but Vera had no idea how to procure one. They would also need a housekeeper, once Max secured a contract at a studio.

"How else will you entertain?" Salka Viertel asked as she strode through the newly painted rooms, rubbing her arms up and down as though the recently vacated house, without even a rug to cover the hardwood floors, or a throw pillow to brighten the faded couch, made her shiver. She had moved here from Vienna with her husband, a playwright, before the war, and assumed the queenly position of connecting those who needed help with those who could dispense it. She was the epicenter of émigré life in Los Angeles, and her house on Mabery Road, a two-minute stroll from Vera and Max's, was brimming with recent arrivals from Europe, many of whom were desperate for work. Everyone knew Salka, and knowing her brought you closer to knowing everyone else, from picture people, such as Garbo and Chaplin, to famous musicians, such as Stravinsky and Korngold, along with a host of aspiring artists whom she nurtured and included in her Sunday salons.

"I know a very nice Dutch woman," Salka announced, glancing up into the corners of the living room, which glistened with spiderwebs, "who used to be a pediatrician in Rotterdam. Hilde Assendorp. She's looking for housework. The two of you will get on well."

Michel gave Vera and Max a few of the old lawn chairs from his property so they could at least sit in their garden and take a coffee, just as in Sanary, Max joked. The house itself came with furniture, even if it was overly ornate and belonged to the last century, all dark wood and crushed-velvet chaises, but none of that mattered to Vera. She walked through the dusty rooms, tearing off sheets from wingback chairs and pulling the heavy floral curtains aside to let in the light, and glimpsed the sea through the dusty windows. She could smell the salt in the wood, and the clean pine scent of the trees surrounding the garden, and when she closed her eyes and listened closely, she heard the tide rolling in and out.

The next morning, while she was still in her dressing gown, Michel rang the bell. They thought he had come with more lawn furniture, whispering to each other about how they would politely decline the offer, but when they opened the door, he held up a letter, his lined face jubilant, his gold-rimmed glasses catching the morning sun.

"I think you've been waiting for this one," he said, handing Vera the envelope.

The first thing she checked was the postmark date: September 9. Three months ago. She broke into a sweat, trying to open the envelope with her fingers. Fearing tearing the letter, she waited while Max frantically looked for the letter knife, finally finding it in a kitchen drawer, and then, with the utmost care, she slit it open.

He now hovered next to her, and they glanced at each other with a mixture of fear and hope, so

palpable she could almost taste it, before she un-
folded the letter.

They read it quickly, racing through the hum-
drum descriptions of farm life, scanning for any hint
of bad news, but there was none. Lucie was healthy,
it had been a very good harvest, they had canned
fruits and vegetables for the winter. **We must exist
in the quietest corner of France, and we thank
God for blessing us with such calm. I will write
again soon. Sending love and prayers.**

Vera fell into Max's arms, crying out of relief, and
Michel hugged them both, and after a few minutes
they were all cautiously laughing and shaking their
heads, embarrassed by their fears and making vague
admonishments that there was no use in overreacting, the war would end, normalcy would return,
and in the meantime, look at this glorious summer
day in the middle of December.

A few weeks later, Vera walked along the same
esplanade where they had stopped their first day
in Los Angeles, which she had learned was called
Palisades Park. She passed the twisted Monterey
cypresses that barely elevated themselves above-
ground, as if the earth had an abnormally strong
gravitational downward pull on their branches,
causing the trees to grow horizontally, flat-topped
by the strong winds. **What kind of tree is this that**

cannot grow upward as nearly all trees do, she thought, touching its thick rough bark.

Old-fashioned orchestral music floated over from the pier. She clutched Agnes's letter, folded in her coat pocket, as though by her carrying it around, Lucie would sense Vera's protection. That night, she had read it over and over again, repeating certain lines to Max, imploring him to confirm it was a good letter and Lucie really was safe, even though the letter stated this plainly.

"Vera," he had said, sipping a glass of sherry, "you can't worry so much. Otherwise, you'll go mad."

Those words circled in her head as she entered the pier: **Otherwise you'll go mad.** She knew he was right, as he was right not to seek out a sign in everything; that also drove people mad. Their new neighbors Conrad and Pauline Leland had come to the door with a bouquet of yellow chrysanthemums as a welcome gift. He was a physicist at Caltech. She had grown up in India and played the sitar, carrying a Bohemian air about her.

The minute they left, Vera violently threw the flowers into the bin, much to Max's amusement. Of course, he understood. In France, chrysanthemums were reserved for funerals, and in Russia, one only gave yellow flowers to the sick.

Vera paused before the glassed-in merry-go-round, the aquamarine and violet horses flaunting manes of flaming pink and silvery white. A boy on a black pony banged his harmonica against the brass pole. When she glanced down to retrieve a lighter from her purse, she spotted a little white sock on the parquet floor, and wondered where the other one was. In the wrong moment, a child's lost sock would cause a sinking heaviness in her stomach. But today, she felt a cool indifference. Perhaps the careless mother who had lost the sock was now scolding her child, pointing to his raw pink foot, warning that the child would fall ill. Or perhaps the child had purposefully abandoned it, knowing this would annoy his mother. These unsentimental thoughts comforted her, and she inhaled the cigarette smoke, holding it in her throat for a moment, relishing the burning sensation.

She strolled past news vendors, ice cream stalls, and stands for renting bait and fishing rods. Young runaways hawked their wares on a tartan blanket: chewing gum, metallic-gray abalone shells, coral beads, bits of misshapen sea glass. She felt them watching her, with their hooded eyes and sunburnt faces, as she made her way up the length of the pier. **What must they think of me?** she thought. **A lonely woman with leather gloves the color of butter. A woman who comes here for the garish attractions, for the Ferris wheel and cotton candy, sickeningly pink.**

An idle woman who has no work, no necessity in life, seemingly childless.

She envied Max.

Today, he had left the house in a hurry, rushing off to the appointments that Michel had arranged for him at the studios. One at Paramount, the other at MGM, which Max favored, because MGM made big splashy musicals, and they had an enormous music department teeming with renowned musicians, many of whom were from Europe. She vaguely wondered about the interviews, and if he would return home dejected, fretting that he was a failure like Petrovitch, or roaring with optimism, the promise of a contract within reach. Either way, she already saw herself sitting by the fire while he recounted each and every detail, from the interviewer's ridiculous bow tie to how many films he would be expected to score over the course of a year. During these monologues, she followed along just enough to inject a comment at the right moment while her mind swung, like a pendulum, from deep worries to minute domestic concerns: Should they buy a new icebox or repair the old one? They could buy a new one, but only if Max secured a contract at a studio, as everyone said he would. If not, they certainly couldn't afford a new icebox. They could go to the Jewish Free Loan Association, or the Jewish Social Service Bureau, which gave émigrés money to start businesses, such as a shoe store or a grocery, but such an endeavor felt unimaginable to Vera.

And how long, Vera wondered, glancing up at the slowly rotating Ferris wheel at the edge of the pier, would she have to wait for Agnes's next letter?

CHAPTER II

LUCIE

When she woke up, her breath stood in the air, as white as smoke, the tip of her nose chilled, her cheeks wet with tears.

Lucie drew the covers close, the recent nightmare still rolling through her mind: she ran in the Tuileries Garden, laughing and yelling to her mother, who chased her under a bright yellow sun. Balloons escaped into the sky, blue, red, and orange orbs floating toward wispy white clouds. She hid behind a fat hedge, tricking her mother, waiting for her to uncover this good hiding place, but then, while she was hiding, within the span of seconds, the sky darkened, and it was time to go home. She called out for her mother. She called and called and then started running back the way she'd come, the garden dark, the green benches deserted, the balloon seller gone. She knew that she was lost, and tears streamed down her face, but she kept running into the shapeless night until she woke up, her chest pounding, muffling the urge to cry out, because in this house, displays of emotion were unwelcome.

So many times, Agnes had to shush her and then guide Lucie into another room, close the door, and explain that crying or yelling or raising one's voice, especially over a trifle, even if Thomas had stolen her favorite ribbon or teased her about her hair, would not be tolerated. When she said this, her voice turned hard and stern, but her eyes were soft, recalling, Lucie thought, how it used to be. Before they came to this farm, and before her parents left, if she cried after getting hurt or after a bad dream and her mother was not there, then Agnes would pull her onto her lap and run her warm palm over her back, whispering, "When I was little, just like you, my sisters teased me relentlessly, but it hurt even more when people told me it was nothing, that I was making a fuss on purpose."

She sat up, her heart still crashing around in her chest from the dream, but also it was Christmas. Her parents might come for her, surprise her on Christmas, and Lucie willed that today was the day she would see them again. She kept still for some minutes, listening for them, and heard the sisters preparing breakfast in the kitchen, the clatter of knives and forks, the sweet earthy smell of baking bread wafting up the staircase. The other children must already be sitting around the tree, decorated with apples and candles, their shoes, left before the fireplace, filled with little presents from Père Noël.

Lucie put on her slippers and slowly came down the stairs, clutching the banister, still hoping that maybe her parents might be standing there with outstretched arms, ready to whisk her away, and yet she knew they wouldn't be.

The living room, decorated with streamers, with the pretty fir tree in the corner, and filled with warmth and chatter, with sighs and gasps of surprise, allowed Lucie to forget the terrible dream. She felt happy when she touched the new red ribbon tucked into a discreet roll inside her boot, and when she cupped the orange in her other boot. There was even something else: she unwrapped a soft square of gold foil and out tumbled a new dress for her doll, sky blue with black shiny buttons, and she knew Agnes had made it, having spied her knitting the blue dress over the last few weeks.

Beneath the tree, next to a few unopened presents, Lucie stared at the nativity scene. It had captivated her from the moment the sisters had brought it out weeks ago, in preparation for the holiday. She now lay on her stomach, chewing on a piece of candied fruit, and inched closer to the beautiful little figurines: Mary, draped in heavenly blue, her head bowed, bent over baby Jesus, who was arranged on a little heap of hay. Joseph, kneeling on one knee, prayed next to the shepherds, along with a few peaceful sheep. There was also an angel in the corner, golden wings outstretched, blessing the birth. Lucie reached out to touch baby Jesus, but then caught the disapproving eye of Agnes's sister and withdrew her hand, pretending that she had never intended to touch it.

Later that day, the fading light cast a purplish tint over the frosted fields. Nearly magic, the way colors changed, Lucie thought. Against the window, her warm breath left a small circle of condensation before slowly vanishing, and then she left another breath, and another, watching each disappear in the same way.

The bedroom door opened, and from the smooth swish of her dress, Lucie knew it was Agnes.

"Lucie," Agnes whispered, holding an envelope in her hand. "Come."

Together, they sat down on Lucie's bed, the coverlet left untucked, but Agnes didn't notice. Carefully, she slid a letter out of the envelope and immediately, Lucie knew it was from her parents.

With one arm wrapped around Lucie's shoulders, her other hand holding the letter out before them, Agnes read aloud: "'We miss you terribly and think of you every day. Cold wind sweeps through the city, which is full of canary yellow taxicabs and garbage trucks and loads of glamorous lonely people, and barely any trees . . .'"

After she finished reading, Lucie had so many questions, none of which Agnes could answer to her satisfaction. She couldn't tell Lucie where her parents were, or when they were coming back, or why they hadn't taken her with them. This last question caused Agnes's face to redden, her eyes watering slightly when she explained in a shaky voice, "They knew it was safer for you here, with me. They wanted to protect you . . . You are the most precious thing to them."

"Is it still safe here?"

Agnes clenched Lucie's hand and forced a smile. "Yes. Yes, it is." She paused. "But don't say anything about this letter. Think of it as a secret gift, not to be shared with anyone else. Do you understand?"

"Yes," Lucie managed, her voice barely audible, "I understand."

That night, yellow taxicabs and enormous garbage trucks filled her dreams, along with glamorous women in fur coats who smoked long thin cigarettes and wore black silk gloves, until she realized that every one of these women was identical to the one before, and they all looked exactly like her mother.

CHAPTER 12

SASHA

DECEMBER 7, 1941,
LOS ANGELES, CALIFORNIA

On that blindingly bright Sunday morning, the year closing in on him, Sasha was driving down Pico, his tongue burnt from drinking too-hot coffee over a late breakfast, mulling over what he'd read in the trades and listening to the football game between the Brooklyn Dodgers and the New York Giants. Sasha rooted for the Giants, who were ahead. **How much longer can I do this?** he wondered, aware that he'd been in town for almost three years and he was still writing one-offs for Columbia and other studios around town, churning out schlock, working on his own ideas at night, directing his own pictures still an elusive dream. Nothing had ever happened with **Cyclone**, which Warner Bros. had briefly expressed interest in, and then

Wyler had optioned it to direct, but the six-month period had ended, and he hadn't renewed it. Charlie kept saying that at least Sasha had a foothold, but he wanted more than a foothold, and had begun doubting his decision to even come out here, although the thought of moving back home felt worse than failure. But he'd recently written a little Western, tight and lean, about two brothers in love with the same woman. It wasn't the kind of lighthearted commercial picture Charlie said the studios wanted, but so what? He was thinking of calling it **Clementine**, already envisioning how to direct it, and make it with just a little money. And if the movie was a success, he thought, then it could be a stepping-stone . . .

He shifted gears, and a car suddenly swerved in front of him.

The car sped ahead, and Sasha stayed on its tail, wanting to race, when he heard John Daly's wooden voice announce, **"We interrupt this program to bring you a special news bulletin. And now we take you to Honolulu: 1234. Hello, NBC. Hello, NBC. This is KGU in Honolulu, Hawaii.**

"We have witnessed this morning the distant view of a battle off of Pearl Harbor and the severe bombing of Pearl Harbor by enemy planes, undoubtedly Japanese. The city of Honolulu has also been attacked and considerable damage done. This battle has been going on for nearly three hours. It is no joke. It is a real war."

Sasha pulled to the side of the road, cresting over

the curb and nearly hitting a palm tree. Hunched close to the radio, he gripped the steering wheel, his whole body coiled and tense. He thought of his mother in New Rochelle listening to the broadcast in her stocking feet. He thought of all the neighborhood kids in the Lower East Side obliviously playing in the snow while their parents froze in hallways and bathrooms and living rooms, staring at the peeling wallpaper, the kettle screeching to a boil, wondering how much longer this world would last.

This past June, his mother had received a letter from her second cousin that the Germans were advancing into Riga, and that they were killing all the Jews and gypsies as they went, taking hundreds into the Rumbula forest to be lined up and shot. The lucky ones were rounded up and put into ghettos on the city outskirts, which was where her cousin was now. Leah told Sasha about this over the phone, her voice thin and soft. Sasha pictured the Rumbula forest, recalled running through its narrow grassy paths, among the silvery birches that cast long skinny shadows before him, interspersed with lambent sun. Other forgotten childhood details jolted him, as if they carried an electric charge: In winter, snapping off icicles from the overhanging eves for swordfights with the other boys in an imaginary war. Finding his mother's engraved wooden box pushed under the armoire. He'd opened it and, knowing he shouldn't, had lifted up his grandfather's tallit folded over the silver kaddish wine-cup. Then, he saw the corner of the photograph stashed into the folds of the tallit: a soldier sitting under the apple trees, with one knee up and the other leg outstretched, and even though he had a gun slung across his chest, his face was soft, his eyes laughing at something that had just happened. Sasha had quickly turned over the photograph and read: **September 1915.** His mother's handwriting had sent a chill up his spine, and quickly, he'd put the photograph away, not wanting to touch it, as if it might burn his fingers.

All that followed after those moments alone in the car appeared oddly abstract, as if some unthinking force drove him forward, maybe the force of escape and the force of ambition: two seemingly opposite impulses he held within himself. The desire to run from something and the desire to run toward another thing—he couldn't tell which motivated him more when he stood in line at the US Army draft office that afternoon.

He wanted to go to Europe, to defend the place he'd been born. The Germans had already taken Latvia and the other Baltic states, and from what he gathered, the Germans under Hitler were much worse than in past history, though during the First World War, they were, according to his mother and her family, brutal and unbending, killing livestock and burning fields to the point of starving the local population. Leah said they would have gone hungry if it were not for a few kind soldiers who periodically snuck them an extra chicken, medicine for typhoid, a bushel of potatoes. She added, her eyes flashing with irony, that these helpful soldiers were Jews, German Jews but Jews nonetheless—some of them even had family from Russia, who then found themselves as both strangers and brothers to the shtetl Jews.

During the required interview, the recruiting officer wondered aloud, "Why not the communications department? That's what you're already doing. And we need men who know how to operate a camera, to record what's happening over there. How about it?"

"Listen, I don't wanna be taking pictures of the action from some rooftop or making little films about how great army life is." Sasha leaned forward. "I wanna be in the thick of it, without any lens or typewriter getting in my way. You know what I mean?" This war could be the worst crime of the twentieth century, and he yearned to be on the ground, shoulder to shoulder with the other soldiers, witnessing the enemy up close, close enough to see their mouths quiver and the snow dusting their eyebrows, and to see if these Germans were fueled by manic violence or if they were just as afraid as he was. Sasha wanted to understand what kind of men they were, and what kind of man he was.

The recruitment officer tilted back into his chair. "Okay, kid. Here's your chance."

. . .

Back in his car and driving toward the ocean, the direction he always went when he needed to think, he glanced up at the crystalline blue, emptied of clouds. He parked on Ocean Avenue and walked the short distance to the pier. It was another world out here in California, without winters, with nothing to brace himself against, the city not really a city but just little populated pockets sprinkled up and down the coast, and the wide boulevards that cut inland, leading to the mountains. Wherever he ended up, he would miss this place.

He took in the sea, as though a million tiny mirrors reflected off its surface. Ocean Park Pier, with its wide vistas, the long wooden walkway barely tethered to the city, the tides ebbing and flowing beneath its planks, lured him. It seemed the only place still immune to the news of war, as army vehicles already patrolled Little Tokyo, machine guns aimed at the deserted storefronts. Soon, LA Harbor would be closely guarded by sentries, and perhaps even Ocean Park Pier, with all of its amusements and diversions, would shut down too.

His forearms pressed against the railing, he stood next to a few lone fishermen who surveyed the sea. Faint tinny music floated over from the carousel, music for children, and the scent of fried dough emanated from the churro stand, setting his mouth watering.

Out of the corner of his eye, Sasha noticed a woman at the tip of the pier, staring into the horizon, seemingly unaware of all else: the pelican skimming the water's surface, the light laughter trailing from a couple wrapped up in a tartan blanket, the strong cigar an old fisherman smoked while angling for his line to tighten with a potential catch. The red sun began sinking into the sea.

The wind lifted up her hair from her neck, and he saw that she had left her hat and handbag on a bench nearby. Something about those abandoned belongings made him approach her, to see if she was all right, but in that moment, she swiftly turned away from the ocean and knocked into him, their shoulders colliding.

He apologized, and she said it was her fault, she wasn't looking where she was going. Her French accent sounded like gold twinkling in the dark, and her smudged eyeliner lent her a forlorn intensity, her dark eyes boring into his. She shivered in the wind and then glanced away.

He gestured to her purse and hat. "Are those yours, over there?"

"Oh, I forgot . . ." She paused, hugging herself. Goosebumps rose up on her flesh. She wore a wedding ring, a delicate gold band that flashed against her olive skin. Looking back out at the ocean, she continued, "It's hard to imagine that Pearl Harbor is that way, not so very far. And yet we're standing here as if nothing has happened. But we're surrounded now, on all sides."

She looked at him earnestly, expecting him to agree with her sentiments, of which he felt uncertain. Did she want him to share in her frustration because the fisherman was still fishing, the couple still cajoling each other over some private joke, the sunset still beautiful, while the Germans marched on Moscow, and only hours ago Japan had attacked America?

"I don't think nothing has happened." He paused. "I joined up today."

She gripped his hand, her palm alive against his, but then her cheeks flushed with embarrassment, and she withdrew it.

An expectant pause hung between them, his pulse hammering through his veins. The wind rippled through her blouse, and with the light falling so softly and perfectly over her face, he could see why directors called this the magic hour.

He wanted to know why she was all alone on a day like this. But he was unable to think of what to say, his mind jumbled from the heady jasmine perfume that rose up from her skin and the delicate blue veins pulsing beneath her neck.

"The light's fading." She gestured to the last slice of sun sinking into the ocean. "I should go." Glancing up at the sky, she seemed to fear that Japanese paratroopers might land on the pier any minute.

She shook her head. "But I don't want to go; time stops here. It's peaceful." He thought she must have a husband waiting for her somewhere. Maybe he was sitting in a restaurant booth, starting to worry. Or maybe dinner stood on the dining room table, growing cold.

"I know," he said, meeting her gaze, and he saw her eyes flicker with something lost. "When I first moved out here, I couldn't believe that when I drove down Wilshire Boulevard, I could see the ocean, even from miles away, between buildings, and over buildings. I love it out here too, on the pier. At the edge of the world."

She smiled politely, and he felt her retreating.

He picked up her things, and when she took her hat and purse from him, their fingertips brushed, and he wondered if she also noticed that sharp current passing between them. Walking away, she crushed her purse and hat to her chest, thanking him again, before breaking into a half run. He watched her cream blouse and dark hair recede into the purple twilight.

That evening, after a simple dinner at the Green Cat, Sasha dialed his mother. He anticipated her shrieking at him for joining up, after all she had sacrificed, and here he was, volunteering for an early death.

Instead she said, "This war will be even more

terrible than the last one. I feel it in my bones." She fell silent, which was something he had witnessed many times. She could be cooking, or ironing a shirt, or sharply complaining about the upstairs neighbors, and then she would just stop and stare out the window. Sighing heavily into the phone, she added, "War stirs up so many old ghosts. I don't want you to become a ghost too."

"Come on, **mamele**. Don't get so morbid."

"I'm gonna send you a keepsake in the mail, something for good luck, something from the old country . . . God knows you'll need it."

"I still have a few weeks before training camp."

"Where's that?"

"Don't know yet."

"You'll visit me beforehand, yes?"

He said of course, and then she grumbled, "What kind of son wouldn't see his own mother before going off to war?"

"Hey, Ma, the call is getting expensive—I'll see you soon. Promise."

Gently placing down the receiver, Sasha lingered over his desk, feeling the weighty silence that always followed a phone call with his mother, her disappointment and worry palpable, even from such a distance. His notes scrawled on sheets of yellow lined paper for a crime picture he'd been tossing around appeared silly to him now, as if he hadn't dashed it all down yesterday in a fervor of misguided confidence. Already, he felt these notes had been written by a naïve, younger self, even if this self had existed only twelve hours ago, before he pulled over to the side of the road and listened to the world change, before he stood in a line that snaked around the draft office, sharing cigarettes with all the other guys who carried the same pounding urgency to fight.

CHAPTER 13

VERA

NOVEMBER 1942,
SANTA MONICA, CALIFORNIA

The strangeness of those first months in Los Angeles stayed with Vera, even though two years had passed. It was as if she'd taken a new lover but still found parts of his body surprising and foreign, despite having acclimated to his overall newness. She was occasionally unsettled by the empty wide boulevards and withered palms, and the gnarled cacti that peppered the steep hills rising up along Roosevelt Highway.

She was often uncertain of the time of day, as well as the season, which engendered a dreamy rootlessness as months slipped through her fingers like sand. Many of their friends had surrendered to time's fluidity here, but she resisted it, knowing that in Europe, which held Lucie in it, the war raged on.

And people asked so many questions here: **Where do you live? How much do you pay in rent? Where do your children go to school?** Before she could answer, they gave her advice: **Join a church or a social group, don't complain or criticize, abandon your mother tongue and never look back.**

"Never look back" was a particular favorite because Eleanor Roosevelt had said it. Yesterday, when she was standing on the corner, weighed down by net bags filled with groceries, waiting for Max to pick her up, an older man with matted hair and a rucksack approached her. He said he was a traveler. She couldn't take her eyes off his bottom teeth, which were all bashed in and broken, like a pile of rubble. He asked if she was a movie star and if he could have her autograph. When she said no, he started to guess where she was from. "Georgia? Alabama? Mississippi? Kentucky? I bet you're from Kentucky. No, I take it back. Georgia. A Georgia peach."

She kept shaking her head, feeling slightly threatened, but she thought it was better to smile. If she said anything more, he would pounce on her French accent, and she didn't have the energy for the bevy of questions that would surely follow, about why they had left France, how long the war might last, and so on—none of which she thought suitable to discuss with a perfect stranger, whether it be this vagabond or the waiter at their favorite Chinese restaurant who often chatted them up as though they were old friends, asking about Max's work at the studio, and if he had met any big stars. A European waiter would never do this, as there were certain unspoken rules everyone followed. Here, an amiable openness permeated every encounter, and she never knew exactly how to react or what to say.

But sometimes it was nice, how people smiled all the time, even if they didn't mean it. Better than that perpetual Parisian scowl, Vera thought. And the women, the way they brightly chirped hello and kept smiling long after the conversation ended—their white gleaming teeth almost sent Vera into a trance, and she found herself smiling back, baffled by their persistent cheerfulness coupled with this American compulsion to compliment. During the process of making "small talk," the interaction proved incomplete without a compliment, and only later on did Vera realize she must dutifully return the compliment, after which the woman would inform her that her Bakelite bangle, intricately carved in the Oriental style, had been purchased on sale, at a great discount, and sometimes she might even name the exact price, which left Vera confounded, as if the woman was both chastising herself for wearing something new, while praising herself for striking a bargain. In Paris, if a woman liked your handbag, she might bestow it with a fleeting, appraising glance before ignoring it completely. Any mention of where it was purchased, or the cost, was unimaginably uncouth.

Nonetheless, everyone from the neighbors to the mailman was so friendly and welcoming, she felt touched by their natural playfulness that held so few barriers; she marveled at how easily they accepted her, a refugee, with her bad accent and her shyness. And even if such friendliness was superficial, as some of their European friends grumbled, what did it matter? When Pauline walked outside in her robe and bare feet to fetch the paper and saw Vera doing the same, she stood on tiptoe and waved energetically to Vera over the hedge, her unfixed hair catching the sun, and in that moment, Vera's heart lifted, so grateful to say hello back, as though she belonged here too, among the wet grass and hummingbirds and the low drone of lawn mowers. Fanning herself with the morning edition, Pauline had called out yesterday, "Oh, Vera, I just love your robe. Is it from Paris?"

She nodded, slightly embarrassed by the attention. And then she forced herself to say, "Where did you find that charming turban? It suits you perfectly."

And even though she still couldn't get rid of her thick accent, her English was improving with the help of her tutor, Peter, Salka's son. She couldn't believe that the boy had been born in Dresden as there wasn't a touch of Europe on him, collegiate and winning in his pressed khakis and confident smile. After an hour of halting but good-humored conversational English at the kitchen table, he often left her in a lighter mood.

But there was no accounting for the hollow absence of work. Last year, she'd finally abandoned the World War I novel, after multiple drafts, with Leon's words ringing in her ears: **Historical novels should reflect the present state of things. If not, then why write them?** She attempted to write a few short stories, but the sentences felt as thin and colorless as water, the characters inconsequential, and she abruptly stopped midway through, disgusted with her efforts. It was grinding, putting pen to paper, frozen at her desk, gazing out the window at a hummingbird, sentences as fickle and flitting as the hummingbird she watched, which never settled on any one branch, choosing another and then another. Sitting here, grasping at straws, as an American would say, she missed that momentous stream of productivity, her fingers tapping down on the keys, that punchy definite sound steadying her.

Lately, she had been writing various observations in her notebook, wondering if the details would ever cleave into a narrative, or even spark the possibility of a poem, but they remained lines strung absently across the page, as mundane as the bedsheets Hilde hung up to dry in the sun. And when she reread what she had written the following day, she hated it:

Bulbous geraniums burst from
their troughs, voracious for
admiration.
When the unfiltered sun shines,
it punishes me, exposing
every flaw,
But once in the shade, I am
chilled.
Among all this bracing beauty,
there is no comfort.

To avoid confronting those fallow hours, when thoughts of Lucie would often send her into an anxious spiral, Vera did the shopping, even when the icebox was fully stocked, distractedly wandering through the grocery aisles filled with citrus fruits. She was learning to drive, and took coffee with Pauline in the afternoons, and played a weekly round of golf with Elsa and some other women from the neighborhood, but none of this provided the old sensation of time suspended, when she was lost in a silky cocoon of her own making, creating worlds within worlds, multiplying her singular life into many lives: the lives of old men, disgruntled servants, or boyish German soldiers who didn't know why they were fighting. When interrupted, she used to look up from the page and stare vacantly into the middle distance; it took her a moment to tear herself away from those other realms and ask, "Yes, what is it?"

She knew that if she couldn't write, she must do something else. Something to at least help the war effort. One afternoon, she waited in line at city hall to join the Women's Auxiliary Forces, thinking perhaps there was a secretarial role where she could type and take dictation. She imagined getting lost in the monotonous work, submerged in the din of typewriters clacking away, ringing telephones, the shuffle of papers, and hoped this work would provide a kind of comfort. Nothing close to the ecstasy of inhabiting other minds and worlds, but a clear defined task to focus on besides her own personal plight. She could no longer tolerate her overwhelming uselessness, which induced a thick self-loathing that nearly choked her.

She stood in line for a long time, out of place among all the confident, outspoken American women, thinking about how Max teased that she'd be assigned to some canning factory out in Riverside or asked to operate a sewing machine, when they both knew she couldn't sew, but she brushed aside his jabs, straightening her shoulders, getting ready for her turn at the front of the line. But when she uttered her name, the older woman sitting behind the folding table barked: "American citizen?"

Vera's face fell.

The woman said hurriedly, "I'm sorry, honey. Maybe you can sell war bonds."

In the end, Max helped her get a job volunteering for the European Film Fund, an organization to help European immigrants relocate and settle in the United States. The fund was run by director Ernst Lubitsch and Paul Kohner out of the Paul Kohner Talent Agency on Sunset Boulevard in Beverly Hills. Vera worked there three days a week, settling behind a typewriter to compose letters on behalf of European refugees who had moved to Los Angeles and were in need of money, jobs, or affidavits. She wrote to filmmakers who agreed in advance to donate one percent of their fees to the fund, and she called the Hollywood Canteen and other venues after their benefit performances to collect the promised donations. She often had to telephone the heads of major studios, her voice shaky over the line, fearing her accent would cause them to hang up, but the secretaries were solicitous, and after speaking to their bosses, they said to expect a check in the mail. Sometimes, they put Vera through to one of these powerful men, brusque and harassed over the phone, but willing to write a check. Many of them were Jewish, with roots in Eastern Europe, and writing checks alleviated their guilt.

Driving slowly home from work, she felt her cheeks burn with shame, realizing how lucky she and Max were compared to these struggling refugees, many of whom would receive barely enough money to survive, compared to Max's generous salary and five-year contract, which allowed them to live comfortably in a house overlooking the sea.

And then, of course, there were those still in Europe, begging to get out, but everyone knew nothing could be done for them. At least, she reminded herself, staving off panic, Lucie was safe with Agnes.

Many of their friends and family were trapped in France, writing letters bloated with hope, gliding over the fact that they couldn't leave, their tone sounding as though they had chosen to stay, to avoid disrupting a child's schooling, or because an ailing parent could not be easily moved. Max's brother, Paul, had been fired from his position at Banque Lazard, and yet his letters remained flippant and casual, just the way he always was.

Elsa had heard barely any news of her mother in Berlin, but last week she received a short note from a friend by way of England that her mother had been rounded up in a truck with many other Jews and deported to the east. "She won't be able to endure the harsh conditions of the work camp," Elsa worried. "She's already in poor health, with her asthma, her lungs are weak, I can't imagine her lifting stones, or whatever it is they have them do there." Katja, one of Vera's only friends who had remained in Paris during the occupation, wrote that there were mass deportations from Drancy, but she hadn't heard of any other deportations in the rest of France, and for this coded message, Vera was relieved.

Other people from the past that she used to know visited her at odd moments, as though they were figures in a dream, such as the flower seller on the corner who used to put aside peonies wrapped in brown paper for Vera, knowing it was her favorite flower, or Lucie's primary school teacher, incredibly strict about handwriting, who once made Lucie cry because she kept reversing her **b**'s into **d**'s. What had happened to all those people? And did they wonder what had happened to her?

Yesterday an army truck had hauled away the neighbors' donation of bronze animal figurines that had decorated their front lawn, and Vera watched while the men picked up the mother doe and baby fawn, along with a reclining cherub, his head tilted coquettishly to the side. She noticed the sandbags piled up outside of Santa Monica city hall in case of an air raid, along with the multiplying number of military trucks cruising the main boulevards, and the placards that had sprung up overnight directing citizens to bomb shelters.

She bought war bonds and planted a victory garden, although her tomatoes refused to ripen, remaining stubbornly green even after Pauline showed her how to prepare the soil, explaining about fertilizer and planting schedules.

Many of their friends, such as Elsa and Leon, had to forfeit their radios and cameras to the government because they were German nationals, but at least, Vera thought, they weren't interned in camps like the Japanese, which sent a chill through her when she pored over the photographs in the **Los Angeles Examiner** of Japanese families standing in line at Union Station, saddled with their suitcases and their children, to live in the Santa Anita Race Track, where primitive barracks awaited them. The mothers, neat and dainty, appeared calm; they stood upright, holding their children's hands, trying to convey safety, but the children, dressed in their little suits and dresses for the journey, stared out at the crowd with fearful eyes, wondering why they had to leave their old lives so suddenly. Each time Vera saw one of these photographs, she felt a stab of recognition before folding the paper away.

Vera knew they were the enemy, of course; in every grocery store or gas station a poster commanded patrons to keep quiet because the Japs might be listening, but she couldn't help being revolted by the pamphlets that arrived in the mail about how to tell the difference between the Japanese and America's Chinese allies, with various anatomical descriptions, including a crude illustration of a Japanese body, pointing to the nose, the eyes, even how the feet were apparently different. She threw these things out immediately, not wanting to look, her stomach turning, knowing that in Germany and many other parts of Europe, the same types of images circulated, but of Jews.

A sense of suspicion hung over the city, and now everyone proceeded with an uneasy calm; Leon and Elsa did not speak German in public, and the Japanese disappeared, the flower markets shut down, Little Tokyo a sudden ghost town. Even knowing this, she admired the soldiers in their pressed khaki uniforms striding down the street, such confidence pouring off of them, reminding her of the man from the pier the day of Pearl Harbor. She had lingered there with him, longer than she should have, the sun dipping into the flat ocean, the light sliding into a golden pinkish hue that made everything appear softer, more fluid and malleable, and wondered if she would ever feel like herself again. Sometimes, when she read Ernie Pyle's column about troop life in Europe, she feared what had happened to him.

The war consumed Vera. She tracked every news story, especially those about France, and listened to every radio news broadcast, which often followed a lovely piece of classical music. Yet many of their friends appeared entirely unfazed, or at least pretended to be.

Today, the papers announced: "France Is Overrun: Nazis Reach Marseilles after Hitler Scraps

Armistice Pact." The free zone no longer existed, or as the reporter put it: "The last vestiges of a 'free' France disappeared from the map of Europe today."

When Vera read it, she felt sick and furious. Furious that Max had only frowned and then kept chewing on the heel of a baguette, brushing the headline away as easily as he brushed the crumbs from his lap, his only comment being that once again, they exaggerated events to sell more papers.

Vera stopped short on the stone-lined path leading to Salka Viertel's house, recalling Max's stoic reaction this morning, a renewed sense of indignation bubbling up inside of her. The door, painted a deep red, was ajar. People had already arrived for the Sunday cocktail party, the yellow light warm and inviting through the picture windows, the smell of heavy cigar smoke and strong perfume lingering on the footpath. Salka always insisted they come over on Sunday afternoons for goulash and endless rounds of Ping-Pong, as if her "European salon," as she called it, could compensate for the inherently ghostly quality of Sundays in Los Angeles.

"It's temporary," Max said, referring to the broken armistice. He lightly stepped onto the next moss-covered stone.

"You don't know that," Vera retorted, recognizing Renee, the dermatologist from Paris, walking in front of them, carefully holding her son's hand.

"Roosevelt will fix it, you'll see," Max replied.

Vera shrugged at the pointlessness of thinking anyone could fix anything.

At the party, no one mentioned the broken armistice. They gossiped about Alma Werfel's Bénédictine addiction, and that Heinrich Mann had recently moved into a shabby apartment house on Montana Avenue, which resembled derelict barracks. "Tragic, considering that his own brother lives in a veritable paradise on San Remo Drive," Elsa whispered to Vera.

Vera sighed, used to the routine gossip and intrigue, even enjoying it at times, but then she noticed Renee, who sat quietly next to her son on the living room couch. Vera hadn't seen her since New York, and remembered that her son had been injured in an air raid. He sat very still on the couch, his head cocked at an odd angle.

Arnold Schoenberg's severe voice cut through her thoughts. "I wrote to my son-in-law, who just arrived in New York by way of Cuba, don't get mixed up in anything political. Don't contradict anyone, don't argue, just keep your head down. And don't talk about what you've seen in Europe. No one wants to talk about that."

Vera turned to him, catching Max's look of alarm before she spoke. "If we remain silent, what will happen to our families and friends left behind? Shall we just watch them perish while we drink champagne?"

Schoenberg's large nostrils flared. "That's not what I meant."

"What did you mean then?"

"What I think he means is that Americans don't debate the way we do, about politics and such, and it could create unnecessary tension in certain situations, for example, at the studio." Max paused, looking over at Michel for encouragement. "At the studio, we do not discuss the political situation in Europe, no matter how dire it seems. It's simply not done."

"I see," Vera said, the heat crawling up her neck, but she didn't see, and felt betrayed by the way Max always sought to smooth things over.

During dinner, she stepped out onto the veranda and inhaled the sea air, feeling the weight of the evening lessen slightly. It was good to be alone. She stared at the long strip of highway running beneath the bluffs, headlights beaming forward, hurtling into the night. A cool breeze brushed over her face.

She wished she could fold away her worry about the broken armistice, reminding herself that they were lucky compared to many other refugees who suffered much worse.

Through the French doors, she saw them all sitting around the dining room table, constantly reminding one another of their adaptability and happiness, spooning goulash into their mouths, her husband among them, while Europe burned. Part of her yearned to join them, to feel that temporary warm glow that held fear and doubt at bay, if only for a little while, but something within her wouldn't allow it. She watched them half longingly through the glass. They were only trying to enjoy themselves, to make the most of things. To live.

She crushed her cigarette into the balustrade. The moon her only light, the dampness of the ocean crept over her while they toasted, sherry glasses raised, faces flushed, laughing at a joke, Max loosening his tie, settling into the convivial glow, free from the weight of her thoughts, the oppressive stream of which he could hear just by looking at her. Even Renee was laughing now, with her arm wrapped around her son, whose eyes fluttered closed.

And here I am, alone with the night, Vera thought. Time shuffled forward and back; her disorderly mind left her unable to control which memory arose when. A cerebral land mine.

The glow of the moon gave her pause. Did Lucie see the same moon through a farmhouse window while listening to the grim rumble of German troops advancing? Or did she fall asleep to the raspy breath of her puppy, warm fur coiled into the crook of her arm? Did she see her mother in the moon, as some of the children at Gurs had claimed they saw their fathers in its dimpled pale surface?

"Are you all right?" Elsa's voice cut through the dark as she closed the patio door behind her.

Vera kept staring at the moon. "I don't know anything. And I keep envisioning the Germans flooding into Oradour-sur-Glane."

Elsa nodded, pursing her lips.

From inside, Oscar Levant, a student of Schoenberg's, played the first chords of his new concerto, the melodious introduction floating through an open window.

Vera continued, her voice trembling, "And it's so odd to see all the sunbathers on the beach, and the fruit piled high in the supermarkets, and golfers with their clubs sticking out of their cabriolets, and people drinking champagne, as if there isn't a war."

Elsa whispered, "What should we talk about, then? That people are dying? That they're murdering all the Polish Jews while we sit here and sip champagne? It's not that we don't **want** to talk about it. **We can't.**"

Vera wiped her eyes with the back of her hand.

Elsa sighed, her tone softening. "Everyone here has a story to tell. So many stories. If we listened to them all, we would be flooded with sadness." Her eyes flitted over Vera. "Try not to take everything so hard."

A hot embarrassment coursed through her. She knew that she wasn't the only one to leave someone behind, to mourn a country, a city, a daughter. An entire life. She was selfish, clinging to what she didn't have, when everyone else had also lost so much and yet they managed to carry on somehow.

Or at least they were better pretenders.

She watched Elsa return to the well-lit dining room. Immediately, other guests surrounded her as if to close a gap in the air.

How will I even know if she's all right?" Vera said, her voice hoarse, resuming the argument they had started before Salka's party. They undressed, the massive floral bed between them. "As we speak, the Germans are most likely occupying Oradour," she added, her head buzzing from too many Kir Royales.

Max faced her, his shirt unbuttoned, revealing his wooly gray chest the color of steel. "Just stop. Stop torturing yourself." He motioned to her nightstand, where Vera kept the letters. About every four months a letter from Agnes arrived. It once took six months, which was agony.

"There hasn't been a letter in months. Who knows what the situation is like now?" Vera snapped. She thought back on the last letter from July: a sketch of Lucie, bow in her hair, a frilly collar. Agnes wrote about apple picking, butter churning, that summer had arrived early, L. finding a dead finch under her windowsill, the mare about to give birth. **Lucie named our new wobbly colt Vivi, after you.**

Vera's tears fell onto the navy ink, blurring it.

Vera also sent letters to Agnes, unsure how many were getting through, if any, and she was also careful not to reveal too much, just enough to paint a picture of their life here, for Lucie to understand.

"What I mean is, we are free and Lucie is safe, and soon we'll be together again." The strain of the evening was evident on Max's face, despite his tan.

"The Germans are flooding into France. How are you so calm?" Her voice jumped at the end of the question, but she tried to keep it level, imagining Pauline and Conrad inadvertently listening in on their argument through the open windows.

Max hung his shirt on a satin hanger. "The precise wording of the article was that the Germans 'did not appear to have made any gesture toward complete occupation.'"

"They have occupied the entire south. That means **complete occupation**," Vera said, tugging on each finger of her silk glove before pulling off the whole thing.

Sitting on the edge of the bed, Max unlaced one shoe and replied that of course the news was troubling, but the French people were not in support of the Nazis, not at all, and this was important to keep in mind. "In Lyon, the entire street emptied so no German would feel he had been 'welcomed' by the local population," he added.

She unclasped her necklace, the pearls spooling heavily into her palm. "So, the expectation is that the French will not cooperate. Is that it?" Transferring the pearls into her other hand, Vera added, "You know as well as I do what happens to people in wartime. They would steal food from a hungry child, a wife would sell her body for a few drops of petrol, they'd even sell their own grandmothers." She replaced the pearls in the velvet-lined box on the dresser, recalling what the French police had told her in Nîmes. "You really believe that those petty French farmers will sacrifice more than they have to? Or the shopkeepers who used to cheat us, and the waiters who always recommended the most expensive wine on the menu, thinking to themselves, **They are Jews, let them pay!** Will they risk their lives for the Jews? Of course not."

Now she was yelling. She couldn't stop, even though the windows were wide open.

Max stared at her gravely and then went over to close the windows. "I didn't realize you held such a low opinion of . . ." He paused. "Of people. French people."

Vera unzipped her evening dress, letting the silky folds fall away from her shoulders. **The war did this,** she wanted to say. **It changed me.**

Overnight, they had become hunted pariahs, outsiders to their own lives.

She still felt a pang, remembering when they left Paris for Sanary-sur-Mer in the middle of May while the Nazis swept across Europe: Denmark, Norway,

Belgium, Holland. Following each surrender, Max and Vera braced for when the Germans would reach Paris.

When they left their apartment, no one had helped them; no one asked where they were going. From her third-floor window, Madame Allard silently watched Vera and Max lug their suitcases into the courtyard. And the concierge, with feigned interest, wondered why they were leaving so soon for summer holidays, when he probably already was imagining what valuables they had hastily left behind that he could filch. When he adjusted the gas meter in their apartment, or stopped a leak under the kitchen sink, his eyes would rove, lingering over the crystal vases, the Persian rugs, the grand piano, and the antique violins hung up on the wall of Max's office, the surroundings no doubt confirming his belief about Jews and their wealth.

Compared to many people they knew, Vera was aware, they had been smiled upon by Fortuna herself. Trying to lighten the moment, she remarked that Thomas Mann had managed to keep all six of his children so close he could swat them whenever he wished. She'd seen him routinely order Klaus under the dining room table when he disobeyed his father, treating the boy like a dog. "How unfair, that this man, who doesn't even like his children, sees them every day, while we're separated by oceans and continents."

Max leaned on his side, regarding her from the bed.

She only wore a slip now.

"What are you smiling at?" she said, putting her hands on her hips.

"You're beautiful. Ungodly beautiful. Say I'm not lucky, but I'm the luckiest man alive."

She sighed and went over to him, straddling him on the bed. He still had all his clothes on, his fingers interlaced behind his head. "Everything will be all right." He smiled faintly. "I promise."

"You always say that."

"But so far, we've managed to make a real life here. And Lucie is safe."

"Yes, but . . ."

He drew her into him, the sharp hurt of the evening softening a little. She gazed down at him.

"I'm sorry," she whispered, and then burrowed her face into his neck, breathing in his warm skin, her weight sinking into his weight. His hands spread over the small of her back, holding her in place, and a sweet, distant memory resurfaced: she was twenty-two again, honeymooning on the Venetian Lido with him. They sprawled over the fine warm sand, their bodies beaded in salt water. She held up a book as the only shade, the sound of seagulls and melodious Italian overlaying her thoughts. In the afternoons, a small plane from Bolzano ferried baskets of wild Alpine strawberries to the Lido, which they ate by the handful, the pink juice streaming down their wrists.

The next morning, Vera woke with a start, and for a moment she glanced around, the surroundings blurred, before the paisley wallpaper reminded her this was Santa Monica, not Sanary, even though shadows from the trees played across the ceiling in the same pattern, with the familiar scent of orange blossoms bullying into the room. Her temples pounded from a hangover, and then she recalled having sex with Max, the blackout curtains drawn so tightly she could barely see him. He fell asleep quickly afterward, and Vera, her eyes adjusted to the dark, had stared down at her naked body splayed out on the bedspread, the side of her foot pressed up against Max's warm, motionless leg.

She now listened to him puttering around in the kitchen, and she anticipated the rich aroma of coffee that filled the house on Sundays. The maid, Hilde, was off today, so it would just be the two of them.

As she turned onto her side, a dream resurfaced. They moved through the floors of their Paris apartment in the birdcage elevator, all the way up to the top, Lucie clenching her hand more tightly during the surging acceleration before the elevator dropped down again and leveled, allowing them to exit. When they stepped into the foyer, her blurry image reflected back at her in the cloudy mirror, a wedding gift from her father that she had always found too ornate. She couldn't see Lucie in the mirror, but she knew that Lucie was there from the feeling of Lucie's hand in hers, slightly sweaty and warm, her grip slowly loosening as the elevator exhaled a mechanical sigh and clanged back down through the floors.

Vera went downstairs, tightening the sash of her silk robe.

Max sat in the dull light coming through the diamond-paned window. He had parts of the Sunday paper scattered over the breakfast table, and leaned over a section, his hand roving through his hair, as if trying to locate something in that mass of graying black.

Pausing on the threshold, she felt the days folding in on themselves, their length shortening little by little with winter's approach. A photograph of grinning RAF members, caps jauntily tipped at an angle, thumbs up, posing on a runway, with the headline "London Elated by Triumph; Axis Tasting Punishment!" caught her attention. Another headline proclaimed that the Japanese population had been evacuated from the entire Western Seaboard, followed by multiple exclamation points.

"Good morning," she said, leaning against the stove.

Max glanced up from the paper, his eyes uneasy.

Already, he had smoked a pack of cigarettes. She could tell from all the butts littering the ashtray.

He kept raking his hand through his hair.

"Things don't look good," he blurted out.

Her pulse quickened. "What happened?"

He flicked his index finger against an article buried in the back pages. "France issued a new decree that all Jews must wear the yellow star. It has been in effect since May 29th."

The china-blue walls and the ticking clock felt oppressively tranquil. Her stomach clenched, and she pressed her lower back into the knobs of the stove. "Even children?"

Max took off his spectacles. "I don't know." He started to pull another cigarette from the carton but thought the better of it. "Agnes would never follow such a decree. She would keep Lucie looking the same as always, blending in with the other children, as we discussed."

"Yes, of course," Vera said softly, barely able to get out the words.

He flung the newspaper onto the table and stood up, staring out at the garden. On the grass, fallen avocados had been ripped open by crows. Puckered figs, the color of bruises, nestled within the flat green tree leaves.

Vera came up behind him and wrapped her arms around his middle. He also wore a robe, flannel, and she rested her head against his back, breathing in the lingering scent of sleep. She knew that he worried not only about Lucie, but also about his brother and his parents, and whether they had already been rounded up in Paris, as many other friends and relatives had been.

She whispered into his back, "You must be thinking of Paul."

He turned around, his eyes watering. "He hasn't written since August."

Then he pulled her into his chest, and she listened to his drumming heart.

CHAPTER 14

LUCIE

NOVEMBER 1942,
ORADOUR-SUR-GLANE, FRANCE

Lucie and the other children balanced on wooden crates, peering through the farmhouse windows, the morning crisp and blue. Their breath left white marks on the glass as they watched the German officer survey the inside of the house. Lucie thought the German looked elegant in his olive-green uniform with the little silver cross dangling from the collar. Solange whispered that he was as handsome as a prince, with those golden eyebrows. The other children hissed, "Don't forget he's a kraut!"

They listened to the soldier explain to Agnes's sisters and their husbands, in a loud performative voice, that within the next forty-eight hours various members of his unit would be billeted in the farmhouse. He paused and glanced around at the drafty rooms, with the high vaulted ceilings, as if calculating how many of his men could reasonably fit under the roof. Then he added that their family would live in the two rooms at the back of the house, off the kitchen, where the housemaid currently resided. "You'll have to let the maid go," he added. "There's barely enough space as it is."

Agnes and her sisters nodded, their hands shoved into their apron pockets, their eyes trained on the floor. The men also averted their gazes, and Lucie wondered why they were all so quiet and still. Even Giles, the border collie, sniffed and roved around the room, when normally he would be lying on the rug by the fireplace, his nose buried in his front paws.

Then the officer awkwardly reached into his coat pocket and thrust some wilted wildflowers in the direction of the women.

For a tense moment, it seemed as if no one would accept the flowers, until Agnes's sister Marion stumbled forward and took the bouquet, before making a big show of rushing off to find a vase.

That night after dinner, the sisters lingered in the kitchen, as they often did, while Lucie played marbles with the other children on the rug next to the unlit hearth. The husbands sat nearby, watching the children play. Sometimes Lucie stared at the men, trying to discern what they were thinking beneath the sweaty sheen of their faces, their pronounced knuckles gripping the armrests. When they caught her eye, they would make some quip to lighten the mood, something that Lucie never entirely understood but pretended to because she wanted them to feel happy and to laugh. Then she returned to the reassuring clink of the marbles, only to feel their worried eyes on her.

In the evenings, Agnes lay beside her on the narrow bed and read a few old letters from her parents. This was only allowed at bedtime. During the day, she must remember that the wife of Agnes's cousin in Reims had died, and finding himself a widower, unable to care for his five children, he had sent Lucie to Agnes when the war broke out. She almost started to believe that she had a father in Reims who was a pharmacist, and that her mother had died of throat cancer. It seemed more real than the vague way Agnes talked about her real parents, who had left two years ago. Whenever she pressed for more information—how far away were they, and when were they coming back—Agnes always said that they were not too far away, and they would come for her as soon as the war ended.

"Shall I read the one about the ice cream shop?" she asked in her customary way, rubbing her eyes, which were slightly red and puffy.

Lucie nodded, pulling the quilt up to her chin,

aware of the faint buzz of mosquitoes circling in the unseasonably warm night.

"'My dearest L.: The ice cream here is delicious. There's even an ice cream stand in the shape of a bulldog. You walk into the shop through his open mouth! The children read comics and run barefoot all day. Chewing gum is also very popular. Many children, and some adults, eat with their mouths wide open! It's quite funny, as you know how much Papa hates bad manners. Sometimes when we're out at a restaurant, he can't stop himself from staring at someone across the way with her mouth hanging open full of food. I tell him to just ignore it, but he really can't stop himself!'"

Agnes and Lucie laughed, and then she nestled closer to Agnes. "There are restaurants where they are? And children?"

"Oh, yes." Agnes sighed. "It seems so."

"Do you think they went back to the house on the sea? Near the beach?"

"I don't know," Agnes said, furrowing her brow. "It doesn't say."

Lucie inhaled her lavender-scented blouse, which made her head heavy. Agnes read on about a caramel-colored cat that visited in the evenings for milk. Then some cursory questions for Agnes about Lucie's health, and if she was able to get any schooling at all, inquiries that Agnes glided over, her soft voice a stream over rocks.

As she descended into sleep, Agnes's intonations

melded into her mother's voice. During the day, Lucie couldn't recall her mother's voice, and even had trouble remembering her face unless she took out the photograph: her mother standing in front of a spouting fountain on a gravel path, her hand resting on a giant pram, where Lucie slept, apparently swaddled in muslin, according to Agnes, who also said that Lucie only slept when wheeled around the Tuileries Garden and howled the moment the carriage stopped. Her mother wore a cloche hat, so it was difficult to see her hair, but it was bobbed. Her face was blurry beneath the rim of the hat, but Lucie could make out her defined cheekbones and lively eyes looking at the camera with incredulity, as if having a baby was the rarest of gifts.

The following morning, Lucie woke up alone, but she could tell that Agnes had slept with her all night from the bed's disarray. Agnes only did this when Lucie had a fever. She touched her forehead. It felt cool.

Downstairs, at the long oak table, it seemed as if all the sisters and their children had evaporated. Only Agnes sat there, waiting for Lucie with some bread and jam and tea spread out on the table.

She motioned for her to sit and eat.

Lucie sat down, suddenly uneasy. She stared imploringly at Agnes, who wouldn't meet her gaze.

Instead she fiddled with her watch, saying that it was broken again. "Silly old thing," she repeated.

Lucie tried to eat, but the bread and jam moved around tastelessly in her mouth, as if she were chewing up paper. Then she noticed her suitcase standing in the doorway and her heart accelerated. She leaned forward, and asked in a low whisper, "Are we going to meet Mama and Papa in the place with the bulldog ice cream shop?"

Agnes smiled tightly. But then she stopped trying to smile, the depressions under her eyes more pronounced, as if she'd barely slept. "I'm afraid not."

She put down her watch on the table, as if to restrain herself from playing with it. "We've decided it would be best if you lived with the Sisters of St. Denis until the war ends."

"When will the war end?"

She stroked the top of Lucie's hand. "Hopefully not too long from now."

"Are the Germans going to take me away? With the rest of them?"

Agnes clenched Lucie's hand. "Who told you that?"

Lucie instantly knew she had made a fatal error, repeating Thomas's comment. He had fisted her dark curls and pulled hard while telling her that the Germans were coming for her. The other children stared at her with renewed interest. He was the eldest boy and seemed to know things.

When he let go, she punched him in the neck and he yelped like a kicked dog.

Lucie focused on the porcelain plate before her, on the little blue flowers circling the rim, on the jam smeared over the hard bread.

"Who said this to you?" Agnes repeated, calmly now.

"Anyone," Lucie said, her face reddening.

"No one," Agnes corrected her.

"No one," Lucie repeated, upset that she had used the wrong word, which happened when she got nervous.

Agnes sighed and held her hand. It felt uncharacteristically sweaty, not the cool, dry one Lucie had expected.

In the car, she hugged her doll to her chest, the only thing Agnes had allowed her to take. None of the letters or even the photograph of her mother was allowed. Agnes explained that she would keep it all for her at the farm, so that the letters and photograph would not get lost or damaged, but Lucie felt unconvinced.

Through the car window, the leaden sky promised a storm. The dog Giles barked furiously from behind the fence where the cows and pigs were corralled. He kept clawing at it, trying to leap over, and a few times he nearly made it. Someone yelled at him in the distance from the stables. Lucie wanted so much to run out of the car and fling her arms around his neck, feeling his warm bristling fur, but she knew this was impossible.

Agnes pulled on her leather gloves with finality and started the car. Watching the farmhouse recede into the grayish sky, flanked by fields of lavender, Lucie felt a strangeness settle over her. No one had said goodbye, as if the stones of the house had buried the rest of the family, even though it was a normal Saturday.

She looked anxiously at Agnes. "Will you visit me?"

Agnes checked the rearview mirror. "Of course."

"When will you visit?"

"Oh, as soon as I can." A heavy pause hung between them.

Agnes kept looking into the rearview mirror.

The road curved around a field of sunflowers stretching toward the sky. The bright petals and wooly brown middle made Lucie want to roll down the window, but she restrained herself. Inside the car, the air felt dense and secretive, and Agnes seemed to want it this way.

About an hour later, Lucie jerked awake, looking out the window at the rolling hills in the distance and the dense green bushes along the road, the quaint houses spaced far apart from one another. Agnes pulled onto a smaller road, shaded by overgrown trees, with branches that stretched overhead, as if they were trying to touch, a shadowy tunnel of leaves.

Up ahead, the church's steeple punctured the sky. "Are we here?"

Agnes nodded.

Clutching Agnes's hand, Lucie stared at the spherical hedges lining the path leading to a sky blue door embedded in the convent's archway. Agnes tugged her along, her jaw tensing. But before she even rang the bell, the heavy door swung open and two nuns flew out. Long black gowns covered their shoes, lending them the appearance of levitation. Lucie stared up at their white habits, as if dove wings sluiced through the air on either side of their heads.

They were Sister Helene and Sister Ismerie, but Lucie quickly forgot who was who and only noted that one nun was slimmer and younger. They smelled of wet wool and Marie-Rose talc.

The Sisters seemed quite pleased that Lucie had arrived at this point in the school year, as this would give her time to adjust to her new surroundings before the Christmas holiday. They made quite a fuss over this, as if such timeliness was something to celebrate, whereas a dull panic had begun to spread through Lucie. When would she see Agnes again? How long would she stay here? And who were these other pupils, as the nuns kept calling them, and what were they like?

Agnes knelt down, gazing at her.

One of the nuns rested a hand on Lucie's head.

She wanted to shake it off.

"Don't be afraid," Agnes whispered. "It's better here." Steadying herself, she let her hand graze the purplish gravel lining the circular driveway. Lucie wanted to ask if she had done something wrong at the farm, if Agnes's sisters hated her for some unnamable reason, which she knew they did.

Agnes smoothed down her hair, and smiled because of course it had already tangled despite how carefully she had brushed it out the night before. Then she kissed Lucie on the forehead, a dry quick kiss, as if she were only strolling out for a quarter of an hour, implying none of the urgency and importance that the nuns placed on her departure.

Sister Helene carried her suitcase and Sister Ismerie spoke in hushed tones to Sister Helene as Lucie tried to keep up with their swift pace, straining to hear their conversation.

"She's baptized at least," Sister Helene said, glancing hopefully at Lucie. "Perhaps she even knows her catechism. The governess explained that the parents have been missing for two years, and the situation in Oradour has recently become quite . . ." Sister Helene hesitated. "Untenable."

"Yes, well, with the broken armistice, we must take every precaution." Sister Ismerie gave Lucie a long look. "Show her the dormitory," she added before striding off.

Lucie followed Sister Helene down a long white corridor. Arched windows looked out onto a rose-mary garden encircled by stones. A statue of St. Augustine feeding a tiny bird perched inside his open palm stood near a gurgling fountain. Plaster fell off in chunks from the moisture in the air, the floorboards soft and creaking beneath her feet. At the end of the hall, they reached a large room where Sister Helene said she would sleep with the other girls. Tall narrow windows admitted a syrupy light shimmering with dust motes.

The empty room appeared even gloomier, and Lucie's chest tightened, rejecting everything she saw. There were no freshly cut flowers or dogs roaming about, no one practicing the scales on the piano, no voices arguing or laughing, no calves being born or litter of kittens to fawn over, and if she reached even further back, to when she lived with her parents, other details came to mind that certainly could not be found here: marble sinks with golden faucets, mosaics tiling the entryway, her canopied four-poster bed, the big black car her father drove on Sundays with the top down. She glanced at the rows and rows of perfectly made beds and shivered.

Sister Helene smiled down at her. "Here we are then."

Lucie focused on her youthful face, sprinkled with freckles, and her brown eyes, flecked with green, which seemed to laugh behind a veneer of seriousness. Swallowing hard, Lucie nodded.

Next, Sister Helene took her to Mother Superior's office, which was richly furnished with a velvet chaise longue and even a radio. Sister Ismerie, who Lucie now realized was the Mother Superior, sat behind a large wooden desk and stared at her gravely. Lucie suddenly felt as if she had already done something wrong, and that sharp nervousness returned, the same feeling that made it difficult to find the right words for things. Then Sister Ismerie started talking, and at first, because of the nervousness that rushed into her ears like an ocean, Lucie only heard bits and pieces: she wouldn't be able to wear her old clothes anymore; she would be given a school uniform. "Every day you must wear it." Sister Ismerie's voice pierced through the oceanic rushing, and Lucie regained focus. "And there will be no dolls or toys allowed during the school year, and no thumb sucking either."

Sister Ismerie sighed heavily and shot a despairing look at Sister Helene.

Standing in the middle of the office, Lucie memorized their faces, and noted that Sister Ismerie was older and fatter with deep creases around her mouth and across her forehead, and Sister Helene was slight and fragile-looking. She seemed almost too young to be a nun.

Sister Ismerie said something under her breath and massaged the rosary beads on her desk. Then she fixed Lucie with a disapproving stare, and Lucie remembered to take her thumb out of her mouth, wiping the saliva on her skirt.

"Your new name is Lucie Ladoux. This is what Madame Agnes has instructed. You must forget your old name and your old home. These are the rules now."

Heat flooded Lucie's face and she felt the urge to protest, but then she sensed Sister Helene's quiet fearfulness and Lucie knew better and followed along, just as she had acted on the farm, silently accepting the story that she had left behind her father and siblings in Reims to live with Agnes.

Sister Ismerie touched the gold cross resting on her large bosom, which jutted out like a shelf. Lucie stared at the gold against the black, reminded of one of her mother's evening gowns, Lucie's favorite, because of the gold against the black, its theatricality and specialness always attracting her.

Sister Ismerie rose up from her chair, and she appeared much taller and wider than before, like a blackbird fanning out its wings. "Do you understand what this means?"

"Yes," Lucie said.

Even though everything else had changed, at least she could still keep her real name. Lucie.

That first night at the convent, she fought against the impulse to cry, telling herself that soon Agnes would come for her, and she would see her parents again. Under the thin woolen blanket, she hugged her knees to her chest, trying to get warm. Spidery tree branches tapped against the windowpanes, a cold wetness seeping into the walls. The heavy breathing of the other girls, as they tossed and turned, their errant coughs accompanied by persistent sniffles rushed into the darkness. She tried to ignore it, but the rustling and sighing of the others intensified the longer she lay still.

Lucie pulled the blanket tighter, wishing she could at least have her doll, but the nuns had burned it. She still saw the doll's head crackling in the flames, her yellow hair singeing until it turned to black ash. They thought she didn't see from the hallway, but she had peered around the corner into the kitchen. Sister Helene stood there silently while Sister Ismerie strode around the kitchen energetically explaining that it was for the best; there could be no evidence that they were hiding this child, disobeying Pétain's orders. "We cannot spare one thing," she added, also throwing Lucie's tartan dress, silk underwear, and patent leather shoes, along with some papers and documents, into the fire.

When the nuns emerged from the kitchen, Lucie stared at them, her back pressed against the cool wall.

Sister Helene gave her a sympathetic smile, which Lucie resented, and then handed her a school uniform along with the scratchy white nightgown, which she wore now.

Feeling a light hand on her shoulder, Lucie jerked up in bed. A girl stood there, her flat hair falling around her oval face, her round eyes scrutinizing Lucie.

"Don't worry," the girl whispered. "It's just me."

"Who are you?"

She smiled. "Camille."

Lucie pulled the blanket around her. "That was my doll's name."

Camille perched on the edge of Lucie's cot, hugging herself to stay warm. "They don't allow toys during the schoolyear."

Lucie swallowed down the sharp lump gathering in her throat. "I know. They burned Camille."

"I'm sorry," the girl whispered.

Lucie nodded, tears welling up in her eyes. "They thought I didn't see, but I did see."

Camille touched the side of Lucie's face. "It's not

so bad, once you get used to it here. The last time I saw my parents was Easter."

"Well, I'm leaving soon. Agnes is coming back for me."

Camille nodded, her eyes round and shining. Lifting up the blanket, she shimmied underneath it, her long legs pressing up against Lucie's, generating heat. Propping her head up in her palm, she lay on her side, facing Lucie. "Did you know," she whispered, "that Sister Ismerie makes Sister Helene clean out her chamber pot? Every morning!"

Lucie wrinkled her nose.

"Doesn't that sound beastly?"

"Yes, beastly," Lucie reflected, admiring Camille's light hair, so straight and flat, perfectly parted down the middle. Camille shook her head, burying a muffled laugh into the crook of her arm. Then she took a deep breath. "And did you know," she asked, her breath close and sweet, smelling faintly of chamomile tea, "that Sister Helene, last Christmas, broke the rules because they found a chocolate bar in her cell, under her pillow. She loves sweets. She can't help it."

Camille's silky hair carelessly brushed Lucie's bare shoulder. "What happened to her then?"

"Sister Ismerie ordered her to fast for three days and three nights. She was not even allowed one drop of water." Camille's eyes reflected the stark moonlight filtering in through the elongated windows. "Beastly."

"Yes, beastly," Lucie agreed. After a pause, she asked, "How long have you been here?"

"I just turned nine." Camille paused, calculating in her head. "I've been here for two years."

"Oh," Lucie said. "I'm only six."

Camille rolled over onto her side. "Well, good night then."

She nestled her head into Lucie's pillow, pulling the blanket up to her ear, her eyes slowly closing.

Lucie whispered, "Good night."

CHAPTER 15

VERA

NOVEMBER 1942,
SANTA MONICA, CALIFORNIA

Two weeks later, on a Saturday afternoon, Max suggested they take a drive. The setting sun cast a wintry orange light over the hillside. As they drove down the winding road to the highway, Vera took in the unruly cacti, dirt with flashes of green, interspersed with magenta bougainvillea that she found overly sensual, lush and loud. The straight blue line of sea framed Max's profile. Now on the highway, he accelerated and the sudden speed rushed through her. A few clouds, tinged with gold as if a flame flickered within their dense interiors, caught her attention. Only here, Vera thought, were clouds inflamed.

"Have you met any nice women at the EFF?"

She recognized that tone, a gentle, prodding insistence that emerged when he wanted her to do something she disliked, such as play golf with him, or take up bridge. These days, he wanted her to make more "woman friends," as he called them. She knew he worried about her, immobilized at her desk, flooded with thoughts of Lucie in France, and when Europe would be liberated, as if Roosevelt himself had hired her as a war strategist.

Filtering through the radio, Vera Lynn's silky voice interrupted her thoughts, singing that horrid song "Lili Marlene."

"There's a nice Dutch woman, Afke," she offered half-heartedly. "Her desk is next to mine. She used to be the first violinist in the Amsterdam Sinfonietta, but now, of course . . ." She leaned forward and angrily switched off the radio.

"What have you got against Vera Lynn?"

"I can't stand all these romantic war songs. It's not how it really is. For anyone."

"No, of course not." He slowed a bit. "But sometimes people need to listen to music for enjoyment. For pleasure." He said "pleasure" as if she withheld it from him.

She flashed him a look.

"Take, for instance, the troops. Do you think they would want to listen to Schoenberg's dissonant notes, like nails screeching over a chalkboard? Or Vera Lynn?"

Staring out the window, she crossed her arms over her chest.

"Fine, then," he said. "We'll stick to Mozart."

They ended up going to the pictures that night. Before the film, a newsreel played, showing a hulking US tank rumbling through the North African desert, leaving dead German soldiers in its wake, faces slack against a blanket of sand. In the next frame, Italian soldiers begged to join the Allies, the camera panning their soulful faces. US infantrymen marched along dusty roads, brandishing the American flag, as a stiff male voice recounted American victory after American victory in Algiers. Max ate his popcorn loudly, relishing the butter and salt, shaking the bag every so often, something he never would have done in France. In fact, he never even ate popcorn in France. But no one noticed, as they were all eating loudly too.

Shifting in the velour seat, Elsa's **We can't** circled through her mind. It was the same reason why they didn't show any footage of the Himmler program liquidating the Jewish population of Poland, in particular all the elderly, children, infants, and cripples. They didn't show the sealed freight cars packed with people, or that when the cars arrived at the camps, half of the passengers were already dead from the chlorine and lime previously sprinkled on the floor.

Vera had read this in the **New York Times**, buried as a special cable toward the back of the paper, buried, it seemed, to everyone but her. Suddenly chilled, she realized that she'd been sweating all through the newsreel, sweating even now as Judy Garland played the piano and sang, with Gene Kelly by her side, about love.

When they got home, there was a letter from Agnes, postmarked in August four months earlier, before the broken armistice. Somehow it had gotten through, even though all mail between the United States and France was now suspended. Vera felt unsettled after reading it, putting down the letter and picking it up again, only to revisit the same words: **It's been a fine summer, filled with long peaceful days . . . We captured butterflies and then let them go again. We made wreaths out of wildflowers. Lucie looked just like a princess.** It wasn't like Agnes to sound so whimsical, to mention nothing of schooling or health or other practicalities. The letter, Vera decided, was intentionally blithe, masking something worse.

Vera wanted to talk about it, but Max was suddenly preoccupied with his own concerns, locking himself away in his study late into the night, cigarette smoke floating up from under the door, the sound of the piano vibrating through the wall.

Standing on the other side of the door, Vera knew

he was composing a piece of symphonic music, which was his specialty, but the work was arduous and exacting, as each piece of music was set to a specific scene, as well as a specific piece of film.

Cradling a glass of red wine in her palm, she knocked anyway.

When he opened up, she told him about the syntax of Agnes's last letter, and he accused her of pouncing on a vague sense of unease with the aim of nursing it into a crisis, which she then would implore him to fix when there was nothing to fix.

"I don't have the energy for imaginary problems," he said, pressing a tumbler filled with ice and whiskey to his temple.

"How do you know this isn't real?"

"I don't. That's the problem," he said before closing her out of the room.

She fumed on the other side of the door, and then threw the glass of wine against it.

He didn't open up.

She felt nothing after throwing the glass. The scattered shards bathed in wine were only a mess. Kneeling down with a tea towel, she picked up the pieces one by one and threw them into the bin.

CHAPTER 16

SASHA

AUGUST 1943, TROINA, SICILY

After a month of fighting in the unrelenting heat, the hot dry air stinging their eyes, the hillsides full of stones, cacti, wandering donkeys, and camouflaged panzers, they captured the strategic hilltop town of Troina, sending the Germans into retreat.

Troina was theirs for a few precious days, the respite as glorious as biting into a ripe fig, or taking that first sip of red wine in the shade of a bombed-out church. Old men and women brought over fruit, pasta, and flowers, and cursed Mussolini, spitting into the dust. In part, it was a show; only recently these same villagers had praised Il Duce, performing the Hitler salute for their invaders, but then again, Sasha knew it was human nature to survive, to want to live. And their joy at the American arrival felt real, as warm and melodious as the Italian language that softened the atmosphere, tinting everything with beauty. It reminded Sasha of how a cameraman once explained the trick of putting silk stockings over the camera lens to diffuse the light into a gentler, more appealing image.

When they set up camp, schoolchildren watched them from a distance, but then slowly, they gathered around Sasha and his buddies, who flashed their big American smiles. The children came closer, lightly touching their sleeves and their steel helmets that rested on the ground. One girl traced the red-and-green badge on Sasha's uniform with her pinky finger.

This country was too beautiful, too abundant, for war. Breathing in the scent of alfalfa and jasmine from the surrounding orchards confused him, made him feel as if he'd waded into some thwarted dream instead of taking over evacuated enemy territory. After ambushing seven Germans inside a stone barn, they walked back out and looked up to find plump green grapes hanging down from a wooden trellis. Sweet dusty juice filled their dry mouths, while at the same time, Sasha was acutely aware of all that fresh death on the other side of the wall.

Afterward, they went through the dead Germans'

backpacks for reconnaissance purposes. In one pack, wedged between the pages of a journal, a guy in his unit, Nick Lambert, also from Los Angeles, found letters from the kid's mother asking him to send her shoelaces from Italy. Nick had studied German in college, and apparently Düsseldorf was out of shoelaces. The guys from Intelligence had trained them to hand over the smallest of details; for example, if the factories that manufactured shoelaces no longer operated, it could mean that other industrial branches in Germany might be stalled.

Still, confronted with the fact that this German kid had a mother somewhere, writing to him, expecting shoelaces, expecting him home alive, gave Sasha the shivers every time he sat down to write a letter to his own mother on V-mail stationery. He kept it light and brief, as they were instructed to do. He wrote that the vino wasn't half bad, the mosquitoes so bloodthirsty he slept with a net over his face inside the pup tent. He signed off: **I'm getting all your letters. Hope you're getting mine . . . Love, Sasha.**

He also kept a notebook for ideas and details he didn't want to forget, like the German mother who wanted shoelaces, or the American deserter who had been caught pretending he was an Italian POW, only to get thrown back into combat and killed the next day, or the way a woman silently watched him from a doorway, her son's arm in a cast. The kid incessantly tugged on her skirt, asking for something, but she kept watching Sasha and the other troops, her eyes dark, distrustful.

There were other things he wished he could forget, plaguing his dreams, things he couldn't bring himself to write down for fear that, once committed to paper, the images would never go away, a gruesome looping merry-go-round burning a hole through his head. The senseless brutality he witnessed every day, the sheer scale of it, was worse than any crime scene he'd reported on, and for the first time, he found himself wordless, all language melting away.

The shock of what he'd seen could flatten his mind into a numb, humming blankness, and once, when he was in this state, he chanced upon a schoolroom, the doors flung open because of the heat. He stopped, watching the kids hunched over their desks, writing. The teacher leaned over a thick book propped up on the lectern, mumbling out phrases in Italian, pressing his finger into the page to keep his place.

Sasha's chest went tight with something he couldn't at first identify, but the way the man hunched over the book, his long beard skimming the pages, hurtled Sasha back to the drafty yeshiva basement on Rivington Street, the teacher intoning that today they would review the fifth book of holiness in the **Kedushah**, the Issurei Biah: forbidden sexual relations. Sasha and the others stirred with nervous excitement. The teacher explained that the outlandish coupling between members of the same sex, between a man and an animal, between a man and his stepmother, and so on, were strictly forbidden. Sasha's sides hurt from suppressing his laughter, and Zundel looked as if he were hyperventilating—he kept gulping down air—while another kid nearly fell off the bench trying to contain his laughter. The teacher continued, "But the most common sin is adultery. If a child is born out of an adulterous union, especially if the woman is already married, such a child is a **mamzer**, and the curse of this sin will last for ten generations, forbidding the **mamzer** and his offspring from entry into the congregation of the Lord." Sasha stared at the yellowed pages of his prayer book, at his bitten-down fingernails, at the scarred wooden table, to mask how naked he felt, stripped of every shred of clothing, as though the teacher were speaking about him in front of the entire class, pointing to various parts of his anatomy in a sarcastic, knowing manner.

Sasha hunched over, shivering in the dry hot air, and opened his eyes to Nick's mouth, too close to his face, saying, "Hey, you okay, buddy? Here—" He took out his canteen. "Drink some water. You look dehydrated."

Sasha rubbed his forehead, feeling slightly sick, but he couldn't help remembering that after the incident, he ran home in such a blind confusion that he knocked into an apple cart, overturning it, the peddler swearing, unable to erase the word from his mind, unable to stop thinking about the first time he'd heard it, back in the old country, just before they left for America. He was about six, and through the wall, he heard Aunt Raisa thank God that Leah and Sasha were finally leaving because their house would be tainted, cursed, if anyone ever found out that a **mamzer** lived under their roof. Uncle Isaac retorted that she couldn't blame a little boy for the sins of the past, and when she challenged him, he nearly shouted: "**Do not wag that evil tongue of yours!**" Sasha froze against the wall, holding his breath, his face hot, knowing that the dirty word she had used was meant to describe him. Something he had done wrong. Something inherently corrupted.

"Better?" Nick asked, his eyes searching Sasha's face.

"Yeah, thanks," Sasha said, wiping his mouth with the back of his hand.

"We should get back to base. Come with me?"

Sasha nodded, and they walked together, not saying much, the dusty streets eerily silent.

After Troina, they moved on to Palermo, for two last days of R&R before hitting mainland Italy. Young partisans mobbed the cobblestone streets, roaring with pleasure when the sight of their American green tanks with the white star came into view. They could barely drive forward with the cheering crowd pressing on all sides. A kid even jumped on the back of the jeep, hanging onto the spare tire, shaking his tiny victorious fist in the air. From balconies, women threw garlands of flowers, the white gardenia petals raining down on their helmets like snow. Young men ran alongside the jeep, clasping Sasha's hand in both of theirs.

He refilled his C rations, got new socks and to-bacco, and wished he could smoke at least one good Havana cigar. Sitting on the cool church steps, he peeled some oranges from a grocer who had insisted on giving them away for free. An animated back-and-forth ensued between them until Sasha relented; he saw how badly the man wanted to give him the oranges, and that there was power in benevolence, even if it amounted to gifts from a modest fruit stall swarmed by flies off the main square. Even if it amounted to Sasha and his outfit tossing chocolate bars and Spam into a crowd of children as they motored past the pinched, hungry faces.

On their last night in Palermo, the army organized a USO show. They all felt jittery, knowing that at dawn they would lead an assault on the mainland to secure Naples, a German stronghold. Shoulder to shoulder, they packed in front of the makeshift stage with a single upright piano and a microphone stand. Sasha joked that at least they'd see Marlene

Dietrich's legs before biting the dust tomorrow. A few guys laughed, but their sunburnt faces seemed ashen and drawn.

First, Al Jolson performed "My Mammy," a song about traveling a thousand steps just to see your mother's face. A thin guy accompanied on the piano, his fingers flying over the keys. Jolson outstretched his arms, and sang as if this were his last show, his face upturned to the sky when he held the high notes. Everyone clapped and cheered, and brotherly emotion surged through the crowd, as well as a shared homesickness, nerves collectively sharpening at the prospect of what tomorrow would bring. Sasha swallowed hard, not wanting to think about it, not wanting to think about anything other than this moment.

The master of ceremonies then introduced Anna Lee. They had expected Dietrich, but when they saw Lee walk onto the stage in a long columnar dress the color of midnight, Sasha forgot all about Dietrich. She apologized because she couldn't sing or dance. "Oh, this is embarrassing, isn't it?" she asked in a quivering voice, but they just smiled stupidly, filled with silent admiration, until someone shouted from the crowd, "We love you, Anna Lee!" and she laughed, shaking her head, and the sight of her laughing made them all start clapping until she cupped the microphone and sang, in a low, uneven voice, "When the Lights Go on Again All Over the World."

After the show, Sasha snuck backstage and found her dressing room door ajar. She sat before the vanity mirror, an army blanket wrapped around her shoulders, shivering slightly in the damp room while applying more blush to her cheeks and sipping a thimble of brandy. In the mirror, he assessed her cool patrician beauty before rapping on the door.

"Yes?" she asked, startled.

"Miss Lee," he said, growing self-conscious of his unshaven face and dirty fatigues, "I was wondering if you'd be willing to take a message for me back home."

She shook her head, her dangling earrings swinging gently, and said she couldn't possibly. So many soldiers had asked her to ring their mothers, their girlfriends, their little sisters back home; if she said yes to one, she'd have to say yes to all.

He explained it wasn't a message to his mother or anything like that. It was just one word, for Charlie Friedman.

Her penciled eyebrows pinched together. "My agent?"

"He's also my agent."

She gave him a disbelieving smile

"I'm a writer." Just mentioning Charlie and work

made him feel close to that life again, the electrifying staccato punch of those keys and the rewarding **bing** at the start of a new line.

She asked if he'd written anything she'd heard of, and he mentioned **Cyclone**, which Charlie had finally sold to Paramount last year. George Stevens had directed it, and given the strong anti-German theme, the film had done great. Ironic, Sasha thought, how from one day to the next, a script was either "clannish" propaganda or a great story to fight the Nazi menace, as **Variety** claimed in a review.

Her easy, lighthearted laughter filled the room, and she poured him some brandy before raising her glass to his. "All right, so what's this message?"

"Cigars," Sasha said after taking a long sip, the brandy warming his insides.

"That's it? No name?"

"He'll know who I am."

"Okay, soldier," she said, her eyes softening. "Whatever you say."

CHAPTER 17

LUCIE

JANUARY 1944, ST. DENIS CONVENT, SOUTHWESTERN FRANCE

Lucie copied down the Latin conjugations written in slanted cursive from the blackboard. When she glanced out the window for a moment, the raw icy sky made her shiver in her seat, the gray so dense her head felt even heavier this morning, especially after last night's air raid. In the middle of the night, they had filed out of the dormitory and crossed the courtyard, their nostrils tingling from the smell of burnt wood, before descending into that cold, dank shelter, where they squatted on dirty canvas mattresses. With a heavy wool blanket around her neck, Sister Ismerie explained that they had to stay here until the bombing stopped, but even she flinched at every blast, half hunched over, her face waxen.

When dawn approached, everyone sighed with

relief, thinking it was almost time to return to the dormitory, when a shell exploded right next to the shelter. Smoke funneled in through the cracks, and it felt as though the ground beneath Lucie's feet shook and broke apart. She cried out, grabbing Camille's arm, thinking that any minute they would fall into a harrowing dark pit.

Sister Margot now pointed to each conjugation with her long wooden stick, its tap-tap-tap running through Lucie's head like music, the monotony of it almost lulling her into believing that last night belonged to a bad dream.

Next to her, Camille gave her a secret smile because they both were waiting for Sister Margot to lose her train of thought, as she often did, with those spectacles that continually slid down her elongated nose, and her watery brown eyes that squinted out at the rows of girls, searching for the answer to a question she had already forgotten.

"Now," she resumed after a prolonged pause, "who can tell me which one of these is the infinitive future of '**religare**,' meaning 'to bind fast, to moor'?"

Lucie's hand shot up first, ready with the answer: "**religaturum esse.**"

Sister Margot sighed. "Perhaps, Lucie, we should give someone else a chance today."

At the tail end of her sentence, the door swung open and a German soldier strode into the classroom, followed by Sister Ismerie, her eyes combing through the rows before settling on Lucie. She tried to say something about the **Feldkommandantur**'s visit, but the soldier's right arm shot out, as straight as a rod, and he barked, "**Heil Hitler.**"

Sister Margot hesitated, throwing an uncertain glance at Sister Ismerie, before she repeated "**Heil Hitler.**"

The soldier began pacing the length of the room. He paused, scanning the faces of the girls, all of whom sat straight up in their seats, hands folded neatly on their desks.

"As you can see, we only have French students here, from good families," Sister Ismerie said, motioning to the class. "Their education has remained uninterrupted, as we have managed to remain entirely disconnected from the war, and from—"

He gestured sharply for Sister Ismerie to stop talking and walked in between the rows, surveying each student.

Sister Ismerie stared desperately out at the leafless trees.

He stopped next to Lucie's desk.

Sweat trickled down her sides, the back of her neck prickling with heat. His cedarwood scent filled her nostrils. This was the moment she had been trained for, the moment when she must recite her name, age, and origin without a hint of hesitation. "You cannot show one ounce of doubt," Sister Ismerie had coached her. "Otherwise, like an animal, they will smell it. And once they sense something amiss, only God can help you."

Those words thundered through her now. She sat so still, she almost stopped breathing.

He stared down at Camille's desk and jerked up her chin with his black-gloved hand, forcing her to meet his gaze. "What is your name? Age?"

"My name is Camille Bonheur. I am eleven years old."

"Where are your parents?"

She swallowed hard, her cheeks inflamed. "They run a cattle farm in Normandy."

Lucie knew this was Camille's story, the one she had to practice, because her parents were fighting in the Resistance, a fact that had circulated among the pupils in hushed admiring tones. No one knew Lucie's real story, that her parents had left her with Agnes and she had lived on a farm for two years before coming here. Because she was a Jew. No one knew except for Sister Helene and Sister Ismerie. If she told anyone, then the Germans would surely come for her. This is what Sister Ismerie had drilled into her from the very start. But she couldn't help it. She had told Camille the truth, and Camille only hugged her afterward. Then they pricked their fingertips with a safety pin and mashed them together, and Camille announced that now, they were sisters. Blood sisters. "Anything that happens to you happens to me," she had said gravely.

The soldier let go of Camille's chin. "Why are you so far away from your family?"

"This is where my mother is from, originally, and they wanted me to have a good Catholic education."

Unsatisfied, he moved on down the row.

Lucie wanted to give Camille an encouraging smile, because she had done well, but no one moved. She forced herself to stare at the flaxen braids of the girl seated in front of her. If asked, she could feel the words on the tip of her tongue: her name was Lucie Ladoux, she was from Paris, her parents had an antique shop on Rue de Rivoli, and she had four older brothers.

But she didn't have to say it because after a few more minutes, the soldier walked out with Sister Ismerie, leaving them all in stunned silence.

Sister Margot shuffled around some papers on her desk, muttering nervously to herself. Then she finally looked up, squinted out at them, and said, "Take out your lesson books. It's time for dictation."

After this, Sister Ismerie grew much stricter about Lucie and Camille retreating to their hiding place, even when there didn't seem to be a threat. Just the sound of the front bell, with its piercing aggressive ring, prompted Lucie and Camille to run into the padded alcove behind Sister Ismerie's bed and close the little door behind them.

A few weeks later, after the bell rang, they were

sure the German had returned with that gruff voice and heavy footfall from what they could hear in the alcove. And it wasn't just him. They heard at least two others speaking German. Clutching Lucie in the darkness, Camille whispered, "He's come back for me."

"Don't worry," Lucie whispered. "They'll never think to look behind Sister Ismerie's bed. Who would ever want to get that close to her!"

Everyone joked about how unattractive Sister Ismerie was, with her broad shiny forehead and awkward gait, her hands as big as a man's. But in that moment, Lucie saw that Camille couldn't laugh. She only gripped the hay sprinkling the floor, convinced she was going to die.

Lucie held her close. "Think of something else."

"I can't."

Lucie started to tell Camille a story, about how a magical fairy cast a golden net over the convent whenever danger neared, protecting them. "The net makes the convent invisible to anyone wishing to harm us."

Camille shook her head, a tightness spreading through her chest. "He's here now, and it's only a matter of time before—"

Lucie interrupted, "Let's play the remembering game." She smiled, trying to block out those menacing sounds reverberating from the kitchen. First, they would raid the kitchen, confiscating all the flour and milk, and then they would come for them.

She felt the urge to clench her fists and dig her nails into her palms, but she must be strong for Camille.

"What kinds of dresses did your mother wear?"

"I don't know," Camille whispered, her voice catching in her throat.

"Just tell me something."

"She didn't wear so many dresses. But there was one . . ." She stopped at the sound of Sister Ismerie coming down the hall, the Germans walking with her. They couldn't make out what they were saying.

Lucie tugged on Camille's sleeve. "What was it like?"

Barely able to get the words out, Camille said in the faintest of whispers, "Blue velvet, the color of the sky, with a black sash. She wore it on Christmas."

Then they heard the front door open, and after a few suspended moments, filled with Sister Ismerie's high, affected voice bidding the Germans good day, it closed again.

Both of the girls exhaled, relieved in the dark. After a pause, Camille asked, "What did your mother wear?"

"I remember a long black silk dress, embroidered with golden threads. She only wore it on special occasions."

"Where do you think they are now, your parents?" Camille's large eyes shone expectantly.

"I don't know. But I always imagine them in a sunny place, warm and peaceful, close to the sea. Far away from here."

They heard the approach of Sister Ismerie, and then the little cubby door opened. The Sister's face shone with sweat, but she was smiling.

"Girls, you can come out now. They only took some food. It was very good of you to hide so quietly. You must always do this."

CHAPTER 18

VERA

JUNE 1944, SANTA MONICA, CALIFORNIA

With every day that passed, the Allies won another city. The Americans had just taken back Rome—a photograph in the paper showing Italian peasants tossing flowers at US tanks plowing through rubble. Last night on the wireless, that reliable British voice reported that the Nazi rail lines were in chaos. Every major yard from the Bay of Biscay to Cologne had been blasted to pieces. As Max and Vera listened together on the living room sofa, the windows open to the sea-scented air, Max gripped her hand, his eyes lit with euphoria, the same euphoria that Vera saw on every other face wherever she went; in the elevator, on the streets, and especially at the office, the other women carried that tense, hopeful gleam in their eyes. She could tell they were afraid to trust it entirely, but the shared feeling was infectious, all of them tingling with the sensation that the war was nearly over, and the Americans had won it.

She wanted to believe it too, but she didn't dare get caught up in it. No mail had come in almost two years, and to fill in this blank absence, she'd come up with the most gruesome stories of what had happened to Lucie, the worst scenarios parading through her dreams, which continued to haunt her during waking hours, of what she might find when the war finally ended, when she could go back to France. One dream she couldn't shake: Lucie had drowned, and when Vera found her, all that was left was a shred of cloth mixed together with skin and bone that she could tuck into her palm.

She remembered listening to the wireless in Sanary, alone on the couch that evening in June four years ago, when the German advance on Paris was inevitable, and witnessing the dark eclipse the light. But now, Max believed, for the first time, the tide was shifting, the Allies undoing much of the damage and maybe even reversing it, pushing back the Germans. He gripped her hand tighter. "We're going to win."

Their next-door neighbors Pauline and Conrad were already talking about a trip to the English countryside, a honeymoon put on hold because of the war. Max was whistling again, composing a symphony in three movements: flight, struggle, and rebirth, with a choral section at the end. "It's shorter and lighter than what I've done in the past, without the fourth movement. I would say it's a sinfonietta," Vera heard him explaining to Michel over the telephone.

Even the mailman moved with a lighter step after months of trudging down the street, his canvas bag dolefully banging against his side as he went from door to door, everyone dreading what bad news he carried; now they opened their doors before he was even half up the block. He tipped his cap with a flourish after he handed over the mail and announced that by way of England, some letters from France were making it through, and it wouldn't be much longer now, she'd see.

She closed the door behind her, her breath shortened, her heart pounding with dangerous hope.

And then a few days later, on June 6, the wireless announced that the liberation of France had begun: "Allied naval forces supported by strong air forces began landing Allied armies this morning on the northern coast of France." Max picked her up in the living room, accidentally knocking over their coffee cups on the low table, her stocking feet dangling a few inches above the carpet. He held her so tight she almost couldn't breathe.

She whispered, "It's nearly over. Nearly. Just a few more months, maybe less."

He placed her back down, his face flushed. "We'll go straight there and get her."

. . .

Elsa and Leon came over later that day with champagne. Pauline and Conrad were also there. They drank in the garden to a crooning Frank Sinatra while Leon and Max took turns imitating General Eisenhower, shaking their fists in the air, proclaiming: "This is the Europe we came to free!"

"Will you move back to France, after the war?" Pauline asked, sipping champagne. They sat in the shade at the edge of the garden.

"Oh, I don't know," Vera said, stretching her arms overhead. The fig tree was beginning to bloom, and she inhaled its deep rich scent. "We've gotten used to life here. And France is not the France it once was. What is there now? Ruins? Collaborators? I'd rather raise Lucie here, free of all those old associations. I want her to have a new start. I want that for all of us."

The next day, Vera walked into the extra bedroom that would become Lucie's room. She touched the faded yellow wallpaper, and imagined it replaced with pink rosebuds leafed in green. It would be too bold to actually replace the wallpaper now, even if the room needed brightening. But she did allow herself to buy one dress for Lucie, which she kept in the packaging, hidden in the back of the closet.

A crossed-back pinafore dress, mint green and dotted with flowers, with little pearl buttons down the front. She couldn't imagine Lucie fitting into the dress, it looked so big on the hanger, a size eight, but that was her age now.

Sitting down on the twin bed, Vera imagined Lucie playing with her dolls in this sunlit room, the animated stream of her make-believe talk floating through the house. Glancing at the pink bedspread and lace pillows, the very pillows Lucie might soon lay her head on, she felt a stab of anxiety but pushed it away. Oradour was in a peaceful corner of France where there had been no fighting. And soon, she thought, the town would be liberated along with the rest of the country.

Daringly, she filled every room with freshly cut flowers. She planted rosebushes in the garden, willing the light pink buds to bloom early. She hung a wooden bird feeder from the fig tree, hoping for bluebirds, harbingers of luck. She fixed her hair more often, and bought a set of colored ribbons, wondering if Lucie still liked her hair plaited. For Lucie's room, she found a porcelain figurine of a black cat licking its white paws that looked just like Mourka.

She acted as though any day now, Lucie would come home.

This morning, Vera sat at the kitchen table drinking a glass of orange juice. The sun shone, dissipating an early mist that hung over the mountains. She heard the birds rustling in the trees and Max dressing upstairs. In the distance, someone mowed their lawn, and from the tennis court next door, she half listened to the ball repeatedly strike the rackets, followed by Conrad's muffled grunts, indicating that Pauline was winning.

The sounds of Sunday, Vera thought, turning the page, scanning the headlines: "Stunning Blows Strike Foe in Pacific Arena: Saipan is Stormed," "Allies Landed Men Months Ago to Dig Sample of Normandy Soil," "Landing Puts End to 4-Year Hiatus: Fiery Renewal of Battle for France."

And then, up in the corner, a smaller article stood out: "A Martyred Village—Wrong French Town Burned."

She sat up in the chair. The article had been reported by French headquarters in London. She kept reading, an odd needling numbness spreading through her:

On Saturday, June 10th, beginning in the early hours of the morning, all the men, women, and children in the sleepy French village of Oradour-sur-Glane were shot and burned to death by the Nazi SS Division, on the charge that the population gave shelter to Resistance fighters and hid explosives. The men were locked in barns and shot to death, and the women and children burned to death in a locked church. A total of 642 townspeople—245 women, 207 children, and 190 men—were massacred.

Ironically, a German general stated in Neue Zürcher Zeittung that "the massacre was committed in error," instead intended for Oradour-sur-Vayres, a town a mere 17 miles away, where German troops suspected that members of the FTP (Francs-Tireurs et Partisans) were sheltering ammunition as well as an abundance of rationed commodities.

Putting down the paper, Vera swallowed hard, staring at her coffee cup, her chipped nail varnish, the china-blue walls, the large clock hanging over the swinging door. She closed her eyes, as if to hold time in place, as if nothing had changed, and maybe nothing had changed, but then the paper lay there, with the evidence printed. If she kept very still, it all might disappear.

Max swung through the kitchen door. He wore his white trousers for golf.

Gripping the kitchen table, her hands shook.

He poured himself a cup of coffee from the French press on the stove.

She held her breath, watching him dump a teaspoon of sugar into his cup, wanting to preserve these last moments before everything would change.

Stirring the sugar, the teaspoon hitting the porcelain to create that high-pitched ting-a-ling sound, he turned toward her, the sun slanting across his face. He had just shaved. The lime-blossom scent he doused on afterward filled her nose.

He smiled, but his mouth looked crooked. "Is everything all right?"

A thick sheet of water rushed over her, his voice faintly calling from above. He looked confused when she started to talk, until she realized that she was sobbing, making deep guttural sounds.

He came toward her and knelt down to her eye level.

She shook her head, squeezing her eyes shut, her stomach clenching. She couldn't catch her breath, but she wanted to tell him herself, to stop him from reading those terrible words.

"Max," she said, grabbing onto his arm, knocking over the orange juice.

The juice soaked through the paper and dripped from the edge of the table onto the floor.

She swallowed down a surge of vomit.

"Vera, what is it?"

She gestured to the wet newspaper.

He delicately lifted up the wet sheet of paper and started to read.

"My God," he whispered, his expression hollow, the air dense, interspersed with the cry of seagulls and the dinging of an ice cream truck winding its way down to the beach. The thud of an errant tennis ball hurled itself against the side of the house, having sailed over from Pauline and Conrad's court.

"Sorry!" Conrad yelled over the wall.

They sat as still as statues, holding hands across the table, their wrists sticky from the juice, the transparent print seeping into the wood.

Max's voice, faint and unsteady, cut through the quiet. "What are we going to do now? What are we going to do?"

He covered his face with his hands. She kept staring down at the soaked-through newspaper. An overwhelming numbness pulsed through her, as though a lead apron were draped over her chest, stifling all feeling, all movement, all thought. Everything went colorless, the kitchen monochromatic. Max, with his gray hair and white golf shirt, was a newspaper cutout.

He kept shaking his head and started to manically clean his glasses with a square of silk. "I don't understand," he cried, his face naked and vulnerable. "I don't understand how this happened. I don't understand."

She sat very still.

There was nothing to say.

CHAPTER 19

SASHA

JUNE 1944, OMAHA BEACH AND
NORMANDY, FRANCE

The fire-swept beach blurred with bodies, most dead, some still alive, and Sasha yanked soldiers, one by one, from the rough surf, onto the sand toward a medic. The guys screamed as salt water rushed into their wounds, but Sasha kept running and pulling them out along the open beach as he gained more ground. An ammunitions truck burst into flames, lighting up a few soldiers, and two other guys stared in confusion before they were shot down by machine gun fire. Seconds later, another man stepped the wrong way, and a land mine blew him up, his body arcing into the air. Panic rang in Sasha's ears, his heart bursting, knowing his only purpose was to deliver this one piece of information and then get the hell back.

He stumbled over corpses, dismembered limbs, and almost staggered into the surf, but all the dead bodies blocked him, piled up like sandbags where the tide broke. Lurching back onto the sand, he fell over something, his chest smacking into a corpse, and the idea of just lying there, playing dead, crossed his mind, but he forced himself up and sprinted, blindly and hysterically, down the beach.

Minutes felt like hours, until finally he spotted Taylor hugging a nearby seawall with another soldier. Taylor was smoking the butt end of a cigar, and Sasha screamed out: "E-I exit's open!"

"Who blew it open?" Taylor yelled.

"I did."

"All right." Taylor spit out his cigar butt and ordered Sasha back to the breach, and he and the other men would follow. Sasha knew he'd have to run back into that hellish nightmare. But he did it, plunging through it, knowing any minute a Nazi bullet might shoot through his head, as guys all around him caught bullets in their necks, their backs, their chests.

They kept moving inland, at a crawling pace, through the immense tangle of hedgerows where German snipers hid, and through small hamlets where French peasants cowered in their farmhouses. Teenagers from the Free French Forces filtered back and forth across enemy lines, sharing information about German positions, and they elected one kid, Gussie, as their unit's mascot. He spoke pretty good English, and he was always joking and laughing over any small thing, the gap between his two front teeth seemed to widen the more he laughed. One night, after they secured Colleville-sur-Mer, Gussie liberated a bottle of calvados from an empty bar. Sitting at the deserted tables, they passed around the brandy until there wasn't a drop left. No one said much; they were just glad to sit at a table and drink out of a glass, almost feeling human again.

To recuperate and wait for replacements, Sasha's outfit bivouacked on a wide château lawn in the village of Colombières. They wrote letters home under the generous shade of pine trees, while Red Cross girls served up coffee and doughnuts. They threw around some baseballs, which landed in rosemary bushes. Nick and Sasha played poker for long stretches until they got tired, and Sasha napped on the grass, a Raymond Chandler novel open and facedown on his chest. His mother had included it in her last care package. He pictured the winding roads through Laurel Canyon, the cool blondes lounging by swimming pools, the way Marlowe was always in his car, driving and mulling over some detail of a case that would later be the key to everything. Closing his eyes, Sasha almost believed he was back there.

. . .

The next morning, Sasha and a few guys from his unit, Nick and Gussie included, strolled into town, hoping to find more brandy and cigarettes. Gussie boasted about a flirtation with one of the Red Cross girls. Sasha kept worrying about land mines, even though they were walking on cobblestone streets; he knew the forest was littered with them, and tried to reason with himself that they could walk freely here. They passed buildings peppered with bullet holes, followed by entire bombed-out blocks.

Up ahead, an old man pushed a wooden cart overloaded with bedding bound together with rope. A woman trudged a few paces behind, lugging a sack over her shoulder. They both wore faded black clothing, and with their austere white hair and wizened faces, they appeared like figures out of a fairy tale, as a kind of warning or bad omen. A chill passed through Sasha, reminding him of his mother's Baba Yaga stories about a forest witch who stole newborns in the night. She used to tell him that he was the only child Baba Yaga had let her keep.

Rounding the corner, Sasha sensed commotion along the main street culminating in the square. Gussie and the others lagged behind at a tabac, but Sasha followed the townspeople, who spoke in animated tones, gesturing with impatience. The street hummed with a carnivalesque quality. A few men from the Resistance, their rifles slung across their chests, walked along with the crowd. One of them gave Sasha a grim smile. The general pace quickened and Sasha kept up, seeing that in the square, men were cutting and shaving off women's hair; this was the main attraction, and the crowd jeered at the women, forming a loose semicircle around them. Some children watched and laughed because the adults were laughing, but otherwise the children looked ill at ease, confused to be celebrating punishment. One woman knelt down and cried when she touched her newly shorn head. A few tiny nicks on her scalp glinted in the sun. Another woman jerked away, but a man held both of her hands in his while another man fisted her hair. Nearby, a young woman, wearing red lipstick and a silk floral dress, casually sat on a bench while a man cut away. She didn't protest or scream, like the others, but only stared vacantly ahead, her mouth slightly parted.

Then there was a shift in the air; one of the shaved women started walking away with a bundle in her arms. Barefoot, she wore a thin slip. She walked swiftly, and townspeople ran after her, heckling, calling out names, but she kept walking and Sasha strode parallel to her, and he saw that she held a baby in her arms. The baby was about six weeks old, from what he could tell, with a mound of dark hair, its tiny face scrunched up in sleep, its miniature hands fisted into its cheeks. The crowd chanted

"collaboratrice putain" with the force of a battle cry. The townswomen spat on her and laughed, their wooden heels clacking against the cobblestones.

The shaven woman had no one, only the baby, whom she clutched close to her chest. She stared straight ahead, her cheeks burning. Someone had used red lipstick to paint a swastika on her forehead. Sasha saw she had nowhere to go, but could not stop; otherwise the crowd might descend on her and yank the baby from her arms, the living evidence of what she had done. Seeking refuge, her eyes met his, and in that moment, seeing her chapped lips, protective eyes, thin dirty neck, and the shame that coated her every gesture, recognition pierced him, circling back to his birth. In a flash, the harsh morning sun shining down on her shorn head, he knew his father must have been a German soldier instead of the story his mother spun: that her husband, a Russian Jew from their village who had died during the first year of the Great War, was his father. Why else would they whisper **"mamzer"** behind his back? Why else did she never talk about him? Why else?

On some level, he'd always known this, haunted by the hidden photograph of the soldier in field gray against the tree, a photograph he periodically sought out, desperate to know who his father was, and desperate to link omissions, silences, and shame into a story he could understand about himself.

He held up his arm to the crowd and walked over to her. The crowd stalled, unsure of what to do.

Nodding to the Resistance fighters, he pretended to have a plan, and they nodded back, and somehow, within the span of a few minutes, the crowd dispersed, seeking another target, or maybe they just grew bored.

Too afraid to look at Sasha, she whispered **"merci"** over and over again. Gently taking her by the elbow, he guided her to the only place he could find, an empty doorway shaded by an overhanging portico.

She sat down there, the baby stirring, and she slumped against the wall.

When he walked away, he heard the baby begin to wail, his cries gathering force and intensity, despite her shushing, or maybe because of it.

CHAPTER 20

LUCIE

AUGUST 1944, ST. DENIS CONVENT,
SOUTHWESTERN FRANCE

At first light, she ran behind Camille, following the flash of her thick golden hair around the corner. When she caught up to her, they balanced on the wooden benches beneath the window for a better view of the road. Listening hard, they heard distant cheering and honking, and then the distinctive thundering of "La Marseillaise," the national anthem.

"Do you think the Americans are here?" Lucie wondered.

"They've come to save us." Camille sighed, her breath smudging the windowpane. "And they're so handsome," she added dreamily, even though she'd only seen a few snapshots of American soldiers in the newspaper.

Camille's eyes then filled with light, the same light Father Belanger said had encircled Mary during the Annunciation, and Lucie knew the war was ending.

The doorbell rang, and Sister Ismerie ran to open it, trying to appear calm and overcome her old anxiety that it might be the Germans. Camille immediately clasped Lucie's hand, her eyes frozen, waiting, followed by the sound of the door opening and exclamations in French. A woman's voice, high and sweet, rang through the corridors.

"My mother is here!" Camille gasped. She pulled Lucie along, and they ran barefoot, hair loose around their shoulders, sleep still in their eyes.

Sister Ismerie and Sister Helene stood speaking with an elegant couple with light hair and light eyes, smiling expectantly. The man wore an officer's uniform with the tricolor badge around his arm, the woman a smart jacket cinched at the waist and wide-legged trousers. Their eyes lit up, and the woman cried out when Camille ran to them. She knelt down to catch Camille. Then the man picked her up and hugged her close, as if he might crush her.

They were all crying and laughing at the same time, while Lucie sucked her thumb. She watched the reunited family from behind the massive black habit of Sister Ismerie, who was also overcome with emotion, describing the events leading up to this point in a flustered, excited tone. Suddenly, Camille had transformed into someone else: a daughter in her father's arms, her head pressed against his chest, her face relaxed, her mother stroking her hair, which gave off a lustrous sheen in the early summer morning. To Lucie, her old friend appeared beautiful and foreign, locked in their embraces. Everyone spoke at once, except Lucie, who became a shadow, a faint smudge on the wall, invisible even to herself.

Sister Ismerie ushered Camille's parents into the vestibule and closed the front door, shutting out the exuberant shouting and music coming from the town square.

"Now," Camille's father began, trying to assume a serious tone, although he couldn't stop smiling, "France has not been entirely won yet. We're still pushing the Germans across the Rhine, and pushing them into Berlin might take some time yet. Many more months, possibly."

He paused, running a hand through his thick hair.

Camille stared at her parents. She didn't even notice Lucie anymore, standing there pitifully behind Sister Helene.

Her mother continued, "What we're trying to say, Camille, is that we can't take you home yet. There are militiamen and collaborators all over. It's still unsafe."

She turned to Sister Ismerie. "It would be best if she stayed here and began the school year with the rest of the girls in the fall."

. . .

In Sister Ismerie's office, they discussed the recent liberation of Paris, and how hopefully now the rest would go quickly, God willing. Lucie lingered near the open door, waiting to see if they would mention when her parents were coming. Or maybe Camille's parents had news of Agnes, who hadn't written in such a long time. Agnes might retrieve her first and deliver Lucie to her parents, who were probably waiting nearby. Or maybe her parents had moved back into the Paris apartment, putting everything in place for her arrival. Yes, Lucie thought, that seemed sensible. Lost in the swirl of her thoughts, she faintly heard Camille's mother say, "And I hear you have been a great friend to our Camille."

Camille beamed at her. "Lucie is my best friend."

Lucie smiled dumbly back at them.

"And where are you from, dear?" her mother asked.

"Oh," Sister Helene interrupted, "she came to us about two years ago, delivered by her governess."

Camille's parents nodded.

Sister Ismerie lowered her voice: "From Oradour-sur-Glane."

"Oh," the mother gasped, her gloved hand flying to her mouth.

The father lowered his head.

Lucie swallowed, wondering if they could hear her heart thrashing in her chest.

Camille sat on her mother's lap, her eyes half closed, her bare feet skimming the green carpet.

"Would you know anything about the deportees, about those who were interned?" Sister Helene asked in a hushed and hopeful tone, as if asking for more sugar when there was none.

Camille's father sighed and shifted positions in the creaky wooden chair. Then he said, from what he'd heard, the deportees, including many political prisoners caught fighting in the Resistance, were located in camps across Germany and Poland, and they would not be back for some time.

He shook his head and ended his little speech with a dry cough.

Sister Helene sat there staring, her hand on her heart. Camille's mother continued to nod, as if the conversation still continued.

Instinctually, Lucie wiped her saliva-coated thumb on her nightgown, unable to tear herself away from the horribly silent scene, and at the same time, she wanted nothing more than to run to her secret place, the dry, cool hay-filled cabinet where she had hid many times before today.

Lucie knew the convent. Even if the meals consisted of lentils with little rocks in them, tightly rationed milk and casein cookies, that terrible pumpkin compote and desserts made with colored gelatin, she suddenly wanted to stay here with Camille, eliding the question of the future. A natural affinity coursed between them: Lucie following Camille, like a distorted shadow, and Camille the bright blazing light that everyone praised.

Of course, it hadn't always been easy here. When the nuns saw Lucie, they sometimes crossed themselves as if she were the devil because of her knotted hair, a halo of tangles, along with her perpetually ink-smudged collar, and those questions she posed during religious lectures, such as: **If God is so powerful, why did he let Jesus die?** And: **Where is God now, during the war?**

But Lucie had Camille. On the weekends and during holidays, the other boarders returned to their homes, leaving Lucie and Camille alone together. The nuns allowed the girls to skip Mass, and supplied them with old Catholic propaganda magazines, which they consumed on their cots, lying on their stomachs, their stocking feet lolling back and forth.

The convent buzzed with news of the Allied landings in France and the German defeats on the Eastern Front. Sister Ismerie and Sister Helene shut themselves into Sister Ismerie's office every evening, removed their coifs, and listened to the old crackling radio broadcast the Free French; unbeknownst to them, Lucie and Camille crouched on the other side of the door, trying to hold back their laughter at having escaped their beds unnoticed. During the day they flew down the long corridors and stairwells, cheeks feverishly red, too excited to eat or sleep. They couldn't sit still to peel vegetables or embroider, and between the heat and their mosquito bites and scabies, they were constantly itching and moving, willing the moist stone walls to crumble.

But the conversation she'd witnessed in the office, between Sister Ismerie and Camille's parents, kept running through Lucie's head, and she feared what had happened to Agnes, and why Camille's parents were so upset by the mention of Oradour-sur-Glane.

But what haunted Lucie the most was their silence.

After Camille's parents left, Sister Helene's concern for Lucie intensified. She tried to brush out Lucie's hair when it was wet, she promised it would hurt less, but Lucie still jerked away. At bedtime, she lingered next to Lucie's cot, sometimes laying a cool hand over her forehead, sometimes smoothing her hair back from her temples in a rhythmic calming motion. She urged her to eat more, to stroll the beautiful parks, to see the goldfish in the ponds. "You should go outside, take some air," Sister Helene kept saying. "It's not a danger anymore."

Lucie felt too tired even though she slept for hours at a time. A hollow, dull pang replaced her former defiance, and she stared listlessly at the sun-bleached curtains in the dormitory, never bothering to push them aside.

Finally, Camille and Sister Helene persuaded her to take a walk one evening. "Down to the Garonne

River, just for an hour," they chimed. It was still warm in those first days of September. Lucie didn't have the energy to protest, and the wispy pink clouds appeared magical against the purpling sky.

On the street, the crowds and the noise distracted her. To focus, she stared down at her worn sandals and noticed how ugly they looked, thinking about how many times the sandals had been repaired only to break again. Camille picked up the pace, pulling her past the bombed-out rail station. Sister Helene walked a few feet behind them, calling out, "Girls, look at the reblooming roses! And those hats in the window: Which one is the prettiest?"

Lucie nodded, overwhelmed by all the different faces on the street, the clack of wooden heels striking the cobblestones, the women with their rouged cheeks and strong perfumes.

On Quai de Paludate, she noticed a mother with a small child. They walked down the street swinging hands and singing a nursery rhyme, and the sad familiar song about a little lark cut through her: **"Alouette, gentille alouette, alouette, je te plumerai."** It was a song her own mother used to sing when she bent down to tie Lucie's shoelaces. Her mother didn't sing often, except when performing certain tasks, such as tying laces or blotting out a stain from a blouse, because she found such things tiresome and irritating, so it was better to sing, she always said. The faint image of glancing down at her mother's upswept hair, her white neck bent over Lucie's shoes while those verses floated above them, gave her a shock. **"Je te plumerai le bec, je te plumerai le bec,"** the woman continued, pulling the child along.

Lucie watched them go, entranced by the fluttering black ribbon attached to the woman's straw hat. Then heat flooded through her, and she was taken aback by the sharp invasion of such a specific memory when she couldn't even recall her mother's face.

She started running, bumping into people as she went. Distantly, she heard Sister Helene calling after her, but all that mattered was the faithful rush of her own ragged breath.

The cobblestone streets and little storefronts, the streetlamps and soft sky, blurred at the edges of her vision. She focused only on the forest up ahead, yearning for the cool pines redolent with sap and resin, and the relief it would bring to throw herself onto the shaded ground and scream into the dirt.

CHAPTER 21

SASHA

SEPTEMBER 1944,
NEW ROCHELLE, NEW YORK

Gray morning light filtered through the wooden shutters. The early-morning fog, thick and soupy, cradled him. His eyes involuntarily closed again, hurtling him back to Omaha Beach, the sky lit up with machine gunfire. His chest hit wet sand, and then a dismembered ear washed up on the shore next to him, carried inland by the rough and bloody surf.

Sasha moaned, instinctually palming his shoulder, where he'd gotten shot six weeks ago by a German sniper hiding in one of those hedgerows when they started their advance into the Longny forest. He was lucky; the bullet didn't hit any bone, organs, or major blood vessels, but it left pieces of itself in there, pieces he could still feel. His CO sent him home early on medical discharge, arguing that he couldn't do much fighting with his arm in a sling, suffering from a nasty infection that set into the wound ten days later. Languishing on clean white sheets in the field hospital, he pictured his infantry division pushing the Germans back across France, all the way to Aachen in a relentless offensive, while he lay there, useless, listening to battle updates on the radio, or overhearing the nurses talk in promising tones while they changed his dressings. It was during this time, his mind restless, itching to jot down tidbits of scenes, lines of dialogue that might turn into something more, when he started to think about his next script.

He wanted to make a film about the war, but not the war itself; he had no idea how to capture the vastness and scale of what he'd seen, and everyone knew war was hell. They didn't need a movie to remind them. More interesting was the war's psychological effect on those who returned, on their morality and their sense of justice after witnessing so much senseless bloodshed. How could they all live in the world again, after years of violence, willfully forgetting their humanity to survive? Turning this over in his mind, Sasha began to sweat, remembering the men in his unit who were hit by friendly fire a few days after Normandy, and how they had to swiftly bury them and move on. Or the time his friend Nick killed an Italian soldier who was running toward them, surrendering, yelling with his hands up, but Nick, in a panic, started shooting, and when they went over to the body, they saw the soldier was only a kid, fifteen at most. How, Sasha wondered, would these guys return to their office jobs, pushing paper across a desk, looking present-able in a gray flannel suit, after what they'd seen?

He asked the same thing of himself, but writing had always been his way out, and it would be the way out now, if only he could use both of his hands. He would call it **The In-Between Man,** he thought. In that moment, he jerked up in bed and asked if they had a pen and paper lying around that he could use. One of the younger nurses smiled at him indul-gently, but then the head nurse, an older wisecrack-ing lady, pulled the curtain aside and said, "To do what? Write the Great American Novel? Rest is what you need. Not paper."

Unlike so many others, he survived the war, but it had nothing to do with any particular skill, or cun-ning, or talent. Death was a random selector, and the thought of this, along with a rotating host of disturbing images, plagued him relentlessly in those first weeks, when he was staying at Dubrow's house, his mother nervously fluttering around him, every-one asking if he was all right, coupled with that con-stant refrain: **Look forward, not back.**

It must have worked. He only looked back in dreams, his mind careening with land mines and hedgerows, lost children and dead horses, and that shaved woman with the baby, the way he had left her in an empty doorway. Before they mobilized, he saw her again, sitting in the back of an open truck with a bunch of other women, all of them half naked and shaved, their eyes lowered as people shouted, throwing rotten fruit and garbage at them. The truck moved slowly, allowing everyone a good look, but the sight of her made Sasha shudder, thinking about what kind of life her child would endure, with such a heavy past; he would never be able to outrun it.

His mother had made up a bedroom for him, with a desk for his typewriter and clean new socks neatly balled in the top dresser drawer. But sitting on the edge of the bed, staring down at his bare feet sinking into the rose carpet, he was more unsure than ever of his place in the world. He felt like a caged animal, undomesticated and restless, pacing from one end of the room to the other, glaring out at the placid greenery while everyone moved silently and carefully around him, as if he were a grenade that might come unpinned at any moment, as if he might start screaming at the slightest irritation. The comfort was plush, suffocating. Sure, he enjoyed lighting a cigar at night, and he no longer slept with his rifle, but he was uneasy, plagued by headaches, sleeping in short spurts and then up in the middle of the night, drinking scotch in the kitchen under the bright light of the bulb. And he wanted to start writing **The In-Between Man**, but his arm was still in a sling. He took it out and typed down a few lines, but instantly that fiery ache returned in his shoulder, spidering down his arm, forcing him to stop. "Sasha, what are you doing?" his mother barked from the hallway. Always she had this innate sense of when he was causing trouble. Wincing, he put his arm back into the sling just as she appeared in the doorway.

She eyed the typewriter. "You were typing."

He shrugged, and even that small movement hurt.

"Why can't you just rest?"

Sasha stared at the typewriter. "I want to work. It's all I want to do."

Leah marched into the room, and from the desk drawer, she took out a pencil and a sheaf of lined paper. "Tell me what you want to write. I'll take dictation."

"Okay," Sasha said hesitantly. "But you won't like it."

Leah brushed away his comment and set the paper over a book on her lap, the pen poised in her hand.

"The thing is," Sasha began, "the hero is as bad as the bad guys. You see, Jack, he fought in the Pacific and grew close to two other guys in his unit. Now they're back in New York, trying to fit into society again, but there's not much that separates the bad from the good after what happened to them in a Japanese POW camp, where they used to fantasize about robbing a bank, describing how they'd do it, down to the very last detail. After a big bank robbery happens in Midtown, Jack instantly knows his war buddies did it, and he has to decide whether or not to turn them in. In the end, he helps his buddies escape out of the country, because if given the chance, he would have done the same thing. That's what I want to say. Because that's the truth. It's called **The In-Between Man**."

Leah was still writing when Sasha finished talking. After a few minutes, she looked up at him. "Why would you want to make a picture like that?"

"Why not?" Sasha asked, trying to mask his irritation.

"It's like there's no difference between right and wrong."

"I'm not saying that . . . What I'm saying is that it's more complicated than the way I used to think about things, with bad guys who were all bad, and good guys who were all good. That's not reality. That's not human nature, and it's not how the world works . . ." He stopped himself when he saw his mother's distraught expression, as if she might start crying, and he couldn't bear it when she cried.

Rarely did she let him see her cry, but the times that she did, especially when he was little, he would stand there motionless, watching her, his arms hanging limply at his sides, racked by the sense that he had caused it, and that he was unable to make things better again. Her face, suddenly distorted by sadness, made her inaccessible, and he felt afraid, as if he bobbed in a vast ungovernable ocean, a tiny lone speck compared to her crashing emotion that threatened to swallow him whole.

Just then the phone rang and she sprung up to answer it, deftly leaving the room.

"Oh, hello, Charlie," he heard her say from the hallway, relieved that the charged moment had dissipated. He got up from his desk to take the call.

When she handed him the phone, her eyes still flickered with injury, as if they had argued, over what he wasn't sure, but then Charlie's jovial voice filled the line. "Sasha! When are you coming home?"

"What do you mean? I've been home for two weeks, trying to recuperate, but my damn shoulder—"

"I mean when are you coming back to LA!"

"Soon, I hope. So, I've been thinking about a new—"

"Listen, Sasha. Do you remember a kid named Lambert in your unit? Nick Lambert?"

"Sure," he replied, fearing the worst. He leaned into the wall, steadying himself. "He's a good kid."

"His father, Robert Lambert, contacted me. He's a producer in town, and about a year ago, I slipped him the Western you wrote before you left, **Clementine**, and Lambert heard about how you helped Nick and the rest of his unit on Omaha Beach, and now he's all fired up about **Clementine**.

He wants to put up the money for it, so get back here as soon as you're able. Okay?"

"Okay," Sasha said, and as quickly as Charlie had got on the line, he got off, leaving Sasha standing there against the wall, clenching the receiver in his hand, relieved Nick was okay, and only after that sank in did he begin to feel excited about **Clementine**, and pitching **The In-Between Man**. He went back into his room, and started to pack.

On his last morning home, around three a.m., Sasha crept downstairs and sat at the kitchen table, not bothering to turn on the light. In his palm, he clenched the red ribbon his mother had given him from Russia, for good luck. "Something from the past," she had said, "to keep you safe." He had pinned it to the inside of his fatigues, and by now, it was discolored with sweat and blood.

Sasha laid it out on the cool wooden surface, next to his glass of scotch, and just stared at it, somehow knowing it was his father's. He rested his head on his forearm, stretched out across the table, and tried to imagine what it had been like between his parents. He tried to imagine his father, and wondered if he was anything like him, disbelieving the story his mother had always told him: that his father had joined the Russian army, as all the men did, and died early into the war, on the Carpathian pass. Then why the sense that he was marked in some way, if she was merely a widow, like so many other women in their village, left husbandless after the war? Why the shameful silence when he was little and he blurted out questions about his papa, missing him, wanting him to come back? Why did they have to endure the neighbors' spiteful glances, or the way his aunt and uncle looked at him with sadness and distaste?

This wasn't all he remembered.

Other things, blurry and faint but memories nonetheless, had started to come back to him during the war, and continued to gather intensity now that he was home with time to think. A golden pocket watch someone used to dangle from a chain before him, swinging it like a pendulum, and the sound of rueful laughter at his fascination with the watch. He tried to grab it mid-swing, and when he succeeded, a male voice, deep and resonant, said in Yiddish, "Good boy, my boy."

His mother's hair smelled of cigarettes, but only sometimes. He didn't like it.

The black boots at the foot of the bed. He put his little bare feet inside of them and tried to walk, falling down. Always falling.

Digging and digging through snow to find a chocolate bar that his father had hidden for him. When he found it, his hands red and throbbing with cold, his mother scolding him for not wearing mittens, her voice jumping with concern. His father laughing. Always laughing. "He's okay." He gestured to Sasha. "Look, he loves chocolate."

· · ·

The sky started to lighten when he heard his mother's footsteps on the stairs, her tired sigh, and then she appeared in the doorway, her face creased with worry. She had aged during his time away, the depressions under her eyes more pronounced, her hair thinner, her back slightly hunched, and he felt a rush of guilt for all the fear and anxiety she carried because of him.

"What were you doing down here, sleeping with your head on the table, in the dark?"

He gestured to the picture window. "It's almost morning."

She sat down across from him, rearranging her quilted robe. Then, with hesitation, she touched the frayed ribbon. "You kept it."

He felt the old urge pounding in his chest, making his throat close up, his voice winnowing down to a whisper: **Tell me about my father.** As he started to ask, she sprung up and hugged him, her small frail body crushing into his. "It protected you," she said, her voice breaking. "I protected you."

He gripped her arm and buried his face in the crook of her padded elbow. She wept into his hair, her breath short and jagged, and he sat here with her, not asking about the past. That's what she wanted, because the past, he realized, was another country, with borders he shouldn't cross.

CHAPTER 22

SASHA

OCTOBER 1944,
LOS ANGELES, CALIFORNIA

On his first night back in town, Charlie took him to Romanoff's in Beverly Hills to celebrate his return. He even surprised him with a chocolate cake decorated with K rations and lined with Sasha's favorite cigars, Optimos. Charlie had reserved a table outside in the garden, and the night wind was warm and dry, the sky above them as black as velvet with little stars burning into it, pinpricks of brilliance. Sasha looked up and felt as if he could drink up the sky and everything in it before he dove into his pitch for **The In-Between Man.**

When he finished, Charlie took a long sip of scotch, hesitating, and Sasha recognized this tactic of his, not wanting to admit he disliked it right away.

"Listen, Sasha," Charlie began, but then Sasha blurted out, "You hate it."

"Not quite **hate**, but why make a picture like that at a time like this? People want to celebrate the good things in life . . . They're tired of the war."

"But it's not about the war . . . It's about what comes **after**, how difficult it is to feel . . . normal again." His eyes wandered over to the bar, where a few guys in uniform, recently discharged, stood drinking in silence amidst the celebratory air.

Charlie noticed them too and then met Sasha's gaze. "You okay?"

"Yeah," Sasha said. "As long as I keep writing and telling the stories I need to tell."

Charlie raised his glass. "I'll drink to that." He paused, a slow smile spreading over his face. "And to **Clementine**. Looks like you got your shot at directing."

Sasha jumped up. "What do you mean?"

Charlie leaned back into his chair, grinning. "I told Lambert over the phone that he could have the script for free on the condition that you direct it."

Sasha flung his arms around Charlie in an unexpected rush of affection, and Charlie slapped him on the back, laughing and saying, "Glad you're home, kid. Glad you're home."

Two weeks later, Sasha found himself at Romanoff's again. Cigarette girls glided around the perimeter of the dining room, ignoring Sasha's attempts to flag one of them down for a cigar. But the clink of crystal tumblers, the beautiful women throwing back their necks in laughter, the band playing Benny Goodman, all distracted Sasha from the tingling expectation that coursed through him after having just met with Robert Lambert out in the San Fernando Valley at his sprawling estate. They discussed casting and prep time for **Clementine**, and Lambert explained that he had a fourteen-day slot open in January on the little lot he owned; it even had an Old West town built into it already.

But, Sasha thought, watching the cigarette girl make her way toward the bar, anything could happen: Lambert might get cold feet, run out of money, or back out for some unforeseen reason. Sasha took a long swig of vodka, relishing its abrasive sting. He would revise the script over the next ten days, and by January, he'd be directing a picture.

A waiter passed by, ferrying a sizzling lamb chop, and Sasha realized he was hungry from having skipped dinner. His mouth watered at the thought of sausages on buttered toast, his favorite here.

The bartender, a young kid with slicked-back hair, vigorously shook vodka and Cointreau, adding a splash of apricot liqueur at the end. Sasha tried to place him, but the nattering debutantes at the bar were distracting. In high chirping voices, they discussed the possibility of wearing an off-the-shoulder dress to a luncheon. He was about to lean

over and order another vodka when the cigarette
girl appeared before him, packs of Chesterfields and
Camels artfully arranged and cellophane-wrapped
in a tray poised beneath her voluptuous breasts. He
took in the short flared skirt and cheap perfume,
her hair molded into conical points on either side
of her head.

"You got any Cubans?"

"We're out," she said, gazing flatly into the mirror
running behind the bar, reflecting Romanoff, in his
signature white dinner jacket, holding court at the
corner table, snubbing patrons and spoon-feeding
steak tartare to his two bulldogs.

He bought a pack of Camels, and she slipped the
quarter into her front pocket before turning away,
not acknowledging the tip.

"They had some Romeo and Julietas in last week.
Rich and strong," the bartender said.

"Yeah, I prefer La Aroma de Cuba, if given the
choice."

"No choice tonight," he joked, funneling a to-
mato juice cocktail into a long glass. He expertly
sliced a lime and wedged it onto the salted rim, and
the way he cocked his head at a jaunty angle brought
Gussie to mind, the French kid who helped them
out in Normandy.

In the long mirror, Sasha watched the padded
front door swing open as more people streamed into
the place.

"You okay, buddy?"

"You just remind me of someone I used to know."

The boy shook his head, clearing empty tumblers off the counter. "No one dead, I hope. That's bad luck, you know. Even if I'm his exact semblance, do me a favor. Don't tell me about it."

The bartender went on about how his mother, a devout Catholic, saw his dead father every evening sitting at the edge of the bed, asking for his usual whiskey on ice. Sasha half listened, his stomach growling, remembering when they played a joke on Gussie and pretended to drive away while he was flirting with a farmer's daughter, talking to her about how the birth of a colt was full of warmth and blood and new life while caressing her hand. Midway through his seduction, Gussie noticed the departing jeeps and the rest of the guys laughing. He quickly kissed her on the cheek and jumped into the back seat, his regular place next to the driver already occupied. Sasha rode in the first jeep, looking back at Gussie, who was still grinning at the girl.

A few minutes later the jeep hit a land mine, killing the man in the passenger seat and tearing off the driver's legs. Gussie came away with a few cuts and bruises, but that was it. Such chance, luck, fate, or whatever you wanted to call it still gave Sasha the chills, and he shook his head, knowing how very little separated anyone from death, as it was always breathing beneath the surface of things, slumbering and waiting until it arbitrarily plucked you from this earth.

"No, not dead," he told the bartender. "Maybe it's good luck."

When he got home, a letter from his mother awaited him, unusually thin. He opened it, and a clipping from the Scarsdale society pages announcing the engagement of Margaret Altman to Bobby Schneider fluttered out. A blurry photograph of Margaret smiled back at him, and he remembered the mystified look she'd given him when he told her that he was moving out to Los Angeles, as if it were the most ungodly, foreign place in the world.

He stuffed it back into the envelope and flung it across his desk. **You see,** he heard his mother say. **That could have been you, and I would have finally been happy.**

He was supposed to call his mother tonight, but it was too late, and he was grateful. Instead, he started banging out notes on his script, working until his eyes burned and the last light went out on the street.

Sirens blared in the distance, echoing off the ocean as he tossed and turned under his sheets. Another brushfire probably raged in the canyons.

He would eventually have to make the disappointing call to his mother. He was supposed to go home for the holidays, a date she hung her heart on, but now, with shooting scheduled for right after

New Year's, along with casting and prep, he had to stay here. He imagined the withholding silence that would settle over the line after he explained this—a silence that felt worse than any reprimand or guilt-laden comment.

To drown out the blaring sirens, the neighbors Gloria and Ray turned up their radio and Vera Lynn's elegant voice sang that old wartime favorite, and for a moment, Sasha felt at ease; he used to listen to this song during Operation Torch when none of them could sleep.

With sirens cutting in and out of his dreams, he was brought back to those cool little beds of North African sand, his fingers sifting through the fine granules as he stared into the night sky vibrating with hot white stars, as though each one contained a heartbeat. Just as they nodded off, that sultry American voice drifted across the desert dunes from a hidden German loudspeaker, cutting into the dead quiet. "Hello, boys. Hello, Big Red One! Wake up . . . This is Axis Sally bedding you down for the night." She told them not to bother searching for the loudspeaker, buried in the sand somewhere, under a land mine. "Churchill is smoking his cigars, watching all you GI Joes die, he doesn't give a damn. You should ask yourselves: Why are you fighting for the Brits and not for us? Pretty soon, the Germans will be toasting their victory in Moscow, while in the Pacific, the Japs butcher you by the thousands."

Into the darkness, someone yelled, "Finish your damn report already and play our song." All the soldiers laughed, and they burrowed deeper into the black cool sand, waiting for it.

"Here's a nice little lullaby, and while I'm singing sweetly to you, imagine your wives and high school sweethearts spreading their legs for those draft dodgers and good old 4-Fs. Good night, boys. Sleep tight."

The ghostly sound of a harmonica accompanied her smooth voice, which trembled over certain notes of "Lili Marlene," a song that sent him into rich and sonorous dreams.

CHAPTER 23

VERA

OCTOBER 1944,
LOS ANGELES, CALIFORNIA

I t was very difficult to get an appointment," Max explained in the car on the way over. It had only been a few months, but already Max was pressing her to see specialists—psychiatrists, psychologists, herbalists—thinking all these appointments would help her come to grips with what had happened at Oradour.

Turning onto Bedford Drive, Max added, "I had to pull some strings." He called his cousin Dr. Adler, asking him to put in a call to Dr. Bettelheim, as the two had been colleagues in New York, and for this, they were lucky, Max reiterated. "Try to have an open mind," he said, parking in front of a low brick building with white shutters.

. . .

Dr. Bettelheim sat in a leather armchair with a notepad balanced on his knee. The cream carpet and dark paneled walls, combined with the walnut desk and leather furniture, made it seem as though Dr. Bettelheim had been planted into this scene with such perfection that his expertise was indisputable. He instantly reminded Vera of a turtle, with his small rounded head tilted to the side as he gazed at them inquisitively, his wrinkled neck straining out of his collared shirt. Leather-bound volumes of Goethe and Heine lined the shelves, and a gilt-framed diploma from the University of Vienna hung behind his desk.

He leaned back into his chair and gestured for them to sit on the couch opposite, giving Vera a half-hearted smile before directing his gaze at Max.

Clearing his throat, he then repositioned his body before beginning to speak. "Dr. Adler provided me with a general sense of the trouble, but it would be immensely helpful to hear it from you, in your own words." His thick Viennese accent struck certain vowels with unintended emphasis, simultaneously relaxing and jolting the senses into submission.

Sensing their hesitation, he explained that he was from Würzburg, but he came to New York for a fellowship at Mount Sinai Hospital, in the psychiatric department.

Sighing, he laced his fingers over his knee. "My particular area of research is hypermnesia. The opposite of amnesia. An uncontrolled ability to recall memories which are physically painful in their vividness and intensity. And these memories flood back all at once, with overwhelming power, and on their own volition. What happened yesterday sparks something that occurred three years ago. For example, I treated a German businessman whose textile mill was 'Aryanized' in the thirties. He had to flee the country, and he immigrated to Brooklyn, where he and his wife started up a stationery store. But a few years later, the store failed, and yet he not only felt the failure of that store closing down, but with it, all the memories and fears associated with the loss of his textile mill came rushing back as well: the incessant anxiety of the SS knocking on the door, their hiding in the pantry for three days, waiting for exit visas and then escaping their Berlin apartment in the dead of night. The two events coalesce into one. With each new distress that occurs, the patient experiences not only that failure, but every failure that preceded it, creating a cumulative effect."

Vera nodded, noticing that Max's hand had inched across the leather couch toward hers, but she felt no desire to hold it. Of course Max wanted so badly to give what she had a name instead of the wordless, inexhaustible range of emotions that punctuated her days. But when that unwanted darkness

seized her, it was not necessarily connected to a particular memory or event, as the doctor described.
Her dark moods could be provoked by the color of
the walls at a particular moment, the sight of children playing at the beach, or a recent dream. The
slightest thing—a word, a scent, an object—left
her defenseless. And this defenselessness had only
worsened.

"That's very interesting," Max said, nodding at
the doctor, whose small obsidian eyes scanned their
faces.

"And how," Vera asked, "do you treat these dis-
orders?"

"We prescribe antidepressants, tranquilizers, barbiturates . . ." His voice trailed off, and he impatiently waved one liver-spotted hand through the air.
"But we've never entirely cured anyone of the nightmares or the hypermnesia." He attempted a kindly
smile. "It's still early days. Now," he said, frowning
down at his notepad, "if you could explain the trouble, in more detail."

Vera could tell that Max was nervous as he began
to speak. He had high hopes for this doctor, as if
a doctor could fix her somehow and shake out the
grief. The clock on his desk sedately ticked as she
half listened to Max explain their attempts to find
out more about the massacre, but it was challenging.
They scoured reports and newspapers for more details: Was it only the town itself, or did the Germans
also target the surrounding farms and hamlets?

Were there any survivors even though the initial report claimed there were none?

Finding out more about what happened at Oradour had grown into Vera's obsession, a solitary one, while Max retreated into his work. He had just been assigned as the head composer for **Music for Millions,** a film with June Allyson and Harry Davenport, that the studio expected to win the Academy Award, which he said would secure him an extension on his contract, adding another five to seven years.

Vera resented and also understood why he worked so much, envying him for having something real to disappear into, when she had only shreds of news, theories and statistics, unsubstantiated reports. Her job at the EFF temporarily relieved her from this searing uncertainty, the dullness of the work blunting her senses, until she returned home to her real life, and then the pain came blazing back. The moment Max woke up, he dashed to the shower, after which he gulped down his coffee with still wet hair and, smelling of soap and starch, grabbed his pockets to check for keys and cigarettes, planting a perfunctory kiss on Vera's cheek seconds before the car door slammed and he roared away to the studio, waving as he went. She sensed his fear that if he lingered too long, she might burst into tears, which she hadn't done in weeks, but nonetheless, he sprinted from the house as if it were on fire.

One of their worst fights happened unexpectedly,

when she was pulling on her stockings, and he called from the hallway, "See you later on," as if by not being dressed quite yet, she had intentionally stalled him.

He tugged at his collar. "Vera, I've got to—"

"You're doing it again." She now had on her stockings and was zipping up the back of her skirt.

"What?"

Pale light filtered into the hallway.

He stood on the landing, his jaw tensing.

"You're doing **that**." Vera pursed her lips, waiting for him to confess, but he just stood there. "Your performance of being so very rushed and short on time, when we both know you don't actually have to be at the office until nine." She said this crisply and cleanly. No weepiness or intimation that things would turn tearful.

"But you know that I have to—"

She cut him short. "It's not as if I'm trying to drag you down into the morass of my suffering at any given moment."

"Oh, come on. That's a bit of an exaggeration, even for you," he said, attempting to lighten the mood.

She fixed him with a stare. Underneath his congenial expression, she saw that her observation disturbed him. Her heart accelerated, and she relished the leap in her blood, readying herself for a fight. He tried to embrace her, to make it up, but his warm pity repulsed her and she pushed him away. He staggered into the wall, and for a moment, it all seemed oddly comic: his overly wounded expression, her exaggerated malevolence. Two actors in a play.

Taking out a cigarette, she still felt the sting of that recent argument, and wondered if this was the sort of thing one talked about in analysis. When she drew deeply on the cigarette, the familiar burn in the back of her throat brought her brief satisfaction, before she noticed Max's amiable expression and she felt a renewed anger with how oddly inflexible he had grown about the details of the massacre, reluctant to consider alternative theories.

Dr. Bettelheim cleared his throat after Max finished explaining that Paris had only just been liberated, and the war still raged in the rest of France. "But you see, Vera is obsessed with finding out more information, and yet we can't—there simply isn't enough access and the reports are spotty, and frankly, at this point, we're dogs chasing after our own tails."

Vera shook her head, almost afraid to speak because she didn't trust herself. She might start screaming. Taking a deep breath, she began slowly, her voice shaking, "But what Max seems intent on ignoring is that, for example, it was recently reported that a boy survived the massacre by hiding in his family's attic before fleeing into the forest. For some reason, he had not attended school that day, just as Lucie wouldn't have, which is why he was able to hide and flee. The same thing could have happened to Lucie. She could still be alive."

"It's highly improbable," Max said gently. He exchanged a knowing look with the doctor.

Vera snapped, "It isn't highly improbable."

"Well," the doctor interjected, leaning forward, his wrinkled hands spreading over his knees, "even if Lucie hasn't died in that particular massacre, from what we've heard about the roundups and camps, you must be prepared to discover the worst."

"I am prepared," Vera said, but her voice sounded small and tight.

"In the meantime, you mustn't stop living," Dr. Bettelheim added.

Vera glanced at the clock again. Only a half hour had passed. The whole point of this visit was for the doctor to confirm what Max had already pleaded with her to consider many times, but in his pleading, he grew prodding and intrusive, flickering around her like an agitated moth.

The doctor gestured for her to say more.

Vera drew her knees tightly together and hugged herself, as if to stay warm, even though it was stuffy inside the office, the afternoon sun heating up the cream carpet and the leather sofa to the point of discomfort. "I understand that I can't do anything from here. That it's useless to torture myself over reports and details that keep changing every day—"

She broke off, refusing to tear up in front of this doctor, who surely wanted her to because that's what people did in places like these. As though crying would open some secret door to health when it only made her feel overly self-conscious, the sole focus of his keen bright gaze.

Max passed her a handkerchief. She balled the silk into her fist.

"She wants to go back to France, to Oradour, as soon as it's possible," Max interjected. He struck a match to light a cigarette and then sank back into the couch. Taking a long drag, he added, "I don't think she should go back there, into all that death."

Vera bristled at his scolding tone, the same tone one might take with a child who has misbehaved. As he stoically brought the cigarette to his lips, a cool arrogance radiated from him.

"I understand Vera's reasons for wanting to witness the place of death. It speaks to our need for closure, for a sense of an ending. Without this, it's very difficult to move forward." Dr. Bettelheim gave Vera an uneasy glance. "Which leads us to my next point."

Max leaned over the marble coffee table, ashing into a shallow amber dish.

Dr. Bettelheim clasped his hands together, almost as if he wanted to celebrate something. "You must try for another child. It is the only way forward, the only way to inject meaning into your life again. Otherwise, this interminable waiting, this uncertainty, will continue to hold you in its grip."

They walked out of the office's sequestered calm into the garish sun, the passing cars and lunch-hour foot traffic disorienting. Vera sought shade under a restaurant awning, leaning into the cool brick. Max faced her, his hands resting on her shoulders, and he started to say how relieved he was to hear the doctor's diagnosis. It was something he had been hoping for because now they had a chance to begin again.

She started to shake, avoiding his eager gaze.

He forced a smile. "We have some guidance now, a real expert opinion."

She finally looked at him, trying to find the Max she had loved, the Max who used to sing to Lucie before bed, and make paper dolls on the living room floor, and hold Lucie high above the waves at Sanary. In the shade of an umbrella, set back from the shore, she had watched, quietly nervous each time a new wave broke and relieved each time Max held her up above the surf.

Pressing her back into the wall, she gestured to the space between them. "I don't want to be a mother again. I can't be anything to anyone again. Do you understand?"

He stumbled back and said that it was too easy to give up, and he wasn't going to give up. "It's not that you **can't**, Vera. You just don't **want** to."

Then he turned away, walking into the shimmering concrete, ignoring the people passing by who openly stared at them, wondering why she was sobbing, crushing her hat in her hands, and why he seemed disgusted by such a display of grief.

CHAPTER 24

SASHA

DECEMBER 31, 1944,
LOS ANGELES, CALIFORNIA

Sitting across from him, her elbows resting uneasily on the white tablecloth, Sasha's date looked everywhere but his face. She shifted in her velvet evening gown, with the puffed sleeves and high neckline, her hair swept up into an elaborately coiled design, a maze of auburn and gold. From the curtained stage, Dinah Shore's deep voice filled the microphone, singing "Speak Low." His friend Dex had set him up for New Year's with Helen, who worked for the naval auxiliary core and was a friend of Dex's girl, but he didn't know her at all. She looked just as uncomfortable as he was, having a first date on New Year's, a night burdened by heightened expectations.

They sat far back from the stage, gazing into a sea of close round tables. Little lamps illuminated laughing faces, with mink stoles thrown over bare shoulders, and he wondered if he should have taken her to the Cocoanut Grove instead. But here at the Mocambo, the damn parrots, cockatoos, and seagulls cawed to the music, causing a racket, their feathers aggressively fanning up in their glass cages that lined the walls—an odd attraction of this place.

When he complimented her dress, she passed him a fleeting smile, but then the ambient ephemera took over again: the swirl of waiters, cigarette girls, and festive balloons that crowded the low-ceilinged ballroom. A bottle of chilled champagne balanced in the ice bucket, and Sasha realized he'd already drunk most of it, while she'd barely sipped hers.

She realigned the cutlery while the waiter took their order, her nails shiny red against the silver.

He leaned over his plate. "Is everything all right?"

She produced another polite smile.

Some friends were supposed to meet up with them here, and he found himself hoping they'd come sooner, especially Dex, who now served in the coast guard after his ship, the **Yorktown** got torpedoed in the South Pacific. He was on the half that didn't blow up.

Hunched over the silverware, she whispered, "I just don't like New Year's."

"Wanna get out of here?"

"Oh, no. It's lovely."

Her retreat into stiff formality made him clumsy. Reaching for her hand again, he tipped over a champagne glass, bubbly liquid cascading over the tablecloth. When he signaled for the waiter, his elbow knocked the salt and pepper shakers to the floor, and at the sight of spilled salt, he swiftly picked up the shaker and tossed more over his shoulder.

It was something his mother always did, to ward off bad luck.

He tried again. "You sure? I mean, if you want to leave, we can leave. It's for show, this place. The crowd, photographers, the people."

The band started prepping for the next set. He was about to tell her that whatever it was, they'd order another bottle of champagne and wait for a slow song, but then he thought about the shoot starting next week, adrenaline coursing through him, and at the same time, he revisited some preliminary scenes for **The In-Between Man**, a welcome distraction to the mounting pressure. Sasha still couldn't believe shooting for **Clementine** would start in ten days. Jesus, he thought, that was soon. Too soon.

The overhead chandeliers dimmed, accentuating the glow of the table lamp. The first day of shooting loomed, and they only had fourteen days to shoot the entire movie, with only so much daylight for the scenes in Griffith Park. Sasha worried that Lambert might stick him with a bad cameraman, but at least Lambert couldn't push his mistress for the lead anymore; by a stroke of luck, Charlie had somehow twisted Mayer's arm to get him to release

Hedy Lamarr temporarily from her contract to do this little film.

He willed himself to feel as excited as Charlie was about the movie, but he couldn't stop mulling over all the little details that might go wrong on set. Things he couldn't foresee because he'd never done this before, and Charlie's half-joking advice about skipping lunch to stay on schedule didn't help much. He also worried that Hedy, who was such a big star, would sense his insecurity, like an animal smelling fear, and if the rest of the crew got a whiff of this, he'd be finished.

His date stared down at her charm bracelet and tugged at the miniature ballet slipper.

"You wanna dance?" he asked.

They were playing Count Basie's "Rusty Dusty Blues," the sax rich and voluptuous. He took her onto the dance floor and felt her body adhere to his, submitting to the music and to the other bodies spinning and dipping around them, half-closed lids and closely held hips, women's powdered cheeks resting on silk lapels.

Sasha held her velvet back, feeling it shift beneath his palm. Her hair smelled of apricots, and when he glanced down, she had assumed the same dreamy expression as the other women, as if they had all agreed to swoon and be swayed by the music and the men.

He dipped her, the tendons in her throat tensing,

and the effort of holding her like that caused a quick bright pain to spread over his shoulder for a few moments. She peeled back up, a flush tinting her cheeks, and he forced a smile, not wanting to draw attention to his wound.

She was about to say something when the set ended and everyone erupted into applause. The dance floor thinned and couples retired to their tables. The elaborate sound of a gong signaled that only ten more minutes remained of the old year.

As he took her by the elbow, turning toward their table, a woman seated on a curved banquette near the far end of the stage gave him pause. Her broad bony shoulders drew together when she leaned forward, allowing a man to light her cigarette. For an instant, the flame illuminated her features: dark, almond-shaped eyes, an elongated nose and sharp cheekbones, her face composed of competing angles that failed to create the symmetry of conventional beauty. Rolling waves of dark hair fell around her shoulders, diamonds glinting in her ears. She was a mirage of light and shadow, encased in a violet gown the color of a bruise.

Faintly aware of his date heading back to the table where they would sit in mild silence for the rest of the year, he maneuvered toward the woman's table, straining to decipher the mix of French, German, and English that they spoke. He wondered about the man who sat next to her. He looked older, with tired, small eyes. Sasha's heart lifted at the thought that he could be her brother or uncle. Now she spoke to the other woman, who wore a silk turban and a long coral necklace. The man noticed Sasha staring and said, "Happy New Year!" with a congenial smile, because it was New Year's Eve and everyone wanted to feel brotherly and forget about the war, at least for one night. Sasha tried to smile, but he couldn't take his eyes off her. A palpable sadness encased her while the other man poured her more champagne, and the turbaned woman told a joke that held no interest. She existed in another realm, causing her to appear disembodied, not entirely here.

Dex and his girlfriend, Ruth, were waiting for them at the table when they got back. He had his arm thrown over Ruth's shoulders, and she told them some convoluted story about the party they'd been to before this, at a club on the beach where she was a member.

"Oh, it was dull." Dex sighed.

Ruth punched him in the arm and smiled at Helen. "You always say that about my friends."

The countdown started. People blew into their miniature golden paper horns and drummed their palms against the tables. The birds were getting restless, cawing irritably in their cages. Silver balloons, held overhead by a net, would soon shower down on them. Everyone wore those pointed little hats, tilted at an angle, plumed and glittery. Helen put one on and took a bite out of her dark chocolate cake, the prongs of the fork lingering in her mouth. On stage, a voluptuous Betty Grable look-alike motioned to an oversized clock they had wheeled out, indicating only seven minutes remained, her lovely arms imitating the slow-moving minute hand.

"Hey," Sasha said over the noise, "I gotta hit the head."

Helen grabbed onto his wrist, staring up at him imploringly. "Don't miss it!"

"Course not," Sasha said, getting up. He threaded his way through the crowd, trying not to stare directly at the woman's table, which was to the left of the stage, but out of the corner of his eye, he realized she wasn't there with the rest of them. His eyes roved through the tightly packed room, straining to see around columns and checking the bar.

Running out of time, he took stock of the dance floor. She wasn't there. Again, his gaze traveled back to her table, and he noticed that the two men and the turbaned woman were craning their necks in the direction of the exit, a plate of untouched profiteroles before them. He ran toward the exit, squeezing between chairs and nearly upsetting a tray of champagne cocktails a waiter balanced overhead.

Stopping short in the hallway, he found her waiting at the coat check, the ticket poised between her gloved fingers.

He came toward her. "Happy New Year."

As if his voice had roused her from a dream, she

replied, "Happy New Year to you too," in a beautiful French accent that hurtled him back to the pier, the day of Pearl Harbor, with her standing there, the sun descending into the ocean. **It's her,** he thought, his heart in his throat, making it hard to speak.

She half smiled and flicked her hand in the direction of the hanging coats. "I've been waiting here forever. The girl said she was coming right back . . ." Her voice trailed off. There was something in her faraway expression, a restlessness that hovered around her like a fine mist, as though she wanted to be anywhere but here.

The crowd started counting down from sixty, and he felt a heated pressure, reminding him that Helen was waiting, he was being rude, when he wanted nothing more than to stay right here.

The woman sighed and rummaged through her clutch, fishing out a pack of cigarettes. Strong foreign ones.

He flipped open his lighter, the blue flame wavering between them.

She bent toward it, and he caught her scent of jasmine and something sharply citrus. Inhaling, she said, her mouth blooming with smoke, "Thank you."

"My pleasure." The words caught, making him sound nervous, adolescent.

Her eyes flashed conspiratorially when the gong went off, followed by applause and drunken laughter, the band rolling into the celebratory tune, "Accentuate the Positive."

She lightly touched his shoulder. "You're missing all the fun."

"I don't think so." He stood so close he could have traced the slant of her eyebrow with his finger. Her black pupils engulfed almost all of the deep brown.

She kissed him on the cheek, tantalizingly near his mouth, whispering, "It's bad luck not to kiss someone on New Year's Eve."

"It'd be even worse luck not to get your number," he whispered back, catching her elbow.

She shook her head, as if such an idea were outlandish, ridiculous.

He looked around for a scrap of paper, rooting through his pockets for a pen. He would give her his number, in case she changed her mind, but a crowd of garrulous drinkers trundled down the hallway in the same moment that the hatcheck girl appeared with a long mink coat.

The drinkers were singing "Auld Lang Syne," draped over one another, crowding the counter and shouting for the hatcheck girl to hurry up already.

Slipping on her fur, she mouthed "Good luck" before walking down the hallway and opening the padded leather door into a starless night. Her perfume lingered in the smoky air, and the way she half looked back, as though she regretted leaving the club as well as staying, as though she regretted everything, even herself, made him want to know her.

.   .   .

Primly alone, Helen waited, the table strewn with streamers. She sipped a glass of champagne while he explained that the line for the bathroom had been long, and before he knew it, the gong had gone off. His words hung unconvincingly in the air.

She tore at the edge of a paper doily. "Happy New Year to you too," she said.

At home alone after a silent car ride in which Helen's disappointment was palpable, Sasha spread out on the cool sheets, the open window inviting the fragrant night. The strong dry winds made everything tremble. The woman entered his thoughts again, her long angular frame trailing down the padded hall before she opened the door into the night, as though she existed outside of time. When he watched her walk away, a sense of loss streamed through him, as though something precious and rare was slipping from his grasp.

CHAPTER 25

VERA

JANUARY I, 1945,
SANTA MONICA, CALIFORNIA

She watered the orange trees, the thin stream sputtering over the roots, her bare feet sinking into the grass. A hummingbird quivered in front of the magnolia tree, searching for succor in the blossoms before flitting away. The new year shimmered with a belated, vengeful heat, the wind fiercely dry. They called it the Santa Ana, and it tightened her skin, cracking it in places.

Wiping her forehead with the back of her hand, she felt Max watching her through the kitchen window, but that hard-edged stone of resentment lodged within her, which she had cultivated and polished over the past months, kept her from turning around and waving, as she might have done in the past.

Last night, she'd felt ugly and ungenerous sitting

there among the others. Leon and Elsa told German jokes, and Max drank champagne as if it were water, his thigh pressed up against her thigh, his hand searching for hers under the table. As the night wore on, his desire grew treacly, and she wanted to get away from him. It reminded her of how in bed his clammy feet traveled over to her side, rubbing up against her calf suggestively while she feigned sleep.

As she sat there in that curved booth, watching the birds aggressively fan their jewel-colored feathers against the gilded cages, the turning of the old year into the new only made Lucie seem less real, adding another year to the distance between them. Vera could barely contain her alarm, smiling tightly at their comments while imagining her own face collapsing, her skin no longer adhering to bone, her bones disintegrating into dust.

Just before midnight, she'd lied and said she had a headache, getting up to go, ignoring Max's beseeching look. She thought he would at least follow her out, but this time he didn't.

Upset by her own selfishness and feeling as though she'd played the martyr, a role Max accused her of relishing, Vera repeatedly rang the bell for the coat check girl. No one came, and she stood there listening to the chorus counting down the seconds until the new year.

And then, that attractive American materialized,

smiling as if they shared some private joke. The way he unselfconsciously approached her, his presence filling the hallway, and the conversation he started as though they already knew each other, implying that only time and distance had unfairly kept them apart, made her feel persuaded in his favor. Perhaps he reminded her of the young American GIs pictured in the newspaper, liberating town after town. They were celebratory, aware of their potential and the potential of the world, infusing hope into places where she saw none. Compelled to say something to him, she made some banal comment about the new year, and this light banter had made her feel young, pretending that she also had nothing to lose.

When he asked for her number, she felt bad for him because, of course, he had no idea. She kissed him, her lips skimming his strong jaw, his pulse racing when she whispered into his neck, "Good luck," which she sincerely meant because luck wasn't a joke. It was cruel and merciless. She recalled the exhilarating run down the foothills of the Pyrenees, gripping Elsa's hand, believing they were lucky, and maybe they were, then.

Ever since the appointment with Dr. Bettelheim, Max's insistence that they try for another child had intensified, lacing the air with want and expectation. Vera thought it was Max's way of silently retaliating against her indecisiveness, but there was a startling aggressiveness to his insistence. When the lights went off, his weighty frame rolled on top of hers, and he caressed her face with the intent not just to seduce but to impregnate. Max began tracking her temperature, and the most likely hours of ovulation. He made charts on graph paper and urged her to see a specialist. He said they still had a window of opportunity, given that she was thirty-two, parroting the words from a manual that Vera had found between the pages of the phone book listing fertility doctors.

She tried, at first, to change her mind. Perhaps it wasn't wrong of him to want this. Elsa agreed, explaining that he was only trying to mend things, to move forward, somehow.

She dropped the hose, watching the water seep into the dirt, darkening it, and went to turn off the spigot. She didn't bother coiling up the hose, and instead left it stranded in the high grass. Through the kitchen window, she watched Max drying the porcelain teacups. She wondered if he would look up. She wanted him to notice that she had abandoned the hose haphazardly, willing him to comment on it so she could start a fight.

An empty flowerpot propped open the back door, and she wandered inside, sitting down at the kitchen table.

He dried a saucer, placing it inside the cabinet, and then turned toward her. His inquisitive, prodding look caused her insides to sharpen. "Elsa telephoned. She asked us over for bridge and oysters this afternoon."

Vera pressed her palms against the sides of her turbaned head. "We just saw them last night."

He thrust out his chin. "You don't want to go, then?" His sleeves were rolled up from doing the washing, and he pushed them up even more, revealing the bulbous blue veins running down his tan arms, spreading out into the tops of his hands. He had vigorous, able hands from playing so many instruments and composing so many scores, hands that still wanted so much more out of her, even after that blotch of blood in her underwear last week.

It's finished, she thought.

He took off his glasses and rubbed his eyes. "Just tell me what you want. Oysters and bridge, or we could go to the pictures. I hear there's something good playing at the Aero. A Western."

"Let's go to the pictures," Vera said, her realization so loud and clear, she almost wondered if he could hear it too: **I'm going to leave you.**

Max nodded and turned back to the sink.

She swallowed hard, feeling as though she had already said it as she watched him dry the last teacup.

CHAPTER 26

SASHA

JANUARY 1945, LOS ANGELES, CALIFORNIA

Driving home, he itched for a vodka to dampen the mixture of adrenaline and exhaustion coursing through him after the first week of shooting. Unbelievably, they were on schedule, making their days, even with Hedy's wardrobe crisis and Bob, the male lead's, initially wooden performance. Today, during the bar scene, Bob improvisationally grabbed Hedy's hand across the bar, and then Hedy softened, allowing for the chemistry to come alive between them. After that take, Bob loosened up, and his next scene clipped along at a much faster tempo.

Despite the first week's disappointments and unforeseen difficulties, Sasha's anxiety that no one would take him seriously proved untrue. He worked fast and decisively, changing a line that hit the wrong note, or deviating from his boards if a scene felt off, and everyone followed his lead, which in turn bolstered his confidence. The best part was having control over the story—not just writing it, but also deciding how it was told. And now, from the first line he had typed on his Royal, to the final roll of the credits, everyone on this picture was working to create his singular vision.

Now forced to witness the war from the sidelines, he would never experience what it would feel like to push those bastards back into Germany and see it through. But here, he'd tell this story from start to finish, without the interference of some hack director trampling on it or life intervening in some unforeseen way. And only he would be responsible for its failure or success, a pressure that fueled him forward.

Cigar dangling from his mouth, Sasha sped through the city, the light falling, a transparent crescent moon taking shape. Soon, the ocean would come into view, and the intensity of the day, with all of its little emergencies, would fade a bit.

As he pulled up to his house, the ficus trees offered shaded respite from the sun that bleached other streets, the concrete shimmering, mirage-like. He relished the crunch of leaves beneath his tires as he parked and, killing the engine, he stared out his window, watching his neighbor's son, Christopher, play handball against the rickety garage door of the apartment building across the street.

When Christopher waved, Sasha got out of his car, bringing over a brown bag of groceries. He did so every week, and every week the boy's mother left a note in his mailbox, in flowery cursive script, thanking him for the canned beans and sardines, the tuna fish and Coca-Cola. He never saw her during the day because she slept then and worked nights as a maternity nurse. It was another piece of the story he'd learned from Christopher, who said "maternity" with care, rolling over each syllable after which he went on a jag about how angels hovered in heaven, waiting to be born, but someone had to die for one of these babies-in-waiting to replace them, so it all worked out in the end.

"Hey," Sasha said, setting down the grocery bag on the concrete ledge that ran the length of the driveway.

Christopher kept playing handball, his cheeks molting pink from exertion. "Where ya been all day?"

"Shooting."

He hit the ball harder against the garage. "Out on the range? Will you take me? I'm a good shot."

Sasha laughed and said sure, but that wasn't what he'd meant. From behind the kitchen curtain, he sensed movement.

Christopher said he had to go, hugging the brown paper bag to his chest.

Sasha walked back across the street, mulling over

the call sheet for Monday, his thoughts flitting from notes that he had for the actors to his script for **The In-Between Man**, still in need of revision. And then he felt that sharp twinge again—every time he thought of her he felt it, similar to how he could be pointing and instructing the actors or bringing a cup of coffee to his lips when, instantaneously, he'd feel that tingling race down his arm or a dull aching pain spreading over his bad shoulder. Thinking of her was like that, catching him unaware, his mind tunneling back to how she wore grief as if it kept her alive, and when she wished him good luck, it was as if luck were an uncertain, untrustworthy thing, reserved for others. He wanted to know why her sadness seemed impenetrable, her self-deprecating manner hinting at something worse, something she was ashamed of, something she refused to forgive herself for . . . He wanted to know everything about her.

CHAPTER 27

SASHA

FEBRUARY 1945, VILLA AURORA, PACIFIC PALISADES, CALIFORNIA

After they wrapped the second week, Hedy invited Sasha to Villa Aurora, which she described as a slice of old Europe. At first, Sasha declined—he had to prep for next week. They were behind schedule, and still had a few more days of shooting left, including some big scenes—but when her new boyfriend, Otto Beckmann, the German artist, picked Hedy up, he insisted that Sasha join them, and Sasha gave into his jovial persuasions.

Sasha drove with the windows down, the sinking blue sky falling over the hills and the highway. The ocean was restless, waves towering to a full foamy height before crashing against the shore. Up ahead, Otto's bullet of a car veered over the yellow line and then back again, Hedy's silk scarf flickering in the wind, an emerald flame. Sasha followed Otto now, unsure where this house was. The sharp turn onto Sunset was a surprise, and then another quick one folded him into the hills, shaded by brush, sage, and eucalyptus trees. Otto slowed on the dirt road that zigzagged upward, cutting into the mountain, before he turned onto a shaded side street.

From here, Sasha made out parts of a Spanish villa, but the curved whitewashed wall and hedges hid most of it. Beyond the house, the Santa Monica Bay flashed with the illuminated pier, its steel roller coasters set against the blurry horizon.

Otto and Hedy walked toward him, speculating about who would be here. It was someone's birthday, a German writer Sasha didn't know. He heard a piano thundering over the din of dinner-party talk.

They made their way down the terra-cotta steps into an open-air patio, which had a lily pond in its center. Otto called out, "Sorry we're late, Elsa. But we brought a little treat for you. An American director, Sasha Rabinovitch."

The woman, Elsa, smiled up at him from the patio, the silk folds of her peridot kimono hanging down from her outstretched arm. "Please. Come inside." Sasha sensed her sturdy womanliness, her leonine grace, and liked her immediately.

She slid her arm through his and led him into the house. Two tortoises traipsed ahead, leaving a wet trail along the terra-cotta stones.

In the entryway, the scent of roasted meat hit

him and his mouth watered. "It's delicious, my duck," she said, as if reading his mind. In the same breath, she directed a housemaid to refill champagne glasses, gesturing toward the living room, where a swirl of men in cardigans and monocles conversed in a cacophony of German, French, English, and Russian. They reminded Sasha of Fritz Lang, whom he met a few months ago at a party. Lang had just finished directing **The Woman in the Window,** and he wondered if Lang might even be here.

Stepping back for a moment, he marveled at the beauty of the place: the whitewashed walls emanated a serene coolness, and views of the sea filled every window, while eucalyptus trees shaded the backyard, the leaves shimmering in the setting sun. Leather-bound novels lined the bookcases, and a gleaming black Steinway stood in the corner, where a man sat, studying some sheet music. An unbridled vibrancy pulsed through the room, as if the air were made of ideas—poetic, political, sharply satiric. Sasha caught bits and pieces of these conversations that rose up from the din: the incurable problem of music in films, if anyone would dare to return to Europe after the war, and was Germany forever ruined, its great cultural history swallowed up by the Nazi horror?

His mother had always wanted him to stand in such a room, and she had believed college was the way inside of it, and maybe it was, for some people. But he had done it his way. He recalled their recent phone conversation when he had told her he was finally directing his own picture, and yes, there was even a love story baked into it. She paused before congratulating him, but it was in her suspension of breath, the warm moment gathering around them, when he finally felt the rush of her approval.

Hedy took his arm, drawing him farther into the living room. She smiled playfully. "It's nice, isn't it? Our little European colony on the Pacific. Almost like home."

"Is it?" Sasha wondered, catching the regret in her voice.

"Otto's over there," Hedy said, motioning to his gleaming bald head. She steered them toward the open balcony doors, where Otto raised two champagne glasses for them. Whispering while she walked, she told Sasha that Leon, Elsa's husband, could be quite witty, his books sold extraordinarily well, even in America, and he thought very highly of himself. Sometimes too highly. And he was sexually ravenous.

"You know from experience?"

She gave him a little shrug. "Of course not. But I know about the little black notebook in which he records every ejaculation, the duration of it, what he ate beforehand, and how much he produced."

"What?"

"Elsa told me about it once. She doesn't mind his little book, but she gets furious when he breaks the rules and allows a woman to spend the night. Once, after he did this, she served them breakfast in bed, just to make a point. Strawberries and champagne. Leon found the whole episode hilarious."

"I bet," Sasha said.

"Hello, my **Vögelchen**," Otto said, handing Hedy a glass of champagne.

She draped a languid arm over his shoulders and sighed, motioning to Sasha. "He refuses to do more than three takes."

"I'll do more takes if you want to kill every ounce of spontaneity."

Hedy rolled her eyes. "You see what I mean?"

Sasha smiled, leaning against the stone balustrade, taking in the dry yellowish bluffs and palm trees, wondering what kind of life they lived out here, so far from town. Nestled within the swirl of animated conversation, he felt oddly familiar with its foreign cadence and timbre, soothed by the sound of languages he didn't understand. From the living room, someone started playing a few chords on the piano before breaking into a melody that cut to the quick: Sasha balanced on his father's shoulders, the passing tree leaves brushing his outstretched hand, his father whistling this tune, the pressure of his large hands clutching Sasha's small legs to keep him fastened there, Sasha laughing, fearful and giddy. The forest grew denser, his father kept singing, the sky lightened above them.

He turned to Hedy, his heart in his throat. "What is that song?"

She didn't hear him at first, laughing at something Otto had said, her porcelain skin flushed from the champagne. "Sorry?"

"The song," Sasha pressed. "Where's it from?"

"Oh, it's an old one . . . We sang it all the time as kids. **Ein Männlein steht im Walde ganz still und stumm.** A little man stands in the forest, completely still and quiet." She smiled at him, her eyes radiant with the past, and then whoever was playing started a Bach piece, the notes light and scampering.

Putting a hand on his shoulder, she said, "Sasha, are you all right?"

He must have looked undone by the song, by the sudden memory that plunged him back into those early years that his mother would never talk about. He replied, "Just tired from the week."

Elsa came out onto the patio and announced dinner, motioning for everyone to follow her into the dining room, which was on the far end of the house.

Sasha followed Hedy and Otto, their laughter reverberating in the vaulted hallway that connected the living room to the dining room. He paused for a moment, hands in his pockets, vaguely aware of the elegant staircase that led up to the second story, still unmoored by the sensation of wobbling on top of shoulders, the exhilaration of feeling closer to the trees, to the sky, to his father.

Passing under the whitewashed archway, he happened to look up and see a defined ankle, followed by the curve of a calf. He caught his breath when her dark eyes, rimmed with kohl, bored into him with startled delight.

She stopped in the middle of the stairs, her mouth slightly open, and then, in a moment of confusion, she ran back up.

All the air drained from his lungs, as if someone had punched him in the stomach. He exhaled, pivoting on his heel. Then a slightly older well-dressed man stormed down the stairs. Sasha recognized him too, from the club, but he didn't notice Sasha, consumed by what had occurred upstairs, muttering to himself in French before he disappeared into the dining room.

She returned, standing at the top of the stairs, gripping a metallic clutch. When she saw him, she broke into a faint smile before walking down at a measured pace.

He felt that same suspension of time and space, as if she were a magic trick, and there was no dinner party occurring in the next room, no applause, no wineglasses clinking or chairs scraping against the floor. They stood in a velvet cave, rife with anticipation of his hands cupping her bare shoulders, his mouth on her neck, her perfume flooding his senses.

"We haven't officially met." She held out a satin-gloved hand. "Vera Volosenkova." She raised an eyebrow. "And you are?"

"Aleksander Rabinovitch." He reached for his full name, when normally he would have just said Sasha, but next to the way she held herself, shoulders thrust back, her gaze intent and expectant, "Sasha" didn't sound good enough.

She smiled, and his heart lifted.

"Russian?" she asked.

"Yes."

"You have no accent. Is my accent very bad?"

"You have a wonderful accent."

She smiled again, and he felt as if his chest would burst. Then she touched his arm, lowering her voice. "I don't want to go in there."

He inhaled, breathing in every trace of her: jasmine and twilight, dewy grass after the sun has disappeared behind the trees. Luminous and sheer. He craved to feel the curve of her waist running under his hands, her protruding collarbone pressing beneath him, her breath sweeping over his skin.

He took her hand. "Then let's get out of here."

Her eyes widened and she seemed about to laugh. "Really?"

The back of his neck tingled. "Really," he said. "Come with me."

They sped toward Malibu, blond bluffs abutting the highway, the ocean a flat blue line, her hair whipping in the wind.

"You know, I saw you before."

"New Year's Eve."

He shook his head. "Ocean Park Pier. The day of Pearl Harbor."

She turned toward him, her cheek pressed against the brown leather headrest, and searched his face. "You became a soldier."

He caught her eye before refocusing on the road. "Yeah."

"And now you're home," she said, her voice as warm as the sun.

CHAPTER 28

VERA

FEBRUARY 1945, MALIBU, CALIFORNIA

They pulled up to Las Flores Inn, a glass stucco box perched over the water with a sign out front that promised sea lions at play. Walking into the dimly lit restaurant, she stared out at the windswept beach and indigo sky through the windows that wrapped around the room and said, "Perfect."

She didn't know why she was here, or what he was thinking right now, about her, about this situation, but an unexpected recklessness had urged her to drive off with him, erasing all those questions for the time being. And within that erasure, a sense of freedom rushed into her, something she hadn't felt in a long time. Something she craved, to step outside of herself, as if stepping out of an expensive dress and leaving it in a puddle on the floor.

They slid into a booth next to the window, and he ordered them clam chowder and saltines, sand dabs and shrimp cocktail.

When the vodka tonics came, Sasha raised his glass, the ice clinking against it. "To the future."

Her eyes glistened with uncertainty. "To the future."

The waves rose, a shimmering wall of green, before breaking.

Bing Crosby's "White Cliffs of Dover" played on the chrome jukebox lit up in ghoulish neon lime, and she wished for a song that wasn't so popular, a song that wasn't about the war. The euphoria of the car ride, the sense that they had escaped something together—she didn't want to lose that feeling.

He shifted in the booth, finishing off his vodka before ordering two more.

Vera still nursed hers. "When I saw you on New Year's Eve, I was miserable."

He reached across the table and took her gloved hand in his. Her eyes locked with his, and she realized she was shaking, biting her lower lip.

"Was that your husband I saw at the party, coming down the stairs?"

She breathed deeply. "I left him two weeks ago. Leon and Elsa have been so kind, letting me stay at Villa Aurora. But today I told Max that the minute this terrible war ends, I'm returning to France. He's very upset about it."

"He doesn't want to go back?"

"It's more complicated than that."

"Anyway, I . . ." He paused. "I don't care if you're married or moving away, like you say. I only want to be right here with you, in this booth, looking at the ocean." Their eyes met again, their shared gaze eliding the past and the future, and she wondered what he was running from, sitting here with her, a woman who was also running. Running from that shameful mistake that throbbed through her veins every minute of every day. She could never escape it, but tonight, she decided, offered a reprieve, motoring toward her like a rescue boat, its red light blinking in the dark.

She slid her gold wedding band over her knuckle and then back down again, and noticed the way he took out a lighter, debating if he should smoke, before sliding it under the butter plate. She noticed everything, and it made him nervous, understandably, but that's what writers do, even when they're not writing, she thought.

"Don't you speak any Russian?" she asked, her fingertip still tracing the scalloped place mat.

"Yiddish."

She smiled.

Sasha threw up his hands. "What's so bad about Yiddish?"

She stared into her drink. "Nothing."

He explained that they all spoke it growing up on the Lower East Side.

"And you live here now?"

"Yeah, I make movies."

She nodded and dipped a shrimp into cocktail sauce before setting it on her plate. "Little golden America," she murmured.

He asked if she meant **goldene medina**, the golden land, which was how everyone in the old country referred to America. "A few weeks before we left Riga, we became suddenly richer, more important, even though we hadn't even boarded the ship yet. My mother always used to laugh because when we got here, we lived in a tenement flat, worse off than we were in Russia." He paused. "We shared a bed that folded out of the wall. My mother worked for a tailor. Day and night, she was in that little shop."

"And your father?"

He looked uncomfortable, and she regretted asking. Falling silent for a few minutes, Sasha said, "He died before I was born."

The waitress cleared their plates, leaving the saltines that Vera now broke apart. Not taking her eyes off the tiny pieces, she said, "My father and I used to mock the poor Jews who flocked to America, as if America was so much better. As if America, with its promise of money, heals every wound." She shook her head. "And here you are, an example of the American dream, as they say." She looked up at him. "Well, as it turns out, we should have emigrated too. But we waited too long. And then it was too late."

. . .

The waitress approached with the dessert menu, her high chirping voice listing cream pies and tapioca pudding, none of which they wanted. Sasha waved her away, and Vera stared out at the ocean. He pressed her hand between his, and she felt the pressure of her wedding ring between his palms, and wondered if he felt it too, a reminder that she still technically belonged to someone else, the little piece of gold symbolizing a promise that she was now breaking. But Max had broken something deeper, his the greater betrayal, and she recalled the first moment of it with utter clarity: when he stared at her through the detention-camp fence, only worried about his own survival, Lucie erased from his mind. In that moment, the promise between them began to shatter, splintering over days and weeks and years. Splintering into now.

Pushing that thought away, she suddenly got up and slid into his side of the booth, allowing her skin, her breath, her wild heart, her body to take over, to direct her. Her hands rested on the back of his neck, her eyes fluttering closed, and he found her parted lips and closed his eyes too, and she braced for the sensation of falling. He drew her close, his palm spreading over the dip in her lower back, pulling her into this shared desire that obliterated guilt, remorse, the past and the future, vibrating only with now.

She whispered into his neck, "Let's spend the night together, at least."

In the spectral moonlight, half covered by the sheet, she cradled her head in one arm, the other hand balanced on her hip, holding a cigarette. The motel room was simple and clean, with windows opening to the sea, and oil paintings of the redwoods. They were lucky, the motel clerk said; this was the last room. Otherwise they would have had to try farther up the coast. Smoking in bed, she contemplated how easily they'd decided to stay for the night, as though they were conspiring outlaws, muffling their laughter as the hotel clerk unlocked the door, eyeing them with distaste, probably thinking this was how all lovers acted.

Once the door closed behind them, they couldn't wait to be unencumbered by clothing, her shallow breath in his ear, the real smell of their bodies beneath her sun-filled perfume and his cigars. The zipper almost broke on the side of her dress, but she didn't care. She clamped her legs around him and pulled him into her with her thighs, squeezing both his shoulders, but then he yelped out in pain, half collapsing onto her chest, laughing at himself, explaining his shoulder injury from the war, and then she held his head to her chest, whispering, "Sorry, sorry," while he kept laughing, and then he begged, half joking, "Don't hurt me," and she said, laughing quietly, "I'll try not to," but, she thought, that was the promising delight of first encounters: this gleaming, clean slate, without any hurt yet, without any history. Unlike the way she and Max could flash around the wounds they'd given each other at a moment's notice, calling up banks of resentment, and the sadness beneath it, their mutual pain right there beneath the surface, waiting for the tiniest scratch to unleash it.

Afterward, he traced the fuzziness of her earlobe while she stroked the dark hairs on his chest, their legs intertwined. Her head on his heart, he traced the long line of her neck, and then followed the curve of her body until he couldn't reach any farther, stopping at her abdomen, the white raised scar beneath his fingers.

She glanced up at him, her eyes liquid in the moonlight. "She wouldn't come out any other way." Shifting positions, she drew the sheet around her. "When they brought her to me, the first thing I said was 'Welcome to the world. I promise it's not so bad.'" Vera shook her head. "I lied to her." When she told Sasha this, that moment felt so close, as if she still held Lucie to her chest in a bundle of muslin, peering down at her closed eyelids, translucent, as delicate as flower petals while she slept, and Vera watched over her, willing the moment to never end, willing that she could always hold her this closely, protecting her from the world.

They had left the windows open, and the breeze now lifted up the wooden blinds before they clattered against the window frame, the night air carrying the scent of salt water and dank seaweed. Sasha swallowed and drew Vera closer. "My mother was married for ten years before she had a child. My grandmother said dybbukim whisked away her unborn until one day they got tired and gave up. Then I came."

Vera lay still, listening intently.

"The funny thing was, her husband apparently really wanted a child and complained about not having one all the time, blaming her, and then, after he died, she had a son, and my grandmother always said it was revenge, a punishment for saying all those years of childlessness were my mother's fault."

The sharp white of the moon bullied through the blinds, bars of light patterning over the sheets and their bodies. "Your father?" she asked, confused.

"What?"

"When you said 'her husband,' did you mean your father?"

"Yes, that's what I meant," he said quickly.

"It's terribly hard to lose a child, or to be unable to have any, especially for mothers," she replied, sensing that he didn't want to talk about his father.

"But we shouldn't compare tragedies. For example, the way people talk now: he lost all his family in the camps, as opposed to just one sister, or she lost her husband and her children, as opposed to just one child, or someone's entire village has been erased off the map, with no one and nothing left, so then they get the prize. They look at me, a selfish woman mourning only one daughter while living in a nice house, far away from the destruction, and I know they think I'm ungrateful, while they cling to that insipid phrase 'Life is a gift.'"

She turned onto her side to face him.

"Who do you mean by 'they'?" he asked.

"You know. That faceless chorus always judging you, deeming everything you do as either praiseworthy or terribly wrong."

"Yeah," Sasha added softly, "I know what you mean."

She curled up into the crook of his arm, and felt his warm pliant skin against her cheek, and closed her eyes, shutting out the white walls, the crashing waves, the sound of a couple stumbling down the hallway. She wanted to shut out everything and listen to the rise and fall of his breath, proof that he was still here, that she was still here, and that the night still held them. The sky lightened into a silvery gray, and sleep finally took her, dreamless and rich.

CHAPTER 29

VERA

FEBRUARY 1945, MALIBU, CALIFORNIA

Her eyes closed, fluttered open, and closed again, the unfamiliar motel bathroom blurring in the corners of her vision, until she looked up, her chin dripping water, and caught Lucie in the mirror. She was eighteen, fully grown, calmly watching Vera, as though reassuring her that it was all right. **Believe me**, she seemed to say, and then the image vanished and Vera reeled, gripping the sink, and whispered into the still air, "Lucie? Lucie?"

In the milky dawn, she steadied herself against the door frame, her heart pounding. She watched Sasha sleep, the room filled with the sound of the ocean tides rushing in and then receding back out again. She could listen to it forever, the sound a sanctuary, as she knew that if the tides stopped, it meant the world had stopped. Glancing around the room, she noted the same paintings of the redwood forest on the walls, her silk evening dress hanging over the chair in front of the armoire, and Sasha still here. Last night, meeting him on the stairs at Villa Aurora and then impulsively leaving with him wasn't something she would normally do. But the meaning of "normal" or "expected" didn't amount to much anymore.

She went back into the bathroom and waited in the blue quiet, willing Lucie to reappear, but the visitation, or whatever it was, had passed. Still, Vera remained there, wondering whether if she sat very still on the bathtub ledge, it would happen again. Closing her eyes, she tried to feel Lucie's presence, but she only heard seagulls' cries echoing off the ocean, and then water running from the neighboring bathroom, and the sense that the day was beginning.

She got back into the bed with Sasha, self-conscious in her nakedness, tucking the sheet around her. She hadn't been naked in front of anyone else except for Max. He knew her body, its idiosyncrasies, and this shared intimacy grew over the ugly parts of themselves, but she didn't know how she really looked to someone else, in this unfiltered, unmarried light. His back faced her, and his olive skin, the broad outline of his shoulders, appeared so different from her husband's back. The sight startled her, and yet she reached out and touched his shoulder, holding her breath, wondering about the war, where he was when he got shot. What he saw and experienced, and carried within him now. He twitched in his sleep. Did the image in the mirror mean that Lucie was dead, a secret signal to Vera that she had finally crossed over into another realm, spirited outside of time? Or was she still alive, closer than before, and that was why she came to Vera, to convey her proximity, and perhaps, Vera considered, her palm cupping his warm shoulder, had Sasha even triggered Lucie's appearance?

She sighed and turned onto her back, staring at the white ceiling, wooden beams running through it, realizing how it looked, waking up in a cheap motel room on the beach next to this American, even if he seemed so wholly good, bursting with optimism, with the idea that you could just leave a room if you didn't want to stay in it, and you could fight a terrible war and return unscathed, sleeping soundly through the night.

Reaching over to the nightstand, she found a pack of his cigarettes and pulled one out, sinking back into the headboard, Max's voice in her head: **This is how you deal with your grief? Sleep with an American? As if he could ever understand you? It's embarrassing, Vera . . .** She lit the cigarette, holding the smoke in her throat, trying to push his voice out of her head—was she imagining Max's thoughts, or were these her own?

Sasha stirred. He turned toward her, his eyes opening, searching for hers. She discarded the cigarette in the ashtray next to the bed and sank down to his level, and for a moment, she allowed herself to be captured by his sweetness and light, by his sincere happiness at waking up next to her, as though this were the first morning of their lives.

He asked if she was all right, pulling her close to him, and she hedged, mentioning the vividness of a recent dream, afraid to tell him about Lucie in the mirror. It was too soon. He said he also had strange dreams, dreams that felt like they would never end, before admitting that he'd watched her sleep. She blushed, self-conscious again, and then she got up to dress, allowing him to see her in this unadulterated light, realizing how different it felt to walk across the room and slip into her dress while he watched her from the bed, closely and carefully, unlike Max. They'd grown so used to each other, they didn't really see each other anymore, their bodies muted, daily exchanges as colorless as water, unless it was a fight, both of them electrified by the anger, and only then did she feel close to Max again. No, she thought, the black silk cool against her skin, that wasn't a way to live, ricocheting between nothing and rage.

.   .   .

Over breakfast, Sasha asked how she got to America, and if it was difficult to get out of France. Haltingly, she recounted the story of how they had to flee, forced to leave their daughter, Lucie, behind.

"I believed the free zone would stay free, and we'd get her back. That the war would end soon." She scrutinized the silverware, pushing the prongs of the fork into her index finger. "I was wrong. About everything. We had to leave quickly. Our governess, Agnes, took Lucie to her hometown, and hid her there. For two years she wrote me letters. Coded, of course, but I knew Lucie was well looked after. Children become letters—a woman told me this at Gurs. I suppose that woman felt sorry for me, but the phrase still haunts." She stopped to observe the waitress balancing a tray laden with plates.

"I'm sorry." His eyes softened, not looking away as she'd thought he might.

Through the window, Vera stared out at a few swimmers subsumed by waves, little dots in green foam, and continued. "Last June, the war almost seemed over, with the Allies flooding into France, liberating town after town. I had so much hope." She stared at him. "You know?"

"Yeah," Sasha said, leaning toward her across the table. "After D-Day, it felt like the end was close. But it wasn't. Still isn't."

She lit a cigarette, clenching the lighter with too much effort. "It felt so close for us too, as if I could almost see Lucie before me. But"—she exhaled a mouthful of smoke—"Agnes lived in Oradour-sur-Glane, where she was hiding Lucie." After a moment, she saw from his expression that he registered the town, remembering what had occurred there.

"In my mind, she's still four, wearing that black pinafore and reciting those patriotic French songs." Her eyes widened, glistening with tears.

He leaned forward and placed his hand over hers. "Oh, God, Vera. I'm so sorry." And then he said all anyone wants is to survive, to live; that's what she had tried to do for Lucie, hiding her in that town, but how it happens is up to fate and circumstance. He told her that during the war, he wasn't some hero who deserved the Purple Heart; he only wanted to survive, to get through it. "If I'd stopped even for a second to look around that beach, or stumbled and didn't keep running, I wouldn't have made it . . ." He trailed off, passing a hand through his hair, and she wondered if he was trying to reassure her, to convey that she had acted to the best of her abilities, given the immediate decisions those days demanded, and that the slightest hesitation would have killed her, and killed Lucie.

Tossing a crumpled bill onto the table, Sasha whispered, "Let's get out of here."

He guided her down the rickety wooden steps leading to the beach, the wide-open sky a relief from the oppressive clamor of the restaurant. They walked along the lapping shoreline, his hand finding hers, their strides coalescing into a shared rhythm; she felt his calluses, and then the softness in the middle of his palm. They came to the black wet rocks that encroached on the sand, where they couldn't walk any farther without crawling over them. She hooked both arms around his waist and tilted back, as if he were a sturdy tree, the sun delicious on her skin.

Closing her eyes, Vera pictured Sasha fighting in France, breathing the same air as Lucie and walking beneath the same sky, and she wondered if he would somehow lead her to Lucie.

CHAPTER 30

SASHA

FEBRUARY 1945, MALIBU, CALIFORNIA

The cold ocean washed over their feet, and his head lightened in the sun, and he was aware again that they were new to each other, despite how at home he felt with her. But the morning was fragile, the air made of glass, her movements so quick and bird-like that it startled him when she took out a cigarette, her hand cupping the blue flame until it lit, and asked about his film.

Sasha shrugged. "We have three more days of shooting. I hope by the end of it, there will be something there. Something good."

She slid her hand under his shirt. "It will be good."

They turned back toward the restaurant, which from here looked like a tiny box on stilts. She picked up a violet seashell, a miniature fan in her palm, and asked him what it was like, to write screenplays.

While Sasha talked about starting as late as possible into the story, his thoughts were on Vera. He didn't know how she would ever fully recover. All she had was the official record of the massacre, her daughter's name missing from the list of the dead, a name that would forever remain unaccounted for. Sasha saw it on Vera's face, that whisper of hope trailing her, driving her to search further and further, until what? She found a record of death? Something tangible that would prove Lucie's fate?

His hand spread over the small of her back as they walked. "You don't want to spend a lot of time on backstory. That just weighs everything down, makes the script cave in on itself."

That whisper of hope suggesting Lucie might not have died and could be alive somewhere else, somehow, this type of hope was the worst kind.

Then again, he'd seen amazing things: families hiding in a hole in the forest; tunnels dug deep beneath the border through which the lucky few passed into Switzerland; children stowed away in cellars who managed, somehow, to quietly stay alive.

But the thought seemed far-fetched, a fantasy of the living about the dead.

Sasha drove her back to Villa Aurora, and the image of Vera getting out of the car, still wearing her black evening dress, a disbelieving smile playing across her lips and the small wave she gave him when he drove away replayed in his mind.

They had shared the night together, but at the same time, he didn't know if she would see him again. Plagued by uncertainty and guilt over her daughter, Vera couldn't be with him, or maybe with anyone, he realized, until she knew the truth. He felt a sharp stab at the thought of not seeing her again; it took him by surprise, the sense that she was already slipping away from him and there was nothing he could do about it.

He recalled the moment when he woke up next to her, and she was already awake, her dark liquid eyes abstracted, captivated by a parallel life that washed over the present, muting it, as if she'd been somewhere else, far away, maybe reuniting with her daughter in dreams. And then it jarred him when she asked about his dreams, as if she knew he'd dreamed of his father. The dream started the same way as the memory: He was riding on his father's shoulders through the Rumbula forest, the sharp smell of pine trees gathering around them, branches crunching under his boots as he sang about the little man alone in the forest, his voice melodious and sweet, the two of them laughing, Sasha's hands cupping his stubbled cheeks. He didn't want to let go, but his father started rushing, rushing him back to his mother—he had to leave now. At the house, his mother pulled him from his father's shoulders. Sasha cried, as if he'd been pulled from the world.

· · ·

At the moment, his outfit, the 16th Infantry, was pushing through Faymonville into Belgium to breach the Siegfried Line. He had a map tacked up over his desk to track them, putting a red pin in every city they took: Kreuzau, Vettweiss, Gladbach, Metternich. Sasha knew that even if the Germans retreated and surrendered without much of a fight, his unit still fought the harsh cold—frostbite, trench foot, and damp fatigues—as they trudged across icy landscape, wrapped in snow capes, white blankets, anything to blend into the snowy background. Keeping track of the guys eased some of the guilt that he wasn't with them, seeing it through to the bitter end, while at the same time, he felt lucky to be home, working, with all his limbs, and his mind, intact.

Are you even listening to me?" Hedy snapped the next day on set.

"You're worried about the scene," Sasha said, trying to focus, but these last days of shooting had dragged, leaving everyone restless. And Charlie had just submitted **The In-Between Man** to the major studios. The response wasn't great.

The light was fading, and Ernest, the cameraman, signaled that they needed another take, fast, before the sun went. With only a few days left of shooting,

Lambert sat in a director's chair, his heavy tweed thighs jutting out, arms crossed over his chest, nervous they might go over budget.

Sasha scratched his neck. "Two more takes. Hedy, let's try it out with the kiss on top of the hand. And then we'll wrap."

Sasha walked to his car, the sky purpling, mulling over tomorrow's call sheet, depressed by the studios' response to **The In-Between Man**. Charlie had called him last night with the news that they found it un-American and unpatriotic—no one wanted to touch it. Sasha argued that it dared to show humanity in its true light, not how it's supposed to be, and it frustrated him when Charlie served up the same pat response about writing more sympathetic characters. He didn't understand why characters couldn't be sympathetic **because** they were deeply flawed and the audience witnessed them grappling with their flaws instead of skipping around as if they were the greatest people on earth. Thinking about this, he half listened to Lambert trying to convince him to come to Chasen's for ribs and chili. "I hear they have a barber and a sauna in the back," Ernest added, and then the second AD mentioned that Gary Cooper played Ping-Pong there on Friday nights.

But Sasha knew how these evenings went. After Chasen's, they'd move on to the Troc, or La Rue for another drink and then a nightcap. His first AD,

Jack, was going to a fight at the Hollywood Legion Stadium, which was vaguely tempting, but he owed his mother a telephone call.

On the way home, he stopped at the grocery for a pint of vanilla ice cream and root beer for Christopher. The boy usually waited up for him, hawk-like, on the cracked apartment steps, but when Sasha pulled onto the street, he wasn't there, the windows dark.

He propped up his feet on his desk and ate Christopher's ice cream straight from the carton. After the operator put him through, the telephone rang and rang.

Maybe their dinner guests were still there, or it was bingo night at the country club.

When he was about to hang up, Dubrow's muffled voice flooded the line. "Sasha?"

"Yeah?"

"Oh, I'm glad you called."

He abandoned the spoon in the ice cream. "Everything all right?"

"Your mother. She's been complaining. I told her to see a doctor, but she refuses."

"She hates doctors. Thinks they make people sick."

Dubrow sighed. "Don't I know it." And then he broke into a litany of her symptoms. A swollen stomach, pelvic pain. Her skirts and slacks didn't fit anymore, tight around the middle. Yesterday the housekeeper said she'd found some bloodstains in Leah's laundry.

"Could you put her on, please?" Sasha asked.

The line crackled with static, and then Dubrow's voice intoned her name. It took a while. Sasha started pacing the small length of the room, holding the phone up against his ear, watching the cord's curlicues elongate into a reluctant line.

"Sasha?" She sounded out of breath.

"Ma?"

"You called later than usual."

"Okay," he said, trying to detect something different in her voice.

"Don't call so late next time."

"How are you, Ma?"

"Me?"

"Who else do you think I'm talking about?"

She laughed a little. "There's nothing new over here. Just a mountain of snow in the driveway, the streetlights are out, and Doris threatened to quit again."

"Hmmm," Sasha said, noticing Gloria's kitchen light flickering on, followed by belligerent yelling.

"How's the picture going? Something about an outlaw? I don't know why you don't make something more romantic. A love story. Everyone loves a love story."

He sank into his swivel chair. "There is a love

story in it . . . remember?" The ice cream carton left a creamy halo on the desk. "Ma, what's going on? You're talking too fast, like you don't want me to know something."

"For crying out loud, I'm fine. Everyone's making a big fuss over a little bit of indigestion. They call it irritable bowel syndrome. I've already boiled the skin of a pomegranate, dried it, and ate it with a dash of beeswax and a spoonful of egg yolk, and washed it down with a shot of vodka, the way we used to do it. Already I'm feeling better. Probably just too much cake. You know, wintertime, that's what happens. Everyone comes over for tea, and they bring me a cake, I bring them a cake, we eat too much cake." She drew a breath and then said if she had grandchildren to chase, she would be slimmer and healthier, but because he refused to settle down, she only sat on fancy couches, forced to admire pictures of other people's grandchildren. While eating cake. "'He's so smart,' 'he's the best baseball player,' 'she has her mother's eyes'—do you think I enjoy listening to this, nodding and smiling and feeling humiliated that I have nothing to show for myself? Nothing," she repeated, more to herself than to him.

He almost mentioned Vera, to stop her lamentations, but he thought better of it. Yes, she was Jewish and Russian, but not his mother's type of Russian Jew. She would get suspicious. Instead, he would write to his mother about Vera. She couldn't talk back to a letter. He'd dated Christian girls before, Polish ones from Coney Island, with their dark lipstick and tight sweaters, and his mother had coolly dismissed them, knowing it wouldn't last. But this was different.

CHAPTER 31

VERA

FEBRUARY 1945,
SANTA MONICA, CALIFORNIA

Vera rang the doorbell, her chest tight with anticipation. When he had dropped her off at Villa Aurora last Saturday afternoon, she doubted that she would see him again, already thinking of their night together as a present she might occasionally unwrap before she returned to the agonizing wait for the war to end.

Then that night when the phone rang, she picked up, half hoping and half fearing it would be him.

"When can I see you again?" he asked, his breath filling the line, and she stammered that she wasn't sure, her voice thick in the back of her throat, the race of her pulse making her hands shake. He invited her to dinner at his house next weekend, and then the phone call ended as abruptly as it had begun, and she held the receiver, staring down at the little black holes embedded in the mouthpiece as if something of him lingered there.

Over the course of the week, she almost told Elsa that she had seen Lucie in the mirror at the motel the night she spent with Sasha. And that the mirror-Lucie had grown into a beautiful eighteen-year-old who wore a yellow blouse with puffed sleeves, her hair finally brushed. It almost seemed as though Lucie pitied Vera for still being here, tormented by the past, whereas she appeared untouched by it.

From across the street, the popping of a toy gun made her flinch. A kid in a cowboy outfit sprawled out on the sidewalk, playing dead, while another boy twirled the gun back into his holster. A girl watched them, her hip jutted out in disapproval. From over the adjoining hedge, an old woman peeked at Vera and clucked her tongue, puckering her thin lips.

Vera felt her cheeks burn, wondering if the woman detected the guilty heat pouring off her, despite how much Vera tried not to feel it.

The old woman still stared, her crooked mouth hanging open.

Vera looked away, studying the power lines overhead, disbelieving that she was actually standing here, on his doorstep, all knotted up with nerves, anticipating how his touch lit her up for those temporary seconds, but then she felt ashamed of this pleasure. Maybe she only saw him to keep the lights on for herself, so that when she found Lucie, there would be something of herself left to give.

The door swung open and Sasha stood there, sweating slightly in a button-down shirt through which she detected the faint outline of an undershirt, a truly American fashion. He broke into a relaxed smile, and explained, while herding her inside, that he hadn't heard the bell and he was cooking something in the back, and would she like a glass of wine?

A towel dangled from his shoulder, and she tugged it off, twisting it around her wrist.

"Hey, I need that," he said, pulling her close; he gave her a long searching kiss. He tasted of cigars, wine, pepper. "Keep me company," he called over his shoulder, and she followed him, taking in the living room, the low-slung chairs and a white wool rug over the blond wood floor, a glass coffee table with slanted chrome legs. Vera followed him into the narrow galley kitchen, and wondered if he could sense her nervous indecision.

Leaning against the opposite counter, she watched him stir the sauce simmering on the stove.

"This is a recipe from an Italian lady who used to live one floor up from us," he said. "Tedora Binaggi. She cooked all day, and I would smell the garlic and the olive oil and tell my mother that she had to cook like that. The Jews and the Italians, we were all kind of crammed together."

Vera nodded, struggling to imagine how he had lived, recalling her time in New York: looking through the frosted hotel windows out onto other windows, feeling crushed by the rush of business-men in overcoats barreling down the sidewalks. When she took a few sips of red wine, her limbs loosened, and she felt more at ease.

He talked while he cooked, opening drawers and sprinkling salt and chopping parsley, whereas the rare times when she cooked, she had to concentrate, finding all the cutting and the peeling burdensome, her mind drifting until suddenly the pot boiled over with foamy water, burning out the flame beneath it.

He turned off the stove and transferred the pasta into a colander, tossing it before drizzling it with olive oil. He joked that the army had refined his cooking skills as he reached for plates, and closed a drawer with his elbow.

She watched as he carried their plates to the table, his back moving underneath his shirt, his stride long and confident in his slacks. "Holed up in pup tents, in the middle of the Algerian Desert, feasting on K rations; anything tasted good under those condi-tions." The dining table was already set, long thin white candles waiting to be lit.

Vera sat down opposite him.

He poured more wine into their glasses, and for the first time, he seemed self-conscious.

"This is wonderful," Vera said, draping the nap-kin across her lap, and he said that she was probably used to cooks and servants. "I can tell, just by look-ing at you."

She blushed.

He poured more wine into their glasses. "My mom moved away from the city. She doesn't lift a finger anymore. They have a maid who cooks and cleans and whatnot, but I think she misses it, doing everything herself. She sure gives the maid grief."

Vera smiled into her wine. "You must think I'm spoiled."

He pinched his fingers together. "A little bit."

She laughed and said the food tasted good. Very good. "See, I'm not spoiled. I even like your spa-ghetti."

He leaned back into his chair and gave her an ap-praising look. "I'll cook for you anytime. Anything you want."

She blushed again. He referred to the future so casually, as if it were a given. But it was cruel to en-tertain it, and cruel she'd even come here tonight, giving him that hope. She took a hasty sip of wine and tried not to look at his open face, and instead asked how the film was going. He sighed and ex-plained that they'd finished the shoot, and now they were cutting the film.

"Are you happy it's done?"

He smiled halfheartedly and said of course, but the movie he really wanted to make had just got-ten rejected by every studio in town. Shrugging, he added, "They only want to see America as one hundred percent good, including any American who ever fought in the war."

"No ambiguity . . . all black or white?" she ventured.

"Exactly!" Sasha said, newly frustrated.

"They might not understand what war does. How it threatens a person's"—she searched for the right words—"sense of himself, and of the world . . . undoing all that was previously known and trusted." She paused, her brow furrowing. "We should see ourselves reflected in your flawed characters. That's more honest, more truthful, as opposed to some beautiful lie."

"Yes," Sasha agreed, gazing at her from across the table. "It's more interesting that way. More real."

Vera felt a pang of recognition because he was describing her struggle. She berated herself for leaving Lucie in a country overrun by beasts. In rarer moments, she told herself that she had tried to save Lucie from deportation and death, but she had failed, and she couldn't stop hating herself for this mistake.

"What are you thinking?" Sasha asked, reaching for her hand across the table.

"You've made such a nice dinner, and I don't want to ruin it . . ." Sweat sprung up between her breasts, trickling down her sides. When she picked up her fork again, her hand trembled, and she felt as if he could see right through her. "You shouldn't waste your time with me."

The open French doors allowed in a gentle breeze.

From the radio Josephine Baker's velvety voice was singing, "I'm feelin' like a million."

He stood up and held out his hand, urging her to dance with him. Her heart lifted at how little he wanted, while trying to suppress the memory of Max taking her to see Josephine Baker in **La Revue Nègre**, in celebration of their engagement. They ended the night with cocktails at Fouquet's, squeezed into a banquette, bathed in the amber glow of the chandelier.

Sasha and Vera danced, maneuvering between the furniture. Luckily, she didn't know the next song—it only pulsed with this moment. A woman's low throaty voice sang about love on a summer day that withers away too soon, as short-lived as a rose in full bloom.

The lit candles cast a flickering gauzy light over the walls. Putting her cheek against his chest, she felt his warm palm press into the small of her back, his fingers tapping lightly there, in time with the music. She squeezed her eyes shut, listening to the rise and fall of his breath, focusing only on this moment. Their movements slowed until they stood still, kissing and touching each other in the middle of the room, not even realizing that the radio had cut to a jingle for Palmolive soap, or that when he carried her up the stairs, the candles continued to burn on the table, where they'd abandoned an uncorked bottle of red wine that would spoil overnight.

. . .

She sat up in his bed, naked under the thin sheet. Now, in the stillness, after that tension she had felt through dinner, almost unbearable, had broken, after their bodies had reunited and intermingled and they knew each other again, she felt a sense of release, sated and hollowed out by their exertions. The air between them was languid and soft, and she enjoyed this interval for its fallow, blank quality, her mind finally quiet, her body motionless, the constant recriminations from that invisible chorus temporarily muzzled.

She stared out at the dark coast. The walls were made of windows, except for the back one, with the bed's headboard pushed up against it. It was almost the same view from Villa Aurora, but closer and lower, without the grand sweep of things, yet between houses and palm fronds, she glimpsed the ocean. Gathering the sheet around her, she stood up and walked around the room, while Sasha drowsily smoked one of her French cigarettes.

She ran her hand over his typewriter and pressed a key, recalling the sound of work and productivity. A pile of scripts sat on the desk.

"All drafts," Sasha informed her. "Nothing worth reading."

Also, on the desk: a tin case of Havana cigars and a framed black-and-white photograph of a woman who looked as if she were from another time. A pretty peasant, Vera thought, tracing the frame with her fingertip. Dark eyes peered out with a look of mischievous melancholy, her hair covered by a scarf, the rest of her body obscured by the thick folds of a skirt and heavy overcoat. The woman stood in front of a wooden house, the chimney emitting spirals of white smoke into the winter air.

"That's my mother," Sasha said, the bed creaking beneath him as he sat up. "It was taken when she was young, in Latvia, the year I was born. It was during the war, but she always used to tell me the Germans weren't so bad then. The Cossacks were the worst. I think she still has nightmares about those raids. When she was a child, she used to hide in the neighbors' cellar, praying no one would find her."

Vera nodded, staring at the photograph. "The word 'pogrom' was forbidden in our house, as if just by uttering it, you could summon it." She sat down in his desk chair, tightening the sheet around her. "As a special treat, my father took me to Easter ceremonies at the Russian Orthodox Church. The clanging of the church bells made the ground shake beneath my feet. The priests in white gowns paraded three times around the church, and then a strange old woman sitting next to me kissed me three times while crying out, '**Kristos voskres!**' At home, to continue the festivities, we ate **kulich** and **paskha** and peeled hard-boiled eggs that the cook had decorated with little flowers and crosses on the shells." She laughed and shook her head. "I loved those pretty little eggs and felt so bad when we broke them."

He lit her another cigarette, their fingers brushing when he passed it to her. An ambulance bell careened through the night before fading away. She asked to turn on the radio and he nodded.

"When you were little, did you know . . . that you were Jewish?" he asked, turning onto his side as he leaned on his elbow, as if he were at the beach. She didn't know if he would ever fully grasp where she came from: a place where people didn't walk around proclaiming themselves to be Catholic or Jewish, where one didn't constantly point out where one was from, wearing it like an honorary badge as they did here, as if being from Iowa or New York or Chicago demanded praise. At a low volume, Mozart's **Die Zauberflöte** played in the background; it soothed her.

Vera swiveled in the chair. "Growing up, we never set foot in a synagogue, and we knew very few Jews. Only a tiny fraction of us were allowed to live in St. Petersburg. Most were bankers, like my father, or industrialists and lawyers, and almost all of them had been atheists since the Enlightenment." She paused, musing at the smoldering end of her cigarette, and recalled her father's dismay when reading about the Israelites in the paper. She had asked him, knowing that they were Israelites as well but in some secret way, the better kind, why he didn't just have the family all baptized if being one caused so much distress. She must have been seven or eight, around the time when a child starts to ask such questions. He paled, and then murmured that they would never convert, as if she had suggested something ungodly. He rose from his velvet chair and wandered out of the room, dropping his newspaper on the Persian rug as he went. He had just returned from the Egorov baths, where he often went in the afternoons, and his skin glowed a dewy pink from the steam and birch branches used to improve blood circulation. She pictured his hair, wet and combed back from his forehead, the grooves left by the comb visible, but her question had immediately drained the freshness from his face, and he suddenly appeared gaunt and ashen.

Vera bored her cigarette into the ashtray. He was dead now and she had converted to Catholicism in '39, hoping that might save them. She sighed, aware that Sasha was contemplating her from the bed, probably still thinking about how she went to church and celebrated Easter and didn't know any other Jews. In Paris, they had continued to live this way, whereas he described his childhood as teeming with Jews, all of them squeezed together in tenement blocks, frequenting the same shuls and shops, a closed but boisterous community whose borders he could trace on a map.

He asked more questions about her parents, and how she met Max, and what she studied at university.

Unaccustomed to talking about herself in this way, she imagined as she spoke that he was twisting open a brightly painted matryoshka doll, and each period of her life tumbled out.

Through the windows, the first purplish tints of dawn appeared.

She motioned to the photograph on his desk. "Your mother looks like she's in love."

"Yeah," Sasha said, his voice catching. "I think she'd just met my father when that picture was taken."

"What happened to him?"

From the radio, clapping flooded into the room, sounding like heavy rainfall occurring in some far-off place.

"I don't know." He looked at her, his eyes deepening. "I don't know who my father is. When the war started, her husband left to fight the Germans, and my mother had an affair with another man. A German soldier. At least that's what I think happened."

"And then, when her husband came back?"

Sitting on the edge of the bed, Sasha stared down at the hardwood floor, his forearms resting on his knees. "He died before he could find out."

The orchestra began playing one of her favorite pieces, the Largo from the second movement from Dvořák's **New World** Symphony. It always reminded her of the sky just before dawn, as it looked now, a deep blue-violet lightening the edges of it, the birds calling out to one another in the newly minted air. "Did you ever meet your father? Do you remember him at all?"

"Yes," Sasha admitted, his voice breaking. "But it's so faint, sometimes I don't know if he's real . . . He left when the war ended. I must have been around three." He looked away from her. "I've never told anyone this." He stubbed out his cigarette before lighting another one. "I shouldn't talk about it . . . I'm sorry."

"You did nothing wrong," she said, growing upset on his behalf, at the shame marking his face. "You were just a child, born into this world. They gave you a name, and they gave you this past. You didn't choose it." She went over to him and put her hand on his shoulder, careful not to press down too hard.

"What do you remember?" she whispered. When his father left, he had been younger than Lucie, but he still remembered, even as an adult, and this fueled her with the promise that Lucie wouldn't forget, even if years passed until she found her, even if she never found her.

He frowned, looking down. "Little things. The smell of his boots. A song he whistled. Being lifted up into the air . . ."

She sat down next to him on the edge of the bed. "Does your mother ever talk about him?"

He crossed his arms over his chest, and she

worried that perhaps she had asked too many questions too soon. The clarinet now played the main theme, the room stirring with tranquil melancholy.

"I wanted to ask her about him . . . many times." He paused. "But she worked so hard to protect me, to make me feel like any other kid whose father died in the war, because that's what happened to most of the fathers in our village. But mine was different, and so I was different. It started to get obvious, the way people belittled her, the way they shunned me. We would walk into a store, greeted by whispers, disparaging glances. Even her own family held us apart. That's why we left Russia. For a new life, you know?"

"Yes, I know," she said quietly, thinking of Max, how he grasped after this new life, refusing to look back, as if the past were a trap. She drew a breath, choosing her next words carefully. "But it seems as though your mother loved your father. That it was real love, and not something she regretted."

He picked up the lighter from the nightstand, observing the flame's flickering appearance and disappearance subject to the pressure of his thumb. "Why?"

"She took a very long time to remarry. Perhaps she was waiting for him. Even if he eventually died, or they lost track of each other after the war, maybe she couldn't let him go, afraid that if she remarried, and started over, he would fade away." The violins swept into the melody, liberating the clarinets, lightening the emotion, making it more fluid. Tears sprung into her eyes. She had listened to this piece countless times over the years, the music conveying all that she had lost, and the hope she still harbored. "And it was probably painful for her, to come to America. By doing so, she severed the possibility of ever seeing him again. It's quite final, to come here." She pinched the bridge of her nose, squeezing her eyes shut.

"Hey," Sasha said lightly. "Shouldn't I be the one crying here?"

She laughed half-heartedly and cupped his cheek, wondering if he looked like his father, and if his mother saw traces of him in Sasha's face, and if this was a comfort to her, or a torment, or something in between.

Dabbing her eyes, she motioned to the map on the wall. "I see you're also tracking the war. I have the same one spread out on my desk. That way, I can better understand . . ." Her voice trailed off.

"What's happening in France."

She nodded. "Are we close?"

"Getting closer," he said, walking over to his desk. "Another month, maybe two, at most."

She bit her lip, trying to suppress that searing anticipation that flashed through her with every Allied victory, shortening the time between now and when she could return and search in earnest. As if reading her thoughts, he said, "Maybe she's alive. Somewhere."

"Maybe," Vera whispered, peering at him.

Perhaps she wasn't crazy. Perhaps this wasn't a fiction she'd created in her mind, "to cope," as Max said. Her heart lurched into her throat, and she started shaking. He held her to his chest, and the pressure of his body made her choke up. She started to say that she was terrified to go back, because hope was a trap, and as long as she resisted it, she could protect herself, but only a guttural yelp tumbled out.

A few moments passed, and then she looked at the photograph of his mother again, her enigmatic smile, dark hair framing her white oval face. "Your mother looks happy there, but also slightly sad, as if she knows it can't last forever, that intense pure feeling."

Sasha moved behind her, and she let the sheet fall away from her body. He wrapped his arms around her, his mouth resting in the crook of her neck. Together they looked out at the silhouette of rooftops and palm trees, with slices of dark ocean in between.

"You saying this can't last forever?" he teased, but she also heard the seriousness in his voice.

She smiled sadly, reminded of how naïve he was for believing anything could last forever.

CHAPTER 32

SASHA

APRIL–MAY 1945,
LOS ANGELES, CALIFORNIA

A gathering dread hung over the short time they had left, until ships would start transporting civilians back to Europe, while at the same time, a beginning stirred between them, however fragile and short-lived. The days leaned into summer, the evening sky full of lingering twilight, and the air grew soft, burgeoning with newness, with possibility. On Saturdays, they sometimes rode bikes along the beach, and as he watched her pedal ahead, her silk blouse billowing in the wind, another image overlapped this one: the day he'd seen her on Ocean Park Pier, wisps of her hair blowing in the wind, the same cream-colored blouse.

They often met in the early evening after work. He'd finish writing for the day and drive over to

Beverly Hills to pick her up from the EFF, where she volunteered, trying to relocate displaced persons recently released from the camps, desperate to leave Europe behind. She would tell him about the cases, her voice hushed with hope, these survivors indicators of life after the war, a life that might hold Lucie in it.

He would then talk about some of his new ideas, running them by her, and she listened, asking questions he hadn't considered before, about a character, or about why he wanted to tell that particular story. When his answer proved unsatisfactory, she would purse her lips, shrugging imperceptibly, and he knew he had to explain it better, make it more compelling, until her eyes lit up with recognition that yes, this was a story worth telling.

He joked that she was harder on his ideas than his mother, a real feat, but then he quieted, remembering how his mother's voice had sounded abstracted the last time they spoke, as if she were wrapped in a cloud, her usual chutzpah muted.

When Vera asked about **The In-Between Man,** he felt a sharp twinge of failure, admitting that it was his favorite idea but it had never panned out. In a few weeks, **Clementine** would be released in theaters, and before that, a premiere. She wondered why he wasn't more excited, and he told her that in his business, things moved fast, he had to start the next project, there wasn't time to linger on past ones, masking the real reason: he could only think of her.

And yet he knew it was a dream, being with her. Of course, like everyone else, he wanted this terrible war to end, but he feared losing her, and feared what she would find in France. Gently, he warned her about the thousands of displaced persons scrambling across Europe, trying to reach North America or Palestine, but she knew the situation from the very letters she wrote, and reminded him of this. Still, he worried she might get swept up with all the refugees, stranded in some DP camp or detention facility, unable to return to America, but he didn't try to dissuade her from going, or forbid it, as Max had done.

And so he began making a mental list of who had useful information about Oradour-sur-Glane, about hidden Jewish children in France and how to find them now. Starting with Gussie, he typed out a short telegram, knowing he had returned to Paris:

Need help locating a French Jewish girl. Mother in Los Angeles, daughter was hiding in Oradour-sur-Glane, last seen there. Any ideas? Much thanks. Yours, Sasha.

If he got a lead on what had happened to Lucie, he would start digging, like the way he used to as a cub crime reporter. In the meantime, he tried his best to contain Vera's fears, but it felt like catching a shadow, her thoughts catapulting into worse ones. He often found her up in the middle of the night, smoking, staring out at the dark shifting ocean, deep in thought, and he would sit next to her on the window seat and hold her hand. She seemed grateful that he didn't talk, or try to cajole her into believing the best, as so many others did, given the surging optimism of those days. Instead, he let the stillness encircle them, the silent night a comfort, and it reminded him of childhood, the way his mother sometimes sat, as quiet as a statue, staring out a window, the past vibrating through her every particle.

CHAPTER 33

VERA

APRIL–MAY 1945,
LOS ANGELES, CALIFORNIA

They tracked the news reports, listening to the radio in his living room as they followed the Allied advancement, unstoppable at this point, Sasha said, reminding her that it was different now, the war really was ending, unlike after D-Day nearly a year ago. What they didn't talk about was the uncovering of the concentration camps, the thousands of bodies, the crematoriums, the evidence of torture, or how those found alive hovered on the brink of death from disease and starvation. Vera knew Sasha avoided it for her sake, focusing only on the victories and the captured cities, repeating that the Germans had lost all resolve, it was only a matter of days.

· · ·

Last month, Max had found out that his parents died at Auschwitz, but his brother, Paul, had miraculously survived Treblinka, escaping with a group of others on the day of the camp uprising, in August of '43. He ran thirty kilometers before finding shelter in a hay loft belonging to Polish farmers who agreed to hide him. Hearing the story, Vera pictured Paul's long lean legs sprinting through the forest, his insouciant manner charming the farmers, buying him time. Paul now longed to immigrate to America—**the only place**, he wrote, **for any of us.**

Max now clung even more fiercely to life here, recoiling from Europe because it had taken everything from them, and he believed the taking would only continue, agreeing with Paul's sentiment. Apparently, according to letters from friends who had survived, Jews were still at risk, especially those who were returning to their homes in Poland, where pogroms had broken out. In Paris, Jews were met with indifference at best, or received as unwelcome reminders of the occupation, and when they tried to reclaim their property, they experienced a hostile resistance on the part of the French people, who refused to return what they had taken.

She went back to the house in Santa Monica Canyon to comfort Max, sitting with him in the still living room, holding his hands in hers, the only sound the ticktock of the varnished grandfather clock in the corner. Hunched over, he stared at the elaborate pattern in the Oriental rug, unable to look at her, saying very little. The shock of his parents' deaths had paralyzed him; he could barely hear what she was saying. Gently, she explained that she was going back to France when the war ended, hopefully in a few weeks, given the recent news reports. "If you want to go back there, go back. But I can't go with you," Max said, his voice breaking. She nodded, unable to absorb his loss as hers already felt so great; it left no room for his, and she felt guilty about this, while at the same time she resented him for not sharing more in her grief, and she sensed that he also resented her for the same reason. She recalled that day in October, standing on the sidewalk after the session with Dr. Bettelheim, when a certain rigidity formed between them, their relationship turning from a liquid to a solid.

At Villa Aurora, the émigré group still gathered for weekly cocktails and literary salons, and Vera purposefully left Sasha out of these engagements. The idea of parading him around in front of Max was unseemly and cruel. With the old crowd, a jagged freneticism ran beneath their conversations; they rejoiced in the war ending, while staving off a deep dread as they learned who had died, whose house was no longer standing, whose neighborhood had been reduced to dust. They commiserated over

Roosevelt's sudden death, all of them shaken, and then a few days later, the beloved war correspondent Ernie Pyle was shot down in the Pacific. They'd read his columns religiously, along with the rest of America, and Vera feared these deaths, two in a row, signaled a waning victory, but Sasha reassured her it didn't.

Sometimes, a good piece of news lifted everyone's spirits: Leon's niece had come out of hiding in Lille; in Vienna, Michel's family home was still standing. Elsa's cousin had survived Auschwitz and recently wrote from a DP camp that he was trying to come to America, but it would take a very long time to get a visa. Reading the letter, Elsa couldn't believe his optimism, given that his wife and two children had died early on in the war.

"He's still alive," Leon reminded her, his eyes twinkling with irony. "Maybe he has already found a new wife."

But then some darker piece of news would surface, punishing their momentary levity. "The death toll will be more devastating than we can even imagine," Max warned Leon, after hearing that Alain, an architect they had all known in Paris, had died after Dachau was liberated.

A few days later, when Elsa and Leon asked her how long she would stay in France, and what would happen if she didn't find Lucie, she said she didn't know, and she could tell they thought such a move was rash and inexplicable, that she was throwing herself into an abyss. "Will you be there for . . . the foreseeable future?" they wondered, trying to grasp a semblance of a plan.

Foreseeable future. She considered the term. Was anything ever foreseeable? Of course, they wanted to think of life in predictable little steps, one event leading to another, success following success, punctuated by the occasional failure, but still expecting an overall arc of progress. Most people thought about the future in this way. She used to be one of them, sailing through her days blindly confident in all their plans for Lucie, staying up late with Max discussing whether or not to spend the summer holidays in Sanary, or on the northern coast with friends, infusing exaggerated importance into such decisions while engorged with the conviction that each day would follow the next, filled with these tidy little plans she had arranged, as though sliding clear glass beads onto a string, the clink-clink-clink of the beads never failing.

Vera still secretly hoped to find Lucie in the mirror again, waiting for another sign. One morning, when Sasha was still asleep, she went into his bathroom and noticed his regiment badge attached to the bottom corner of the mirror with a russet ribbon pinned to it. She asked him about it over black coffee and strawberries. "Is it from a girl, back home? Someone you were in love with?" She'd read a spread in **Life** magazine about what soldiers carried with them during the war: letters, snapshots of sweethearts, a tiny cross attached to a string of rosary beads small enough to fit into the palm of one's hand.

He stood up to put his coffee cup in the sink and then leaned against the kitchen counter, facing her. "My mother kept it as a good-luck charm; I think it's from my father. I kept the ribbon pinned to the inside of my fatigue jacket the whole time." He paused. "But I want you to have it now."

"Me?"

"Yeah," he said, leaving the room for a moment.

Sitting down again, he placed the ribbon on the table. "Take it with you, back to France. Maybe it'll give you good luck too."

She shook her head, letting out a disbelieving sigh. Yesterday, the discussions at Villa Aurora had been particularly dispiriting; all seven of Leon's brothers and sisters had been killed at Buchenwald, and Elsa's mother was shot on arrival at Auschwitz. Vera had started to fear that Lucie had ended up in one of these camps, harboring the morbid image of the heart necklace lost in one of those immense piles she'd seen photographs of, piles of jewelry, or shoes or eyeglasses, published in the newspaper to demonstrate the Nazi terror.

Pressing her hands into her temples, she squeezed her eyes shut for a moment. "I don't know what I'll find. It could be worse than I imagined. Worse than Oradour. Maybe Max is right . . . It will be like running into hell." She touched the ribbon, as though it were a sacred object, the only link to his father. "I can't take it from you."

"Please. Let me give it to you . . . It's the least I can do."

His comment brought tears to her eyes. Sasha didn't shut out her suffering or change the subject when she became difficult, circling the same worries over and over again even as the words remained words that couldn't change anything. She often burst into frustrated tears, and he told her that he understood, looking unflinchingly into her eyes, without trying to ease her into a better mood, something Max had often done. Max used to undermine her fears by explaining it wasn't so dire when it actually was. She would resent him for his false optimism, but at the same time, she would wish he was right. For Max, her grief proved a burden, causing him to lash out in weaker moments, making her feel guilty about her guilt, or sad about her sadness, one painful emotion weighing down another. Vera still recalled Max closing his office door in the evenings after dinner, letting his music embrace him, disappearing into the sound when all she wanted was to disappear too.

. . .

Sasha placed the ribbon in the center of her palm and then closed his hand over hers. "Do you ever think about finding your father one day?" she asked him. She often imagined Sasha as a little boy, his mother pretending he had a different story, for his protection, to shield him from shame. And yet, even though he and his mother left their little village behind, Vera sensed that Sasha still carried this buried story beneath the one he had been instructed to tell. Did Lucie, she feared, also feel ashamed of herself, and of who her parents were? She must have been asked to erase certain parts of her story to survive. Was she ashamed of being Jewish? Did she even know that she was Jewish? Did she remember anything from before?

It haunted him, and her heart went out to him, knowing that he wasn't free of it because no matter how hard we try, Vera reflected, no one can fully escape the unfinished business of the past.

"I've thought about him. But I wouldn't know where to begin . . . or if he's even alive." Sasha paused, giving his next words gravity. "And he might not want to be found."

Vera felt the pressure of his hand, its heat seeping into hers, and her heart ached at the thought of Lucie feeling this way too, convinced that Vera had abandoned her for a lack of love, when nothing was further from the truth.

Vera said that sometimes people had to make choices they later regretted with every fiber of their being. "Who knows what your father was up against?" she added, breaking into a half-hearted smile. "You know this better than anyone—with your conflicted heroes who often do the wrong thing, eaten away by guilt."

"I guess, you're right," Sasha admitted, squeezing her hand for a moment before releasing it.

She stared at the ribbon, a red streak in the center of her palm. Sitting here at the kitchen table, hearing lawn mowers droning in the distance, a car door slamming out front, the stillness of the morning light and the weight of the gift in her hand attempted to repair a moment from the past: reading the newspaper in her kitchen, the bright green morning streaming through the windows, Pauline and Conrad playing tennis next door, the ball slamming against the wooden fence—"Sorry!" they yelled out carelessly—while she kept reading in a state of numb shock about the massacre, the floor flying out from under her. But she felt differently now, in this moment pulsating with faith, with all that was not yet lost.

"Listen," Sasha said, cutting through her thoughts. "I know someone who could help you. His name is Gussie Lustiger. He's a French kid, fought in our outfit, but he's in the Resistance, did a lot of translating and scouting . . . The point is, he's back in Paris now. I have a hunch he could at least point you in the right direction to tracking her down. I contacted him. He's making inquiries." Sasha explained that Gussie couldn't write much, it was still too risky, but Gussie guessed that hundreds of children were still in hiding all over the country. "Once you get there, talk to him, he'll have names, I'm sure, people you need to contact, places you should go."

"Sasha!" She threw her arms around him, and he pulled her onto his lap. Maybe Lucie was hiding in a barrel, as Malka Mannerfelt, Elsa's youngest niece, had done for over a year. Maybe in a Polish hayloft, like Paul. Maybe. Various scenarios rushed through her now, but she couldn't speak; her voice was trapped in her throat, knotted with fear and yearning.

CHAPTER 34

SASHA

MAY 1945, LOS ANGELES, CALIFORNIA

The next afternoon, Sasha drove over to MGM, his palms sweating on the leather steering wheel, still processing what Charlie had cryptically relayed over the telephone this morning: L. B. Mayer, the most powerful studio head in Hollywood, wanted to meet him. Apparently, he'd seen an advance screening of **Clementine** and was intrigued. Sasha had pressed, "What do you mean, 'intrigued'? Did he like it?" and Charlie had shot back, "Do you think he sits down to discuss movies he doesn't like?" Charlie then told him that many of his writer clients, some of whom were quite successful, had been working in this town for years without once treading on Mayer's snowy white carpet. "What I'm trying to say is: don't fuck it up." And then the line went dead.

Because of Mayer's tight schedule, the meeting had to take place this afternoon, at three o'clock. As he drove over there, Sasha's thoughts careened between trying to anticipate what Mayer would say and Vera. The conversation they'd had in the kitchen yesterday morning replayed in his mind, revealing a growing desire to go with her and help her navigate the ruins of Europe. But the feeling was new and unformed; he didn't trust it enough yet to propose the idea.

When the guard waved him through the Culver Gate, his body tensed up with renewed nervousness as he thought over his plan for pitching **The In-Between Man** to Mayer. Charlie had submitted the script to MGM a while back, and they had passed, but now, maybe he could convince Mayer. This could be his only shot to talk about **The In-Between Man** in his own words to one of the only men in Hollywood who could make it happen.

On the lot, Sasha walked past New York Street, leafy and lined with brownstones, and next to that, a bombed-out European street, complete with loose cobblestones and grinding tanks, the director shouting at some AD through a bullhorn to get more snow. Taking in the re-created war scene, he wondered if Mayer saw through the loads of mistakes he'd made as a first-time director on **Clementine**. Or maybe it was the writing that Mayer liked and not the directing, which pricked Sasha with doubt, his dream of directing another picture, of doing this steadily as a real job and not just as a one-time lucky shot because he'd saved Lambert's kid on Omaha Beach, a delusion.

Quickening his pace, he ran through his pitch, reciting some key points under his breath: "This is a picture about America after the war, struggling to put itself back together again, and about all the men who fought in it now returning to normal life. After witnessing such horrors, how do they wear a suit and tie, ride the train to the office every morning and come home at night to a family, a wife, dinner waiting on the table? This is a story for them, and for our country. For all of us." He stopped short, letting a flock of showgirls pass, their sequined feathered costumes flashing in the sun. Before he crossed the street, a silver Rolls-Royce lumbered by with Clark Gable in the back seat dressed as a sea captain.

Sitting in the waiting room of Mayer's office, he felt intimidated by how grand and gleaming everything looked, as if every chrome door handle had just been polished, every green lawn outside mowed to perfection. His mother would have been impressed by the private elevator, the wood-paneled waiting room, the battalion of secretaries speaking at a library whisper while they typed away, and the overwhelming sense of power that vibrated behind every heavy door, as if the longer he lingered in these halls, the better the chance he might just catch some of it. Fleetingly, he thought about the last time he'd called his mother, just a few days ago, and Doris had picked up, saying his mother wasn't at home but at the doctor. When he pressed for more details, she said, her voice dropping a register, "She hasn't been feeling her best," before adding, "I'll tell her you called, dear."

When one of the secretaries ushered Sasha inside the office, he glanced up to find a plaque hanging over Mayer's door engraved with MGM's famous motto—**Do It Right, Do It Big, Give It Class**— and again, the thrill of being admitted into this world, however temporarily, ran through him like an electrical current. The white leather walls, white marble fireplace, and white grand piano amounted to an intentionally blinding brightness after the dim waiting room, and striding through the door, Sasha felt the plushness of the cream carpet under his shoes. Before him, a fortress-like marble desk curved around Louis B. Mayer, who sat with his hands folded in front of him, contemplative yet also ready to strike, Sasha thought. Four white gleaming telephones, all within his reach, waited to ring.

In front of the desk, a lone leather chair.

Mayer gestured for him to sit, a thin smile playing on his lips. He held out his small well-manicured hand, barely reaching across the wide expanse of the desk as if the gesture alone should suffice.

Sasha shook it. A fleshy, warm hand.

"Sasha Rabinovitch, wonderful to meet you. Wonderful."

"You as well, Mr. Mayer."

Mayer threw up his hand in an effete gesture.

A figurine of a golden horse hovered at the edge of the desk, along with a fountain pen in its ink pot. Behind Mayer, on the credenza, various photographs encased in heavy silver frames stared back at him: Herbert Hoover. J. Edgar Hoover. Cardinal Spellman before a crowd.

Mayer settled sideways into his chair, crossing one gabardine pant leg over the other. "You're from the old country."

"Yes." Sasha shifted uncomfortably in his chair. He gulped down air, suddenly nervous again. "We came over in '22."

"What part?" Mayer asked.

He didn't want to talk about the old country, but Mayer seemed intent on unrooting some common thread between them, no matter how insignificant.

"Riga. You?"

Mayer shrugged. "Belarus."

Sasha nodded, his anxiety mounting.

"And I hear you got a Purple Heart fighting over in Europe."

"That's right."

"Ah," Mayer said, and Sasha willed him not to ask more, not wanting to talk about any heroics when the war was a bloody mess; some made it out, some didn't. Distracted for a moment, he ran a hand over his clean-shaven face and felt the tiny nicks along his chin that he'd patched over with little pieces of toilet paper. While speeding up Venice Boulevard on the way here, he'd discarded the pieces into the warm wind.

Mayer began to speak, but then a female voice cut through the intercom, "Dr. Marmorston on line two." One of the white telephones rang, and Mayer picked up. "Put her through," he barked. His voice softened into a cloying gentleness. "Hello, Doctor."

After the call, he poured himself a thimble of scotch from the bar caddie behind his desk, offering Sasha one.

"That was one of my doctors, a specialist in the endocrine glands. Force of nature. Dark, powerful, beautiful. What a woman." He laughed to himself, as if recalling a particularly erotic episode. "So," Mayer said, swiveling his giant white leather chair to face Sasha. "I'm impressed. **Clementine** was a good little picture that you made on a shoestring budget, and the performances are gold."

"Uh-huh," Sasha managed, wondering where this was leading, and readied to launch into his pitch.

Mayer took a breath, but then Sasha cut in, unable to contain himself, "So I wrote this script, I know your people might have read it once, but—"

Mayer swatted away his comment, his impatient hand slicing through the air, his grandfatherly eyes glinting with mischief as he pulled out the coverage on **The In-Between Man.** He started reading aloud: "'This picture is highly un-American, showing our boys, who risked their lives over there, in a bad light. No one wants another war film, especially not one as pessimistic and unpatriotic as this thing.'"

Mayer stopped reading and tossed the coverage aside. "I guess we better make this damn script of yours. And you're gonna direct it."

Sasha held his breath, trying to contain his racing pulse. Mayer's words were so surreal, he almost feared he misheard them.

Seeing his confusion, Mayer grinned. "Charlie knows how much I wanna steal Humphrey Bogart away from Warner. So he passed Bogie **The In-Between Man**, and Bogie loved it. He wants to star in it, on the condition that there's a part for Bacall. They just got married." Mayer took a breath. "Charlie said great, but only if you direct, and we make it."

His heart beating in his ears, Sasha managed, "When do we start?" Charlie hadn't even hinted at this, giving him a hell of a surprise, and Sasha could already hear Charlie's satisfied laughter rippling over the telephone line later today, when Sasha would call him.

"Bogie's available end of August. He's wrapping up a little picture with Bernhardt right now, at Warner's, about a guy who tries to kill his wife but doesn't succeed . . ." Mayer grunted.

Then he pulled out a box of cigars for Sasha. "Havanas."

"Thank you," Sasha said, plucking one out.

Mayer smiled thinly, revealing a row of little carnivorous teeth. Then he stretched out his hand to shake on it. "Welcome to the big leagues, kid. Don't blow it."

Sasha walked out into the brash sunlight. A clutch of women in nurse outfits waited outside a sound stage, extras for a hospital scene. He smelled orange juice in the air, and watched a cheerful group of children heading toward the MGM schoolhouse, all of them child stars on long-term contracts. White rosebushes lined the sidewalks, and hummingbirds trembled before him and flitted away. The colonial-style schoolhouse, the vintage streetlights, and the modern commissary done up in the current streamlined décor all presented a unified front of effortless luxury. It was a city within a city, and he could see why people lived here and went to school here, and never wanted to leave.

He got into his car and started the engine.

Switching on the radio, that peppy Dick Haymes song "In My Arms" was playing again, and he switched it off. Driving down the wide-open boulevard toward the ocean, into a dry soft wind, the excitement of making his dream script was mixed with fresh confusion, leaving him unsure of what he should do. Part of him wanted to go with Vera to France. Before this meeting, he'd imagined the possibility of writing over there, and helping her connect with Gussie and his old colonel, Taylor, who could also be useful. But now the choices tore at him; if he left for France, he would threaten his one, possibly only chance of directing in Hollywood with the most powerful studio in town. He'd been chasing this moment for years, never quite managing to gain entry into the inner sanctum of success. And now the door had opened: all he had to do was walk through it.

And if he did this, he might lose Vera forever.

CHAPTER 35

VERA

MAY 1945, SANTA MONICA, CALIFORNIA

The streets came alive with celebration, manic with the news that Hitler and Goebbels had committed suicide. Vera's heart hammered in her chest, anticipating the official German surrender and, with that, a free, unoccupied France. Her mind swirled with what would help her find Lucie, and what she could bring for her. She thought of the mint-green dress, stowed away in the closet of the house she had shared with Max. No, she wouldn't take it. She shouldn't even touch it, adhering to the Jewish custom of never buying anything for an unborn child, or even giving the child a name until eight days after the birth, because such arrogance would summon the Angel of Death. In part, she blamed herself for buying that dress for Lucie, and planting roses in the front garden, and her plan to repaper Lucie's future bedroom after D-Day, when she had imagined Lucie home, but it was this misguided certainty during those first June days that signaled the Angel of Death, like a bell in the night, to cause the massacre. Of course, Vera knew this was impossible. She didn't have that kind of power, no one did, but logic began to slant and leer at her with its gimlet eye, whispering suggestions in the predawn hours, when her defenses were down, convincing her that she had failed as a mother, and the failure was irreparable, eternal.

Vera recalled her Gentile friends buying trunk loads of white lace layettes, arranging the nursery with utter confidence that soon a real baby would exist there, staring up at a mobile of stars from an elaborate wooden crib. Jews could never afford to be so sure, so certain that their children would live. Perhaps this was why so many Jewish songs were composed in a minor key, a current of melancholy running beneath every good, hard-won thing. Max once explained this as they listened to Schoenberg's **Kol Nidre** at the Hollywood Bowl on a warm November night. She looked back with nostalgia at that time, when she still received letters from Agnes, when France still ran through her blood, when she still believed it was home.

A part of her wanted to see Max and to talk to him about the return, to ask what he thought. He might point out details she had overlooked, or mention people she had long forgotten who could help, but she stopped herself from indulging in this fantasy. He wanted nothing to do with her, or with France. His survival depended on it, and to protect him, she left him alone.

That night, Vera and Sasha went out to celebrate with Charlie and Jean: the German surrender was surely imminent, Sasha was going to get to direct **The In-Between Man**—for MGM, no less—and a trial screening of **Clementine** had been well received. At Perino's on Wilshire Boulevard an ambient peach glow bathed the curving banquettes and saturated-pink tablecloths, the vested waiters circulating among the tables. With the low-hanging chandeliers and blush carpet, the place felt like an exclusive living room for the rich and famous, a place where Jean and Charlie seemed entirely at ease. Vera sat next to Sasha, holding his hand under the table. Every so often, they would exchange a look full of all that they felt, knowing that this was probably one of their last nights together. Today, she had packed and sorted in a panic, worrying over small things such as what gloves to bring, or how many pairs of stockings she would need, to mask much larger, looming anxieties: Leaving Sasha and America behind, maybe for good. Whether she would find any trace of Lucie. And France, her beloved country, now so changed, so corrupted . . . She could barely stand to think of it. Yesterday had been her last day working at the EFF. The other women threw her a small celebration, with flowers and champagne arranged on her desk, a surprise when she returned from lunch. She was moved by their generosity, knowing she would miss them, after the many months they had worked alongside one another. She still felt their tight embraces, their smooth silky blouses and reassuring floral perfume. Breathing deeply, she squeezed Sasha's hand, trying to focus on the dinner conversation. Charlie discussed casting for **The In-Between Man**, and Sasha said he was hoping to get Edward G. Robinson to play one of Bogie's old war buddies, but he wasn't sure if they could get him. Charlie remarked, "He'll want to do it. Trust me."

Jean gave Vera a sardonic wink. "He said the same thing to me, and now look where I am."

Charlie elbowed Sasha, "Hey, did I ever tell you the story about Jean and Louis B. Mayer in Paris?"

Jean took a long drag. "Oh, please. Don't dredge that up," she said before excusing herself for the powder room, motioning for Vera to follow her. When they rose from the table, a waiter appeared, deftly cleaning off the tablecloth with a thin silver instrument, banishing the remaining bread crumbs with a flourish before blending back into the blush-colored walls.

· · ·

Vera and Jean reapplied lipstick in front of gilded mirrors. A young black woman in an English maid outfit sat in the corner with a silver tray placed on the side table, for tips. Jean rapidly brushed her hair with a miniature brush, moving it in quick circular motions. She shook her head, testing out her work. Then she turned to the side and smoothed down the front of her dress, staring at herself in the mirror. "Can you tell yet?"

Vera lit a cigarette and stared back at Jean in the mirror. "What do you mean?"

She smiled. "I'm pregnant."

Vera took Jean's gloved hand. "That's wonderful news."

"I'm only four months along." Jean turned away from the mirror and leaned against the black marble countertop. "Charlie's coming around to the idea." She sighed, snapping her clutch closed. "Hopefully, he'll start behaving now." Jean bestowed her a bright quick smile, chasing away doubt. It was an enchanting trick, and one that Vera had never been able to perform. A thick wave of longing washed over her for those sequestered months, the baby untouchable and protected, floating within the chamber of her body.

They pushed through the swinging door, dropping some spare change into the silver tray first. At the end of the carpeted hallway, Sasha waited, his eyes searching for hers in the dim lighting, and she remembered when she'd seen him standing in a similar way, in a similar place, on New Year's Eve.

In the car, Sasha lit a cigarette and suggested a drive down the coast. He kissed her on the neck and whispered into her hair, "I'm sorry about tonight. That we had to sit there with those two when all I wanted was to be alone with you. I miss you already."

"Me too," she said.

A gentle wind blew through the trees, the velvety May night sifting through her hair, licking her bare shoulders. She put her palm on the back of his neck, already wistful for the small glimpses of a life they might have had.

He accelerated through a yellow light, the night air potent with urgency, with the sense of having so little time left. The passing streetlamps cast a bracing white light over his face before it darkened again. He drove down the incline to Roosevelt Highway, mired in fog. She didn't ask where they were headed. Maybe he would take her back to Las Flores Inn, where they had spent their first night together, or maybe he would keep driving up the coast. His jaw periodically tensed as they stared at the long stretch of black highway ahead of them.

. . .

He put on his signal and pulled into an empty parking lot overlooking Will Rogers State Beach. The lifeguard tower stood empty in the stark moonlight. Sasha got out of the car and went around to the trunk, pulling out a blanket and picnic basket, motioning for her to follow. She closed the passenger door and stood against it, surveying the windswept coastline, and then she gathered up her thin crepe evening gown and stumbled down the bluff, her bare feet plunging into the cold sand.

They built a bonfire and shared a bottle of red wine. They were the only ones on the beach, and Vera felt the weight of her departure accumulating, like stones gathering in the pit of her stomach. Together they stared out at the ocean, passing a cigarette between them.

She ventured, "It's a wonderful film, **Clementine**. You should be proud."

He shrugged, his forearms tightly wrapped around his pulled-up knees. "I asked my mom to come out for the premiere, it was something we always used to talk about, but she's too busy."

"Too busy?"

"With these women's clubs, I guess. A club for one-world government. A club for the peaceful use of the atom. Thursday morning poetry lectures." Chin on his knees, he kept watching the dark moving ocean. "And she's supposed to rest."

"Is she unwell?"

Sasha sighed. "She says it's just indigestion, but Dubrow is worried."

They waited for the silvery glimmer of grunions to appear along the shore, and with every crashing wave, a light show of mating fish flashed before them.

He seemed nervous, gazing out at the sea, and took a long sip of wine before steadying the bottle in the sand. "I've been thinking . . . about coming with you to Paris. To help you find Lucie."

"Oh, Sasha," Vera said, her stomach dropping with the thought of how much he would be giving up. She started to explain, but he interrupted.

"I want to go. And we have time to search for her, if I come with you now, before I need to be back for filming."

"Sasha, you can't abandon your movie. I won't let you. I know how much you've wanted this, and to now just—" She broke off and their eyes met, his disappointment palpable. He listed all the ways in which he could help, and that she shouldn't bear it alone, no one should, but she flung her arms around him.

Holding him tight, she whispered, "I have to do this on my own. I've always known it. It's my own bright torture. It can't belong to anyone else."

He looked into her eyes for a long moment. "Okay," he said softly.

The embers from the bonfire smoldered. He wrapped his arms around her, pulling her close again, both of them watching the waves cresting and breaking. She felt his heart beating against her back. The fire had burned down. The fish wildly flipped in the surf with the high tide rolling in, and crystalline stars dotted the sky, vibrating with so much life, vibrating with the past and the future.

CHAPTER 36

LUCIE

Morning light, the color of syrup, poured into the dormitory. Suddenly, the church bells began ringing, a great breaking wave of joy cutting through the stillness.

Lucie sat up in her cot, gripping her knees to her chest, and waited for Camille to wake, tracking the steady rise and fall of her breath, her lank hair fanned out on the pillow, the dusting of copper freckles on her nose. Her eyes flickered open and she fisted the sheet for a moment before jumping up and flinging her arms around Lucie.

"It's over, Lucie! It's over. The war is over," she said breathlessly. The other girls stirred, sitting up in their cots, bleary-eyed, wondering about all the fuss, but then, as quickly as a match sparks a flame, they were clamoring for their smocks and dresses, for their stockings and ribbons, their voices rising into a crescendo of exaltation and worry, of speculation and wonder.

The heavy wooden door swung open and Sister Ismerie stood there beaming before bellowing out: "Charles de Gaulle announced on the wireless that the war has been won! The Germans have surrendered! Girls, get dressed. We will meet in the dining hall at half past eight."

Lucie dressed, watching Camille and the others, happiness radiating off of them as bright as the sun. It was hard to look too closely, knowing she would never experience this feeling in the same unbridled, careless way. Her mind raced with the terrible questions that had haunted her for years, and today, she feared, would be the revelation of her fate. Images from the tapestry hanging in Sister Ismerie's office rushed before her eyes: Jesus encircled by flames, furious angels descending, St. John supplicating beneath a roiling sky, decrying the apocalypse. Where were her parents? Would they come for her now? Was it too late? And Agnes . . . what had happened to her? She never forgot the expression on Camille's mother's face when she heard Lucie had come from Oradour-sur-Glane, as if it were a cursed place.

She tried to pull on her tights, her hands shaking: the punishment for her sins would be the revelation that her parents would never return. Breaking into a sweat, she chastised herself for speaking out of turn in class, for not listening, for having dirty nails, for the bad things she and Camille often whispered about the nuns, huddled under the covers at night, giggling over the gray wiry whiskers that sprouted from Sister Margot's chin, and Sister Ismerie with all that garlic stuck up her nose, to fight the grippe, she said, but no one believed her—it was the devil she feared.

Bending down, she fastened the buckle on her shoe, sliding the thin leather strap through the metal clasp, when suddenly, Camille threw her arms tightly around Lucie's waist, lifting her up a few inches from the ground, spinning them both around the room. Lucie went rigid, overwhelmed by the spinning, the noise, but then her chest loosened with warmth as Camille's voice rang out, "Don't be afraid! I'll never let go!"

A few hours later, carloads of families began arriving at the convent to celebrate, honking in a cloud of dust. Some even waved the French flag out of their car windows, the blue, white, and red rippling in the wind. Brothers and sisters tumbled out of the cars, while parents nervously stood in the courtyard, waiting for their daughters to emerge from the convent.

Lucie stood watch from the dormitory window, praying that one of these cars might be the big black one her father used to drive, and then her mother would open the car door and peer around expectantly. Lucie barely remembered her face, but she would recognize her—of course she would. She held her breath, hope pounding through her, while a sense of desertion crept over her chest, like an insidious, thick moss.

All the girls were outside now, hugging their siblings in the bright sunlight, the parents laughing and chatting with the Sisters. Someone had brought a basket of ripe plums, and Lucie noticed the bright red juice running down their wrists as they feasted on the fruit, swatting away an occasional bee. And then a little white dog leapt out of the window of a parked car, racing around the crowd in happy circles, the circle growing larger and larger with each lap. The children laughed at the misbehaving dog, and the parents applauded when a father opened a champagne bottle, the cork popping out, sailing over the dog. The church bells continued to ring.

At the edge of the crowd, Camille stood between her parents, hugging them close. They were tall and fair, and Lucie thought they appeared as virtuous and benevolent as the good kings and queens from fairy tales, but they would spirit Camille away, back to their enchanted land, and Lucie would be left here, alone. Hugging herself, she watched the empty road.

CHAPTER 37

VERA

JUNE 1945, EN ROUTE TO PARIS, FRANCE

On the voyage over, Vera kept having the same dream. Lucie jumped into a swimming pool and sank to the bottom. Vera dove in after her, but when she reached the bottom of the murky blue basin, she couldn't find her. Then she looked up and saw Lucie floating on the surface, the distorted sunlight filtering through the water, backlighting her body, a blurry silhouette. Vera propelled herself upward, trying to swim as fast as possible, but she could barely move, the water resistant and viscous. She woke up still struggling to break the water's surface, to save Lucie, but she had a cruel certainty it was too late. Sitting up and switching on the light, she reached for the nightstand, to touch the envelope that contained Gussie's address and the red ribbon.

She thought back to her last morning with Sasha, the sky promising rain. He'd driven her to Union

Station, and during the car ride, the pit in her stomach grew heavier and heavier, the air between them dense with sadness. Through the window, even the palm trees looked sober against the gunmetal sky, no longer their frivolous selves. At the station, she would catch the train to New York, a journey of over three days. From there, she'd reserved a berth on one of the first ships traveling to France. Most of the passengers were war brides, sailing back to reunite with their husbands, who had remained in the army, stationed across Europe, and during her first few days on board the other women assumed that she too had a sweetheart awaiting her, which made the separation from Sasha even more bittersweet. She still felt his strong embrace in the drafty station, the way he insisted on waiting with her until the very last call to board, their hands tightly intertwined. He said to expect letters, and she promised to write, and he looked at her with the hope that this was only farewell, not goodbye, never goodbye.

Smoking on the deck of the ship, Vera strained to see the coast of France through the misty horizon, but another day still remained before they would dock at Marseilles. Various pieces of information cycled through her mind as she prepared herself for what, if anything, she might uncover. When they had first learned about the massacre last summer, the extent of it was unclear, but she had been methodically amassing information, discovering six people had escaped the massacre, none of them children, and one woman survived by throwing herself out the back window of the church. These details trickled out of news reports from France, and from Katja, who sent news. Her husband, Robert, a member of the Resistance, had returned home from prison last month. She wrote that he weighed only eighty pounds.

Stubbing out her cigarette on the railing, she realized that she didn't miss Max, even though she had once envisioned that he would be here with her, on their way back.

A few days before her departure, she returned to their house to retrieve some clothes for the trip. Not expecting Max home, she used her old key, letting herself in, only to find Hilde in the kitchen preparing coffee, the counters immaculate and gleaming. She had been singing a popular song, her heavy Dutch accent bending the English lyrics into a faintly recognizable version of Sinatra's "Head on My Pillow." When she saw Vera, she emitted a surprised yelp, and then glanced down at her stocking feet, as if Vera had caught her exposed.

"I'm sorry, Hilde. I should have rung the bell. I didn't mean to scare you."

Regaining her composure, Hilde said, "Mr. Volosenkova is in the garden." She arranged the chrome coffeepot onto a tray with some biscuits and napkins.

"I only came to retrieve a few things. There's no need to disturb him."

"Oh." She tried to assume a neutral expression, but Vera could tell that she was affronted. Hilde had always favored Max, showering him with great sympathy after Vera left. Even beforehand, she did little favors for him, such as ironing his cravats and organizing his desk, whereas she often left Vera's skirts unpressed, and ignored tiny stains on Vera's blouse cuffs, which Vera would discover later when she was already out and it was too late to change.

She thrust the tray toward Vera. "I was just about to take this out to him." Softening, she added, "He will be so happy to see you."

Vera found him sitting in one of the wicker garden chairs that she had always intended to throw away. He was leafing through images of paintings by Churchill, bucolic scenes of Cannes and Antibes, printed in **Life** magazine.

She carefully lowered the tray onto the coffee table, overhearing Max's muffled laughter from behind the pages. She sat down across from him, adjusting her blouse, and felt the sun pierce through the clouds. The morning had been rainy and soft when Sasha left for work.

He cast aside the magazine. "I wasn't expecting you." His unshaven face, and the coolness in his voice, unsettled her. He smiled thinly, smoking a cigarette brand she didn't recognize, and despite how fastidious Hilde was about his clothing, she detected a small rounded stain on his white collar, which was slightly frayed at the edges. His remoteness made something inside her lurch forward in an attempt to retrieve their old dynamic.

She commented that he looked thinner, and he scanned her face; she tugged off her gloves. "I didn't mean to barge in like this. Hilde was quite surprised."

"You can come home whenever you like."

"I didn't think you would be here, on a Thursday."

He explained that he'd been working around the clock on the musical **Good News** and had taken the day off. "They want the score to sound lush and melodious, like Brahms but not as difficult. Fluid and digestible." He paused, allowing the irony to settle over his comment. "Turns out I'm quite good at that."

She nodded, and a warm familiarity flickered between them, reminding her of all the times they had discussed his discontent with the studio, and how she'd consoled him. Sitting before her now, he appeared satisfied with the work, describing the high demand for this type of music in cool objective terms.

Squinting into the sun, he added, "I hear you're running around with an American director."

She studied the overgrown grass, and the thought of Max and Sasha meeting each other made her cringe, while at the same time another part of her wondered what it would be like. She already knew what Max would say: Sasha came off as brash, too American, a roguish filmmaker with a New York accent, from a poor family, from some shtetl—what could they possibly have in common?

Everything and nothing, Vera thought.

Max leaned forward. "And he's a war hero?"

"Yes," Vera said, noticing that the whites of his eyes looked milkier. "But I'm leaving for Paris tomorrow."

"Is he accompanying you?"

"No."

The scent of Hilde's spiced honey cake wafted through the open kitchen window, and the sound of a faucet running and then turning off sounded oddly reassuring, as though the ordinary hum of domesticity could muffle all this unpleasantness. The screen door banged shut as Hilde emerged from the house carrying out the honey cake. Vera's mouth watered. She had forgotten to eat this morning, having drunk too much coffee, and now her legs felt unsteady.

"You always knew that I would go back, the minute the war ended, and now it's over, so I'm . . ." She stopped, seeing Max's eyes flash.

He stood up, gesturing with disgust. "You think I don't love her as much as you do? Is that it? That I don't mourn her?"

She tried to swallow.

Hilde stood a few feet away, holding the cake.

"You cling to this fantasy that she's still alive, as though you're the only one who loves her, so that you can be the forever suffering one, while I'm the happy opportunist, glibly living here in **paradise**."

Vera's cheeks burned, shamed by his contempt for her, as if he had kept it hidden all these years but now brandished it about, blinding her with it. She couldn't look at his face. It was too startling, his features contorted, rendering him unrecognizable.

His voice broke. "I still dream about her. Teaching her chords on the piano, singing to her every night before bed, walking her to school in the mornings, and then she points to the faint moon, left over from the night. 'The moon and the sun only share the sky for a short time,' I explain, and she always thinks it's funny, the idea that the sun dislikes the moon because the moon is more beautiful and mysterious. She loved my stories."

He sat down again and stared at his hands, which lay perfectly still on his lap.

Hilde swiftly placed down the cake, the pieces fanned out on the plate, and retreated into the house.

Vera knelt down next to Max, gripping the chair for balance, and with her other hand, she cupped his shoulder. She wanted to say so many things: how wrong she was for blaming him, for making him into the one who didn't care about Lucie, when it was the world that didn't care.

CHAPTER 38

SASHA

JUNE 1945, LOS ANGELES, CALIFORNIA

A thick mist settled over the coast, accompanied by a chilly damp wind that blew through the palm trees. Sasha shivered in his sweater vest, and felt as though the bright beauty of this place evaporated once the sun was gone, revealing its true ugly self: the rash of stucco buildings, low, squat, and hastily constructed; the dying grass; the plaintive cries of gulls echoing off the bay. Or maybe the city just looked ugly because Vera was no longer in it. She'd left two days ago.

Right now, she was on the train en route to New York. For the next two weeks, she would be in transit, so he couldn't reach her, which left him unsettled. She'd given him a forwarding address, Katja's, so he could write her, at least, but this offered little comfort. Part of him still wished he'd gone with her, while at the same time, he was relieved that she had wanted him to stay here and focus on his movie. And yet he ached to see her again.

Driving over to Charlie's office for lunch, he rubbed his eyes, exhausted. He hadn't slept well since she left, the bed suddenly empty and too big, and then his thoughts traveled back to Gussie. Underground operations and Resistance groups had emerged from hiding—mainly focused on capturing war criminals, but also to help victims and former prisoners. Still waiting to hear back from Gussie, Sasha had sent a telegram regarding war orphans to his old colonel, Taylor, who was stationed in Paris at the Hotel Bedford.

A week later, Taylor wrote back:

Utter chaos here. Thousands of DPs released from camps, flooding back into France. Organizations to contact regarding war orphans: Circuit Garel, EIF, and perhaps the Federation of Jewish Societies of France. Good luck, Sasha. Yours, Col. Taylor.

It wasn't entirely impossible. But pretty impossible, given how overwhelmed and understaffed the refugee organizations were, scrambling to tend to the crisis of liberation, with the homecomings and shifting borders as thousands fled from east to west. Bracing himself for the devastation she would have to face, he missed her even more, treasuring the traces of her presence strewn all over his house: a misplaced bobby pin he'd fished out of the drain this morning, a pair of tan leather sandals she'd forgotten in the back of his closet, a few of her silky hairs that still clung to the pillowcase. Their final evening together involuntarily flooded back: the darkening sky that broke apart into a sudden downpour; her suitcases standing neatly by the front door, side by side. When she packed her last small things, she asked him if she should really take the ribbon—it was his father's after all.

She looked at him imploringly, and when she held the ribbon in her hand like that, it was as if she touched the past, jolting it with the present, making it alive and fluid again. Before Vera, he had shoved any memory of the old country and his father into a distant, untouchable corner. It was what his mother did, banishing the past to protect him, so he wouldn't suffer. But what was left unspoken flickered with undeniable heat and regret; he'd always felt it, pulsing through him, waiting to be known.

Touching her collarbone absently, Vera had added, "I gave Lucie my heart necklace before we were separated. Every day, I pray she's still wearing it, because if she's still wearing it, it means she's alive."

He had sensed her superstition forming the equation in her mind that if she took his father's ribbon, Lucie might lose the heart necklace, and she would never find her daughter, just as he might never know the story of his father, as if the two objects and these two histories could interact, porous and transmutable.

They'd embraced. "When you find Lucie," he whispered into her hair, "you can give the ribbon back to me."

At a stop sign, he lit his second cigar of the morning. Almost forgetting to turn onto Wilshire Boulevard, he half listened to the news broadcast: An estimated four million people had turned out to cheer General Eisenhower in a thirty-five-mile motorcade through New York City, Japanese warships had sunk the American submarine **Bonefish** off of Okinawa, and a French politician was sentenced to death for collaborating with the Third Reich. Then they replayed a speech Pope Pius XII had given to the Sacred College of Cardinals a few days ago, and his weary tone, speaking in Italian overlaid by the halting English translation, depressed Sasha even more: "In Europe, the war is over. But what wounds we have inflicted upon each other! These wounds fester with the desecration of a mankind's sacred ideals, shattering our faith. Our Lord in Heaven warns: 'All that take the sword shall perish with the sword' . . ." Static cut into the broadcast before the monotone voice resumed: "We must not grow complacent as danger still very much lurks in Europe. Mobs of dispossessed, disillusioned, and hopeless men swell the ranks of revolution and disorder in search of new false idols, no less despotic and tyrannical than what they have just overthrown."

Sasha accelerated through a yellow light, and a barrage of horns trailed him. He tried to push away the thought of Vera in Paris, a rogue city turning in on itself. From what he'd read, the city was rife with summary executions carried out by the FFI military tribunals, former collaborators now posing as Resistance members, Allied soldiers hungry for a joyride, the general air of criminality and chaos.

The persistent ringing of the telephone woke him up the next morning around four a.m. Dubrow's hysterical recounting of events flooded the line as he explained that Leah had fallen into a coma after they went to seek a second opinion in Rye yesterday afternoon. He was crying, tripping over his words; it was hard to fully understand what had happened. Dubrow cursed himself. "I should have told you about the cancer, but Leah insisted it was nothing. She was walking around, arguing, cooking, going about her business . . . She didn't seem that sick. A little weak, maybe. And then, suddenly, after we went to see Dr. Erlich . . ." His voice trailed off.

"Okay, calm down," Sasha said, his palms slick with sweat, his voice shaking. "I'll get on the first train and be there as fast as I can."

"Okay, Sasha, okay," Dubrow muttered, and then he dropped the phone on the carpet, which resulted in a static thud, until Doris bustled into the room, her concerned voice in the background, before she sighed heavily, placing the receiver back into the phone.

CHAPTER 39

VERA

JUNE 1945, PARIS, FRANCE

On her first night in Paris, the dream of Lucie's drowning revisited her. She woke with a start, the sheets damp, listening to the odd clanging pipes. Staring into the pitch-black hallway, she realized that the electricity had gone out again. She wanted a glass of water, but hesitated. This was not her house, and she didn't feel as though she could freely spring up from bed and putter around the kitchen. At the last minute, instead of staying with Katja, she thought it better to use her publisher's empty apartment, as Antoine was on holiday in Neuilly-sur-Seine. Katja's husband had just returned home and Vera didn't want to intrude on them, further burdening Katja. The only other alive thing here was a gray kitten that slept at the foot of Vera's bed, a silver curl of fur.

She pulled the sheets around her, careful not to disturb the cat, but her heart throbbed.

The next morning, she planned to return to their old apartment. She dreaded it, a sickening fear spreading through her, thinking that Max was right. This was all a terrible mistake, she would find nothing, and nothing would come from it. Even so, she felt the necessity of going home, although most property had been seized under the Möbel-Aktion in '42, the Germans having shipped off all domestic items to the colonized east. Other apartments were looted, even by neighbors. Rarely did homes remain intact. But then again, she had heard that the Germans took over the more luxurious apartments, delighted to find the rooms fully furnished, sleeping on the sheets, dining on the china, and wearing the clothing of those they had murdered.

Quickly, she dressed, imagining what she might find: Would her home be stripped bare, sconces ripped out, grand piano gone, with only a few picture hooks on the walls and an empty chamber pot? Or would she find it untouched? Just thinking about it made her break into a sweat.

On the way out, the concierge commented that the wisteria and lilac had bloomed early this year, and Vera remembered her concierge, Didier, making similar commonplace remarks as he swabbed the entrance hall.

Stalled cars and honking horns, wrought iron

balconies cradling flower beds, the plane trees and untouched monuments and wide-open boulevards rolled out before her. She gripped her purse, afraid to walk these same streets and bump into people she used to know, but she also feared not seeing anyone she knew. She feared the city's familiarity, how even the smallest of details snapped her former life back into focus, as though everything could resume if she only let it. She nearly collided with a young girl who zigzagged toward her on a bike, her bare legs flashing beneath a lampshade skirt.

She kept walking, worried that another bicyclist or pedicab would leap in front of her. A group of American soldiers lounged on a bench, their easygoing voices loose with liquor as they propositioned her. Hurrying past, she pretended not to hear them, and then a gang of children approached, badgering the soldiers for chocolate bars.

Crossing the intersection, she saw a group of boys clamoring onto a German military truck smashed in on the side and abandoned in the street. The boys were using it as a kind of fort, shaking their fists in the air. One of them stood on the hood, saluting people. She passed a bakery that still had bullet holes starring the front window. A long line of women waited in front of it, fanning themselves. They held their children's hands, some of whom twisted away, scowling in the summer heat.

Across the way, racing through Place de la Madeleine, a bicyclist pulled a bride and groom in a wooden cart. They had just been married at the church there, her veil fluttering in the wind, people cheering as they went. Vera stopped a moment to watch them pass. The bride gazed down shyly at the bouquet of roses in her lap while the groom cheered along with the people, as if he had won a prize.

At the edge of the square, an old man was selling used books on a makeshift stand, and the children's book **Les Rêves de Rikiki** jumped out at her. They used to read it over and over, trying to teach Lucie letters and numbers until Max made up funny little poems, waltzing her around the room. The sight of the pale blue book, dusty and abandoned on the cart, made her want to touch it.

The man called out, "If you don't like what you see, I have more to show you, at lower prices."

Hands shaking, she fumbled for her cigarette case and lighter, trying not to think about whether Lucie had ever learned her letters. She had struggled with it, and Vera had been impatient. She smoked, averting her gaze from all that swarmed around her lest a particular café or metro stop unleash an unwanted memory, but she couldn't help but see the English pub where she used to meet Max and his brother, Paul, after work. **Yes, this is Avenue Henri-Martin,** she thought, and an evening leapt into her mind when Paul had discussed the impossible task of joining the Jockey Club, a club that didn't admit Jews, and as the evening wore on, he grew more animated, his determination to become a member comic. Afterward, in the cab, the sky hushed with pastels, Max's coat was thrown over his shoulder, a cigarette dangling from his mouth, and she, in her tweed suit and cloche, described the structure of her latest book; he half listened, composing in his head. He cupped his stubbly cheek, his eyes tired as the cab driver pulled up to their apartment, where Lucie was tucked into bed, and he paid the driver over Vera's half-finished sentence about what Agnes had given Lucie for dinner—**bacheofe**, again, but she loved it.

Someone's shoulder bumped hers, and the recollection skittered away. The man said something under his breath, regarding her in a strange, threatening manner before passing, and Vera realized she looked different from everyone else in her American dress and silk trench coat, her pretty hat set at an angle. He might have assumed that she had benefited from the war by collaborating or black-marketeering, or that she was an arrogant American strolling these streets because America had won the war. She quickened her pace and recalled a heated conversation at a cocktail party, just before she left, between Bertolt Brecht and Thomas Mann. Brecht described Mann as morbidly salivating over how the Germans should be punished now. Then a friend of Elsa's chimed in that she would never return to Germany. She gestured wildly, her heavy gold bracelets clinking.

"For all I know, I might sit next to my father's murderer on a tram, or my grocer could have been in the SS."

"Probably," Brecht agreed. "But the question is whether or not we can disentangle the Nazis from the ordinary German people. Are there really two Germanys? One immune to evil and the other infected by it?" The woman's husband, a famous playwright, then bellowed out, "Now every German has a sad story to tell, as if they had no choice and we should all feel sorry for them." The woman admitted that no nation should cast the first stone, given the collaborators in France, the racist behavior of the English, and how the Russians treated their own people; no one escaped unscathed. "Do you feel shame as a German?" Brecht had asked, assuming the tone of an interrogation officer. "As a human being, I am ashamed," the woman replied.

Vera paused before the wrought iron door of her old apartment building, shaken by the general air of mistrust and blame in Paris, by how collaborators now posed as heroes, denouncing the occupiers whom they formerly embraced. She squinted up at her balcony, where she used to think and smoke, the same gnarled ivy flowing over the balustrade. And the same June air, a mixture of cigarettes and dog shit, linden blossoms and petrol. Gripping the brass door handle, she felt its familiar coolness, and considered her image reflected in the plate glass: green shantung dress, her hair coiled into a chignon, golden peacock brooch and white gloves.

She didn't look as though she had come back to beg.

The door suddenly opened and Vera backed away.

A young man stepped out. He began sweeping the street, occasionally glancing over at her. He had acned cheeks and dark unkempt hair, and swept his little patch of concrete as though the broom were a nuisance designed to torture him.

Vera peered down the street as if expecting someone, focusing on the copse of trees across the way. Then she pretended to check her watch. **What a performance**, she thought. **This is nonsense.**

"Madame?"

"Yes?" she said brightly, masking the tight nervousness spreading through her.

"Aren't you Madame Volosenkova?"

She hesitated.

"You used to live here, before the war? Flat 8F?" He smiled shyly. "Etienne."

Of course. The concierge's son. "I barely recognized you."

He blushed. "I'm studying at the university now."

She nodded, fiddling with her gloves.

"Are you waiting for someone?"

"No, I'm . . ." She stopped, distracted by the sound of a window opening from above. Instinctually, she checked the top floor. A maid fluttered a sheet from a second-story window.

He gestured toward the open door. "Would you like to come inside?"

She didn't move. "Is your father or mother at home? I should speak to them."

"They're at Mass." He propped up the broom against the wall. "Please, come in."

It felt like a dream. She wanted to say yes, the word alive on her tongue, if only she could utter it. Instead, she started to walk away.

"Listen," Etienne called after her. "No one is there now. The tenants went on holiday."

"Tenants?"

"The Russian ambassador, Boris Bogomolov." He paused. "No one has returned. It's quite difficult to reclaim property."

"I didn't come for that." Again, her own voice startled her. Hoarse and full of emotion, revealing too much. She dabbed her eyes with the back of her glove. "I'm searching for Lucie, my daughter. I thought perhaps someone might have come, with some news, or—"

He interrupted, his cheeks reddening. "No one has come, Madame." Then he extended his hand. "But please, follow me."

The apartment smelled strange, as though someone had recently broiled a roast, unlike the scent of

blooming lilies she had expected. She had always
filled the apartment with lilies or roses in spring-
time, but there were no flowers here. The living
room had been entirely rearranged, the piano covered by a tattered bedspread she didn't recognize. An
air of mistreatment and carelessness permeated the
rooms, with coats flung over armchairs, a threadbare Oriental rug embarrassingly too small for the
sitting room, a dirty glass left on the dining table
with the dregs of oxidized wine. Another glass evi-
denced traces of lipstick along the rim. Wandering
through the rooms, she randomly touched objects
to confirm this was real, despite the surreal scene: a
woman's comb with a tangle of blonde hair, a pair
of cuff links in an ashtray, a long rectangular couch
with scuff marks on the bottom. **I shouldn't be here**,
she thought, staring at the pale green curtains and
Max's old deskin the next room. But somehow, she
found herself in the ridiculous position of trespass-
ing on her own life, recognizing things she had long
forgotten: the miniature oil painting of Mourka, the
gold-leaf wallpaper in the study, the cracked mirror
in the foyer. Even the mirrored glass and gilt sconces
still hung on the walls, white stumps of wax embedded in the candleholders.

Etienne hovered behind her. "Madame
Volosenkova, would you like some tea?"

"Are you going to serve it to me on my own
china?"

He shook his head, unable to look her in the eye,

and she realized she had embarrassed him. "I'm sorry."

He tried to smile and told her that downstairs, in his parents' apartment, they'd kept her wardrobe with the trousseau and linens, and the sideboard with the silver. She barely heard him, feeling the ghostly pull of other rooms: her bedroom and office.

Lucie's room.

"It's all right, Etienne. I don't mind if they keep it." Her body moved on its own accord toward Lucie's room, her heart hammering in her chest, faintly aware of Etienne following her, asking if it was really all right to keep everything.

The door was ajar. The walls were blank except for a more saturated cream square where the watercolor of the Tsarskoye Selo gardens in St. Petersburg had hung. A pair of boy's shoes were kicked off next to an unmade bed. The smell of dirt, grass, and restlessness hung in the air. A leather satchel dangled from the arm of Lucie's rocking chair. The needlepoint ballerina pillow that always had rested there was gone.

She squinted, trying to conjure the rarified nursery of cream walls, delicate lace, the crystal chandelier refracting morning light, china dolls lined along the shelves.

Reaching for the door, she found Etienne's arm instead. "If she comes back," Vera whispered, "if she returns . . . if anyone comes here with any news . . ."

"Yes, of course, Madame Volosenkova. I will contact you immediately."

Coming down the stairs, she saw her old neighbor Madame Allard on the landing. Lucie used to play with her daughter Matilde, and the shrill sound of their childish voices scolding their dolls momentarily rang in her ears.

Madame Allard stared at Vera. She held a potted plant, in the process of discarding it, the door to her apartment half open. Then, remembering herself, she put down the pot and rushed to embrace Vera. "You look so well. We were sick with worry. So wonderful to see you again."

Vera pulled back and noticed Madame's short patchy hair partially covered by a scarf. She had always worn it long, in lustrous auburn waves.

"I heard you were in Sanary?" Madame Allard asked, smiling oddly.

"For a short time. Then we went to California."

"California," she repeated, her eyes glistening at the sound of it. A mawkish cry interrupted them. A little boy, around three years old, stood in the doorway, his cheeks smeared with jam.

"Oh," Vera said, relieved by the distraction. "Who's this?"

Madame Allard stiffened. "Jacquard."

Vera bent down and beckoned to him. "Hello, Jacquard."

The boy stared at her blankly.

"He's lovely. Such golden curls," Vera offered.

Madame Allard tugged on the edges of her hair. "Jacquard, go back inside."

She sighed when the boy didn't move, and in that moment, Vera realized he was a German war baby, with his pug nose, rosy northern complexion, his mother's newly shorn hair. And the boy looked nothing like Madame's husband, whom she remembered as dark and Gallic.

The child still stood there, sucking his thumb, but then Matilde, now nine years old, the same age Lucie would be, came and dragged him into the next room. Fleetingly, they exchanged glances, Matilde's clear mineral eyes full of questions. Of course she didn't ask after Lucie, but the agreed-upon silence made Lucie seem even more dead.

The next day Vera was supposed to go to Oradour, and had already booked a chauffeur, but she decided against it, still shaken by yesterday, her old apartment turned into something else, where strangers now lived. Instead, she would go straight to Hotel Lutetia, where everyone told her to look first.

Coming down the marble staircase, she changed her mind again; she shouldn't be weak and avoid the pain of witnessing where her daughter might have died. She had to go now; otherwise she would lose courage.

After a short bout of conversation in which the chauffeur explained that the only way to get to Oradour was by car, all the rail lines had been blown up, they barely spoke the rest of the way, leaving her to her thoughts. She felt the inside pocket of her purse, where she kept Sasha's ribbon, and made sure it was still there.

During the long drive, she kept revisiting something Elsa had said before she left. They had stood in Elsa's kitchen. In the next room, the cocktail party dwindled. The maid was washing dishes in the sink, humming a Viennese waltz. Elsa stared down at her hands, which she pressed against the kitchen counter, her voice faltering. "I'm sorry for telling you the day we crossed the Pyrenees that you would get Lucie back after the war. That by leaving her, you were saving her." Vera reassured Elsa that it wasn't her fault. None of them could have imagined what would happen, but she couldn't admit that she had often replayed that exact moment in her mind: the blue haze of the mountains, sitting there on the scattered pine needles, sharing green pears, listening to Elsa convince her that she was doing the right thing, and Vera's own desire to believe her because it was convenient to believe her in that moment.

When they arrived, he parked outside of the town, as though the place were contaminated. It was late in the day, the low-hanging sun casting a celestial pinkish glow over the ruins. Vera gripped the door handle, afraid to open it and step out. The driver stared in the opposite direction, toward a copse of trees in the distance, his face turned away from the town. Suddenly, she was extremely thirsty, her throat knotting up, and she managed to say, "I won't be long," hoping for some consolation from him, such as **I'll be right here** or **Not to worry**, but he only caught her eye in the rearview mirror.

She made her way over corrugated tramlines running through the streets, touching things as she went: the crumbling brick facade of a boulangerie, the metal sign hanging over the gaping doorway, dust coating her fingertips. Biblical phrases involuntarily reverberated through her: **Dust to dust, ashes to ashes, God gave and God has taken away.** She had never thought of these lines before, but now they found her, demonstrating that this was the way of the world and she must learn it. She tried to imagine Lucie standing in line here at the boulangerie, the way she used to in Paris, jumping on one foot, impatient to get a little treat, before the baker would palm her a sugar cookie in the shape of a heart, Lucie acting as though it were a great surprise, even though she had expected it. Staring into the bombed-out building, Vera saw nothing of Lucie, nothing of anyone. Nothing of nothing.

She forced herself to keep walking, passing by

a Singer sewing machine in the middle of a razed courtyard. A singular fireplace, lined with broken tile, stood nearby next to a rusted-out car. She shivered in the strong sun, feeling as though she shouldn't be here, as though it were a bad omen to witness the aftermath of so much killing.

Rounding the corner, she caught her breath at the rows of white porcelain ink pots, realizing that a school must have stood here.

All of these abandoned objects reminded her of the Roman ruins she had studied at university, but fresh violence festered in these stones, and she sensed, gingerly stepping over the rubble, the ungodliness of this place.

She walked a bit farther on, leaving the town behind, searching for Agnes's address. Burnt fields stretched on without a hint of life. Even the sky seemed empty, a flat expanse of blue with no dimension to it. Her feet hurt, swelling up in the unforgiving shoes, and her breath grew shallow the farther on she walked, even though it seemed a short distance. She stopped in front of a few stone walls, coated in ivy, and a hearth. It was impossible to tell if it was Agnes's house or not, given that all the farms had been burned down. There was nothing left to distinguish one pile of rubble from another. Staring ahead at the long empty road, she didn't know if she should move forward or go back, and from all directions, she only saw dark razed fields. She set her palms on her knees, steadying herself, letting the blood rush to her head to stop the dizzying sensation of the earth tilting upward.

This place had swallowed up Agnes and her daughter, and the crashing sensation of being left motherless and childless—coupled with the stabbing guilt that Agnes had hidden Lucie for her, and perished for it, when Vera had gone free, sailing across the ocean—left Vera breathless. If Vera hadn't asked Agnes to hide Lucie, she might not have returned home to this village. She might have found work with a new family, or she might have taken up an entirely different occupation altogether. She might have even fallen in love or moved to London, a city she adored but had never seen. She might have done so many things.

Returning to the town, Vera carried the grim knowledge that the church remained. Romanesque, red brick, and low to the ground, it was even more modest now without a roof. Blue sky spread above her. Shadows filtered into the nave, light and dark shapes playing across the altar. Someone had left a small bouquet of wildflowers there, now wilted.

This was the place: the last place where Lucie was definitely alive. In the late-afternoon light, the stone and brick appeared flesh-colored, radiating a silent warmth.

Vera closed her eyes, trying to feel Lucie, but all she felt was desertion, and a violence so brutal it shattered time.

Backing away, she held herself close, clutching the sleeves of her blouse, as if she wanted to rend them, to bring the fabric to her teeth and bite through it.

Then she noticed bullet holes in the altar, because the Germans had fired low, to kill the children first.

The chauffeur leaned against the passenger door, chewing tobacco, his arms crossed over his chest. He squinted up at the electrical lines running overhead. A few blackbirds perched on the wires, squawking into the still air. He spit his tobacco into a nearby bush and then opened the car door for her.

On the way back, he considered her in the rearview mirror, as if only a sick person would want to visit that place.

CHAPTER 40

SASHA

JUNE 1945, NEW ROCHELLE, NEW YORK

The living room was hot and crowded, the long dining table laden with fruit and pastries, knishes, pots of herring, pickled vegetables, and thinly sliced black bread. On the train, Sasha had imagined sitting at his mother's bedside, stroking her cheek, saying some last words. But Leah had died at dawn, and he arrived hours too late.

All Sasha had seen of her death was the elaborately carved wooden coffin lowered into the earth while the rabbi intoned uplifting words about her character, a rabbi he had never met before, but someone, Dubrow reassured him, whom Leah had felt very close to at the end of her life. Surrounded by strange faces, many of them tearful, Sasha felt a whistling absence rip through him. These people mourned another Leah, a woman Sasha didn't know, who had served on the Peaceful Use of the Atom committee and organized bridge games and attended poetry mornings at the country club. They nodded knowingly, as the rabbi praised her charitable service to the community, how she had tirelessly organized food drives for the DPs in the camps, collecting sweaters and socks and bedding for the children.

The mother he knew cleaned the apartment every Friday afternoon before the Sabbath, and sprinkled mint leaves in the steaming bath because she loved the smell, and worked long days as a seamstress in a sweltering shop so that he could attend the neighborhood heder after school.

Sasha lay down on his twin bed, staring up at the ceiling, exhausted, listening to the last guests saying their goodbyes. He didn't want to talk to anyone, and only wished that he could see his mother again, with her ball-busting comments and anxious kibitzing. He remembered the day before he left for California for the first time. Leah had appeared in the dusty doorway, holding a jar of spicy pickles and a loaf of brown bread, saying he'd better take this for the journey, her eyes filling with tears when he reassured her that there was a dining car on the train. He wasn't going to starve. They hugged then, and he patted her smooth black hair streaked with gray and closed his eyes, his chin resting on the crown of her head, and he imagined the little town where she was from, where he had been born, and how far they had come together.

Sasha covered his face with his hands, breathing into the warm dark. Just then he heard a timid knock on the door and Dubrow's muffled voice calling out, "Sasha? You in there?"

He got up from the bed and opened the door to find Dubrow standing in the hallway. Sasha motioned for him to come in, but he paused on the threshold, clearing his throat. "Listen, Sasha, I've got something to tell you." He shifted on his feet, his eyes combing the walls, as though he didn't know where to look. Then he took out an envelope from his breast pocket.

"What's that?"

"It's a letter for you." He paused. "Your mother wrote it just before she died." He tried to say something, but the words caught in his throat. "It's about your father." Dubrow started pulling on the moth-eaten edge of his sweater and took a few steps in Sasha's direction.

Sasha stared down at his shoes, focusing on the tiny perforations above the cross-stitching of his wingtips, instinctively doing what he had done during the war: when he had to focus, he would stare at whatever was at hand—for instance, tree bark, its ripped-up roughness, the white underneath the dark outer skin—to stop his mind from racing. He clenched his knees.

Dubrow stood there uncomfortably. "All Leah wanted was to protect you." He dabbed his eyes with a tissue, his voice trembling. "She was always like that, you know, putting everyone else first." He held out the envelope.

"Yeah," Sasha said, taking the letter and slipping it into his back pocket. "She was."

He left New Rochelle as soon as he could after that. It was nearly dark, the train car rattling. The encroaching Manhattan skyline stretched ahead, but tonight it looked foreign and unforgiving, as though he hadn't grown up among those spires and rooftops and flashing neon billboards.

He felt the letter in his breast pocket like a hot iron, willing him to reread it, the rattling train car triggering flashes of the long train journey he took with his mother from Riga to Hamburg: the smell of onions and sweat on their clothing, wide flat wheat fields flitting by, the expectant hope reflected on everyone's faces.

When the train stopped in Berlin, the city blazed with light, the immaculate modern buildings cutting geometric shapes into the sky, the billboards and marquees glowing against the night, the trundling taxis and automobiles honking at irregular intervals coupled with a policeman's strict whistle, and the elegant couples descending beneath the earth to travel in a tunnel, his mother explained, from one end of the city to another. Most of all, he remembered his mother straining to see out the window amidst the crescendo of Yiddish, Russian, and Polish rising up around them like water. He tugged on her coat. It seemed as though a subterranean pull beckoned her off the train, and into the vast wide boulevards lined with majestic trees. Sasha stared out too, watching the well-dressed men striding down the sidewalks as efficiently as machines, briefcases swinging with the utmost confidence, pointing toward the future.

His mother sank back into the seat and pinched the bridge of her nose, squeezing her eyes shut for a moment. Then she pulled Sasha into the heavy folds of her coat and whispered, "It's beautiful, isn't it?"

It hit him now, that moment rushing back to him, the moment his mother recounted in her letter, breeding the crushing disappointment that she never forgot: Berlin, at night, his mother staring through the train window, hoping that he was waiting for them on the crowded platform.

Pulling the letter from his breast pocket, Sasha reread it:

Dear Sasha,
     This letter might not reach you in time, they tell me I don't have much of that left . . .
     So many times, I wanted to tell you

about your father, but I didn't want to
mark you for the rest of your life. Marked
because I had an affair while still married,
an affair with a German soldier, no less—
this made us outcasts, nearly untouchable
in the old country. That is why we finally
came to America, to the golden land.

I met your father at the beginning
of the Great War, in the little town of
Mitau, where I lived with my family. It
is the town where you were born, before
we moved to Riga after the war, to live
with relatives, to escape the influenza
that took my sister and parents from this
earth.

Let me start again: I met your father
under an apple tree during the month
of Sukkot. He leaned against the trunk,
in his field gray uniform, musing at the
landscape, very unlike a soldier, very
unlike anyone I had ever met. I remember
noticing his long elegant hands, and
thought he must be a pianist or a painter.
He was so careful with them, but that
was just his manner. He owned a textile-
manufacturing company in Berlin,
and left behind a Gentile wife and two
young children there. After serving as
a medic on the Eastern Front at first, he
was transferred with his unit to Mitau to

oversee the local population and occupy
the village and surrounding areas.

This is when I met him, under that
apple tree, and I knew immediately he
was unusual, strange and new, someone
from another world, despite the fact that
he spoke Yiddish because his parents fled
Russia when he was a baby. Poor shtetl
Jews like us, so he didn't look down on me.
He helped me; he brought us food during
the winters, and smuggled medicine
for my sister from the army supply. He
sang with us on Shabbat and danced at
family weddings. He sat at our table, and
listened to father discuss the Talmud,
and nodded with encouragement when
Geza, your cousin, dreamed of Palestine,
while we dipped bread in salt and shared
bottles of kvass. He was educated, refined,
cultured . . . he knew about the world and
moved through it with ease . . . he was all
the things I wished for you. All the things
I was not. I loved him.

When you were born, he raised you up
into the air and named you Aleksander,
after Alexander the Great, he said
proudly, but back then, I didn't know
who Alexander the Great was. I was only
happy that he held you close, and sang
you those sweet German songs, and made

sure we had enough firewood, enough medicine, enough bread. My family accepted the lie I told everyone: that you were my husband's son. He had come home on leave once, a few months after I met your father, and that's when I claimed you were conceived, but everyone sensed such falsehood. Everyone knew because with my husband, during our ten years of marriage, we could not conceive, and I believed I was cursed, unable to ever have a child. And everyone knew because you looked just like Lev, with your dark head of hair, and not the flaming red of my husband, and those round inquisitive eyes, the same eyes as Lev. And the way Lev looked at you, with wistful hope, and how he winced when you cried, he could barely stop himself from running to you, or the times he would take you into the forest on his shoulders, singing the songs from his country, hoping you would remember them. When you were teething, inconsolable for hours on end, he dipped his pinky finger into a thimble of cognac and let you suck on it; this calmed you.

Sometimes, he spoke of his life in Berlin, his blonde wife, and his two children, a girl and a boy. He missed his children terribly; he couldn't desert them.

I loved him, even though I knew he would leave us.

The Russians were returning, the war ending, and soon, he would be shipped out to the Western Front. Instead, he deserted with a few other soldiers, in hopes of getting back to Berlin.

I remember the last time I saw him, in my mother's kitchen. I remember every little detail, from the amber afternoon light, to the apple trees outside the window, to the wooden stairs creaking with eavesdroppers. He said he had a life to return to: a family, a business, a whole existence apart from us. His jaw tensed, his eyes filling with tears. He missed his children; he hadn't seen them in four years, but he also didn't want to leave us. Then he reached into his pocket and gave me the red ribbon. Our red ribbon. I used to tie it to the birch tree outside of the barn when we were waiting for him in the loft. A signal for us to meet safely, where we could talk and play with you, where he could hold you close. He would take it off the tree, and next time, a few days later, tie it up on the same branch, the wind whispering: I'm waiting for you. Please, come. And in return for the ribbon, I, devastated but smiling, gave him a loaf of bread wrapped in an embroidered cloth. Little colorful birds stitched into the white. A pattern he could run his fingers over, a pattern that meant: I love you. I'll never forget you.

In the doorway of the house, I watched him walk away.

My mother clucked her tongue, her heavy judgment beginning. I held you close to my chest, you were nearly three, and we watched him disappear into the trees.

All I had left was the ribbon. And you.

Four years later, I sent him a letter explaining that we were leaving for America, breaking our agreement to not send letters, to not write. I didn't know if he'd made it to Berlin. I didn't know if he was even alive. But if he was, I wanted him to know that we were starting a new life. I also told him where and when we would change trains, in Berlin. He wrote back, saying he would be there, that he missed us greatly and he wanted to see you again.

When the train stopped in Berlin, I thought he might come for us . . . I don't know why I thought he might come . . .

perhaps because we used to fantasize about immigrating to Palestine, and starting over with you, but then he would always fall silent, consumed by what he left behind.

The hour passed, and it grew increasingly clear to me that he wasn't coming. He would never come.

I don't know if your father escaped Germany before this horrible war, or if he perished in a camp, as so many others did. I don't know because I never wrote to him again, and he didn't know where we had settled in America. Even though he left us, he continues to crowd my dreams, visiting me at unexpected moments. I see him clearly now, as I lie dying.

Maybe you will find him and the two of you will reunite.

This is my wish.

I don't have much time left, it's coming quickly now.

Your father's name is Lev Perlmutter. His address was Englische Str. 6, 10587 Berlin, Germany.

Sasha: my heart, my blood, my hope.

Please forgive us.

Love,

Your mother

Sasha pulled his coat tighter, trying to block out the conductor's drone. Perlmutter was a German Jewish name, which made Sasha half a German Jew, with a half brother and sister, if they had survived the war.

The announcement for 125th Street startled him, and he stared at his blurry reflection in the train window: naturally, his blue-black hair came from his mother. But the rest—the olive cast to his skin, his defined chin and straight Roman nose—belonged to his father. The lines from her letter reverberated in his head: **Maybe you will find him and the two of you will reunite. This is my wish.**

A handful of passengers filed into the car. A middle-aged woman took out a magazine, the cover showcasing an enlarged black-and-white photograph of the Eiffel Tower shrouded in thick fog with a row of statues in the foreground. The tagline read, **Paris 1945**, implying that it was no longer the Paris of love and light. He could see, as she turned pages, the desolate photographs of monuments and empty plazas that made it look as though the Germans had drained the city of its verve, leaving behind cold anemic stone. He thought of Vera, trying to place her there, and wondered if she'd met up with Gussie yet, and felt a pang because he wasn't with her.

· · ·

When he came into the hotel room, he lay down on the bed, feeling the satiny coverlet underneath his body, and sleep overtook him.

In his dream, Vera smoked in front of the large glass window. She wore a silk robe, her body rippling beneath it, and then she turned around and came toward him. She was saying something in French. He didn't understand it, inhaling the luxurious scent of her perfume, and he kissed her mouth, which tasted of salt and champagne. Then she turned back toward the window, and the window became a Russian forest. She receded into the birches, the hem of her robe lifting in the wind as she walked, the Baltic Sea visible through the trees ahead. The farther she walked, the smaller she appeared among the hundreds of trees, the wind whistling through the branches, creating a hollow, bleak sound that told him he would never see her again.

Sasha woke with a start, reaching across the bed for Vera, before realizing that he'd fallen asleep fully dressed atop the coverlet. Only an hour had passed and it was still night. Fumbling for the phone, he almost dialed her old telephone number in Los Angeles. He desperately wanted to hear her voice, to tell her that she had been right about his parents; they had loved each other, and those memories of his father were real.

He took out a sheet of hotel stationery and started to write Vera a letter, his hand trembling as he held the pen, his chest thundering at the prospect of being with her again . . . Before he had time to think, he wrote that he was coming to Paris to see her, and together, they would find Lucie. Rereading the letter, he then worried she wouldn't want him in Paris. She'd made this clear on the beach that night. But maybe, now that she was there, she had changed her mind.

After this, he dialed room service and ordered a vodka neat, with some olives. Leaning back into the headboard, he tried to think of anyone else he knew in Paris who could help Vera. Then he scribbled down a note to himself, to send another cable to his old CO, Taylor, asking for a list of survivors from Oradour—maybe one of the survivors would remember if Lucie was still living there at the time of the massacre. Surely Taylor could finagle that from Paris.

From the nightstand, he picked up a pulp he was reading and placed it down again, remembering his mother's disappointment when he explained **The In-Between Man** to her while she took dictation, her insistent voice ringing in his ears: **People love romance. Don't mess with that political stuff. It's love they want.** Well, she was right. He needed to weave in a secondary story line for Bacall, who played Bogie's love interest, further complicating his character's moral dilemma.

The telephone rang, the operator announcing Mr. Friedman was on the line. "Shall I put him through?"

"Yes," Sasha said, knocking back the rest of his drink.

"Sasha?"

"Hey."

"My condolences," Charlie said, breathing heavily into the phone. "I'm so sorry to hear about your mother. Sounds like a real shock."

"It was," Sasha said, gazing out at the anonymous city lights.

"Well, I'm sorry. Really sorry." Charlie allowed an appropriate pause to linger there.

Charlie began to tell him about the premiere. Ironically, **Clementine** had premiered last night, and from Charlie's account, it was a hit. "You should have seen their faces. No one walked out, not one person. Even better, I sat two seats down from Bogie and Bacall, and he loved the thing. Stood up at the end, clapping. Everyone noticed, I can tell you."

"Sounds great, Charlie," Sasha remarked, spearing a toothpick through the last green olive. A few months ago, he would have been over the moon to hear this, but now nothing felt clear or simple. "Any reviews yet?"

"Dailies are gonna hit the newsstands tomorrow, but I'm expecting good things. And I ran into Abel

Green." Charlie hesitated, sensing that Sasha wasn't entirely listening. "The editor in chief of **Variety**."

"Right," Sasha said.

"After the premiere, we bumped into each other in the lobby, and he looked pretty damn pleased."

Charlie then started talking about **The In-Between Man**, and how they needed to cast Bogie's old war buddies and the police chief. He could hear the whiskey in Charlie's voice, and imagined him sitting behind his desk, fiddling with that monogrammed Montblanc pen. "L. B. has scheduled the start date for September 3rd." The line went quiet for a minute and Sasha heard some papers rustling around, and then Charlie yelled at his secretary, but it was a muffled yell, as he probably had covered the receiver with his hand out of courtesy.

"So," Charlie's voice returned, clearer now. "How long are you going to be in New York? You sitting shiva?"

They both laughed at the thought of it, as neither one of them put much stock in religion. But then an unexpected tightness gathered in Sasha's chest, rejecting that his mother was really gone, that he couldn't pick up the phone and listen to her complaints, see her face, hear her laugh.

"So, back Monday?"

"Think I'll swing by Paris first," he managed, his voice thick with emotion.

"What?" Charlie shrieked. "For how long?"

Sasha paced the room. "I have to see Vera. I'm going to help her find Lucie."

Charlie stopped talking, which was never a good sign.

"Listen, if I don't, I'll lose her. I just . . ." He hesitated, pieces of the dream returning: the skeletal birches, her tiny form swallowed up by the forest. "I don't want to regret this for the rest of my life. That's no way to live."

"Sasha, this is your chance. I don't have to tell you that. And now you're trotting off to France? We gotta get started on locations, and Bogie has some ideas about the script . . ."

"We'll shoot it on the backlot."

"That's beside the point."

"Look, Charlie. I'll be there in time. I have to go. For a couple of weeks." He hesitated, knowing it would be longer than that.

"L. B.'s going to be livid when he hears this."

"What's there to be livid about? Pre-prep doesn't start until the end of July."

"I've never heard of a director taking off like this, right before the movie goes." Charlie softened his tone, trying a different tack. "Listen. What if you show up, and this dame is with someone else? And you risked everything for her. Then what?"

Sasha stopped before the wide glass window. "I don't care."

"Listen, kid. It'll only cause you heartbreak. And once you're over there, you'll be kicking yourself, wondering why you didn't listen to me in the first place. Come back, Sasha. This movie needs you."

"Good night, Charlie."

Vera's presence intensified in the room, as though she were waiting for him.

Sasha stood up, only partly drawing the curtains closed, so that the morning light would wake him.

CHAPTER 41

LUCIE

MID-JUNE 1945, ST. DENIS CONVENT,
SOUTHWESTERN FRANCE

While unwrapping a tiny morsel of meat parceled in newspaper, Sister Helene read from the blurred print about the death camps and what had occurred there. Another article next to it described the refugees flooding back into Western Europe from the east, and although thousands had perished in those death camps, the Allied forces were scrambling to set up new camps for the displaced persons, mainly in Germany, Austria, and Italy. She immediately thought of Lucie's parents, and pressed Sister Ismerie to bring Lucie to Paris, where all the French deportees were being sent back.

Sister Ismerie sat behind her desk, slowly coiling a string of rosary beads into her palm. "It would only get her hopes up. And when her parents aren't there, she'll want to know why. What, then, will we tell her?" She sighed, her weighty bosom rising dramatically. "We must preserve her innocence," she said, fixing Sister Helene with a steely stare. "And as you know," she continued, getting up from her desk, "innocence is such a fine, fragile thing. It must be protected. At all costs."

Sister Helene's mouth went dry at this reminder. When the war broke out, she'd arrived at the convent on the verge of giving birth, at the age of fifteen. Her mother had sent her away in a rage after finding out that her new husband had impregnated Helene, blaming Helene for seducing him, when it was he who had grabbed her and pinned her to the forest ground. She could still feel the pine cones digging into her spine, and the sound of the serin finches calling to one another from the trees, their bright yellow feathers flashing through the green.

Sister Ismerie took her in, and after the birth, all evidence of the sin was spirited away. A little boy, barely five days old. She still remembered the way he coiled his translucent fingers around her thumb, his uncertain milky eyes, his black hair matted down over his perfectly round head. He was six years old now. Somewhere else.

"It's not right, to withhold Lucie from her parents. Even if they're dead, she might have relatives looking for her."

Sister Ismerie's warm, stale breath swept over her face. She stood very close to her, something she did when she wanted to make a point. "Lucie was baptized. We must ensure her Catholic upbringing to protect her soul. She must not be entrusted to the many organizations that are now claiming hidden children. Now they want all the children back. For their own purposes."

Sister Helene swallowed hard. "I could take her to Paris. I promise, it won't be any trouble." She paused, knowing that Sister Ismerie was about to say no. "I won't involve those agencies. We'll come straight back here if no one has come for her."

Sister Ismerie pursed her lips.

Sister Helene whispered, "It's terrible, what's happened. Not only to her, but to all the displaced children. At the very least we should try to—"

"All right," she snapped. "I'll allow it. Just this once."

This morning, as was the case every morning, Sister Helene found Lucie sleeping at the very edge of her cot, nearly falling off, her sheets twisted and tossed about. Even in sleep, the most natural of states, Lucie preferred disorder. Sister Helene placed a hand on Lucie's sweaty forehead and bent down, giving her a dry cool kiss.

It took two days to get a train. Each morning, Sister Helene and Lucie waited on the drafty platform of

Gare Saint-Jean to see if there was space, but all the train cars were packed full, the station swirling with people. Finally Sister Helene begged the station-master to find them a seat on the night train.

It was a long journey with many stops and starts. Lucie couldn't sleep, worried that they would not find her parents, and then Sister Helene would leave her in Paris, a place she barely remembered. She anxiously wondered how much longer it would take, with all the stops and the tired dirty passengers who stared at them blankly, some of them so thin she could see their veins through their skin.

When they arrived at Gare d'Austerlitz, Sister Helene hesitated in her cumbersome black habit, unsure which way to go, glancing down at Lucie, as if she should know. She clutched Lucie's hand, her palm overly sweaty, and muttered that the sta-tion was so big, and there was no one to help them. Finally, she asked a passerby the way to Hotel Lute-tia, which was where the newspaper had stated all the refugees were congregating, and he explained impatiently how to reach the location via the metro. But Sister Helene did not catch his last few words and was flummoxed, an immovable black figure fro-zen in the middle of the bustling train station. It was vast and noisy, full of harsh echoing sounds and close loud chatter. Sister Helene's eyes kept darting around, peering up at the steel dome and then down again, and this made Lucie even more uncertain. She suddenly missed the convent with its cool stones, the pointed cypresses bordering the property, the weight of Camille's head on her shoulder, the day portioned out into exact, predictable intervals.

"I think we should go outside," Lucie offered.

"Outside?" Sister Helene repeated.

Lucie nodded and led Sister Helene, by her wide black sleeve, toward the exit. They emerged from the station into harsh daylight, with honking cars and trucks rearing into reverse. Miraculously, Sister Helene spied a church tower a few blocks away, as if God had outstretched His very hand to guide them.

For a long time, Sister Helene conferred in low anxious tones with the priest, while Lucie waited in the pew, fiddling with the one possession she'd been allowed to keep: the chain with a small gold heart dangling from it. She felt sleepy, lulled by the sound of their hushed voices, and by the incense-laden air, which carried a bluish tint. The priest instructed Sister Helene to inquire with city hall about the girl's parents, or try Hotel Lutetia on Boulevard Raspail, and Sister Helene, eager to show she knew this much, said they were already planning on going there first, but they had lost their way.

"Oh," the priest said, thrusting his chin forward. "They have everything one could possibly want there. Foie gras, meats and wines, cognacs, while the

French starve after having fought this war for the Israelites." When he said "Israelites," he gestured to Lucie, who stared down at the dusty marbled floor, blood filling her cheeks.

They made a few mistakes, retracing their steps, squinting up at street signs. Sister Helene kept touching her rosary beads with the little white cross hanging from it. On the way there, they passed the Lycée Victor-Duruy. Schoolgirls chattered and yelled to one another gleefully. They were going home for lunch, and their fashionable mothers waited for them outside the school gates. When they saw their daughters, the mothers smiled discreetly, some of them coming over to correct a crooked collar or fasten back a lock of hair that had escaped, but overall, a rush of tender warmth emanated from the waiting mothers, as if they knew how lucky they were to have daughters. Watching them, Lucie felt ashamed in her bedraggled navy uniform and unruly hair, her bitten-down fingernails and dusty socks sticking out of her sandals. Anyone could tell that she was with Sister Helene, who carried a heavy black briefcase with such provincial formality that it was obvious they came from somewhere else.

They walked up Rue de Sèvres and turned onto Boulevard Raspail, and stopped before a crowd gathered in front of the hotel's entrance. Sister Helene crossed herself. Some of the people wore dark threadbare clothing, holding up signs with names on them. Sometimes they let the signs drop to the ground and didn't bother to pick them up. Others slept on the sidewalk, wrapped in thick overcoats even though it was warm.

Sister Helene hesitated before crossing the street, as if mingling with those people would contaminate her in some way. Lucie didn't want to go near them either. But then Sister Helene crossed herself again and grabbed Lucie's hand, pulling her across the street. She began inquiring about where to locate the repatriated, but people stared at her with hollow, uncomprehending eyes, as if the question were absurd. The crowd jumped to life when two Red Cross buses pulled up in front of the hotel. In an animated frenzy, they held up their signs with renewed vigor. Children scrambled to their feet and balanced atop abandoned crates to see who would emerge from those magical white buses. Red Cross volunteers started carrying out stretchers from the buses, weaving through the pressing crowd, and Lucie wondered what was beneath the thin sheets.

Her heart jumped into her throat when people began screaming out names: "Markus Zebelowski!" "Estelle Gobnick!" "Gerard Markowitz!" A woman threw herself at the feet of one of the men carrying a stretcher, blocking his progress toward the hotel. "My husband," she yelled, "Adrien Epstein; he was picked up in Belleville in June 1941 . . . Do you know him? Have you seen him? Is there any news??"

Lucie thought they should look inside the hotel. From the outside, it appeared grand and ornate, with marbled columns and a red-carpeted staircase leading up to revolving glass doors. She pulled Sister Helene along, following the throng of people streaming inside.

A uniformed nurse sitting next to the door sprayed them, and the strong smell of disinfectant clouded the rooms. They both gagged from the spray's pungent smell, their eyes watering as they struggled to regain their sight, and when they did, they found a luxurious lobby. A crystal chandelier hung from the ceiling, faded yellow silk padding the walls, and Lucie stared up at an onyx statue of a maiden in flight, her flowing hair suspended by an imaginary wind. Sister Helene clung to her black briefcase as if it were an anchor, and gestured to the makeshift offices subdividing the lobby. In each office, a bureaucrat interviewed people who were presumably here for the same reason they were.

Lucie paused before a long wall covered in photographs: men in suits, little girls in school uniforms, mothers propping up babies arrayed in lace gowns for a family portrait, a whole elementary school class lined up in a row. Underneath each photograph a caption stated: **Have you seen this person? Picked up in Paris, Marseilles, Lille, in '40, '41, '43 . . . Last seen in Pithiviers, Drancy, Beaune-la-Rolande . . . Left on convoy number 58, 14, 26 . . . for Bergen-Belsen, Auschwitz . . .**

**Large reward if you know the whereabouts of . . .
Forever grateful, huge thanks.**

Absorbed by all the faces, some plaintive, some
dignified, Lucie at first didn't hear Sister Helene's
suggestion that they talk to one of the women in the
gray suits behind the desks because her parents could
have passed through here, or might even be here.

"Lucie," she repeated, gesturing to one of the partitions, "come with me."

She leapt back, staring at Sister Helene, the very
suggestion incomprehensible. "My parents aren't
here," she blurted out. "They're not like these people." The threadbare rug and moth-eaten coats and
overwhelming smell of unwashed bodies nauseated her. Lucie failed to notice other people's bitter
looks when she shouted over Sister Helene's desperate shushing. Her breath grew ragged and shallow as
she continued to explain that this wasn't the kind of
place her parents would like; they would never come
here. "We should leave. We should leave," she kept
repeating.

Finally, Sister Helene managed to speak to a
woman behind one of the desks while Lucie stood
a few feet away from the partition, refusing to be
interviewed, her arms crossed over her chest. She
turned her back to them, watching the hotel lobby
fill up with all these sad people, as thin as rails,
some of them half naked, some of them barely able
to stand, blinking at the faded luxury. She watched
them while straining to listen.

The woman asked for the child's identification papers. She then inquired if Lucie remembered any other family members, aside from her parents.

Sister Helene touched her rosary beads. "She used to talk about her parents a great deal, and her governess, who brought her to us. We were instructed to burn her real papers, in fear of a raid on the convent, in addition to giving her a new last name. Ladoux. Unfortunately, everything else was destroyed . . ." She hesitated. "In the fire, at Oradour-sur-Glane."

Lucie made a slight half turn, watching them out of the corner of her eye.

"I see," the woman said.

"Aren't the Jews, or most of them, being held in Poland? In camps?"

The woman's eyes flickered over Lucie, who was now clearly listening.

Sister Helene leaned in closer. "You don't think there's any chance?"

The woman straightened some papers on her desk. "There's the Central Tracing Agency. And the OSE. You could try there."

"The OSE?" Sister Helene asked faintly.

"The Oeuvre de Secours aux Enfants. It's a Jewish organization that rescued many refugee children during the war and put them into orphanages and homes." Sensing Sister Helene's hesitation, the woman added, "But at least put up a picture of the child on the wall over there, in case anyone is looking for her. Relatives, or a friend, might know what happened to the parents."

Then she motioned for the couple at the front of the line to step forward.

On their way out, Sister Helene froze before the wall of photographs.

Lucie pulled at her sleeve. "If they'd been here, they would have put up my photograph, to find me."

Sister Helene crossed herself before the photographs, unable to tear herself away from the faces staring back at her.

"Please, let's go," Lucie whispered, panicked. "The people. They don't look like people. They look like . . ." She tried to take a breath, but breath escaped her, and then she reached out for Sister Helene. A cold sweat peppered her chest, the edges of the room dimming, and she sensed Sister Helene holding her tightly while shapes swam before her eyes, deep blue and black blotches, as amorphous as clouds.

CHAPTER 42

VERA

MID-JUNE 1945, PARIS, FRANCE

In the cab, Vera stared impassively out at Rue de Sèvres, at the slender linden trees full of green life and the American flags rippling in the wind. Jacquard's golden curls, Madame Allard's regret, and all of those abandoned objects in her old apartment carried a menacing quality, as though she shouldn't have witnessed these things. She cranked down the window to smoke. A couple pushed a pram. Next to the cab, American GIs clogged the boulevard in their high green jeeps. She inhaled deeply. **We're all to blame**, she thought. **Just as much as Madame Allard; just as much as Etienne's parents, who hoarded my silver and probably many other tenants' possessions as well. Just as much as anyone. But I'm worse. I left my own daughter.**

Smoke escaped her lungs. It was an argument she

often had with herself, an argument that Max had refused to listen to anymore. "We had to leave," she heard him say. "Would you have rather died in the camps?"

"Instead we sacrificed Lucie to save ourselves," she shot back. His eyes went dark, and he turned away.

After this, she never said it again, even though she thought it, over and over.

The driver turned onto Boulevard Raspail, and she caught her breath at the sight of the Hotel Lutetia swarmed by refugees, clusters of them camped in front of the marble steps and then many more circling around the block. Poor and dirty in dark overcoats, they perched on their suitcases with dazed expressions, as though the crisp blue sky were too bright, the sun too strong. She focused on the children, with their translucent skin and curved stick legs. They had nowhere to go.

The driver glanced at her in the rearview mirror. "There are many, many, many." He slowed, as if to show her how bad it was. "You want to go here, yes?"

Vera pressed her hand to the glass. "Yes."

She pushed her way through the crowd, trying not to look too closely at the emaciated women in garish lipstick and tilted hats, their fragile frames engulfed by ill-fitting dresses, the men in those terrible striped pajamas. Vera paused before the revolving door, indicating for a woman carrying a small child to go first. "Please, after you," Vera said, but the woman stared back at her.

She glanced down at the woman's tattered shoes, held together by string and tape, feeling the tension of the crowd pressing behind them. She met her gaze again. "Won't you go first?"

The woman shook her head. The child woke up and started screaming.

Vera pushed through the revolving door, assailed by the colorless spray of DDT that bathed her face and hair. An official waved her through, releasing her into the lobby's swirling cacophony. She gripped her purse to her chest, her legs unsteady, the black-and-white parquet floor dizzying. Unsure what to do, she desperately looked at the other people. Some well-dressed men waited in lines, which had formed in front of different desks, and each desk advertised a number, but the numbers weren't in order. Behind each desk sat a uniformed bureaucrat, dutifully typing up some kind of report, or making telephone calls, or speaking to someone sitting on the other side of the desk in a low urgent tone. Numerous chandeliers bathed the chaos in golden luxury, softening the sight of some male deportees at a nearby table drinking champagne and grinning, their faces weather-beaten, their bony fingers clutching crystal tumblers as the waitress brought them bread. One of them fingered the fresh wildflowers in the center of the table with childish pleasure. In a leather arm-chair by the window, a man sat in a long dress shirt, his naked brittle legs splayed out while a nurse tended to him. Having suffered such extreme starvation, he had become ageless, sexless, a remnant of a human.

Vera forced herself to stop staring, but when she let her gaze wander, the disorderly lobby echoing with clacking typewriters and ringing telephones and streams of multiple conversations made her slightly nauseated. She gripped a marble column only to discover it was an ebony figurine of Perse-phone, her head tossed back and arms outstretched, fleeing from Hades. Her hair was suspended in the air, as if a strong wind blew against her.

Copying the others, Vera stood at the back of a line, hoping to talk to one of the officials behind a desk. In front of her, a heavyset man in an overcoat scrutinized the stained burgundy carpet. The other lines barely moved, the people in them resigned to waiting hours, even days, for the slimmest piece of information. As she tried to suppress a rising panic, a sprawling collage on the far wall caught her eye. The wall was covered with fluttering pieces of paper, a photograph attached to each piece. Dates, names, and places tumbled over her as she hungrily scanned the board. She gasped before the image of a young girl echoing Lucie's likeness: two dark braids and a starched lace collar, the girl sat in a chair, a book open in her lap, her eyes restless. **Colette Magineaux, age 6, last seen in Lyon on June 10th, 1943.**

Next to Vera, a teenage boy balanced on crutches, the bandages on his foot beginning to unravel. He chewed on a piece of bread, his jaw working the hard crust. Nearby a woman in a black feathered hat cried on the shoulder of an older man in horn-rimmed glasses who twisted the buttons on his striped pajamas. He gazed unflinchingly at the board. **Perhaps they too are looking for their children**, Vera thought. She almost wanted to ask them if they had looked elsewhere, or knew more about this process than she did, but she knew not to. The woman continued to cry, as though she and her husband were the only two people in the room.

After waiting in line for another three hours, she finally spoke to a man behind a desk. When she told him the last place Lucie had been seen was Oradour-sur-Glane, he shook his head, and said what she already knew: there were only a handful of survivors; she could go there and possibly talk to people in nearby villages, who might know more. But his words sounded stale and tired; he barely made an effort to finish his sentence, indicating what a futile suggestion he thought this was.

. . .

Before she left, Vera pinned up Lucie's school photograph. It was the clearest one she could find, and Katja had advised her to bring it since paperwork or other documents proving Lucie's identity had probably been lost or purposely burned during the war. Thanks to Robert's involvement with the underground, Katja knew that all children received new identities and papers once they were taken into hiding. **It was routine**, she had explained in her last letter, **but please, do not get alarmed by this. A photograph is much more effective than relying on names, dates, birthplaces, which are no longer relevant.**

Lucie stared boldly at the camera, her hair smooth and parted down the middle, braided into a single plait. Vera still remembered the struggle to brush out her hair that morning before school, with Lucie screaming and pulling away, and Max, as always, trying to cajole her into submission.

Vera's hand shook when she wrote under the photograph: **Lucie Volosenkova, age 9, last seen in Oradour-sur-Glane, September 1942. Please kindly contact Katja Donnadieu, 18 Rue Saint-Benoit, Paris, 6th arrondissement with any information.**

After this, Vera went to Katja's apartment. The place was a salve with its scent of cigarette smoke and lemon verbena, the dented-in pillows, the comfortable disorder of books and coffee cups and filled-up ashtrays stashed in unlikely alcoves. When Katja opened the door, exclaiming that she had worried Vera wasn't going to come, in that scolding sisterly way of hers, Vera fell into her arms, explaining everything that she had seen over the past days, the words tumbling out faster than her thoughts.

Katja led her into the living room and sat her down on the couch, bringing her a cool glass of water. She sat next to her, chin in her palm, listening to Vera describe Oradour-sur-Glane, with its the bullet-ridden altar, and the ghostly refugees at the Lutetia, and that wall of photographs. The afternoon deepened, the light falling onto the carpet in fluctuating prismatic shadows.

Outside, the wind sifted through the trees.

"Vera," Katja finally said after a long pause, "what are you going to do now?" She snapped off a purple grape from its stem.

Vera leaned back into the couch. "Perhaps I should return to Oradour, to see if I can find out anything more about Lucie. Ask around in the neighboring villages." She paused. "Sasha also put me in touch with someone who might help. His name is Gussie. He fought in the Resistance; they met during the war. I'm seeing him soon."

Katja nodded. "And also, go back to the Lutetia. Go there every day. You never know, you might speak to someone more helpful, someone who knows more information." Katja gestured for Vera to eat, but her stomach clenched, thinking of that "wall of absents," as they had called it.

Katja cocked her head, listening for her husband, who lay in the next room, wrapped in a heavy blanket on the divan, cushioned on all sides. "He can't bear the weight of his own body. When the sun shines, I can see through his hands."

Vera leaned forward and touched Katja's arm. "What was it like here, during the war? How did you manage?"

Katja ran her fingers through her short dark hair. "It was so quiet. And dark. Most of our friends, you know, were gone, the cafés stood empty, and an odd hush fell over the streets. We were all afraid to look at one another, as if a glance held too long would reveal the shame we felt, living under the Germans. The street minstrels and the flower sellers had vanished, and the little markets all shut, because of the rations. We rarely went out. But we tried to carry on with our lives. And then, after Robert was captured in the beginning of February, I was a wreck. I couldn't eat or sleep. They put him in Fresnes, a prison outside of Paris. The war seemed nearly over, and yet they had caught him. I was sure they would kill him because it was near the end and that's what they do."

Katja leapt up and pressed her ear against the door

of the study, where Robert rested. "His voice is so faint, sometimes I can't hear him," she said, opening it a crack. Pausing, she peered into the dim room.

Then her gaze settled back on Vera. "No one eats in this house. Please, have some."

Vera took a piece of bread, holding it in her hand, while Katja described that when Robert returned, the concierge had made him a clafoutis, with fresh cherries, but he couldn't eat it. The weight of the food would have torn through his stomach.

Katja seemed calmer as she began to prepare Robert's broth. The business of placing the pot on the stove and measuring out exact amounts of water and bone marrow, lighting the flame and watching it take, and then monitoring the dance of the flickering heat consumed her. She hummed as she worked, a nursery rhyme.

Vera watched Katja thinly slice radishes and leeks, considering the essential difference between them. Katja had nearly lost her husband, but he returned in the final moment. They could have a life together again, despite his intermittent fevers and enlarged heart and skin that turned translucent in the sun. As she prepared the broth and cut the vegetables and poured wine for herself and Vera, a silvery blue calm settled over the apartment, the same calm Vera used to feel when Lucie fell asleep against her chest, their breath merged into one breath, their hearts synchronized in a slow steady beating. As on those long, wordless afternoons, when their shared silence carried its own internal music, she now felt no need to fill the space with artificial questions or commentary, but drew pleasure from watching Katja complete these simple tasks, almost as if Vera herself now prepared dinner for Lucie, careful to manage the flame, the amount of salt, willing each bite to taste delicate and supple.

CHAPTER 43

LUCIE

EARLY JULY 1945, ST. DENIS CONVENT,
SOUTHWESTERN FRANCE

Summer was soft, redolent with fig and sap, gardenia and rosemary, trees heavy with foliage, the grass so green it hurt to look at it for too long. Lucie sensed movement—laughter, games, chasing—occurring outside the window, which was half covered by a muslin curtain that occasionally lifted with the breeze, bringing the sounds closer and then farther away.

After the trip to Paris, she spent most of the day on her cot in the dormitory watching the progression of shadows shift and flicker across the whitewashed wall, sometimes seeing that wall of photographs transposed onto it: the baby mouthing a silver rattle, the handsome couple posing in a garden, a girl who looked just like her sitting on a chair holding a book.

She shuddered, often thinking about all those emaciated men milling around the hotel, in those terrible striped pajamas, and the hard expression on the woman's face when she spoke to Sister Helene, and then the deep dread that spread through her when she realized that her parents weren't coming for her . . . Maybe they had forgotten her, or something worse had happened, despite Sister Helene's encouraging words that perhaps they were still trying to make their way back to Paris, from wherever they had gone. A wave of nausea rose up from the pit of her stomach, a blotchy darkness swam before her eyes, and then she reached out for Sister Helene.

She had come to on a chaise longue, a Red Cross nurse pressing a cool compress to her forehead and explaining in lowered tones to Sister Helene that she needed rest, and this was no place for children. Lucie felt calmer, looking into the nurse's deep-set oval eyes the color of turquoise. She wanted to keep staring into the beautiful color, as if looking into an ocean.

On the train ride back, Lucie asked if her parents would ever come for her, unable to ask the real question that ran beneath it: Were they dead?

Sister Helene bit her lip and recited a verse from Second Peter, about the Lord not being slow in keeping His promise, as some understand slowness, and that He is always patient, and He does not want anyone to perish.

. . .

Despite Camille's efforts to draw her out, Lucie insisted on remaining in the dormitory room, on her cot near the window. Camille brought her fuzzy peaches, dumping them onto the bed, and once Camille cupped her palms, filled with crushed rosemary, over Lucie's nose, making Lucie smell what was left of summer. She also reported any gossip, meager as it was, hoping to interest Lucie in school again. The teachers no longer called on Lucie because she barely spoke anymore, slumping sullenly at her desk. She only spoke to Camille, and even that was an effort.

Today, Camille burst into the dormitory. Along the wall, the shadows elongated, signaling the waning afternoon, and Lucie looked forward to the night, when sleep would take her.

Camille's eyes brightened when she sat down on the edge of the cot, clutching a bunch of wildflowers. She smelled of grass and sunlight, a missive of scents from the outside world.

"I have to tell you something." She glanced around, as if other pupils were crowding the room, but of course it was empty, as it always was at this hour.

Lucie raised her eyebrows.

"I overheard Sister Ismerie talking to Sister Helene about you. She's worried that you might fall back into the hands of the Jews"—Camille suppressed a giggle—"who are sending orphaned children to Palestine."

"Palestine," Lucie repeated. The place sounded biblical, dipped in gold.

Camille squeezed her hand. Hard. "My parents are coming to get me at the end of July. I just received a letter from them. You should come with us."

"To live?"

"We have to stick together. Otherwise, Sister Ismerie will keep you here. And after all," Camille continued, mimicking Sister Ismerie's ponderous voice, "Lucie was baptized before coming to this convent, and to protect her soul, she now belongs to the Roman Catholic faith, and it is my responsibility to look after that soul . . . to save it." Camille burst into laughter, drawing her bruised knees into her chest, her chin resting there. "Wasn't that good?"

Lucie nodded, still looking down, unsure of what to say. She couldn't imagine being here without Camille, but she also couldn't imagine what lay ahead, and if Camille's parents would like her, if they even wanted her.

Sensing her discomfort, Camille asked if she wanted to play the remembering game, which had continued between them as a kind of ritual.

Lucie shook her head.

"Come on. I'll go first."

She didn't want to play. The images had grown so faint now, she wasn't even sure those things had ever

existed. Perhaps they were just memories of memories that she'd made up.

"What do you remember about the house on
the sea?"

Lucie looked out at the trees full of overripe fruit.
And then her gaze settled on a lone lemon tree. "I
remember a low stone wall. And lemon trees."

"Oh," Camille said, clapping her hands together.
"That's new."

The image had just come to her, oddly accompanied by the sound of a piano playing in the background. She shut her eyes tightly, willing more to
emerge. Nothing. She sighed, pressing her palms
into her temples. "Your turn. What was it like, before the war?"

Camille flopped onto her back, her tan arms
folded over her head. "Oh, I don't know. School was
school. Boring as ever. But I still remember my old
desk that had a heart carved into it with the initials
A + P. I always wondered who **A** and **P** were."

"Hmmm." Lucie played with a strand of Camille's
hair, scrutinizing it.

"What do you remember about your mother?"

Lucie twisted the golden strand around her fourth
finger. "She had a wedding band that she always
wore stacked on top of another band, all diamonds,
that glittered in the light. Two rings in one. I always
wanted to wear her rings, but she was afraid I would
lose them. I think I lost a lot of things when I was
little. I think I was forgetful and not very careful."

"Oh," Camille said, unsure what to say next. The moment felt precarious.

Lucie studied the worn coverlet, a faded white. "I remember long silk dresses and fur throws. And these kid leather gloves, the color of butter, that she always left on the foyer table when she came home." She paused. "I can't remember her face. Or what she smelled like."

Camille nodded.

Lucie finally looked her in the eye. "Your mother seemed nice when she came here. Is she?"

"Oh, yes," Camille said. "But she was always too busy for a dog. Or for a little sister. Papa wanted another for a long time. Now it's too late." She smiled awkwardly, as if she shouldn't have said that last part.

The late-afternoon light cast a glow over the room, which soon filled with the other girls bustling inside to wash before supper, carrying the heat of the day with them, tossing their sun-drenched blouses into hampers, their chatter as dense as the twittering of birds outside.

Lucie silently watched them teasing one another about some local boys from the village, their movements buoyant, as hair was brushed and ribbons tied and collars straightened. Camille blended into the tumult, suddenly so far away from her, a blur of gold and white.

CHAPTER 44

VERA

JULY 1945, PARIS, FRANCE

A moist warm wind wafted through the trees, and Vera tilted back her head, catching the sun on her face to calm her nerves. She was waiting for Gussie. He had finally been able to meet, but as the minutes ticked by, she started to fear that he had forgotten. She had been back to Hotel Lutetia every day for the last two weeks, but nothing, and she now waited anxiously for Gussie to suggest another path forward.

A man in a rumpled suit strode toward her, much younger than Vera had imagined, with that disheveled hair all the young men preferred these days. A smile spread over his face when he saw Vera. After they shook hands and he kissed her on both cheeks, he remarked that the city must seem quite different to her.

"Yes," she said, "I feel like a stranger, walking around these streets, with so many gone . . ."

"It's entirely Americanized," he remarked before settling down in the chair opposite her. "Well," he said, "when Sasha first wrote to me about your daughter, the war hadn't even ended—it was very difficult to communicate about anything, as many of these operations were underground. But now the main objective is to unify families, and repatriate them back to their countries of origin. Over the last few days, I've done a bit more digging," he said, following the flash of the waitress's thigh as she strode toward them with menus.

Sweat gathered in Vera's palms, and her heart accelerated, while at the same time, she knew this was only the beginning; she shouldn't put so much stock into one lead, one contact. The search would be long and arduous, and if she did this every time even a hint of information emerged, it would flatten her.

Gussie crossed one leg over the other, and before he could continue, Vera blurted out, "I know how hopeless it seems."

He stirred a teaspoon of honey through his espresso and continued to stir for longer than necessary, nodding thoughtfully. "There has to be a survivor who's willing to talk, who might remember if Lucie was still living in Oradour at the time of the massacre." Gussie added, "Sasha already put in a cable to our old CO, who's at Hotel Bedford, to get us a list of those survivors."

From a distance, Sasha was working quietly on her behalf, and she felt a rush of affection for him, thinking about the way he gestured excitedly when he explained a scene, or how he paced a room when he was nervous, and how, when they sat down for dinner, he looked at her as if she held his heart in her hands.

"The hope being," Vera continued, touching the familiar ridge of the pearl-studded combs that held her chignon in place, "she might not have been there?"

The waitress appeared, and for an instant, Vera envied her clear, untroubled face. Gussie beamed up at her, ordering a round of aperitifs, his voice warming with charm and performance. He lifted up a knee, and cradled it with intertwined fingers. "Yes, that's what we want to know. And you should talk to Madeleine Dreyfus, over at the OSE."

"The OSE?" Vera repeated.

"Oeuvre de Secours aux Enfants," he said, and then rattled off the address.

Vera took a ragged breath, wishing Sasha were next to her so she could hold his hand, feel his warmth. She had shrugged off her cardigan, but now shivered in the cool wind. The sun disappeared behind the stone buildings, the footfall of women's high heels striking the sidewalk as they rushed home, and for an instant, Vera remembered being one of these women, in another life. She took out her pad of paper and pencil and asked Gussie to repeat the address of the OSE.

"And you've been to the Lutetia?" Gussie asked, gathering up his bag and umbrella.

"Of course," she replied.

"You posted a photograph with a message about Lucie: her age, where she was last seen, et cetera?"

Vera nodded.

"And nothing?"

"Nothing."

After Gussie left, she walked toward the Seine, the bells of Notre-Dame clanging. The air was soft, carrying the scents of the city: linden trees and petrol, sautéed sorrels and wine. She caught a whiff of roasted pheasant, and her mouth watered even though her stomach tightened with tension—she could barely bring herself to eat anything. She thought of California: the rugged sun-drenched mountains, the pure blue ocean, the simplicity of people's faces, with their bright, quick intimacy, conversations under which Vera could slide her sadness.

She inhaled the murky gritty scent of the Seine as she crossed Saint-Germain-des-Prés. In the distance, Notre-Dame's Gothic spires remained untouched, as beautiful to the Germans as she found them now. American jazz streamed out of an open window, the sonorous trumpet enriching the air. She avoided walking in the direction of her old neighborhood, the 7th arrondissement, a short stroll away. But the place had a gravitational pull, promising it would look and feel the same when she knew it didn't. But Gussie had suggested she return to her old apartment again. He urged her to talk to the concierge, not just to the boy who had helped her last time, to make sure there wasn't any news of Lucie, but she retorted that no one wanted the Jews back in France. "If we were all to come back, then the French would have to relinquish what they stole from us," she said sharply, and Gussie glanced away, not wanting to talk about it.

In the failing light, she crossed the street, looking at the chalkboards propped up on the sidewalk, advertising all the same entrées. Two American soldiers strode by, brisk in their step, tipping their wedged caps. They offered relaxed smiles, confident and unguarded, the smiles of victors.

She studied the boards while out of the corner of her eye, Vera noticed the doll seller assessing her, and a flicker of recognition passed between them. With a pang, she realized it was the same man who used to sell dolls near the Jardin du Luxembourg. He wore that silk scarf twined flamboyantly around his neck, and those hooded eyes peeked out from under his cap, with the same ragged double-breasted jacket with various medals pinned to it, an artifact from the Great War. Some of the dolls had no arms.

Others lacked bodies, offering only heads of matted hair, hanging from hooks with an air of disparagement. A few were still intact, but stripped of clothing, their hard beige flesh reminiscent of the doll Vera had given Lucie for her baptism, with flaxen hair and rose lips. Lucie had proudly named her Camille, which Vera thought fitting as the name meant "serving at the altar." She wondered if Camille was still under that bench in Sanary.

The man craned his neck, trying to catch Vera's attention, but she pretended not to see him, feeling his pressuring gaze imploring her to look back.

A few days later, she sat at her desk in the apartment Katja had found for her. She had just moved in; the rugs smelled of its former inhabitants, who had cats, and on the walls hung paintings that didn't belong to her. Tomorrow she had an appointment with Madeleine Dreyfus at the OSE. And this morning, she had gone to the offices of the EIF (the French Israeli Scout Movement). Gussie had told her that the EIF was another underground rescue organization, posing as a scouting club, that had forged identity papers for Jewish children when the deportations began in 1942. They managed to move thousands of children to Christian families, or out of the country. The building was closed with a handwritten note attached to the padlocked door promising to reopen at three p.m., but when she returned, the door was still locked. She stood there, ringing the bell, staring at the stubbornly silent intercom. Then it began to rain. She hovered under the portico for another hour, but no one came.

Sitting at the desk now, she stared out at the rows of plane trees along the boulevard, the charcoal sky hinting at evening, and she shivered. Not so long ago, she had pretended at life under the palm trees and eternal sunshine, her hand on the back of Sasha's neck as he drove with the top down, the tepid air infused with sea salt. She still recalled the heavy gray sky when he whispered, "I miss you already," sitting in the parked car in front of Union Station, both of them reluctant to get out.

California's great distance from Europe had protected her from what Europe had become. She now understood Max's fear; they no longer belonged here. Instead, Paris belonged to the Russian ambassador who lived in their flat, to the British and American soldiers who strolled their streets, hungry to consume the city's charms, and to the intelligence officers, counterespionage experts, and all those journalists feverishly typing away their impressions of the liberated city in every café and run-down hotel, cigarettes dangling from their mouths. And yet she felt acutely aware of the disappeared: schoolteachers and acquaintances, the cashier at the tabac around the corner from their apartment, their favorite waiter at

Café de Flore, Lucie's little friends and their mothers and fathers, whose absence haunted every street corner, every crowded bistro, every primary school.

She kept thinking of that wall of photographs at the Hotel Lutetia: **Last seen on June 9, 1943 . . . If you have any information kindly contact . . . Husband searching for his wife, Lilian Gosselin, from Dijon, age 36.** These pleading messages entered her thoughts without warning. While riding the tram, she could be staring out at the familiar streets and see a lost grandmother from one of the portrait photographs, waiting in a bread line. She would leap up, breaking into a sweat as the tram sped past, realizing it wasn't the same woman and knowing the real grandmother from the picture was probably dead by now. She had heard that in the camps, the sick and old were exterminated upon arrival because they couldn't work.

Sighing, she laid her fingers on the keys of the black Olivetti lent to her by Katja, and missed her pale green Underwood, still in a trunk, traveling across the Atlantic at this very moment. Katja had urged Vera to write about what had happened to her—escaping from Gurs, crossing the Pyrenees, and moving to California—but Vera didn't know if she could. The story was unfinished, and the knots gathering in her stomach, which had only intensified since her return, implied that it might not end well.

Erratically, she started banging on the keys,

nonsensical letters imprinting the page. She kept going, wincing at the harsh cacophony, until she banged both fists down on the keyboard.

In that moment, the doorbell rang.

She froze, embarrassed by this spectacle. Was she becoming a madwoman, typing gibberish? Standing up, she smoothed down the front of her dress, wondering if it was the landlady, a snow-haired woman who ferreted out gossip, or if the man next door was complaining about the banging.

Pausing before the door, Vera thought perhaps the person had left, but then she heard a sigh, and the air gathered with that particular density of someone waiting on the other side of it.

Drawing open the door, she caught her breath.

Sasha stood there, hat in his hands. He started to say something, but she rushed into his arms, breathing the fresh air he'd carried in from outside, and the familiar cigar scent of his unshaven cheek pressing into hers.

Vera touched his face. "Sasha." She could barely speak. "You're here."

CHAPTER 45

SASHA

JULY 1945, PARIS, FRANCE

His first night in Paris, they talked until early morning.

Vera never got the letter that he sent from New York, and so he explained his mother's death and what she had revealed. While he spoke, Vera stroked his face, her hand falling to his shoulder, resting there, her warmth funneling into him a comfort.

"It's strange, but I already kind of knew, or at least I sensed there was this other story running beneath the story she told me. She tried so hard to keep it from me, but at the same time, there were signs: on her face, in my dreams, and the photograph she kept of him buried inside that box. He must have been close to my age now when they met, judging from the picture." He drew a breath, flooded by the memory of the stalled train in the Berlin station,

the expectant way his mother craned her neck, peering through the dirty window, willing his father to
appear on the platform, to say one last goodbye, or
perhaps to come with them. He didn't know.

Sasha lit a cigarette, passing a hand through his
hair. "I have no idea if he's alive, if he survived the
war, if he would even want me to find him . . ."

"Do you want to find him?"

The question startled him. He rubbed his eyes
and said quietly, "I don't know, Vera. I don't know."

Hunting around for a lighter, he asked if Gussie
had supplied her with any useful contacts, and she
mentioned the OSE, and a few other rescue organizations. She described the Hotel Lutetia, the terrify-
ing wall of absents, how the man behind the desk
there seemed to think her search was a lost cause.
Settling back into bed, she said she was a stranger in
her own city, and explained the disturbing sensation
of visiting her old apartment, now filled with the de-
tritus of other people's lives.

Drifting into sleep, her head on his chest, she
whispered, "Thank you for coming here."

He awoke in the late morning with the image of
his mother's collarbone rising and falling in his
mind, as if she were struggling to breathe, beseeching him for help. Sitting up in bed, he felt power-
less, a hated feeling. Deciding to go out, he dressed

and shaved. Before leaving, he lingered in the semi-darkness of the bedroom a moment, inhaling Vera's perfume.

He kissed her beneath the earlobe. "See you in a little bit, before the OSE?"

Her eyes flickered open, a dense brown. "Where are you going?"

"Need cigarettes. And a paper. Thought I'd take a stroll."

She smiled faintly and then tossed an arm over her face, burrowing back into sleep.

A map folded into his back pocket, Sasha waded through the blue morning, crossing avenues lined with chestnut trees. He wanted to see where Vera used to live with Max—she had described it to him so many times. On his walk there, the towering Gothic churches and curved facades of elegant apartment buildings were impressive, but he couldn't help noticing signs of the recent occupation: sandstone walls pockmarked by bullets, and the stylish women who cycled past, rail thin, with that hungry gleam in their eyes. Posters of film stars were plastered over crumbling brick walls in an attempt to cover up the decay. Sitting against the wall, a little boy played with a tin can. Every time it rolled away, he wailed with renewed frustration.

Up ahead, workers laid down new cobblestones. An older woman selling flowers silently watched Sasha, ignoring the restless child in her arms. These stone streets, with their reticent flower sellers, and crates crowned with small yellow potatoes, were so unlike the flamboyant entreaties of his childhood, where peddlers demanded that you smell, taste, try.

He smiled, thinking of them with affection, the sting of salted cashews hitting his tongue, the peddlers always pressing a little treat into his palm. Later, his mother would yell, waving his pants through the air like a flag, "In the height of summer, who hides a chocolate in his trouser pocket and then lets it melt? Are you trying to make more work for me, on top of all the cleaning and cooking and sewing? Are you?"

"No," Sasha whispered, rounding the corner onto Avenue Constant Coqueline, a narrow side street funneled with hushed quiet. Feeling like a trespasser, he ventured into this shaded green seclusion, scanning each ornate entryway for the number 10.

He found Vera's old apartment at the end of the block. Ivy spilled over the balcony railings, green tendrils against the smooth sandstone. Fine iron grillwork overlaid a pair of glass doors leading into the lobby. He squinted up at the top story, almost believing Vera smoked a cigarette on the balcony, as she had described to him many times, while Lucie played with her dolls under Vera's desk. His mother would have marveled at this place, similar to the exclusive apartment buildings they used to covet. On the rare free Saturday, his mother liked to take him on the subway to the Upper East Side, where she would stop and admire the black lacquered doors with those brass knockers placed in the middle of each one, as though the doors deserved their own little crowns, announcing to his mother that they would never open for her.

Ordering a coffee, he noticed an older man at the end of the bar sizing him up, most likely having overheard Sasha's American accent when he ordered in French, which often induced a ripple of derision, as it did now. He'd picked up some basics of the language in the army, though even what little he knew was rusty. Part of him wanted to remind the man that he'd be speaking German right about now if it weren't for the Americans, but he stopped himself. What was the point? The French knew they had lost, having submitted to their occupiers, some willingly, some not. And now they chose to see themselves as winners. Everyone does that, Sasha thought, so they can hold their heads high.

Catching his reflection in the cloudy mirror behind the bar, Sasha wondered about his father. What was his wife like? And his children? And had Sasha inherited any of his father's proclivities and habits, his tastes and attitudes, or was blood merely biological, carrying none of the ineffable qualities that people often claimed were passed down from one generation to the next?

Sighing, Sasha looked up from his half-eaten dish of hazelnuts and saw Vera paused on the threshold, her silk coat cinched around her waist. She smiled at him from across the dim bar, a smile he'd never seen before. It lit up her whole face.

Coming over to him, she took his arm and whispered, "Shall we go?"

"Yes," Sasha said, "let's go."

CHAPTER 46

VERA

JULY 1945, PARIS, FRANCE

Photographs of children were tacked to the wall next to Madeleine Dreyfus's desk. In one photograph, small children sat in a circle on a lawn, playing a nursery game, a château in the background. In other photographs, older children attempted some form of gymnastics, balancing in a human pyramid, on the verge of toppling. Often, the children looked stiff, arms crossed over their chests, their faces too old for their small bodies.

Of course, Lucie wasn't in any of these photographs.

Vera drew her coat closed, staving off the depressing atmosphere of the gray unheated OSE office, with papers scattered over desks, social workers speaking to parents in sympathetic tones, and the smell of burnt coffee and old clothes. She refocused on the photographs, listening to Madeleine explain, in a mixture of French and English, for Sasha's sake, that the children in the pictures were orphans. Their parents had been rounded up and sent to the camps. Some of the children were French, but most of them were not. They lived in various homes and châteaus, run by Cimade and Secours Suisse and Tante Soly in which Jewish children mixed with French Catholic ones, providing the Jewish children a natural cover. For example, Château de Chabannes near Lyon, and the Rothschild château in Seine-et-Marne.

Vera nodded vaguely, finding it unbearable to talk about all the saved ones, when Lucie had not been saved. Then Madeleine spoke a great deal about the rescue mission in the Haute-Loire region, where a network of villages in the plateau, Le Chambon being a primary one, rescued hundreds of Jewish children during the war, getting them over the border to Portugal and procuring visas for them to immigrate to the United States, or Palestine.

"Palestine?" Vera repeated, alarmed. "Do you think Lucie could be there?" She reached for Sasha, and his warm hand closed over hers.

"I would have remembered a girl coming to us from Oradour." Madeleine sighed, glancing at a stack of documents on her desk. The phone rang, but she ignored it. "I personally went into the camps, Gurs in particular, and persuaded the mothers to give me their children. All of them did. They knew the alternative."

"I was at Gurs. September and October of 1940."

"Before things got bad."

Vera nodded. "I didn't want Lucie there. And I thought they would release us in a matter of weeks. This was the whole reason why I had arranged for her to go with Agnes instead." She took a shallow breath. "It's my fault."

"No," Sasha said, almost rising from his seat. "You had no choice."

"He's right." Madeleine fixed her eyes on Vera. "I've witnessed too many mothers lose their children for no reason other than bad luck: a neighbor who knew too much, a visa that didn't go through at the last minute, the wrong nationality, the wrong hair color, the wrong accent." She shook her head, her mouth a grim line. "The Germans did this. Not you. Never you."

Vera shifted in her chair, that familiar sharpness spidering over her chest, making it hard to breathe.

Frowning slightly, Madeleine leafed through some papers, and then sank back into her chair, pulling out a pack of cigarettes.

"We're trying to locate a survivor of the massacre, to see if they'll talk to us." Sasha paused, stealing a glance at Vera. "What else should we do?"

"I've been turning something over in my mind ever since Gussie called me, about your daughter."

Vera held her breath, too afraid to speak, waiting for Madeleine to reveal something worse. Worse than what she had already imagined. She glanced down, realizing that her hands were shaking.

"If you consider how much harder it became to hide Jewish children with the increased deportations and roundups in the summer of '42, and with having to wear the yellow star, it would have been very difficult to keep hiding Lucie in Oradour after this point." She absently touched her pendant, a low-hanging scarab. Pale gold, it caught the light. "Perhaps they moved her."

Vera nodded, feeling a pang at the memory of Max anxiously reading the paper that Sunday morning, telling her that the yellow star was now mandatory. They were afraid, but at that point, they had no idea how afraid to be.

"Where do you think Agnes would have taken her?" Madeleine lit a cigarette. "Did Agnes have any relatives or friends in other parts of France? Or Switzerland?"

Vera shook her head. "If she dared to move Lucie, it would have been somewhere nearby. She probably didn't want to travel too far as that would raise the chance of being stopped and asked for papers. And petrol was probably hard to come by." Vera paused. "She was a very cautious person. Discreet and fastidious. If she thought to do this, she would have waited until the absolute last moment to leave, perhaps not wanting to risk it."

Madeleine nodded thoughtfully, taking a long drag on her cigarette.

Vera sat down again and pressed the heel of her palms into her thighs. "Do you think there's a possibility that Lucie is alive?"

Their eyes met, and Vera caught the uncertainty on her face, but she also saw a flicker of promise.

"Maybe," Madeleine said.

When she said this, the chaotic swirl of the OSE offices stood still. Vera no longer noticed the multitude of people shuffling in and out, desk drawers opening and closing, the dusty weak light filtering in through the windows, the phones trilling incessantly, the teenagers in ill-fitting suits milling about, presumably DPs who were too old to be classified as children anymore but too young to begin new lives as adults.

Vera saw only Madeleine's gray-blue eyes leaping at the thought that all was not lost. Her hands trembled when she reached into her purse and pulled out the photograph. "This is Lucie."

Lucie looked directly into the camera. The photo had been taken that last summer in Sanary. She perched on the curved trunk of the car, her little bare feet balanced on the license plate, wearing a white cotton frock with sleeves that fluttered out like butterflies. For a brief instant, Vera felt embarrassed by the photograph. It revealed their wealth, showing how privileged Lucie was here, with Mourka draped over her lap, sitting on top of an expensive car, basking in the sun.

"Just before I left, I gave her a necklace, with a small golden heart on it."

Madeleine lit another cigarette, offering it to Vera, then asked if Lucie had any distinguishing marks, anything that couldn't be erased. "You see, we're finding that, after so many years, many of the children don't recognize their parents, especially if they were quite young when the war started. The parents are also unsure, but of course they're desperate to get their children back, so sometimes mistakes are made. Mistakes that are very hard to reverse." She leaned against the desk. "It's been five years. Imagine how Lucie might have changed. Imagine what she looks like now."

"She has a birthmark on the third finger of her right hand. It's a pink blotch traveling up the knuckle, as if she slammed a door on it."

Pale sunlight hit Madeleine's face and illuminated the tiny translucent hairs downing her cheeks. "Well, that's something."

"Yes," Vera said faintly.

Madeleine sat back down and slid a piece of paper and a pencil over to Vera. "I'm going to read you a list of all the known convents in the area of Oradour, in and around Limoges. There's a slight chance Agnes might have taken her to one of these. But even then, it's quite unlikely, I'm afraid . . ." She paused and gave Vera a long steady look. "Are you ready?"

The pencil felt slick in her hand. She tried to swallow but couldn't, her chest so tight she thought it might explode.

"Yes, we're ready," Sasha said.

The air was fresh and cutting, filtering into the green Citroën with its rusted fender and front tire on the verge of going flat. Gussie got them the car from his old literature professor at the Sorbonne, who had coincidentally read one of Vera's novels and admired it.

Sasha accelerated, the outskirts of Paris receding in the rearview mirror, the sky interspersed with pink-bellied clouds, the edges tinged with gold. It would take almost five hours to drive to Limoges, in the southwest of France, near Oradour, where the majority of the convents were.

Vera spread the map over her lap. Her blouse rippled in the wind. She looked up and turned to him, her cheek pressed into the leather headrest.

Lush green fields flitted past, filled with wildflowers. She wondered if Sasha only saw the war in those rolling hills and low stone walls he would have crouched behind. She placed her hand on the back of his neck.

The road stretched before them. Peaceful, green, empty.

"We don't even have a place to stay in Limoges." But she was relaxed because finally she felt on the right path, finding a hotel the least of her worries.

"We'll find a room."

"I know," she said softly, running her fingers through his hair. "I had a dream about Max last night. Well, it started with him. He told me to take Lucie away. We bundled her into the car and I drove. Max stayed behind in Sanary. The ocean waves along the road were so high, towering above us, these dark blue watery columns cresting higher and higher, and I knew once they crashed down, Lucie would drown, but there was no choice but to keep going—" She broke off, and gazed out the window.

Rows of lavender rolled by.

"Did you make it?" Sasha asked.

"The dream ended then." Vera tapped her ring against the car window.

CHAPTER 47

VERA

JULY 1945, SOUTHWESTERN FRANCE

They had been driving for three days, each night returning to the hotel in Limoges, each morning setting out again. They visited two to four convents a day, depending on how much distance they had to travel and the nature of the roads. They arrived after lauds, or before the midday prayer. Later in the afternoon, they tried to get there before vespers.

Each convent had its own distinct character. Some were sequestered, set back from the road, surrounded by copses of trees, the halls flooded with solemn shadows, places so quiet Vera couldn't imagine even one child living here. At the abbey of St. Martin, the nuns averted their eyes, deferring to the Mother Superior, who explained that they had sheltered only four children during the war, two boys and two girls, who were older, all Czech.

"How old?" Vera asked, feeling the blue shadows thicken around her.

"The youngest, Klara, was eleven when she arrived."

Even so, Vera held out the photograph of Lucie, and the Mother Superior snatched it from her hand and, with a sniff, shook her head.

At Bourbourg Abbey, the nuns were younger and more cheerful. They wore light blue tunics with white habits, and Vera felt as though multiple Virgin Marys surrounded her. They spoke in soft, consoling tones, their creamy skin smelling of talcum powder.

Sasha stood respectfully a few feet away, near the door.

"We have a school for girls here. Some are orphans. What is your daughter's name?" the young nun asked while the Mother Superior smiled encouragingly.

When Vera showed them Lucie's picture, they all nodded, but Vera could tell they didn't recognize Lucie and her chest ached. She tried to take measured breaths, but it was impossible. She reached out for Sasha, but instead found her hand tangled in a nun's blue robe. She bestowed Vera with a forgiving nod.

"It's an old picture," Vera explained. "She might not even look like this anymore."

Mother Superior gave her a tired little nod. "Let's take a look."

On the way to the dining hall, passing through the cool dim corridors, the Mother Superior said that all the girls in the school were French, and about half had lost their parents in the war. "The other half are regular pupils, with families to go home to when the term ends. We have forty pupils attending at the moment. There's one who might fit your description. She came to us in the middle of the night. A Resistance fighter brought her to our doorstep. It was pouring rain, a few days before the Feast of the Immaculate Conception. I still remember her blue lips, and she was wearing a thin wool coat, soaked all the way through. She didn't even know her name, or wouldn't tell us. Many of the children had been trained to forget their real names, so we named her Juliette. Juliette Martin. I suppose the choice of 'Juliette' was a little ostentatious, but she looked so sweet and delicate, we wanted to give her a pretty name. She was four years old."

"Four," Vera repeated, trying to suppress the tremor in her voice.

"Yes," the Mother Superior said, before opening the door to the dining hall.

. . .

The girls sat in rows, wearing navy pinafores over white shirts with Peter Pan collars, their hair braided down their backs. "She is ten years old now. Do you see her, over there, at the far end of the table?"

"Yes," Vera whispered. A sharp fear funneled into her throat. She glanced over at Sasha, who looked anxiously across the room.

Mother Superior went to retrieve her, leading the girl over by the hand.

It wasn't Lucie. Vera saw this immediately. The girl had an odd loping gait, and her skin was darker, echoing Vera's olive complexion, as opposed to Lucie's marble white.

The girl glanced up, chewing on her bottom lip. Vera took in her amber eyes and russet-brown hair that, despite the braid, was unruly, and for a moment, although she knew this wasn't her daughter, the girl's imploring gaze urged her to say yes.

Vera could have a daughter again, and the girl could have a mother.

The girl turned away, hiding her face in the folds of the Mother Superior's robe.

Vera shook her head. "I'm sorry."

The Mother Superior nodded, holding the girl close. "The Holy Spirit guides us. We will pray for you."

Vera suddenly grew aware of the other nuns surrounding her, and she felt soothed by the closeness of their warm bodies and the soft fall of their voices.

A sense of mutual agreement rippled among them, and they began to recite a piece of scripture:

Whatever is has already been,
and what will be has been before;
and God will call the past to account.

CHAPTER 48

VERA

JULY 1945, SOUTHWESTERN FRANCE

After they left Bourbourg Abbey, they drove back to the hotel in silence. Her disappointment was palpable; she could almost taste its metallic bitterness. Frowning at the passing greenery, she felt her body tense and coil up, as if the surrounding vineyards, the sky and the clouds, were conspiring against her, keeping Lucie away.

Thank God, when they returned to the hotel, a cable from Gussie awaited them at the front desk. He had managed to locate one of the survivors of the Oradour massacre, Jacques Durand, who was willing to talk. He agreed to meet them tomorrow at noon in Limoges, at Café Chez Marie.

· · ·

Jacques Durand sat stoically at the table, a cane propped up between his legs, his hands resting over its curved top. He had a neat graying mustache and wore a houndstooth cap, the brim casting a shadow over his deep-set eyes. When they shook hands, he squinted at them, managing a brief smile. A basket of stale rolls stood on the table, along with a carafe of water.

Vera poured some water into their glasses.

For a moment, no one said anything.

Jacques coughed into his sleeve.

"Thank you for meeting with us," Vera began.

"Yes, thank you," Sasha added in English, leaning over the lip of the table.

Vera lightly touched his shoulder, indicating that the rest of the conversation would follow in French. It was a little signal that had naturally developed between them, as most people spoke no English, and Vera hoped her impeccable French would help people, like Jacques, view her as one of them, as opposed to another refugee with her hand out.

Jacques nodded and pressed his palms into his cane, as if it were an anchor. "You want to know about the girl Agnes was taking care of on the farm, during the war?"

"Yes," Vera nodded. "Lucie."

His pursed his lips. "Lucie. I remember her. She used to play the piano a little bit. She liked to look at my tools." His eyes watered. "I am a piano tuner.

I have been tuning pianos my whole life." He began to explain that he knew Agnes when she was young. They were in love, but he was too old for her, and their families, both farming families, harbored a mutual hate for each other that spanned a century, over a land dispute. "In retaliation, Agnes's family sent her away to become a governess in St. Petersburg."

Vera touched the top of his blue-veiny hand. "She was my governess."

The man drew a labored breath. "When Agnes returned to Oradour in 1940, I couldn't believe my eyes. Still the same elegant girl. Just a little older." He smiled. "I thought she'd never come home. But with her sisters, you know, she didn't have a good relation." He adjusted his cap.

The awning of the café flapped in the wind.

He crossed his arms over his chest and gave them both a mischievous grin. "And luckily, the Fauchuex family had a piano. An old Schilling Victorian that needed tuning. Already I had been coming there twice a year to tune it, but when Agnes returned, I said it needed tuning more often than that."

He carefully started to deposit some tobacco leaves into cigarette paper. "That's when I noticed Lucie. She was always hanging around the piano, hoping to play a few chords."

Vera interjected, "Lucie played piano with her father. Every night, after dinner."

Jacques tightly rolled the cigarette, licking the

end to make sure it stuck. "Agnes vaguely referred to Lucie as a distant cousin who had come to live with them, but we knew there was no distant cousin. We know everything in these parts." He shifted positions in the rickety chair. "Lucie stayed with Agnes up until about 1942, and then she took the child away right before a German regiment came into town."

"And?" Vera said, sitting very still. "Where did she take her?"

"I don't know. When Agnes returned, she said nothing." He smiled faintly.

"Oh," Vera gasped, clutching Sasha's forearm, her mouth incredibly dry.

"Vera," Sasha said, holding her hand tightly. "What did he say?"

"Agnes took Lucie away in 1942, and moved her somewhere else. He doesn't know where, though."

Her heart lifted and expanded with the possibility of Lucie's nearness, that she could still be living and breathing somewhere, maybe even a car ride away, and various scenarios flashed through her mind: an orphanage, a DP camp, an elderly couple who agreed to hide her in their cellar. "Oh, thank God," she cried, leaping up from the table, not wanting to waste one more minute sitting here, when they could be on the road again, racing to the next convent.

But then she grew aware of Jacques across the table; he regarded her with a pained expression, his face hollow and creased. He bent over his cane and coughed into the crook of his arm before regaining his composure.

A stray dog trotted into the middle of the square before a man pulling a pushcart whistled for it.

They all watched the dog. A hot shame filled Vera for displaying such intense relief when this man had probably lost his entire family that day, and here she was, radiating joy.

The dog paused, debating whether or not to obey its master.

Jacques cleared his throat. "I left early that morning, to tune a piano in Saint-Denis. A Steinway and Sons. From the nineteenth century. The keys always stuck. When I left, I forgot to say goodbye to my wife." He looked down at his hands.

When Sasha offered him a handkerchief, he waved it away.

"Here," Sasha said, half rising from his chair. "Please, take a glass of water."

Jacques sipped from the glass slowly, his face wet and flushed.

Vera watched him with a secret fear, knowing that only a small amount of restraint prevented her from having these lapses, when the uncertainty grew unbearable. She had orchestrated such scenes privately, in the house on Adelaide Drive, before Max came home in the evenings. She recalled the feeling of the wooden floorboards against her cheek after she had pounded them with her fists until her knuckles bled, and afterward tore off her blouse because sweat drenched the front of it. And then, in her slip, shivering, she cleaned up the mess, cursing herself in the aftermath. By the time Max came home, she had taken a long nap, and folded away all that rage for another day.

"In just a few hours, they were taken from me," Jacques said, wiping his eyes with the back of his hand. "Charlotte was engaged to be married." He gestured to the tiered fountain in the middle of the square, the water steadily sputtering.

Afterward, they watched Jacques amble along the square's perimeter with his cane. He waved to a few old men sitting on green benches who were tossing crumbs to pigeons.

Vera looked at Sasha, her eyes damp. "Thank God she didn't burn in that church."

"She was lucky," Sasha said softly. "It all comes down to that."

They looked out at the square to watch Jacques again, but he had disappeared behind the soaring stone church.

CHAPTER 49

LUCIE

LATE JULY 1945, SOUTHWESTERN FRANCE

At the end of July, Camille's parents, Jean-Paul and Marie, returned to the convent to fetch Camille and Lucie. They would take the girls to their summerhouse on the Basque coast, in Saint-Palais, for the summer holiday.

"It's a good place to recover and forget, for all of us," Jean-Paul said to Sister Ismerie in the shadowy vestibule of the convent as they waited for Lucie and Camille to finish packing their things.

The convent was quieter than usual, as all the other girls had already gone home. Before Lucie left, Sister Helene knelt down and took her by the shoulders, her eyes watering slightly when she told her to be good, and to listen to the Bonheurs. Her mouth trembled when she said, "It is the best thing for you."

Lucie nodded, a knot gathering in her throat. And then, unexpectedly, Sister Helene hugged her, pressing Lucie's cheek against her chest, as though she didn't want to let her go. She whispered into Lucie's hair. "Look after yourself. Everything will be all right."

Lucie nodded, taking in Sister Helene's powdery rose scent. Pulling away from her, she knew she had always wanted to leave the convent, had always waited for this crucial day, but now she felt afraid. Afraid to leave the last tie to her parents, and afraid the Bonheurs would not like her, and that it might be different with Camille outside of the life they had shared here. Would Camille have other, better friends, from before the war? Would they sleep in the same room? She didn't want to be a nuisance to the Bonheurs, and she worried that she would be, as Sister Ismerie was always saying that she was such a nuisance, and prayed to God to guide her and show her how to love this child, as though Lucie were a great spiritual obstacle.

In Saint-Palais, Lucie and Camille spent their days wolfing down a breakfast of chocolate milk and croissants before running barefoot through pine needles to the long flat beach. They collected shellfish in mesh bags for dinner. Lucie rescued cloudy pieces of sea glass that she found beautiful, even though

Camille said those pieces were just from old beer bottles, broken down and washed up on the shore, turned into this.

During the long afternoons, they rode rusty oversized bikes along dirt paths, zooming past low stone walls, wildflowers twined around the handlebars for decoration. The surrounding area had only been liberated two months ago, and they discovered a burnt-out door from a jeep lodged in the forest. They cycled past bombed farmhouses, and along a lavender field cordoned off by barbed wire, they dug up cartridges around the perimeter. They touched the cartridges with curiosity before stuffing them into their knapsacks to be examined later, on their twin beds that they'd pushed together into one.

On the windswept beaches, they snuck into blockhouses in search of the fabled poisoned candy that the Germans had sprinkled over the countryside to kill French children before their final retreat, but they found nothing.

When they returned in the evening, Marie commented that the color had returned to Lucie's cheeks, announcing to no one in particular that it was so good for them to be outside all day, by the sea.

At night, they slept with the windows open, listening to the distant waves, to the mosquitoes and crickets, to cats prowling along ivy-covered walls.

With the bedroom door ajar, they overheard Marie and Jean-Paul playing bridge with friends, smoking and talking about the future of the party and the great progress that was being made.

Sometimes Jean-Paul got hungry in the middle of the night and could be found standing at the stove, a faraway look in his eyes as the eggs sizzled and burned. Marie would come in, scolding him, dumping the eggs into the bin and cracking another one into the pan, and they would talk seriously about what would happen when Camille started the Lycée Mondenard in Bordeaux next month. Lucie heard them saying they couldn't possibly leave her at the convent without Camille. "She'll wither away there. You see how attached they are," Marie said. The Sisters would agree to it, Marie explained, because no one had come looking for Lucie, and any link to her family, if they had even survived, had been entirely erased. And as a magistrate, along with his valiant service during the war, Jean-Paul would easily acquire the necessary consent of the judicial authorities to adopt her.

You will come live with us, as Camille's cousin," Marie said brightly the next morning over buttered toast. "And of course, you'll take our name. It's for the best."

Camille started chanting "Lucie Bonheur, Lucie

Bonheur" in a singsong voice, sashaying around the kitchen table in an irritating blur of light and noise that made Lucie want to hide away in some dry dark place. They'd given her a new last name when she started at the convent, Ladoux, so losing it held little consequence, even though last names mattered greatly to Marie, who kept repeating that a new name was a fresh start. Her name before, the one belonging to her parents, she felt embarrassed that she couldn't remember it. Only that it was long and hard to pronounce. A name they made her forget, a name she was never supposed to say out loud.

But it seemed, from her faint memory, that her parents, even if they were Jewish, were no different than the Bonheurs. Her mother also smoked and wore silk slacks and returned in the late afternoon saddled with shopping bags, her peacock-feathered hat slanted at a fashionable angle. Just as she witnessed Camille falling asleep on her mother's pale sweater last night, she remembered lying over her mother's coat, the fur delicate and soft against her cheek, the murmur of adult conversation soothing and distant.

Why had her parents been sent to the camps and not the Bonheurs? Did they not fight hard enough? Why had they so willingly left that long-ago day in the car with smiles on their faces, abandoning her?

Lemons, sunlight, a low stone wall, the smell of rich smoke floating from a lounge chair where her father puffed on a cigar, the newspaper half covering his face.

She caught her breath, squeezing her eyes shut, burrowing into dark memory, trying to retrieve more.

That night in bed, Camille was overly silly, pinching Lucie's arm and babbling like a baby, and then laughing about it.

Lucie kicked off the sheet, scratching at her mosquito bites.

"Mama," Camille called, sitting up in bed. "Mama."

Marie appeared in the doorway, cradling a glass of wine. "What is it?"

"Mama," Camille repeated, creating an awkward silence in the room.

"I'm here, Camille. What's the matter?"

"Mama, please, pretty please sing me the old song, the one from when I was a baby?"

Lucie pressed one of Camille's old stuffed animals to her chest, fighting the urge to dig her fingernails into the inside of her wrist until little half-moons of blood emerged. She found herself yearning to do it more and more, ill at ease with the familial chatter, the disorderly flooding sunlight. Camille's parents touched each other all the time and kissed Camille on the head thoughtlessly. Such displays of affection disoriented her, and she missed the convent's tomb-like silence, the dusty vestibules, the serene stone saints, how the nuns maintained their own circles of solitude, circles that never overlapped.

She had her own circle too, one that never opened except for Camille, whom she had clung to from the very beginning, but now other people invaded this circle: Jean-Paul with his scratchy beard when he hugged her, Marie calmly fixing her hair, various friends and relatives who appeared every Sunday, interrupting one another, hugging and yelling and laughing. She also noticed tumblers still smelling of wine were often left on the dining table from the night before, and the half-peeled carrots on the cutting board attracted fruit flies, and various doors were flung open and left that way, inviting anyone to traipse through a room, unannounced. Lucie resisted the impulse to clear away the glasses and finish the peeling and close all the doors.

Marie perched on the edge of the bed, looking over at the half-open bedroom door, perhaps fearing the roast would burn or her dinner guests would arrive early. They all heard Jean-Paul opening kitchen drawers and slamming them shut, searching for a corkscrew as he did every evening at this hour. He swore, the corkscrew eluding him.

Marie sighed. "'Au Clair de la Lune'?"

Camille nodded, pressing her cheek against the pillow, and Marie began to sing, her thin high voice filling the room. "**Au clair de la lune, mon ami Pierrot, prête-moi ta plume, pour écrire un mot. Ma chandelle est morte, je n'ai plus de feu. Ouvre-moi ta porte pour l'amour de Dieu.**"

Lucie clenched her fists, digging her nails into her palms, feeling the enticing pressure. When Marie finished, she glanced over at Lucie, and her eyes clouded over. Lucie started to suck her thumb, an old disgusting habit from childhood that the nuns had stomped out that she now had started doing again. Marie stared at her as if she were some pitiful creature, a wounded bird or a lame dog hobbling alongside the road.

She touched Lucie's shoulder. "I know how much you miss your mama and papa." She paused, giving her words their full weight. "I'm sure they miss you too, very much."

Lucie jerked away and inched closer to the wall. She wanted to scream and hurl the stuffed animal at Marie, but then the Bonheurs would surely send her back to the convent. "I don't have any parents."

Marie didn't move from the bed.

Lucie squeezed her eyes shut. She couldn't bear to look at the woman's sorrowful face, so full of feeling. Beneath her tightly closed eyelids, she saw dark blue blots within the black. She imagined Marie deliberating over whether she should remain here on the bed, to see if Lucie would burst into sobs, revealing how vulnerable she was, and she wondered if she wanted to be loved by Marie. She steeled herself against such a saccharine impulse and opened her eyes, scrutinizing the paisley wallpaper. She kept staring at it, debating if the paisley was violet or black, her eyelids growing heavy. The design slowly blended into the darkness.

CHAPTER 50

VERA

LATE JULY 1945, SOUTHWESTERN FRANCE

The next morning, they woke up early to reach the convent of St. Denis before midday Mass. It was the last one on the list. She chose her outfit carefully, gabardine slacks and a chiffon blouse, wondering if today would be the day they would find Lucie. The meeting with Jacques had lifted her spirits, perhaps too much, but she greedily grabbed at that hope. Everything felt lighter, pliant with possibility, the sun streaking through the clouds a sign that they were on the right path. She tugged on her pearl earring and took in the passing foliage, bracingly green, still wet from last night's rainfall.

During the two-hour drive they barely spoke, but she enjoyed this intimate silence, was calmed by its weight. After meeting Jacques yesterday, the revelation that Lucie had not died in the massacre infused

her with manic joy, a rush of it. In the little hotel
room later, under the thin coverlet, she and Sasha
found each other again, both grateful for the release
after so many tense days, because the good news
was a shred of something real, something she could
almost touch. White moonlight streamed into the
room, washing over their bodies with bright desire.
His animal warmth surrounded her, and she felt as
contained as the safe, warm hush that descends on
a concert hall before the orchestra begins to play.
When she woke up in the morning, she touched his
hand, enclosing it in hers, and for a brief interval let
herself believe that the story didn't end here. They
would keep searching until the end became the beginning of something else.

When they neared St. Denis, she started getting
nervous again, bracing herself for what, if anything,
they would find.

Sasha smoked and drove with concentration,
mulling something over.

She gripped the door handle when he whipped
around bends in the road. "You're deep in thought."

He slowed a bit. "It's just work."

"What's happening?"

Shrugging, he continued, "Bogart has some notes
on the script. Changes he wants made. They want
me back in LA."

"Will you go?"

"I'm seeing this through with you."

Vera kissed him on the cheek, her mouth lingering there, and then she rested her head on his shoulder.

"And I've been tossing around some other ideas. About the war, about ordinary people who were just trying to survive, and remain human." He glanced over at her and then added, "Did you know that Madeleine Dreyfus was sent to Bergen-Belsen for over a year?"

"No."

"Toward the end of the war, she'd just had her third child, but refused to stop with the rescue missions. She received a call that the Gestapo was about to raid a children's home. Of course, she had no way of knowing that on the other end of the line, the Gestapo held the caller at gunpoint. When she got there to save the children, she walked right into their trap." He pulled off the main road onto a smaller one tunneled by overgrown fruit trees.

Sasha frowned, glancing at the map for a minute. He strained to see around the bend in the road. "It's up ahead, a few kilometers."

She flipped open her compact, powdering her face, trying to contain the mounting sense of dread mixed with sharp hope that this could be it.

Getting out of the car, she stood before the Romanesque church, dark and low to the ground, surrounded by blooming fruit trees and thick hedges. Gripping each other's hand, they walked over the pale gravel toward the sky blue door.

She held her breath, afraid to knock, but then it opened.

A tall imposing nun filled the entryway, her doughy moon face glistening with sweat. "Hello," she said. "Welcome to St. Denis. Please, come inside."

In the vestibule, the spartan walls gave off a moist chill. Weak light filtered through the arched windows along the corridor, and she heard the faint sound of children playing in the yard. Mother Superior, noticing that Vera was trying to see beyond the enclosed courtyard, informed them that this was a convent school for girls, known for its outstanding reputation.

The other nun standing a few feet away timidly smiled at them.

"And this is Sister Helene," the Mother Superior announced. "She may provide a brief tour of the premises, if you would like."

Sister Helene was younger, with freckles over the bridge of her nose, and wore a string of white rosary beads from which hung a heavy wooden cross. The Mother Superior wore an elaborate golden cross that blazed against her black robe, reminding Vera of an evening gown she once had owned, a long time ago.

For a moment, Vera wanted to pretend that she was only here for a tour; the idea felt seductively real.

"No, thank you. We aren't here for that. I'm

looking for my daughter, Lucie Volosenkova. She had been living in Oradour-sur-Glane with our governess, Agnes, who might have brought her here, in 1942, toward the end of the year?" Vera stopped short, seeing the muscles in the Mother Superior's jaw tighten. Sister Helene's cheeks flushed, and she clutched her rosary beads.

Sensing the tension in the air, pierced by a stab of expectation, Vera added, "She would have been six years old at the time."

The Mother Superior replied, "I'm so sorry. We never had anyone here that fits your description. I thought you were prospective parents, interested in our school."

Seeing Vera's expression, Sasha took her elbow and whispered into her ear to press the nun and explain that Madeleine Dreyfus at the OSE said many convents in this area hid Jewish children during the war. "Ask her more questions," he added.

"I'm sure it's a wonderful school," Vera began, "but Madeleine Dreyfus at the OSE informed us that many of the convents in this area hid children during the war. Jewish children."

Mother Superior turned her face toward the window. The morning sun slanted across her cheek before she smiled warmly. "Yes, we've had other parents, such as yourself, knocking on doors around these parts, looking for lost children, but I'm afraid we did not hide any Jewish children here. We had a few French children whose parents were in the

Resistance, and we willingly sheltered them." She paused, giving Sister Helene a pointed stare. "But no Jews."

Sister Helene nodded, her eyes trained on the black-and-white parquet floor.

Vera glanced over at Sasha, and he gave her an encouraging nod.

"May I ask why not?" Vera said.

The question momentarily flustered the Mother Superior. "Well, as you can see, our school is quite well-known in these parts, and we were already full to capacity, with French children from Paris whose families wanted them out of the city during the war. We just didn't have the space to safely accommodate any more children, especially Jewish children, who would have put all of us at risk."

"I see," Vera said, unconvinced, and then she turned to Sasha. "They didn't hide any Jewish children here."

"Really?"

"Sasha, what am I supposed to do? If that's what she says . . ."

"She's defensive," he whispered back, his eyes darting around the vestibule, as if he could find some clue in the stained glass nativity scene, or the marble putti in the garden, with their little dispassionate smiles.

The nuns glanced warily at Sasha now that they realized he was an American.

"In any case," Vera rejoined, holding out a piece

of paper, "I wrote down my address and telephone number here, if something comes to mind. If you hear anything from a neighboring convent or from the OSE that would fit our description, please contact me. Please." Vera's eyes beseeched them.

The piece of paper disappeared into the heavy black folds of Mother Superior's robe. She produced another bright smile, and then announced that midday Mass was about to start.

"Sister Helene will show you out." She turned down the whitewashed corridor, her black robe flaring behind her.

Sister Helene fumbled with the keys to reopen the front door.

When it finally opened, a spring wind flooded into the entryway.

The nun took Vera's hand, her light eyes watering from the glare of the noonday sun. Watching her meek gestures, Vera shivered at the thought of convent life: the interminable devotion, solitude and obedience.

"Madame Volosenkova, may I ask if you have tried the Hotel Lutetia? It appears to be a central point of information."

"Yes," Vera replied. "I went there. Many times."

Sister Helene watched them carefully. "It must be so difficult, this loss."

"We're not done searching," Sasha said in English

before walking back to the car. He lit a cigarette and leaned against the car door.

Vera turned toward her. Slight traces of concern lined Sister Helene's high forehead.

"Thank you for showing us out, and for taking the time to talk to us. Please do let me know if anything turns up regarding my daughter."

Sister Helene continued to hold her arm.

Vera extracted herself, dabbing her eyes with the back of her glove, trying to hide the crushing feeling tearing her up inside. Another dead end. Another failure. Another place where Lucie hadn't been.

"You must take care," Sister Helene said, looking at her with too much feeling, a suffocating sympathy that made Vera want to sprint to the car. "May God go before you, and lead you."

Sister Helene waved to them from the stone steps.

Vera waved back through the dusty windshield while Sasha struggled with the gearshift. She leaned into the seat. The Mother Superior's obdurate moonlike face, which seemed to will Lucie's existence away, had filled her with a tinny hollowness.

Sister Helene continued to wave from the steps.

"She's still watching us," Vera said.

Sasha thrust the stick into reverse, and the car made a guttural noise, resisting the sudden movement. He jerked it back into drive and then into reverse again, saying with effort, "That Mother Superior didn't like all our questions."

"Do you think she knows something, about Lucie?" Vera asked as she jerked down the window to let in some air.

He steered the car back out of the long driveway, straining to see the road behind him, which was obscured by shadows and foliage. The tendons in his neck stuck out, pulsing with effort.

"Honestly, I can't tell. But she protested too much, about not hiding any Jewish kids. What's that expression again?"

"'The lady doth protest too much' . . ." Vera's voice trailed off as they backed out into the main road. She caught the last glimpses of the church steeple slicing into the sky.

"Yeah, that's what I mean," Sasha said. "Kind of reminds me of when you write a scene, and a character is overcompensating for something, so they come across as too happy, or overly righteous . . ."

"So, is this just another story idea for you?" she lashed out, that sharp anxiety vengeful, wanting to punish someone because St. Denis had been the last convent on their list. From here, she'd have to start over. Contact the EIF again, go back to the OSE, locate those Protestant priests in the Le Chambon region who had hidden children in the mountains, but the thought of that made her want to scream— more uncertainty, more obstacles, more people who didn't know anything or just looked at her as if she were mad, searching for one girl out of thousands.

He kept driving, not taking the bait. This incensed her more. "And your idea to write a whole movie dedicated to Madeleine. Are you trying to compare her to me? Because I left my own daughter behind when Madeleine wouldn't leave even one child during the war, risking her life countless times? Is that what you're implying, with all this talk of her? That it's my fault I lost her? Because I'm a selfish, terrible mother who left my daughter behind to save myself?"

"No, I'm not."

Infuriated by his calm refusal to fight, she pounded her fists on the leather dashboard. She wanted to cry, but no tears came, only a hot, white rage, reminding her of those early days after the massacre, when she couldn't cry. She could only scream, filled with hatred for herself.

"Vera," he said, reaching over to her. "Stop."

He pulled over to the side of the road and turned off the engine. The stillness of the countryside filled the small car.

Pressing her damp forehead into the dashboard, she whispered, "St. Denis was supposed to be it. When we were driving there, I felt closer to Lucie, somehow. I felt her in the trees, in the air. And then nothing, nothing again, nothing so many times . . ." Her voice broke and she burst into sobs, boring her forehead into the dashboard again, trying to calm herself against the solid surface, as if it would stop the continuous stream of self-lacerating thoughts.

She murmured into the leather, "We're in a stupid desperate search that will never end, and you don't even have the heart to tell me."

"Vera," he said, taking her hands in his as she sat up. "I don't know what's going to happen. That's the truth."

She leaned her head against the window, exhausted.

Sasha started the car again.

The hollowness returned, so callow and numb, urging her to accept that Lucie was really gone.

He shifted the gear back into drive, refocusing on the road. "We'll keep searching. I promise you."

Catching a glimpse of herself in the car window, she flinched: her smudged eyeliner, blotchy skin, and pained, distraught expression made her unrecognizable. In that moment, a line from Akhmatova swam back to her, forceful and true: **Motherhood is a bright torture. I was not worthy of it.** Akhmatova wrote this about her little boy, Lev, who was separated from her, and Vera now understood this bright torture was a kind of prize that only mothers who actually raised their own children could claim to endure. Not mothers who abandoned their children, or allowed their children to be taken from them. Those mothers had neither torture, nor brightness. Only a relentless negation, like the sound of cranes crying across an empty field.

CHAPTER 51

SASHA

AUGUST 1945, PARIS, FRANCE

The passage of time began to weigh on him with its own special density, and he started to fear that they wouldn't find Lucie. He felt this increasing doubt at dinner, when Vera retreated into long pauses, silently obsessing over where she should search next, or what she was overlooking or looking too hard at. And he felt it in bed at night, when the lights went out and she rolled onto her side, pulling the coverlet over her body, her eyes fluttering closed while whispering "I love you," the whisper of something ending between them.

Today, when the phone rang and the long-distance operator asked to put Mr. Friedman through, Sasha tensed. Over a month had passed since he left LA, and he knew that's why Charlie was calling. When Charlie came on the line, jazz played in the background. It sounded like Duke Ellington, and he pictured Charlie pacing his bedroom, wearing that velvet smoking jacket with the embroidered lapels. A muffled wet cough flooded the line before Charlie asked, "Sasha, you there?"

"Yeah. You all right?"

Charlie hesitated. "Jean left me yesterday."

Sasha had always pictured them together, despite their fights. Worried, he asked, "Her clothes still in the closet?"

"Yeah, but I don't think she'll come back this time."

"What happened?"

"She heard that I was carrying on with Mary Howard."

"Well, were you?" He felt sorry for Charlie's tragic, self-sabotaging nature, realizing that Charlie would never be able to hold on to the one woman he loved.

"Yes," Charlie admitted. "So I called her friend Victoria, who finally admitted that Jean went to Vegas to file for divorce. She's been threatening it for a while." He paused, taking another sip of his drink. "I didn't think she'd actually go through with it, though, especially with the baby on the way."

"Why don't you go get her?"

"Sasha, I'm not like you, crossing continents for

a woman. And for Christ's sake, what in the hell are you doing over there? You don't even speak the language. I thought you'd be back by now."

"I've got to find out what happened to Lucie. That's what I'm doing here."

Charlie let out a frustrated sigh. "You're out of time, Sasha. Bogie is getting antsy about his script notes. Screen tests are about to start. You can't be missing right now."

"So then, where are Bogie's notes?"

"Sasha. Bogie isn't going to write up notes just for you and mail them over in a cute little envelope. He expects to sit down and talk it out, face-to-face. That's how this works."

In an attempt to fend off the sinking feeling that Charlie was right, Sasha shot back, "Everyone's got their panties all twisted up over nothing."

"Don't be a fool. You're closer than you think to blowing this whole thing."

After the call, Sasha went for a coffee at the bar next to the apartment, needing space to think. Even though he didn't want to admit it, Charlie's words stung. He could feel his chance, not just to direct but to direct his own film for MGM, unimaginable a few months ago, slipping through his fingers. Sure, **The In-Between Man** had a start date, and theoretically, he still had time to get back two weeks before shooting, but he also knew Charlie was right. He needed to be there. Then again, Charlie had just blown his marriage because he didn't know how to sacrifice, and Sasha vowed not to fall into the same trap. But it wasn't another woman drawing him away from Vera; it was his movie, his career; it was everything he'd put stock into before he met her. He couldn't simply throw that all away; it would feel like flushing his beating heart down the toilet, but then again, if he wanted to stay with Vera, he didn't see another way forward without doing so.

Two months had passed since his mother's death, but he often caught himself taking out a piece of stationery to write to her before putting down the pen. Twice, he even picked up the telephone and asked the operator to place a long-distance call to New Rochelle, New York, before realizing his error. And sometimes, he pictured her in miniature, sitting on his shoulder, passing judgment like a moody guardian angel, and this feeling, that she was still in the air, spread a sudden tight pain through his chest. He wondered if she sensed, from beyond the grave, that he had gone back to Europe, to his father's Europe, and was now in his milieu, Vera's milieu too, he realized: educated, assimilated, of a certain echelon, and entirely unprepared for what had happened here, the systematic, borderless violence unimaginable, though he didn't know anyone who could have imagined it; it was beyond the pale of conception.

Sometimes, Vera wondered about his father, and

they wondered together, spreading a blanket onto the grass in the Tuileries Garden, a place she reminisced often about taking Lucie on summer days. In the strong sun, the shards of grass appeared greener and more vibrant up close. Lying on her side, she tugged at the grass, watching an errant balloon float upward, only to get tangled in a tree's branches. "It must have been terribly hard for him to leave you and your mother, but he also had this other family— he couldn't abandon them either. It was an impossible choice," she added, and Sasha knew she often thought of her own decision to leave Lucie behind as impossible, and at the same time unforgivable; she tortured herself over it, and she believed his father had undergone a similar torture.

Vera thought aloud, "Maybe he's in South America," faintly recalling the many refugees, on her first voyage to America, who praised the merits of Brazil's climate, while others were intent on Chicago, or Palestine. She turned over onto her back, shielding her eyes from the sun. "And I wonder about his children, if they were able to escape somehow, given their Gentile mother, or if . . ." She sat up and studied the small pile of grass that she had gathered in her palm, as if reading tea leaves. "Maybe they got out in time."

"Maybe," he said, pinching the piled-up grass in her palm and scattering it over the lawn, careful not to upset her with his own misgivings. She had cried when she read his mother's letter, especially when

Sasha told her about the moment in the Berlin train station, when his mother had hoped he would come, and when he didn't, the sense of having been so fully forgotten and abandoned, of not having mattered enough to him, crushed her.

"Once," Vera began, "I was chasing Lucie through the mazes of hedges over there"—she gestured in the direction of it—"and suddenly, she was gone. All I could see was a whirl of green, and the concerned faces of passersby as I screamed her name. Tearing up and down those paths, minutes felt like hours, but it must have been only five minutes until I found her crouching behind a spherical-shaped bush, so happy to have tricked me, but then her face fell when she saw my expression, contorted with so much raw emotion, probably unrecognizable. She started to cry, and I collapsed before her, holding her so tight, I think my ferocity scared her; I didn't want to let her go, ever. Afterward, we walked home in the failing light, and she never hid from me again—" Vera stopped short. "Until now."

The summer wind carried bits and pieces of conversation, errant phrases distracting them for a moment. A woman laughed loudly and then her laugh dissolved into the bright day. A flock of pigeons cooed, pecking at some bread crumbs scattered beneath a park bench. Yesterday's telephone call nudged its way back into his mind. Charlie had ripped into Sasha for still being in France, jeopardizing his career, pissing off Bogart and Mayer, and frankly, Charlie was pissed off too. Before he hung up, he had reminded Sasha that pre-prep started in two weeks. "This movie is gonna fall apart if you don't get back here." And then the line went dead, leaving Sasha fuming, but at the same time, Charlie was right: he was running out of time.

Vera looked at him with uncertainty, as if she could guess his thoughts.

"Have you thought about the DP camps?" he asked. "Hénonville. Landsberg. Gussie said those camps are teeming with orphans. And he knows someone at Hénonville who might be able to help us."

"DP camps, children's homes, convents, orphanages . . . there are thousands of displaced children in France now. Thousands."

"Okay, so, begin with Hénonville, and then—"

"I can't bear to see more places where Lucie has never been."

"You can't be sure," Sasha managed, but for some reason, he felt the same way, that she wouldn't be there.

Vera regarded him intently. "And here I am, dragging you into this endless search, when you should be getting back to your film, back to LA." She paused, her voice catching. "And maybe he's waiting for you to find him."

Hesitantly, he met her eyes, and she embraced him. "Sasha," she whispered, hugging him tightly. "He will love you, as she loved you, as I love you."

He pressed his face into her hair, releasing the

hiccuping sobs that rippled through his chest, the old wound of fatherlessness, inherited and unspoken, tunneling him back to when he used to sit at the kitchen table across from his mother, the sun streaming through the small dirty window, her unnamable sadness, the unrequitedness of it, stretching across time and space, collapsing into now.

CHAPTER 52

SASHA

AUGUST 1945, PARIS, FRANCE

The phone rang when he opened his eyes.
Vera had left an hour ago to spend a few
days in the country with Katja while Sasha packed
up his things. Last night, she had convinced him
to return to Los Angeles and make his movie. They
both agreed that it was for the best to separate in
her absence; otherwise it would be much harder for
him to leave. They each had to go their own way,
she had reasoned, and even though he agreed, the
decision felt wrong, betraying his natural impulse to
never capitulate, no matter how unsolvable a crime
seemed from the outset. Because there was always a
loose thread hidden in the fabric of other details. He
only had to find it.

Hating to admit that he'd failed, and now he had
to pack it in and go home, he still pictured Vera's face

hovering above his when she leaned over to kiss him goodbye. Katja's cabriolet hummed on the curb— they heard it through the open window. Then Vera kissed him on the forehead, a sweet kiss, almost chaste, and he watched her walk away, disappearing through the bedroom door.

When the front door closed, the silence of the apartment rushed in and he welcomed sleep, not wanting to face the day without her.

But then, as he drifted back into dreams, the phone rang again.

He stumbled out of bed, picking up. The operator announced Gussie Lustiger.

"Sasha," Gussie said. "I finally got you in to see the DP camp at Hénonville. Annie Hirsh, she's an American with the UNRRA. I told her you'd be there at noon."

Sasha rubbed his eyes, his head pounding. Next to the phone, he noticed Vera had left the ribbon on the desk, carefully held down by a bronze paperweight in the shape of a cat. He knew she meant for him to take it, perhaps hoping he would share it with his father, if he ever found him. But he decided to leave it here, as a reminder that he loved her, that he would wait for her in a distant city, in another country—it didn't matter how long; he would wait.

"You there?"

"Yeah."

"How about 'Thank you, Gussie'? Or 'That sounds terrific, Gussie'?"

He smiled and lit a cigarette, leaning into the edge of the desk. "Thank you, Gussie. That's really terrific, and it's absolutely the last thing I feel like doing right about now."

"But I thought . . ."

"Vera left for a few days while I pack up my things. I'm going back to California."

"To be honest, Sasha, I think that's a good idea. I mean, what are you doing here anyway?"

Sasha took a long drag and then pulled out a piece of paper and a pencil from the desk drawer. "So. What's this girl's name? Annie something?"

The camp, just outside of Paris, was a miniature city. Across the main entry gate, a banner in Hebrew read, **Kibbutz Hénonville.** Wide unpaved streets, bleak and utilitarian, led to different parts of the camp, all of its various factions attempting to inject some form of masticated hope into its inhabitants. Occasionally, a JDC truck sped by, beeping to signal the arrival of more provisions. Along the main road leading into the camp, a young girl, the hem of her dress torn, pushed a baby carriage. Sasha couldn't tell if an actual baby lay inside of it, or just a bundle of blankets. In the distance, they heard cheering and clapping followed by an outbreak of music that sounded distinctly Eastern European.

"It's a wedding." Annie wiped a stray hair from her face. "Many are getting married and starting new lives." She smiled, her strong white teeth flashing. "Isn't it wonderful?"

Sasha nodded, unconvinced.

Annie led him through the camp with crisp authority, nodding and waving to every teacher, doctor, and fellow relief worker who passed by them. She emphasized that none of these facilities—the schoolhouse, the maternity ward, the blacksmith workshop, the houses of worship, the day cares, the printing presses—would have been remotely possible without such generous donations from the JDC.

She gave Sasha an encouraging look. "American Jews, like us, have been reaching across the ocean to help." And then, remembering the entire reason why he was here, she added, "Gussie informed me of your daughter's age and last known whereabouts. There's the Central Tracing Agency, but it's extremely understaffed and takes months. Public radio broadcasts and newspapers contain lists of survivors and their whereabouts, but in your case, it's quite difficult as she was so young and most likely given another name and an entirely new identity. We'll visit the schoolhouse and the kindergarten, which is where your daughter would most likely be, but of course there are many orphanages and children's homes and foster homes and other—"

"I know," Sasha interrupted, not bothering to correct her that he wasn't Lucie's father. Things were already complicated enough. He took from his back pocket the thin, worn photograph of Lucie that Vera had left in her desk drawer. "Here," he said, giving it to Annie. She studied it for a moment and then brightly looked up at him. "Okay. Let's go see."

A few pregnant women strolled past, kerchiefs covering their hair, conversing in Russian. Across the way, men plastered posters on the side of a brick building that read: **We demand to open the gates of Palestine. Eretz Israel for the people of Israel!**

A mother with two gaunt children hurried by. They wore heavy overcoats in the strong sun.

Annie took a breath and began describing the difficulty of placing the orphaned children that were arriving in droves to the camp. "Do the children return to surviving relatives? Or should they be housed with foster families, to remain in their native countries? Or should we send the children to Palestine for a collective education with all the other displaced children? And then there's the question of how to define a child . . ." She stopped and crunched down on an apple. "Anyone under the age of seventeen is considered a child, but the DPs constantly lie about their age."

"Why?"

Annie waved around her clipboard as if the Messiah himself had given it to her. "It's very frustrating. We never know a person's real age—they adjust on purpose. For example, because children are often sent to Palestine first, even men with beards claim they are fourteen. Yesterday, a thirty-five-year-old woman proclaimed she was sixteen. When a colleague of mine doubted it, do you know what she said?" Annie asked incredulously. "'After all I suffered in the camp, how can you wonder why I look older than my years?'"

"And what about the children? Why do they lie about their age?" Sasha considered if Lucie would do this.

"They lie because they don't want to be repatriated back to their countries. For instance, why would you want to go back to Poland or Czechoslovakia when you could immigrate to America?"

"Little golden America," Sasha murmured, taking in the cloudless sky.

Annie finished the apple and tossed the core into the dust. "Let's go see the schoolhouse."

On the way there, they passed a barefoot kid riding a bike who gave them a toothless grin before pedaling away, his skeletal legs working hard, his suspenders on backwards, crisscrossing his spindly chest. Elderly men in black overcoats conferred over newspapers printed in Hebrew. Sounds of carpentry reverberated throughout the camp, and Annie proudly explained that the DPs were learning useful occupations for Palestine. When they wandered down a narrower road, away from the central activity of the camp, the paths grew shadowy and small, and Sasha felt as if he were intruding on private domestic scenes. A woman bent over a large pail, peeling potatoes, while two babies cried on a pallet in the grass. She yelled at them harshly in Polish and then went back to peeling.

Outside of the maternity ward, two mothers relaxed on a bench in the sun. They held up their babies, turning the infants toward each other while making cooing noises, encouraging the babies to mimic them, while the babies stared at each other with dark, unblinking eyes.

And then the jolt of rounding the corner where a little boy showed off the tattooed numerals on his forearm to a group of other boys. He stopped mid-sentence and gave Sasha a shrewd look that captured, in a flash, the man he would become: suspicious and defensive, grasping after any pleasure, no matter how small and hard-won. Annie pretended not to see him, as though his very presence undermined the project of rehabilitation in which she so ardently believed.

Walking away, Sasha noticed the scabs on the boy's knees and the children's general state of neglect. As though reading his mind, Annie said that when the children first arrived here, they had pieces of cardboard tied to their feet. Like wolves, they traveled in packs. "We called them wolf children." Then she motioned to an open field on the other side of the schoolhouse, where teenage boys played soccer, yelling in a mixture of German, Polish, and Russian. "The fresh air is good for them."

.   .   .

Along the perimeter of the field, the openings of pup tents flapped in the wind, revealing families huddled over tea and makeshift fires, and Sasha recalled the pup tent he had shared in a small Sicilian town, overseeing a German POW camp.

When they arrived at the school, a teacher led a line of small children out of a clapboard house into an adjoining garden, where she would teach them about transplanting seedlings. "Hopefully, within the next year, all of these children will immigrate to Palestine," Annie said.

Inside the schoolhouse, Annie explained how different classrooms separated the children by age. The canary yellow walls smelled of fresh paint, and along with the sound of children repeating phrases in unison, their voices strong and forceful, a sense of industry and cheer permeated the place.

Annie led Sasha into each classroom, quietly opening the door while Sasha scanned the rows of children, their small round faces turned to the blackboard, where the teacher pointed to Hebrew words with a long pointed stick. For a moment, the smell of chalk and disinfectant and the panic of not understanding the lesson brought him back to that noisy restless classroom on the Lower East Side, with its smudged walls and the wooden desks carved with obscenities. He understood no English, and in those first weeks, the boys' jeering freckled faces, with their salami sandwiches and bitten-down nails, felt foreign and threatening. On the playground, they used to rub their elbows into his head, searching for horns. The teacher sharply yelled at Sasha to pay attention, but his head hurt from their pointy elbows, and from all the new words that made him feel as if he were drowning in a bottomless pool.

Leading him out of the class, Annie whispered that the children were learning Hebrew for Palestine.

"Don't they already know Yiddish?"

She stiffened and said that was a bastardized language, a remnant of the shtetl, the pogroms, the massacres.

When he pushed through the door, his mother's constant refrain came back to him: **Yiddish at home, with the family. Outside, English and only English. Learn it better than an American if you want to be American.**

Annie closed the classroom door behind her and leaned against it for a minute. The hallway was uncharacteristically quiet and still.

She looked at him apologetically.

Sasha's shoulders sank. "I guess that's it then."

. . .

They walked back toward the camp entrance, and Sasha asked if the children remembered anything from before.

"Most of them, especially the younger ones, don't. They wouldn't recognize their own parents if they saw them on the street." And then she added that it was really best for the children, to finally have a national homeland. "If the war has taught us anything, it's that without a nation to call our own, we are nothing. Even in America, the Jews could be driven out." She stopped to catch her breath, giving Sasha an admonishing look. "The same thing could happen over there, you know."

He was about to argue with her, but then she motioned to a run-down brick building and announced it was the library.

He didn't care.

He saw only dirt and loneliness.

Teenage boys ran past them, yelling in Russian, one of them carrying something bundled under his arm, while the others looked on covetously.

Watching them run, he knew that the next camp, and then the next, would yield nothing. Annie's voice became a distant echo while she wondered if he had been to the camp in Brochard; it was bigger, the child could be there.

Sasha stared at an old man reciting his prayers,

clutching the fence post. He heard crying babies, and a loudspeaker barking, from some far corner of the camp, directions in Russian, German, Polish, and French. Nearing the exit gate, he almost felt as though he would start sprinting.

"But as I said, there's been trouble getting some of the children back."

He took out a cigarette and fished around for his matches, and she gave him a disapproving look, but he needed it badly. Lighting it, he added, "Sure, you can't track down every single kid." He kicked at a few pebbles embedded in the dirt.

Annie shook her head. "It's not that. It's the Catholic Church. They have such a hold over these children who they hid during the war, oftentimes they don't want to return them to their Jewish families. Or to any type of Jewish organization. Can you imagine? Especially if the children have been baptized, the church believes that these children belong to them now. That they are responsible for their souls." Her gaze shifted beyond the gate, settling on the empty road ahead.

Unsteadily, he ran a hand through his hair, her words spinning through his head, the surroundings altering slightly, as though he had been here before, a warm close recognition pounding through him: the woman's dark laugh on the other side of the rotting fence, the way the noonday light slanted across Annie's cheek, and then he pictured Mother Superior's face, from St. Denis. Her hardness under feigned welcome, protesting too much, and the sharp glance she gave the other nun, a glance that demanded silence, obedience. And the young nun, weepy when they left, clinging to Vera's arm on the convent steps. He distinctly heard her high thin voice, as though she stood before him now: **Have you checked the Hotel Lutetia?**

How would she know about the Hotel Lutetia? A simple nun, in rural southwestern France. Unless she had gone there. With information about a missing child, or to find a missing child.

Annie turned toward him. "Mr. Rabinovitch, are you all right? You look pale."

He flung his arms around her and lifted her up, laughing while he did it, and she started to laugh too, staring down at him, her cheeks flushed, blonde wispy hairs haloing her face.

"I think I just figured something out. Thank you. Thank you so much."

Annie wouldn't let him borrow a JDC truck unless she came with him, saying that its use must be authorized and entered into a notebook, which she continued to explain as he drove them to the Hotel Lutetia in the center of Paris, about forty minutes away from the DP camp.

In the lobby, massive lines formed in front of each desk. Against the walls, people sat, staring into space, playing cards, picking at their nails. He walked up to the front of one line, pushing aside a man with a thick mustache who looked surprised but didn't say anything. The bureaucrat behind the desk, a tired woman in her late fifties, shook her head and said in French that he must go to the back of the line, gesturing angrily at all the people.

He put both hands down on her desk and leaned forward. "I need to see the log that you keep here."

Annie raised her penciled eyebrows, and Sasha motioned for her to come over, explaining to her what he needed. "They must have some record of who has come here, searching for displaced persons. Otherwise, what function does this place have?" His voice suddenly sounded very loud to him, overly confident and commanding, but Annie agreed and spoke to the woman in French.

The woman slowly got up from the desk and went over to talk to someone else behind another desk, motioning to Sasha and Annie. The other man nodded and stood up, disappearing behind a partition. A few minutes later, he brought out a large black leather book. He carried it with two hands and laid it on his desk.

Sasha went over to him, feeling as though everyone watched now: the DPs in line, the tired woman who didn't want to help, and the Red Cross nurses, busy with incoming patients, paused.

Aware of Annie breathing nervously by his side, he started reading the dates and names in each ruled column, beginning in April of 1945, when the first deportees arrived here, the cursive slanting across the page, the saturated blue ink staining the yellowed pages. He lost track a few times, and he went back. There were so many names. He moved to the side of the desk so that the man could help others while he kept reading. April: nothing. May: nothing. He started to doubt that the nun had been here. June, with so many more wobbly signatures: many of the names French, some Russian and Polish ones too. He paused on June 11, 1945: **Sister Helene Bisset of Convent St. Denis, with girl, age 9, Lucie, in search of any living relatives.**

He read it again, his chest pounding, both disbelieving and believing. All else dissolved into the background: the man speaking across the desk with his pungent halitosis, a woman shrieking in the doorway over a lost purse, sirens blaring down the street, the hiss of the chandeliers above him.

The reality of Lucie's existence was here, just under his fingertip, in blue ink, screaming to be seen.

He told Annie to ask the bureaucrat to telephone the convent, to contact Sister Helene. The man consulted a fat telephone book, and after several minutes of muttering under his breath and scrutinizing the fine print, he dialed a number.

It was Friday, late afternoon. Sasha pictured the convent's stone walls, the surrounding rosemary hedges, the sky blue door, the distinct crunch of pebbles underfoot.

The telephone, on the other end of the line, rang and rang.

He could hear it from across the desk.

The man frowned, on the verge of hanging up, until a woman's voice finally answered and he began rolling out a long preliminary good afternoon, "I hope you are well," and finally asking to speak to Sister Helene.

He paused, and nodded to them.

Then he cupped the receiver with his other hand and whispered to Sasha in halting English: "Sister Helene is no longer with the Sisters."

"What?"

He shook his head and said something in French, and then turned back to Sasha and Annie, saying, in a mixture of English and French, that Sister Helene had left the convent quite recently.

Sasha gripped the edge of the desk. "Where did she go?"

The man held up a finger and then, after relaying something in a cursory tone, wrote down an address on a slip of paper and slid it across the desk to Sasha.

After the hotel, he said goodbye to Annie and went to Sister Helene's address on the outskirts of Paris, but no one was at home. Waiting on the street, he leaned against the wall, read the paper, watched the afternoon turn into evening, smoking cigarette after cigarette, uninterested in the rail-thin prostitutes who told him their price and asked for a cigarette in the same breath. He gave them cigarettes and some spare change.

Finally, he went back to Vera's apartment and found a telephone number that corresponded to the address through the operator, and planned to ring in the morning. Maybe she would be home then. His head felt heavy, the adrenaline of the day draining from him, bit by bit. He lay down on the bed, turning his face toward the open window, the pillowcase cool against his cheek, his mind crowded and harried, thoughts racing as to why Sister Helene had left the convent, and if she knew where Lucie was, or if she had only been with Lucie for a short interval before handing her over to someone else.

The sound of thunder gathered in the distance. When he closed his eyes, images of the DP camp rushed into the room's stillness: abandoned children, old men in heavy overcoats, the boy with the faded blue numbers along his forearm. Witnessing the war's aftermath was so much worse than fighting in it, with its rapid violence, beginning and ending with shocking speed: a parenthesis of experience.

The images tumbled into a nightmare, the first one he'd had since last summer, when he was freshly home from the war. The boy with the tattooed numerals tugged at Sasha's sleeve, demanding to know where his parents were, growing more and more agitated that Sasha didn't know. To escape the boy,

Sasha ran up endless paths, leading to decrepit barracks and makeshift huts. He started sweating, nauseated by the mazelike lanes, certain he'd gotten to the center of the DP camp, only to discover it wasn't the center: more clusters of roaming people appeared, and he found himself in the middle of a parade. Young men held up banners with Hebrew lettering, demanding a Jewish state. An older man shuffled along with the crowd and said something in German to Sasha, staring at him with a pale, stricken face.

Something shuddered inside of him, and Sasha knew this man was his father. Realizing that Sasha recognized him, his father started to cry, little tears seeping out of his eyes, and he gestured for Sasha to come closer so that he could embrace him, but then, as strong as a current, the crowd parted them and strangers engulfed Sasha, their expressions desolate and somber, vibrating with an inherent atomization, echoing the diaspora of not just this war but of all the wars and pogroms and massacres that had ever been.

He woke to the predawn light, the sheets damp, his temples throbbing, knowing that when all this was done, whether or not they found Lucie, and whether or not Vera stayed with him, he would find his father.

CHAPTER 53

SASHA

AUGUST 1945, PARIS, FRANCE

Traces of virginity still clung to her: the pointed crisp collar, the white blouse underneath a navy cardigan, the slim pencil skirt and flat black shoes, her thick reddish hair in a heavy braid down her back, as though she were afraid to cut it off and sever the final tie to what she had been.

They sat together at a café in the 15th arrondissement, near where she worked. The neighborhood was industrial, home to the Citroën factory and rough, but Helene had found a job as a seamstress here. She worked every day except today, Sunday. Her new home was a furnished rented room above a tobacco shop. When Sasha and Gussie called her this morning, she had sounded afraid at first, as though he were hunting her down, to interrogate her or berate her, but when he explained, with Gussie's help and constant interjections, that he and Vera Volosenkova had recently visited the convent of St. Denis, and they were searching for Vera's daughter, Lucie, and he hoped she might have some information about the girl, she agreed to meet them here at this shabby café on the water, the Sunday morning sun warming the tabletop. She drank weak tea with no sugar, and the croissants were stale, but she didn't seem to notice.

Staring into the cloudy tea, as if at confession, she explained to Gussie that after Sasha and Madame Volosenkova had left the convent that day, she begged Sister Ismerie to change her mind and tell them the truth. The Bonheurs had picked up Lucie only days beforehand, a sign from God if there ever was one. But Sister Ismerie clung to the command from on high, as directed by the Vatican and the Holy Father, that the church must protect these baptized children's souls, and under no circumstances return any hidden children to the Jews, whether it be the child's mother or the Zionists.

"It's the same thing to her," Helene said, her eyes watering. "But God would never keep a child from his mother. And so I left." She swallowed hard. "I spent days searching for Madame Volosenkova, with no address, with nothing—Sister Ismerie had burned it. I thought I would never succeed." She looked up at him shyly as Gussie translated all that she just said to Sasha.

"And here you are," Sister Helene added in French.

Sasha took her hand.

Church bells clanged in the distance, cutting through the dissonant noise from down the street, which was clogged with students waving the familiar red flag with its yellow sickle and star, hungrily embracing what their parents had feared before the war. The other side always lay dormant, Sasha thought, sharpening itself for new believers.

He realized he was squeezing her hand too hard. Sun splintered through the passing clouds, warming the back of his neck. She blushed and in one smooth motion handed him a folded-over piece of paper. "Lucie is living with this family. They are good people."

Gussie translated what she said, her eyes bright with excitement.

He opened it and read an address, written in fine cursive on paper the color of ivory.

CHAPTER 54

VERA

AUGUST 1945, PARIS, FRANCE

When Vera rounded the corner, she saw Sasha pacing in front of the apartment, studying the sidewalk. It was a shock; she had expected he would be gone, that's what they had decided, but during the long car ride back to Paris, she felt sick over it, anticipating the emptiness of walking into the apartment with him no longer in it. She felt winded, jarred by the sight of him, unsure if he had changed his mind or if something else had changed. Clouds, like pale sandbars, indented the sky. Lavender-tinged, luminescent. Putting down her valise, she brushed aside wisps of hair, and called out, "Sasha!" her voice trembling in the thick air.

The sound of her voice struck him like an electric current, and he ran to her. She started to explain that she didn't mean to return earlier than he had anticipated, but she was so happy to see him again anyway, and she was sorry for—

He grabbed her hand. "I know where Lucie is. She's living with a family in Saint-Palais."

Her knees buckled under her and she reached for something to hold, but Sasha was already there, holding her.

"How?" she managed, her voice barely audible. "How do you know it's really true?"

"I know it is."

She flung herself into him, her chest exploding, her breath rushing too fast, in sharp cresting waves, the trees spinning, the cobblestones flowing like water under her feet, and Sasha whispering into her hair, "It's all right. I'll tell you everything in the car. Let's go get her."

He drove as fast as he could in the same borrowed Citroën, but she willed him to go faster. Her heart beat violently, and she tried to take measured breaths, reasoning with herself to calm down, to wait and see, as so many things were still unknown. What if Lucie didn't recognize her, or didn't want to come with her? Or what if this whole story was a mistake and the nun had the wrong child?

She gripped the piece of paper, staring down at the meticulous handwriting. **Marie and Jean-Paul Bonheur.** Vera rearranged her plaid skirt, wishing she had worn something prettier, something that Lucie would like. Lucie used to watch Vera dress for the evening, mooning over a sequined dress, a ripple of silk. Anything with a sheen pleased her, and she was always upset to discover that the next morning Vera had returned to her normal self, as though Vera's wool cardigan tucked into a pencil skirt betrayed the glamorous apparition who had kissed her good night the evening before.

The afternoon grew overcast, tipping into gray. Vera worried that they would arrive too late, and already the drive was taking longer than the customary five hours because of the poor conditions, with many of the roads in disrepair, or blocked off. "I don't want to scare her, blundering in there at night. It could make the whole event appear even more unreal than it already is. I always pictured finding her in the morning."

He slowed as they approached a railroad crossing.

"I knew it," she continued breathlessly. "That nun at St. Denis wanted to tell me something. The way she stood there on the steps, watching us drive away . . . but I thought it was only the irrational chatter of my mind. I've grown so used to that chatter." She sat up, staring out at the vineyards, and at the blue-shuttered châteaus lording over rows of green.

At the crossing, a freight train sped past in a blur of smoke and steel.

· · · ·

They waited in the car with the windows rolled down, and stared at the stone cottage across the street with roses growing in haphazard bunches in the yard. The red-tiled roof slanted down sharply, housing two small windows framed by pale green shutters. The cottage, nestled and protected by generous foliage, was set back from the road, with rosemary bushes dotting the perimeter, and all the wild roses. They listened to the birds flitting through the trees, the tiny squeak of the weather vane on the rooftop that shifted in the wind. A dog barked in the distance. Vera thought how different this summerhouse was from their old place in Sanary, even though it also stood a short distance from the sea, a bike ride away, but this was the Atlantic coast, near the Pyrenees, a wilder and more rustic landscape, whereas in Sanary they had bathed in the warm Mediterranean currents. Nonetheless, she wondered if Lucie was reminded of her old life, being here, even a trace of it.

She thought she heard a woman's voice call out into the fading twilight, along with the clatter of pots and pans coming from an open window, the air carrying the expectation of dinner. Rising above these sounds, the cicadas chanted from the trees, a deep quivering hum.

She caught movement in the bottom floor of the

house, through the kitchen window, and strained to see more.

"I think you should just knock on the door," Sasha finally said.

"You're not coming?"

He shook his head. "It's better if you go on your own."

She swallowed, her chest needled with panic. Her clammy hands clenched the piece of paper with the address. "I'm afraid."

He squeezed her hand. "I'll be here waiting for you. Waiting for both of you."

Reaching for the car-door handle, about to open it, Vera saw a girl in a floral dress with fluttering sleeves sprint across the field that separated this cottage from the next one, her leather satchel too big for her slight frame. Her movements were coltish, her honey-colored hair a thick sheet across her back.

Not Lucie. Not even close.

Vera inhaled, holding her stomach. She shut her eyes, shaking her head. "Oh, no," she whispered. "It's not her . . ."

"Wait," Sasha said, leaning forward.

The girl laughed and gestured to someone across the field. "**Viens, au ralenti!**" she shouted.

Another girl came into view, wearing a white blouse with puffed sleeves, a pleated gingham skirt. She was smaller and thinner, her dark hair cut short into a balloon of loose curls, her eyes suspicious and then playful when the other girl looped her arm through hers, and for a brief moment the two girls conferred over a comic book. They laughed, theatrically throwing back their heads.

Perched on the edge of the seat, Vera let out a breath, leaving blurry circles on the windshield. "Sasha," she whispered, as if saying it too loudly would threaten what she saw before her and make it disappear. "It's Lucie."

"Yes," he said thickly, "I know."

Vera watched Lucie, marveling at how recognizable certain gestures were: she brushed a strand of hair away from her face with impatience, and her brow furrowed as she examined the comic. She jutted out a hip and cocked her head to the side, the pose she assumed when deliberating something.

Vera looked at Sasha, her voice breaking. "What if she doesn't recognize me?"

"She will," he whispered.

Vera opened the car door, the early-evening air hitting her face. "Lucie!" she cried.

The girl immediately looked up, her face a question, unfolding into recognition, her eyes widening. She inched closer to her friend, but the other girl stood motionless, entranced by the sight of Vera.

Vera ran toward Lucie, her knees buckling, her chest breaking apart, as if she might not reach her, as if at the last moment Lucie would dissolve into thin air.

Lucie stared at her with a shocked, glazed expression, and Vera started to cry, sharp hiccuping sobs that made it hard to catch her breath, her eyeliner running in sticky rivulets, her mouth trembling, wanting to say so much, but instead an odd bleating came out. She threw her arms around her daughter, taking in Lucie's hair and skin, the feeling of Lucie's body relenting, melting into hers.

Vera inhaled, trying to drink up all of Lucie, her heart beating so fast she thought it might beat through the fissures of veins and vessels that held it in place. "I'm here. I'm here now. I'm here," she whispered, pressing her face into Lucie's hair, breathing in her powdery scent, the crown of her head dampening from Vera's tears.

Lucie's birdlike shoulders twitched under the pressure of Vera's embrace, as though she was suppressing a mountain of sobs.

"I found you. I found you," Vera repeated, trying not to frighten her.

Lucie pulled away and stared hard at Vera's face and her clothes, taking in every detail. She didn't seem scared so much as mystified, floating in suspended shock. She instinctually reached for her friend's hand, but the girl had run into the house, leaving the front door ajar.

"Do you remember me?" Vera asked, her voice trembling.

Lucie slowly nodded.

Vera knelt down and stroked Lucie's cheek. The golden heart flashed from a chain around her daughter's neck. The wine-colored birthmark smudged her third left finger.

Lucie gripped her mother's hands as if they might melt away, as if her flesh proved unconvincing. "Why did you leave me?"

Vera started to explain, but she struggled to breathe, as if stuck under a roaring wave at the bottom of the ocean.

Then Lucie flung her arms around Vera, murmuring, "Mama, I thought you forgot me. I thought you forgot and then I thought you were dead," and she started to cry, her slight frame shaking, and Vera clutched her closer, so close their breath melded into one breath, rising and falling, the map of her daughter's body pressing into hers.

Vera tightened her arms around Lucie, tunneling back to those golden afternoons, her palm resting on Lucie's downy back, reassured by the steady rhythm of Lucie's breathing, her fragile head tucked into the curve of Vera's neck, with her smattering of dark hair, eyelids translucent half-moons, asleep to the world.

Lucie looked up, her eyes searching her mother's, a surge of recognition coursing between them, running through Vera into Lucie and back again, an eternal, spinning loop; Vera realized it had never stopped.

AUTHOR'S NOTE

The inspiration for **Those Who Are Saved**:
exile, motherhood, wish fulfillment

Growing up in LA, I shortsightedly felt as though
life were happening elsewhere, as if real culture and
history remained out of reach. I then discovered that
during World War II, many European exiles fled to
Los Angeles, such as novelists Lion Feuchtwanger
and Thomas Mann, writers Salka Viertel and Bertolt
Brecht, musicians Erich Korngold, Igor Stravinsky,
Arnold Schoenberg, and Theodor Adorno, directors
Otto Preminger and Fritz Lang, and so many others.
These exiled artists formed a community congregating and living in some of the very places where I
grew up: Pacific Palisades, Brentwood, and Santa
Monica. They too felt at odds with the city's nat-
ural beauty and ceaseless sunshine, with the brash
Hollywood glamour and the lack of obvious cul-
ture. I began to feel a kinship with these displaced

artists who still clung to the Old World while they were forced to adapt to a new one. I wanted to write about the experience of exile, and this is how the characters of Vera Volosenkova and her husband, Max, were born, as well as their friends and cohorts, who gathered at Villa Aurora, a Spanish-style house in the Pacific Palisades hills overlooking the ocean.

As I was writing about a mother separated from her daughter, and how this causes Vera so much pain, I reflected on the perpetual project of motherhood, full of battle and worry, and how every decision, even seemingly small, trivial ones, can feel like the wrong one, inducing guilt and anxiety. Of course, Vera's choice is heightened by the life-and-death consequences of war; but even today, as a mother, the stakes often feel so high in terms of what you choose for your child, or for yourself. These feelings of guilt and inadequacy helped me shape Vera's intense guilt in the aftermath of her ill-fated decision to leave Lucie with her governess, a guilt that is not shared by her husband in the same way, which also shows how men and women deal with grief, especially around the loss of a child, in starkly different ways.

This story is also inspired by one of my favorite writers, Irène Némirovsky, most well-known for her novel **Suite Francaise,** written during the first years of the German occupation of France but not discovered until the late 1990s and published in 2002, as the manuscript was hidden in a suitcase for decades. Nemirovsky was a Russian Jewish writer living in Paris during World War II. She did not escape France in time, and was killed at Auschwitz in 1942, but she left two young daughters behind who survived the war. In a way, this book is for her, a kind of wish-fulfillment, of what her life could have been if she had gotten out, and come to Los Angeles.

READING LIST

I am deeply indebted to the following books that provided a rich trove of research and inspiration:

A Bintel Brief: Sixty Years of Letters from the Lower East Side to the Jewish Daily Forward edited by Isaac Metzker
From the advice section of the **Jewish Daily Forward**, this book compiles various letters spanning over eighty years, tracing how Eastern European immigrants grappled with their new lives in America.

After Auschwitz directed by Jon Kean
A wonderful documentary that follows six women, all survivors of the Holocaust, who moved to Los Angeles after the war, and in varying degrees, struggled to create new lives while the past continued to haunt them.

Brave Men
   by Ernie Pyle
Selections from Pyle's writings as a war correspondent in Europe during WWII offer a realistic and fresh look at army life in the trenches, field hospitals, and bombed cities, providing unique and specific details.

City of Nets: A Portrait of Hollywood in the
   1940s
   by Otto Friedrich
A seminal history of Hollywood from WWII to the Korean War, featuring various writers, actors, directors, politicians, and studio heads, full of delicious gossip and the backstory to how the most well-known movies from that time period got made.

Conversations with the Great Moviemakers of
   Hollywood's Golden Age
   by George Stevens Jr.
An inside look at how Hollywood worked in the 1940s, and the ways in which it coincided with the war and informed the vision of various directors and writers of the era.

Crossing Over
   by Ruth Wolman
Interviews with Jewish couples who settled in Los Angeles after emigrating from Germany and Austria to escape the Nazi terror.

The Devil in France: My Encounter With Him in the Summer of 1940
by Lion Feuchtwanger

A first-person account of German Jewish writer Lion Feuchtwanger's experiences of internment in France, followed by his ultimate escape from the Nazis. Useful description of the camp's conditions, the types of people who were imprisoned by the French government at the beginning of the war, and how this work camp foreshadowed the horrors to come.

Exiled in Paradise: German Refugee Artists and Intellectuals in America from the 1930s to the Present
by Anthony Heilbut

A central work of scholarship on German exile culture.

Five Came Back
by Mark Harris

A great source on how Hollywood changed as a result of the war, focusing on five key directors who all fought in the war: John Ford, George Stevens, Billy Wyler, John Huston, and Frank Capra.

Hitler's Exiles
edited by Mark Anderson

A personal account of the war from various exiles from different countries, many of whom fled to Los Angeles to start new lives.

The Impossible Exile: Stefan Zweig at the End of the World
by George Prochnik

An account of the agonies and ecstasies of Stefan Zweig, one of Europe's leading intellectuals, who was driven into exile along with many others of his milieu; but this book tracks his personal experience of exile, which ultimately ended in suicide.

The Kindness of Strangers
by Salka Viertel

A beautiful memoir from a female perspective on the experience of exile in Los Angeles during and after the war.

The Long Road Home: The Aftermath of the Second World War
by Ben Shephard

A detailed look at life after the war; Shephard's focus on repatriation of refugees, and the fate of Jewish DPs, as well as the process of searching for lost children, proved particularly helpful.

Los Angeles in World War II
by Ruth Wallach, Dace Taub, Claude Zachary, Linda McCann, and Curtis Roseman

Provided wonderful photographs and explanation of Los Angeles during wartime, from civilian experiences to how the city prepared and weathered the war.

The Mirador: Dreamed Memories of
Irène Némirovsky by her Daughter
by Elisabeth Gille

A beautifully impressionistic account of French writer Irène Némirovsky's life leading up to her deportation to Auschwitz in July of 1942.

Never Look Away
directed by Florian Henckel von
Donnersmarck

A feature film that traces the path of a German artist from his childhood during WWII to the 1960s. A powerful depiction of intergenerational trauma and the inescapability of the past.

The New York Times Complete World War II
1939–1945:
The Coverage from the Battlefields to the
Home Front with Access to 98,367 Articles
edited by Richard Overy, foreword
by Tom Brokaw

Savage Continent: Europe in the Aftermath of
World War II
by Keith Lowe

Particularly helpful in explaining the state of Europe after the war, and how Jews were viewed in its direct aftermath, before the terms "Holocaust" and "survivor" became commonplace.

Shadows of a Childhood
by Elisabeth Gille

This novel traces the wartime experiences of Elisabeth Gille, Irène Némirovsky's daughter, who was hidden and survived the war, and only later discovered the circumstances of her mother's death.

Southern California: An Island on the Land
by Carey McWilliams

A historical account of California, written in 1946, covering all aspects of the state, from the topography and climate to personalities such as cult leader Aimee Semple McPherson and why people from all over the US came looking for a new life in California.

Suite Francaise
by Irène Némirovsky

A beautifully written novel composed during the German occupation of France, told from various points of view.

A Third Face
by Sam Fuller

An autobiography by writer/director Sam Fuller, who fought in the unit the Big Red One during World War II and lived to tell about it afterward, including his experiences as a director and writer in Hollywood in the 1940s and '50s.

The War: A Memoir
  by Marguerite Duras
Written in 1945, this memoir describes Duras's experiences living in Paris during the occupation, including her work for the Resistance and her dealings with a Gestapo officer who was attracted to her.

Weimar on the Pacific: German Exile Culture
  in Los Angeles and the Crisis of Modernism
  by Ehrhard Bahr
The first book of its kind that examines this group of German exiles that escaped Nazi Germany to settle in Los Angeles in the '30s and '40s as a cultural phenomenon that affected the shaping of modernism in the face of National Socialism.

The Wine of Solitude
  by Irène Némirovsky
An autobiographical novel based on Nemirovsky's childhood experiences growing up in prerevolutionary Russia.

ACKNOWLEDGMENTS

I would like to thank my editor, Tara Singh Carlson, who read an earlier form of this book, and with her tremendous combination of faith and endurance, worked tirelessly to bring our vision to fruition. Her honest, meticulous notes and her determination to push me beyond what I thought possible in terms of the narrative and my own capabilities as a writer still astound me; I am forever grateful.

My gratitude also extends to: Ashley Di Dio, Helen O'Hare, Alexis Welby, Sally Kim, Anthony Ramondo, Vi-An Nguyen, Mary Beth Constant, and the rest of the team at G.P. Putnam's Sons.

I am so grateful for my agent, Alice Tasman, for her generosity of spirit, sense of humor, and pluck to keep on going during this long journey. She is my greatest ally, and kept both of our heads above water. And thank you to the rest of the team at Jean V. Naggar Literary Agency: Jean Naggar, Jennifer

Weltz, Ariana Philips, Alicia Brooks, and Maddie Ticknor.

Thank you to Deb Garrison and Lexy Bloom for believing in and fighting for this book, too.

I am indebted to the USC Writing Program, USC Libraries, and the Feuchtwanger Memorial Library, and especially to Michaela Wolf for her research assistance with exile studies, and to Sophie Lesinska.

Thank you to Deborah Netburn, my central point of gravity, for our wonderful friendship and your magic; Cecily Gallup, for her medical advice on gunshot wounds and her friendship; Sara Sandström, my north star in Sweden, for our long walks and talks; Anna Mattos and Carl Hampe, for weathering the storm with us and for our Bulgarian summer; Meghan Davis Mercer, for your insights and our breakfasts; Maya Varnell, for our ballet days and your humor; Laura Regan, for the friendship as we became mothers; and thank you so much to Stephen Kenneally for listening and lighting the way through the dark woods.

Natasha Gevorkyan, thank you for the music.

Thank you to Kaley Giles-Bruess for caring for my children.

Thank you to Rachel Artenian, Evan James, and Alma Santillan for so graciously sharing your office environment.

Thank you to my father, Joel Landau, for supporting me in all things, for the space to write, and the time.

Thank you to my mother, Arlene Landau, for your encouragement to keep writing, despite life's turbulence.

My gratitude extends to the rest of my family: Brad TePaske, Susan Landau, Lauren Cadish, Patrick Griffin, Betty and Anders Westgren, Pia and Birgitta Westgren, and the entire Westgren clan in Holland and Sweden.

Thank you to my children, Levi and Lucia, for understanding how long it takes to write a book and cheering me along the way.

This book is also for Anders Landau Westgren, wherever you are, we carry you in our hearts.

Last but absolutely not least, thank you to Philip for reading this book from its first beginning pages, the countless drafts in between, to this final rendition; I cherish your patience, love, and generosity— I cannot thank you enough.

ABOUT THIS AUTHOR

ALEXIS LANDAU is a graduate of Vassar College and received an MFA from Emerson College and a PhD in English literature and creative writing from the University of Southern California. She is the author of **The Empire of the Senses** and lives with her husband and two children in Los Angeles.

AlexisLandau.com
Instagram: Alexis.Landau